AVENUE OF BETRAYAL

SPIES OF THE CIVIL WAR ~ BOOK 1

SANDRA MERVILLE HART

WILD HEART
BOOKS

For my Family

The characters and events in this fictional work are the product of the author's imagination. Any resemblance to actual people, living or dead, is coincidental.

Unless otherwise indicated, all Scripture quotations are taken from the Holy Bible, Kings James Version.

Scripture quotations marked (NIV) are taken from the Holy Bible, New International Version®, NIV®. Copyright © 1973, 1978, 1984, 2011 by Biblica, Inc.™ Used by permission of Zondervan. All rights reserved worldwide. www.zondervan.comThe "NIV" and "New International Version" are trademarks registered in the United States Patent and Trademark Office by Biblica, Inc.™

Cover design by: Carpe Librum Book Design

Author is represented by Hartline Literary Agency

ISBN-13: 978-1-942265-54-2

PRAISE FOR AVENUE OF BETRAYAL

Sandra Merville Hart has done it again. She's captured time and poured it on her pages. I love the concept of spies during the Civil War and the conflict in Washington City (present-day D.C.) where many residents had southern roots. Romance is intertwined with the conflict of the day, making it sigh-worthy. Hart's extensive research makes this historical romance authentic.

— CINDY ERVIN HUFF, AWARD-WINNING
HISTORICAL ROMANCE AUTHOR OF *ANGELINA'S
RESOLVE*

Sandra Merville Hart's *Avenue of Betrayal* is a look into Washington City—now known as Washington D.C.—during the early days of the American Civil War. It was a city divided, with people who were staunchly pro-Union living side-by-side with those who were fiercely pro-Confederacy. People didn't know whom to trust, sometimes even within their own families. Hart does a wonderful job of bringing that level of uncertainty and angst to the reader along with a gentle romance that must survive the secrecy and divided loyalties.

— PEGG THOMAS AWARD-WINNING AUTHOR OF
SARAH'S CHOICE

I normally don't read historical novels unless there is a fantasy element yet I found Hart's *Avenue of Betrayal* to be a touching story, well-written. This is a captivating novel of intrigue and heartache, and a glimpse behind-the-scenes of a painful period in our country's history. Take it from someone who usually doesn't read this genre. Dive in and enjoy the bumpy ride to true love.

— MICHELLE LEVIGNE, AUTHOR OF THE TABOR HEIGHTS, QUARRY HALL, AND COMMONWEALTH UNIVERSE SERIES

Sandra Merville Hart's *Avenue of Betrayal* is a beautifully written saga of divided loyalties, betrayal, and love. Set in the tumultuous Civil War, Annie Swanson must decide whom can she trust, when both her brother and the man she loves betray her. This story has it all...romance, suspense, and secrets. I highly recommend it.

— ANE MULLIGAN, AUTHOR OF *IN HIGH COTTON*

Lovingly dedicated to Ray, Mary, John, Fran, Scott, Tricia, and Ruth. Thank you for your support.

This book is also dedicated to my husband, who somehow doesn't know that all my heroes include parts of him.

"Therefore, I tell you, her many sins have been forgiven—for she loved much. But he who has been forgiven little loves little."

— LUKE 7:47 (NIV)

Spying took place in many cities and towns in both the North and South during the Civil War. Northern spies in Richmond, Virginia, the Confederate capital, and Southern spies in Washington DC, the Union capital, inspired the *Spies of the Civil War* Series.

Many spies were never discovered. Extreme measures were taken to hide spying activities. Only three or four people in a spy network might know an individual's true identity. Some spies were imprisoned and some were hung. Some individuals confined their spying to a single event, such as a battle. Others created elaborate cyphers to send messages. The longer a person engaged in spying, the greater the risk of getting caught.

How many spies were never caught and took their secrets to the grave? How many swore their children and grandchildren to secrecy before revealing their spying activities during the Civil War?

We will never know.

CHAPTER 1

"*F*ather, is there troubling war news?" Annie Swanson sought to break the rare silence at her family's comfortable yet elegant dining table. Drums, bugles, and banjos from regimental bands camped in the vicinity serenaded them through open windows.

"Hmm?" Hiram Swanson's stare shifted from his lemon cake and focused vaguely on his oldest daughter. "No new clashes on a battlefield that I'm aware of, my dear."

What new misfortune besieged their country? He hadn't been his normal jovial self since returning from the bank just before supper. Something to do with the war? She hid her shudder at possible battles ahead. There'd been plenty of uproar in her city already, starting with the thousands of Federal troops camped in every available field.

"It's good to have the evening to ourselves." Beatrice poked her dessert with her fork.

"Agreed." Annie was glad that her sister, her junior by one

year at eighteen, introduced a safe topic. Division in her country had brought only one bright spot —it had distracted her father from his grief at Mother's death two years before.

"Though I do enjoy our parties more than you." Beatrice wiggled an eyebrow at her.

"You know me so well." Annie laughed. A quiet evening with family and a few close friends was more to her liking.

"Never doubt it." Her face softened as band music grew louder. "Listen to the band. They're playing 'May God Save the Union.' I love that song."

"I love the sentiment behind it." Annie's heart nearly burst with pride as she pushed her empty plate to the side.

Bea ran to the open window, her green satin dress brushing against the lace curtains in her hurry. "Oh, I can't see the band."

"No doubt we'll have an opportunity to attend another concert soon." Annie noticed that her sister's dress was the same one she'd worn to bid her latest beau a safe journey when the sergeant left to defend their country, though she doubted her sister's heart had been deeply touched by his absence. Indeed, she didn't believe that Bea had fallen in love with any of her many suitors. "We don't lack for entertainments. Between our supper parties and soirees, we've personally welcomed many officers to our country's capital."

"Perhaps the bachelors are drawn here by my beautiful daughters." Father's broad chest appeared even broader. "Beatrice, your blond ringlets are the image of your mother to me."

"That you see my mother in me is the highest praise, Father."

Annie, aware that her sister had inherited her mother's beauty, stared at her plate. Though both of them wore their hair swept back in combs, Beatrice's locks fell in a profusion of curls, whereas Annie twisted her straight brown hair into a knot at her nape.

"And my eldest daughter favors my mother's side of the

family." He studied Annie. "Did I ever tell you that you're the image of my sister as a young woman?"

"I believe you mentioned it." At least a dozen times. It was a compliment, though she'd prefer to favor her compassionate mother, who'd been as strong as she was beautiful—the perfect lady. Not that Aunt Victoria wasn't a lovely woman in her own right. She had been a lovely Southern belle in her girlhood, and Annie aspired to become equally graceful. It was simply that no one measured up to Mother. "Thank you, Father. Aunt Victoria is beautiful still. I'm glad to inherit a bit of her beauty."

"You did, make no mistake."

"Aunt Trudy is still my favorite Richmond relative." Beatrice, with one last regretful look outside, ambled to her chair. "She's been faithful in her correspondence even with the challenges of communicating between the North and South."

"I miss my Richmond family, my old plantation home." Father stared toward the window as if seeing his boyhood home instead of the beautifully attended gardens outside. "As for a quiet evening, we may yet have guests after supper."

Beatrice raised her eyebrows. "It's unfortunate your work at the bank spills into your evenings these days. Will it be a quick meeting?"

"Perhaps." He traced his finger over the condensation on his water goblet. "These are difficult days for our customers, and soon may be for us. We must become more efficient with our expenditures in these uncertain times. Don't order any new clothes without consulting me."

"Certainly, Father." Annie met her sister's wide-eyed stare. Their generous father readily agreed to most purchases. Had the war caused a financial setback at the bank? "Does this mean we won't entertain as often?" She didn't begrudge the work of entertaining, though her maids and cook shouldered much of the preparation. It was more that the soldiers she met didn't measure up to John Finn, her brother Will's friend. She and

John had danced together last summer at Will's wedding, and the gallant gentleman with his Irish brogue still occupied her dreams.

"We'll continue our duty to our soldiers." Father drummed his fingers against the white linen tablecloth. "No, we'll host soirees with the same regularity. Suppers less often."

That meant continuing to share hostess duties weekly with her sister. Meeting strangers and making them welcome in her home drained her. Not that she minded adding this task to daily sewing for the soldiers. It was just that, some days were very long.

"Plan on Wednesdays for our soirees. An easy way to save money will be simpler family meals when there are no guests."

"I'll speak to Rebecca." No doubt their cook would take a lightening of her duties in stride, as she did everything else.

"Where is Rebecca?" Father swirled the coffee grounds in his cup.

"Do you want more coffee? She left the pot." At his nod, Annie retrieved the silver-plated pot to refresh his cup, it's aroma rising with the steam. "Has the war hurt us?"

"War?" He scoffed. "This will end with one major battle."

"I'm happy to hear you say so." She sank against the cushioned high-backed chair. Father, a savvy businessman, knew more than she did about such things. "Rumors abound of gloom and doom."

"Any thinking man knows this conflict won't be of long duration." He spoke with hearty reassurance. "Perseverance, my dear daughters. Entertaining our brave officers while they train their soldiers in our fair city is a small sacrifice in light of theirs. This Wednesday, the Johnsons and the Abbotts, including their two oldest daughters, along with some army officers will attend a soiree here."

"Of course." An evening party without supper in two days wasn't a problem. "Do you know a precise number of guests?"

4

After Fort Sumter fell, her father had started inviting an increasing number of government officials, their secretaries, and soldiers to their home. Though Annie didn't send written invitations to the military men and officials, as etiquette demanded before the difficulties, she never complained about not knowing who to expect. Entertaining was a sign of Father recovering from his terrible grief. "One hears so much military news at these gatherings. By the end of the evening, my head reels with new information."

"Oh?" Father clutched his fork. The last bite of moist cake fell back onto his plate. He speared it. "What have you heard?"

"A New York soldier last week bragged of his regiment's accomplishments in erecting a fort. I don't recall details." Her father's tense demeanor encouraged Annie to probe her memories of a rather dull conversation with an Irish officer. Her dreams were of another Irish man, one from Boston whose friendship for her brother prompted him to travel to attend her mother's funeral where he first captured her attention. "Fort Corcoran, I believe."

"Anything specific?"

"Something about cannons and such." Her brow furrowed. "I believe he meant to reassure me that our city is safe."

"Soldiers are very proud of their achievements." Beatrice nodded. "And can be quite boastful over a cup of tea."

"Perhaps they boast too much." Father frowned. With his rather thickset chest and grim demeanor, he looked as if he could best his greatest enemies in the business world.

"Surely no one divulges secret military information?" The mere possibility of federal officers or government officials speaking out of turn chilled Annie. Someone in the Confederacy might twist the information to the South's advantage—and there were plenty of Southern sympathizers in the city, even among their friends. A few families had already chosen sides and moved South.

"Unlikely. Either way, come to me with any military information you hear. I'll decide if it's important enough to report to the authorities." The corners of his mouth turned upward as he straightened his shoulders. "Enough about that. I received a letter from your brother."

"Finally. Are he and Frances coming for a visit?" Annie's spirits brightened. She adored Will and his bride. "What is the news from North Carolina? Has he been unduly affected by the conflict?"

"The big news first." He spread his arms, palms up. "They expect a blessed event in December."

Annie's and Bea's gasps mingled as the sisters looked at each other.

"I'll be an aunt by Christmas." Eyes shining, Beatrice clasped her hands together.

Joy coursed through Annie. "I'll sew little nightgowns as soon as I can spare a moment."

"I'll knit stockings to warm those tiny feet." Bea giggled with happiness. "Christmas suddenly seems a lifetime away. Might we travel there for the holidays as we did last December?"

"Oh, let's go to North Carolina for Christmas, Father." Annie's brother had married a very sweet Southern belle with one major flaw—slaves worked inside their mansion and on their cotton plantation. The happy couple lived with her parents near the small town of Colerain and planned to someday build their own home on the vast acreage. "Order should be restored by then."

"Perhaps the army will require passes to travel even beyond the conflict's end. Let's see how events unfold." Father stared out the window toward the setting sun. "That leads to Will's other announcement."

Annie's heart skipped a beat at his serious expression.

"Before I tell you, I must exact a promise that you will keep this in strictest confidence." His glance bounced from one daughter to the other.

"Of course." Beatrice's fingers tightened on her water glass. "War reduces everyone to secrets."

Annie straightened her shoulders. Her sister wasn't as blind to the murmurings around the city as she'd seemed. "I'd never do anything to hurt my family."

"I believe you." Hiram's glance lingered on his youngest daughter's stony expression. "Bea?"

"Never doubt my ability to keep secrets, Father." She met his gaze squarely. "Especially if doing so protects my family."

"Tell us quickly." Annie wrung her hands. "There can be no question of our discretion."

Father dropped a crumpled linen napkin beside his plate. "Will mustered into the Confederate army."

Annie fought waves of dizziness. Her dear brother…a Rebel?

"He explains that his country is under attack"—he shifted his gaze to his plate—"leaving him no choice but to defend it."

Her blood turned to ice.

Will considered himself a citizen of *another country*? How could that happen? The dratted war had changed everything already. Surely this was a nightmare.

"Your brother is now a Confederate officer. Lieutenant William Swanson of the Seventeenth North Carolina regiment."

❧

"*I* can't believe my luck." Sergeant-Major John Finn stared down the lane toward the mansion. "To be camped near my old pal's family, and we've barely arrived in Washington City."

"The Swanson family lives in that mansion?" Lieutenant Patrick MacDonnell gave a low whistle. As a commissioned officer, he outranked his companion, yet he didn't flaunt his rank. "Your friends have a right good situation, I believe."

"You have the right of it." John surveyed the splendid three-story stone mansion half-surrounded by a semicircle of dense forest. "I was in the home only once on the sad occasion of Mrs. Swanson's death." The unexpected loss had devastated his friend, Will, though his father seemed the most affected. "The family received me graciously, yet there were too many guests to linger in conversation." It was unfortunate because his first acquaintance with the family had been at West Point four years before. Miss Annie Swanson had grown up since their initial meeting. She'd recaptured his attention during their brief conversation.

"Our picket line extends to the woods in back of their home." Patrick indicated the forest with a nod.

"So it does." John glanced behind him on the road they'd followed on their late afternoon walk. "I've had my head buried in writing reports since we set up camp two days ago. 'Tis a pretty lane."

"All the more welcome for the trees shading it. Hot day."

John grunted. He had more important matters on his mind than the scorching sun, and what did the man expect in Washington City in July? "Did you know Will Swanson at West Point?"

"Nay." Patrick resumed a leisurely pace. "I met him, of course, but don't recall any conversations."

John laughed. "No time for us underclassmen."

"Something like that."

"I was privileged to stand up at his wedding in North Carolina, where he now lives with his sweet bride." He'd danced with the lovely Annie. He couldn't forget her, though the miles between Boston and Washington City made courtship difficult...not to mention the demands of running his father's company. He'd allowed dreams of her to wither the same way his other dreams had.

"North Carolina? So, he's a Reb?"

"Not a chance." He clenched his fist. "I'll not hear anything against Will or anyone in his family."

"Meant no harm." Patrick stopped and took a step back. "'Twas a mere question, not an accusation."

"Sorry." John's reaction surprised him. Anger rarely got the best of him. "I've written Will five letters since Fort Sumter fell and received none in return."

"Sent under a flag of truce?" Patrick gave him a wary glance.

"Of course." He was grateful for the process that allowed correspondence between Northern and Southern civilians. "It's worrisome. I want to call on the family." Perhaps his training in this city was an opportunity to court sweet Annie, the woman who'd appeared in his dreams almost nightly. His thoughts flew to the kiss he'd stolen from her under a Southern moon. A smile touched his lips. Nay, not stolen but a sweet gift. "I sent holiday greetings that Annie Swanson kindly returned in December, but my main correspondence has been with Will."

"Who no longer lives here."

"True." John's attention swerved to the impressive house on the right. Not a soul in sight.

"Are you acquainted with Will's father?'

"Aye." It was too much to hope for a chance meeting outside the home. He'd best greet Mr. Swanson at the bank first. "How about a walk to his bank in town?" Perhaps there was still time today to secure an invitation to the home. Their regiment might receive orders to march out the following day. He must not risk losing the opportunity to talk with Annie. Demands from his father and the army had previously made courtship impossible. He sighed, for she was never far from his thoughts.

"Do you know the way?"

"It's on Twelfth Street near Pennsylvania Avenue."

"Too many avenues to keep 'em all straight."

John grinned at his friend's grumbles. "I've only been here once, yet I remember there's only one that matters—the one where the president's house is located."

"And that's on Pennsylvania?" Patrick raised his eyebrows.

"Aye." Afternoon sun had started its descent toward the horizon. "Let's pick up the pace." Lengthening his stride, taking one last glance at the house, he continued the walk to the heart of the city.

❧

"Why do we need a pass? We live just beyond that tree line." Annie clamped back her rising frustration at the two soldiers guarding the road and nodded toward the woods. She'd already stated their names, adding the important detail they were daughters of Hiram Swanson. Most people understood her father's influence. But these men didn't budge.

"Pardon me, miss." The red-haired soldier tipped his kepi respectfully. "But everyone needs a pass. There's a war going on."

"I realize these are troubled times, of course." Annie squelched the urge to ask if the man considered her a numskull. Thousands of soldiers drilled on the grounds of Washington City's public buildings. Distant drumbeats and bugle blasts accompanied her every stroll. Even rifle shots from drills had ceased to give her a start. Not a soul in this city overrun by Union soldiers could miss the reality of their country at war. She sighed. It had been a long, hot day filled with conversation and hard work. "Indeed, we spent the day sewing for our soldiers at the home of a friend. Mrs. Amelia Jackson and her daughter, Miss Esther Jackson, live on New York Avenue."

"We appreciate the clothing, Miss Swanson." The spokesman of the pair flushed bright red, waging an unfortunate battle with his hair. "But it ain't goin' to alter the facts. And the fact is, everyone on this road needs a pass."

Beatrice rolled her eyes heavenward behind her fan.

"That's ridiculous." She lifted her chin. "We strolled past here this very morning, and no one accosted us. What changed?"

Eyes pleading, the soldier laid his kepi across his chest. "The thing that's changed is that the Ninth Massachusetts is camped nearby. That's us, miss."

"As of when?" Determined polite responses might yet win the young man over. Otherwise, she'd have to interrupt her father's work and ask for help, for she had no idea how to go about obtaining the necessary passes.

"Sunday, miss."

Annie raised an eyebrow. "And why does that demand my family to acquire a pass?"

"This here's our picket line, and you're going to need a pass to walk these streets."

"What's the problem here?"

Annie's skin tingled at the Irish lilt in the well-remembered voice. "John? You're here?" Her gaze drank in his green eyes, that wide grin, and...the chevron on his sleeve? Pride flooded over her. He wore the uniform of a Federal officer.

Unlike her brother.

CHAPTER 2

"*A*nnie, 'tis a great pleasure." John clasped her extended hand, joy spilling over at the welcome in her sweet smile and her brown eyes. How was it possible she'd grown lovelier in the past year? A meadow of daisies did not rival her beauty in that yellow dress.

She lowered her gaze as a delicate blush tinted her peaches-and-cream complexion.

"Why, Annie, it's John Finn, our dear brother's friend." Beatrice gave the picket soldiers a sidelong glance. "Fancy meeting a Federal officer who is a family acquaintance at such a fortuitous moment."

The flap of her fan shifted John's dazed focus. "Miss Beatrice." He reluctantly released Annie's hand. "'Tis happy I am to see you both."

"You know them, Sergeant-Major Finn?"

"I do." He turned to Seth Barrows, a private in his regiment. The soldier was only following orders. John's was an enlisted rank, albeit the highest one. Would Patrick take over the situation? John introduced the sisters to Patrick and to the two men on picket duty. "I attended West Point with their brother, William Swanson. I can vouch for the family's loyalty."

Annie stiffened.

Beatrice, her face suddenly expressionless, snapped her fan shut.

Why such a reaction? Had they become Southern sympathizers? Troubled by the possibility, John glanced at Patrick, whose forehead puckered.

"Begging your pardon, suh." Seth's miserable face held determination. "Colonel Cass said no one gets by without a pass or countersign."

"We'll escort these ladies to the Provost Marshal." Patrick tipped his hat at the women. "Our soldiers have the right of it. You'll soon have your pass."

"What about our father?" Annie wrung her hands. "He'll drive a chaise home from the bank in two hours. He's an important man in the city. Will he require a pass?"

"No one gets by without a pass, miss." The guard spoke with increasing confidence.

John, noting Annie's deepening flush, removed his felt bowler hat. One couldn't blame her frustration. Military and civilian passes were a necessary inconvenience of war. "I was on my way to extend my greetings to your father. Let's obtain your passes and then speak to Mr. Swanson."

Beatrice placed a gloved hand on Annie's arm. "It seems we have little choice."

"Agreed." Annie's brown eyes warmed with trust. "We're grateful for your escort, John."

His suspicions melted. Berating himself for his doubts, he offered her his arm.

Annie laid trembling fingers on his jacketed sleeve.

He covered her small gloved hand with his larger one.

Patrick offered his arm to Beatrice, and they set off for the

Provost Marshal. They'd encounter no problems there with their escort, of that, he was certain.

~

"*I*t's good John was there today." With the pass obtained, Annie sank against the cushioned sofa in their downstairs parlor.

"'Tis glad I was to accept his help." Beatrice copied John's accent as she arched her eyebrows at Annie.

"Don't tease, Bea." Annie giggled. "I love the Irish lilt in his voice."

"What makes John so special?" She patted a dainty handkerchief to her moist brow.

The formal parlor with its expensive sofas, chairs, and rarely-used pianoforte slipped away as memories surged of a magical dance in a crowded ballroom. Afterward, they'd strolled in the garden under a moonlit sky, and he'd kissed her. The following afternoon, they'd sat together at dinner and then wandered the wooded country with other guests. The enchanting week remained like misty shadows in her dreams, for she had since received only two letters from him—both holiday greetings.

"Annie?" Beatrice snapped her fingers. "Are you dreaming?"

Heat rose in her cheeks. "John is Will's friend from West Point."

"If memory serves, they attended together one year only." She fanned her face. "Why didn't John complete his education? I was too young to care back then."

"Family obligations." Annie's brow puckered. "He was called home when his father suffered apoplexy. John said he had recovered by Will's wedding though, as the eldest son, he was still needed in Boston."

"Admirable. I wonder if he heard about Will."

Shaking her head, Annie closed her eyes. "You were talking to Lieutenant MacDonnell when John mentioned he hasn't received a recent letter and asked for news of Will and Frances."

The fanning stopped. "You didn't—"

"Of course not. I promised Father." She pressed her lips together. "I told him the happy news and about all the tiny clothes we planned to sew for our niece or nephew."

"Good." Her fanning resumed.

"Father didn't say why we must keep this a secret." Annie rubbed her forehead. Close friends could lend support.

The door opened. "Now, it's certain you girls are ready for a cool drink." Rebecca Parker, who was so much more than their cook, carried a tray with two tumblers full of red liquid into the parlor. "I prepared a nice raspberry shrub to refresh you after that long walk in the summer sun."

"Longer than expected. What a welcome treat." Annie's mouth watered as she reached for the glass. "Thanks, Rebecca."

"Did Mr. Grant give you a letter from your cousin?"

"As soon as we arrived." Annie glanced at the open pages on the side table between her and Beatrice. She longed to see Meg to know how she was coping after losing both her mother and husband. "Meg is well but has postponed her visit."

"How sad." Beatrice frowned. "Can't fault her with soldiers camping on every open field."

Rebecca nodded. "These are uncertain days."

"I worry about our cousin." Beatrice set her half-empty glass on the table and picked up the letter. "She's just now packing away her black clothing."

"She and Thomas were so much in love." Annie sighed. Thomas's parents had lived in Chicago until their deaths. His brother lived in the Territory of Colorado, the last she'd heard, and they were her only family left on Mother's side. "Perhaps she'll come when the turmoil passes."

"With all those soldiers out there, no doubt that will be soon." Beatrice folded the pages.

Rebecca rubbed the back of her neck and turned away.

A door slammed in the back of the house.

"Are Nancy and Hannah home from school?" Rebecca's daughters were the only children in the household at ten and eight.

"Sounds like their slamming of the door." The expression on her brown face hardened. "My girls had to get their papa's help to come home from their school, and that's just three blocks away."

"Oh, I didn't think of children needing them." Annie's brow furrowed.

"Thought those dark days of needing written permission to go from one place to another were behind us." Rebecca twisted her blue-checked apron.

Annie's throat constricted as it always did to recall how hard Rebecca's husband, Tom, had worked to purchase both of their freedoms from a Virginia slaveowner. How fortunate they'd all been that Annie's mother had befriended Rebecca and then hired the couple.

"Soldiers stopped them too?" The letter in Beatrice's hand fluttered onto the lap of her peach dress.

Her body jerked. "Never say they stopped you?"

Beatrice nodded. "We acquired ours this afternoon."

"Well, I declare. Even with you being Mr. Swanson's daughters and all." Rebecca's face relaxed. "I didn't know they asked white folks to get passes too."

"Yes, John Finn happened by and helped us." The deliciously tart yet sweet drink soothed Annie's parched throat, as John's presence had done for her sagging spirits that day. What a wonder that he was camped within a mile of her home. Perhaps he'd make an effort to see her.

"I recall you speaking of him." Rebecca gave her a sly smile.

"Fancy you seeing him with all the goings on here." Her eyes widened. "Ah, he's in the army."

"Yes." It felt as if Rebecca and her family belonged here nearly as much as Annie's own family, and she was glad they were paid decent wages in this home…the same as their butler, housekeeper, maids, gardeners, and stable workers. "He's now Sergeant-Major John Finn of the Ninth Massachusetts."

Rebecca clucked her tongue. "And here in Washington. Imagine that."

Happiness erupted into a giggle at her smug expression. Annie had told her about dancing with John and Rebecca had looked for him to call. So had Annie. In vain.

Until now.

"He know about your brother being a Lieutenant for the South?"

Annie gaped at her. "I didn't know *you* knew."

"I was coming in to clear the table the other night when Mr. Swanson said it." Her face was devoid of expression. "I left right quick. Figured you wanted a private talk."

"It's a surprise." Her tongue stumbled on a word too mild for her despair. Will had often wandered into the kitchen when he was a growing boy, to look for a sugar cake, doughnut, or cookie, requests which Rebecca had indulged with a satisfied smile. Annie wondered if Will's decision hurt her, especially in light of her former life in Virginia. "Father asked us to keep it a secret."

"Reckon he would." She pursed her lips.

"As one of Will's dearest friends, I believe he deserves to know." Annie didn't look forward to telling John. It might sever their friendship. No. A friendship such as they had withstood such adversity.

"Take Father at his word. Tell no one." Arranging her hoop skirt, Beatrice sank against the cushions and closed her eyes. "Unfortunately."

"Why?" Annie glanced over to ensure that her sister's ankles didn't show, as her mother had often done. Good. Only matching peach slippers peeked out from beneath the layers of fabric. Neither sister chose to wear large hoop skirts, considering them a nuisance. Yet, bowing to fashion, both wore smaller hoops.

Beatrice opened her eyes. "Do you remember when Orville Wilcox mustered into the Confederate army in April?"

Orville's mother had been her mother's friend. "Yes."

"Didn't you wonder if the rest of the family were loyal to the Confederacy? There were murmurings about it."

"Well, Southern sympathizers perhaps." Annie had kept her mistrust to herself.

"And the whole family moved to Charleston two weeks later?"

"Mrs. Wilcox lived in South Carolina in her girlhood."

Rebecca's back stiffened. She moved to the window facing the road.

"Don't you see?" Beatrice said. "Father was born in Richmond."

Annie gulped. "His family owned slaves when he was a child."

"They still do." Beatrice nodded. "Even if Papa doesn't. Not now."

Rebecca tugged the curtains half-closed, blocking a gentle breeze entering the three-foot gap in the almost floor-to-ceiling window.

"Father fears folks will doubt us. Yet our loyalty is secure." Annie fingered her mother's cameo broach pinned on the bodice of her delaine dress.

"Neighbors will question our allegiance the same as you doubted the patriotism of Orville's family." Beatrice sipped her drink.

"Not John's friend." Annie lifted her chin. He deserved to know. "He'll understand."

"Will he?" Rebecca, a tall woman who still turned heads in her mid-thirties, dropped the edge of the curtain. "You say he serves the Federal army. Your brother's a lieutenant in the Confederate army."

Annie sucked in her breath. She hadn't allowed her thoughts to focus on that difference. After all, the men had attended school together. Got into scrapes together. Joked together.

Rebecca spun around, her brown eyes darkening. "They're enemies now."

~

"*What* luck that Mr. Swanson invited us to a soiree tomorrow evening."

"'Tis glad I am to receive the invitation." John worked by lantern light inside the tent he and Patrick shared. Rows of them extended perhaps a half mile for his regiment alone. "Who knows what wind will blow the Ninth Massachusetts from such a pleasant location? And he invited me to call whenever I'm able." He'd been pleased with Mr. Swanson's cordial welcome.

They'd scarcely spent a quarter hour with the busy banker, who didn't seem concerned about the need for a pass. "I foresaw this," he'd told them candidly. "We've become a city of tents. Can't avoid such inconveniences with our country at war."

"He must realize," Patrick said, "at least in part, how the army can fill a soldier's days."

"Aye. Did you extend his invitation to Colonel Cass?"

Patrick nodded. "We'll drill tomorrow in preparation for Independence Day parades."

"Our band will play." That same band now played "May God Save the Union," a patriotic tune. Supper had been consumed two hours ago. Camp activities began to quieten.

"They will." Patrick lay back on his cot, hands clasped behind his head. "The colonel must send his regrets. Other army officers are coming. Perhaps a few Northern beauties like the ones we saw today will attend."

"Your betrothed awaits you back home," John muttered.

"No need for that frosty tone." Patrick closed his eyes. "Me heart belongs to my Deborah. No, I'm dreaming of refreshments."

Was that true? Patrick was not one to trifle with a good woman's affections, was he? No, he merely meant to acknowledge the beauty of the Swanson sisters. A man had to be blind to miss Annie's dazzling smile. "I miss my mam's cooking, too, but tomorrow's invitation doesn't include supper."

"More's the pity."

"Expect refreshments." He well remembered their hospitality and anticipated talking with Annie. If not for his da's illness and insistence on John taking over the family's furniture business, he might have been free to pursue her hand.

Free? He chafed under the figurative bit in his mouth, put there by his family's successful business. His first independence since Da's apoplexy had come from mustering into the Union army.

Truth be told, his dreams took him to the West—and he couldn't see the daughter of a wealthy banker wishing to take that arduous journey with him. As things stood, friendship was all he could offer Annie, but, oh, how he longed to court her.

Sweet memories of his time with her at Will's wedding flooded over him.

He set his quill pen aside. His spirit would be more settled to hear directly from Will.

But his sister was here.

A sudden desire to be near Annie compelled him to his feet. Too late to call, but he'd stroll past her home. He stretched. "Think I'll walk before bed."

Patrick grunted. "Today's walk was enough for me. Remember the countersign?"

"Aye." He knew the word to give their soldiers standing on picket—Union. It changed regularly to prevent Southern soldiers and spies from sneaking into their ranks.

John greeted men in the aisle between tents but didn't stop to talk. The sun had dropped beyond the pink horizon. A breeze ruffled his hair, cooling his skin.

The familiar song of crickets accompanied his stroll on lumpy dirt and stone. Just as he passed a farmhouse, footsteps behind him increased in pace. He turned to look.

A stranger, for he knew at least by sight all the men in his regiment, in a Federal uniform with the shoulder straps of a lieutenant. His shoulders tensed. Though the man, above medium height, fought on the same side as John, a fellow couldn't be too careful. His colonel agreed, for didn't his picket line stretch yards from here, standing guard for Rebels? He saluted.

The officer returned the salute. "Sergeant-Major Finn?" Halting an arm's length away, the stranger spoke in muted tones.

"Aye." John didn't recall meeting the brown-haired man with a mustache forming a circle on each side of his mouth. "Do we know one another?"

"My name is Lieutenant Christopher Farmer." He extended his hand. "I work for General Winfield Scott."

"Commanding General of the United States Army—that General Scott?" John shook his hand.

"Is there another?" He smiled a little.

"Of course not." Heat rose in John's face. "A pleasure, Lieutenant Farmer." He glanced at dark woods on either side of the road. Odd place to meet an officer with such important connections.

"Pleasant evening."

"'Tis." John eyed him. The man seemed to have something on his mind.

"Ever heard of the Swanson family?"

"They live in yon mansion." John twisted toward the home. Blocked by trees. Good. Why was Lieutenant Farmer looking for them? He widened his stance.

"You headed there?"

"Too late to call." John stiffened, every protective instinct on alert. Was this stranger's interest mere curiosity for a wealthy family? "My invitation is for a soiree tomorrow evening." Best cooperate since the officer worked directly for General Scott.

"That's very good." Piercing brown eyes raked John's face. "Are you a close acquaintance?"

"I am. Will and I attended West Point together." John would be a commissioned officer already—a lieutenant—had he graduated. He squelched that old disappointment. His education had been a mere stepping-stone anyway, one his da had removed.

"The general learned of the West Point connection today."

Why was General Scott interested in a sergeant-major's friendship with Will?

"Tell me, Sergeant-Major Finn, are you loyal to the Union?"

"What's this?" John stepped back. "'Tis proud I am to stand for my country."

"I expected nothing less." The officer's expression softened. "I'm here to offer a way to further serve your country."

"I'm performing an important task already in the army."

"You can do both."

Curious. The man spoke in riddles.

Wheels struck against stones behind a horse's clopping hooves. A landau approached. John tipped his hat at the driver and his passengers, a couple near his parents' ages. The man nodded, his features barely discernable in the gathering darkness under a canopy of trees.

John turned back. The lieutenant's hand was still raised in

tipping his hat, yet it shadowed his face. "What is this extra duty?"

The officer's gaze followed the landau, now twenty yards distant. "I will speak frankly." He lowered his voice. "Are you aware that Lieutenant William Swanson mustered into the Confederate army?"

CHAPTER 3

*W*ill...fighting for the enemy?

Sweat broke out on John's face. He rubbed his hands over his suddenly wet forehead and his bowler hat toppled to the ground. Was it true? No, it couldn't be, or Annie would have mentioned it. Neither had Hiram said anything. John had deserved to hear this news from them, if it was even true.

"He's with the Seventeenth North Carolina regiment." Lieutenant Farmer picked up John's hat and brushed dust from it. "Did you know?"

He shook his head, his senses reeling. He wanted to yell that it was a lie, yet it was possible. Will's bride was a North Carolinian, a beautiful Southern belle.

"The Swansons didn't mention it when you spoke to them today?"

John pulled himself back sharply. "I'm being watched then? To what purpose?"

"Not you." Lieutenant Farmer shook his head. "The banker."

Darkness thickened under the trees. "I'd best be returning. It's almost time for *Taps*."

"One moment. General Scott is tasking you to discover if Mr. Swanson is loyal to his country."

"Absolutely. He is loyal." No doubt about the father's loyalty —though he now supported the opposite side as his son. John sucked in his breath. Didn't he?

"You know this with certainty?"

John opened his mouth. Shut it. He'd not seen Will's father for a year. Much had happened lately to alter folks' thinking. He'd witnessed friends in Boston embroiled in heated arguments over the country's division. He simply didn't know.

"Hiram Swanson is from Richmond." Lieutenant Farmer peered into the woods. "Some of our wealthy citizens moved to Virginia and other Southern states after the election. They don't care for President Lincoln. Others stayed and are passing our secrets to Confederate friends."

John stepped closer to hear the man's words, spoken in low tones.

"Hiram is in a position to learn military information from his customers." He paused. "He's hosted colonels, majors, captains, governmental undersecretaries...men who know secrets."

John stiffened. "A man wishes to support our officers with an evening's entertainment, and suspicions are his thanks?"

"We are a country at war, Sergeant-Major Finn. We can't turn a blind eye because of a man's standing in the community."

John rubbed his chin. The wealthy must obey the law as well as the poor. "Methinks you're wrong about him."

"Then help me prove it."

Spy on Hiram Swanson? How could he do that to Annie? To Will, even if he fought for the Confederacy? "What you ask is too great a betrayal. This family has entrusted me with their friendship."

"What question is there of betrayal if they are as innocent as you claim?"

They? Never say the man suspected Annie and Beatrice of stealing secrets to help the Confederates? The back of his neck grew hot. "Will ye be sending someone else if I refuse?"

Lieutenant Farmer met his stare without flinching.

"If the deed must be done, I'll do it." The idea of a stranger spying on the family was far worse. He'd prove their innocence and put an end to this nonsense. "'Twill be a pleasure to clear the Swanson name."

"Good. Your country is grateful for this service."

How grateful would Annie be if she discovered him spying on her father? She must never know. "Where can I find you?"

"I'll wait here tomorrow night for a report and give you my direction then."

"Yes, sir." John remembered his training enough to salute. Then the officer was gone.

John spotted a glimmer of light in a house off the road. This sordid conversation had taken place a quarter mile from Annie's home.

Traitor that he was, his eagerness for tomorrow's entertainment turned to dread.

As he headed toward camp, their bugler played *Taps* to end the day. The mournful tune struck a chord deep inside him. He lengthened his stride, intent on the empty avenue with mature trees on the right and left. Dark. Looks were deceiving, especially in times of war. Pickets from his regiment guarded these woods just out of eyesight. Watched his progress on the dirt road, though it was doubtful anyone had heard the whispered conversation.

He clutched his hat. What would tomorrow bring?

Clearing Hiram Swanson of General Scott's suspicions, that's what the new day would bring.

Unfortunately, nothing lessened the despair of learning that he and his best buddy fought on opposing sides.

~

*A*nnie stole a glance at John, who stood with a group of soldiers in the corner of the large drawing room. He talked and chuckled, but there was a tense quality in his stance. His family, though owners of three furniture stores in Boston, were not as wealthy as her father. Perhaps he was unaccustomed to soirees.

"Don't you agree, Miss Swanson?"

Shifting her focus back to her companion, she inclined her head at the bearded military man some ten years her senior. Though she had heard few phrases of his five-minute monologue on his regiment's weaponry, his eager expression warned her not to invite a repeat of the information. "Oh, of course, Captain Wheeler. How clever of you."

He flushed. "Well, it's thanks to the combined efforts of my..."

Annie's attention wandered back to John. Someone smoking a cigar blocked her view of him. Hiding a grimace at the delay in speaking to the man who'd done a fair job of stealing her heart, she craned her neck for a better view.

John looked over. His eyes twinkled at her.

Annie returned his smile, and then, flushing, looked away. It was as if he'd known where she sat, causing her to wonder how many times he'd glanced at her.

Rebecca entered with a tray of iced spice cakes and lemon snaps. This was the third and last round of refreshments she'd offer to guests. She monitored and refilled a refreshment table in the upstairs parlor near the dressing rooms all evening.

The captain's enthusiasm over a cannon almost put her in a stupor. To combat boredom, Annie searched the crowded room for her father. No sign of him. He'd been absent over thirty minutes, so he must be entertaining guests partaking of refreshments upstairs. Military men enjoyed delicacies that reminded them of home. There'd likely be few desserts left at evening's end.

Male laughter riveted Annie's attention to a couch, where Rose Greenhow sat among a circle of Union officers. The widow's lively conversation and merry laughter enlivened the atmosphere, making Annie's job of entertaining guests easier.

A glance at the clock brought a relieved sigh. Ten o'clock. Guests would leave soon. She glanced at Donna, one of the maids. The pretty brunette with curls to rival those of Beatrice was stationed beside a tea tray, where she served tea, coffee, and lemonade. The other maid, Barbara, collected empty cups and dishes off tables without disturbing guests. A striking combination of brown eyes and blond hair coupled with a friendly smile garnered her a share of male attention.

Baskets of daisies, red roses, and lavender from their own garden graced the room with beauty and delighted Annie's senses with their fragrance. Lavender was her particular favorite. Its relaxing fragrance battled the cigar smoke hanging in the room.

Beatrice seemed enthralled with one of the guests. As hostesses, they were supposed to have short conversations with as many guests as possible, and she'd sat with the man far too long. Who was he? Annie craned her neck and then relaxed. It was Lieutenant Patrick MacDonnell, John's friend.

Come to think of it, Annie had been with *this* guest too long. As soon as the captain paused for breath, she stood and excused herself. She'd waited all evening for a moment with John. One guest had just departed, and others would soon follow. She'd invite John to linger.

Pausing for brief exchanges as she ambled around numerous chairs and small groups, it took several minutes to cross the length of the parlor.

John saw her coming. He said something to his companion—a stranger to Annie—and then sauntered toward her.

"We scarcely had a moment to talk when you arrived, John. Are you enjoying the evening?"

"Very much." His eyes brightened. "I wondered if you'd free yourself from your guests to spare a moment for me."

She sighed. "There are a lot of them." That sounded inhospitable. Heat rose in her cheeks. "I didn't mean that—"

"Of course." He chuckled, a comforting sound that invited a person to join in the laughter. "The city hosts many regiments. It stands to reason that affects parlors of its good citizens."

Her flush receded at his gracious response. Over half the guests were strangers to her and he seemed to understand that erected her reserves. Perhaps he even shared the discomfort. "Thanks for understanding." She tilted her head. "I long for news of your family. Shall we sit?"

Green eyes crinkling, he offered his arm. "'Twould be a pleasure."

His Irish accent fell on her ears like music. She placed gloved fingertips on his uniformed forearm, and he led them to a mauve cushioned sofa near the large window in front of the home. With a pang, she released his arm to sit beside him, stifling a sigh that her modified hoop skirt—though half the size of the current fashion—forced him to sit farther away. She smoothed a tiny wrinkle in her pink satin gown. Thankfully, the sheer overskirt with two rows of lace trim at the hem hid the imperfection. With its modest scoop neck and fitted bodice, it was possibly her last new dress for a while. She wanted to look her best for John.

Happiness bubbled over her that he sat beside her in her parlor.

Because his smiling face was angled toward her, her dreams had a chance of coming true.

~

*a*nnie's beauty dazzled John. She was so pretty that he almost forgot they sat in a crowded parlor until he caught a whiff of cigar smoke.

"My sister and I are indebted for your escort to the Provost Marshal yesterday." Annie dimpled at him. "You knew just what to do."

"'Twas a great pleasure." His heartbeat quickened at her smile. Did she realize its effect on him? "Grateful to be of service."

"It was lovely to learn of your military excursions during our walk yesterday." She folded dainty, white-gloved hands in her lap, "Tell me about your family. How is your father's health?"

"Better." John's heartbeat slowed and became heavy. "He has recovered most of his vigor yet hesitates to retake the reins for our family's furniture factory. Despite this, it was my duty to serve our country."

"I'm happy he has somewhat recovered. Who's leading the company now?"

He grimaced. "He is, with help from trusted managers."

"How about your brother?"

Yes, what about Carl? His brother, only two years his junior, preferred to drink and socialize over working in their father's factory or stores. "Our da desires to expand our business. Carl is searching for a new store location in New York City." He left in February, likely spending more time in taverns than locating a storefront.

Annie's forehead wrinkled. "Didn't he also attend West Point?"

"A few months only. His grades weren't high enough to stay." If only John had Carl's opportunities. The weight of the family business rested on John's shoulders. His father hadn't lifted the burden even when his health improved. John had worked dawn to dusk to learn management of the entire business, which had declined along with his father's health. His success only bolted him to the factory as securely as the walls within it. He'd saved the business...and now he was stuck with it. "Carl offered to establish and run the new store." It was about time he accepted responsibility. "Da might allow this."

"Perhaps it will be the making of him." She nodded to a guest passing by but focused on him again quickly. "How are your sisters?"

"You may recall that Patricia and her husband anticipated a baby when we spoke in North Carolina." He smiled at her blush. Was she remembering their kiss? "I have happy news. Phillip was born before I left Boston. He is six months old." He chuckled. "That boy has a healthy cry. Patricia never needs to wonder if he needs something."

"A mixed blessing." Annie laughed. "I'm happy for your family's wonderful news."

"Aunt Madelynn adores her nephew. It's good they only live one street away, as she visits the Lovell home daily. When her beau isn't coming to call, that is."

Annie puckered her lips in thought.

A desire to kiss those lips was too strong. He forced himself to look away. Straight at her father as he entered the parlor with a younger man. Mr. Swanson had been gone the better part of an hour. Not rude exactly, not with a room set aside for refreshments and his daughters in the parlor as hostesses.

Next time, John resolved to follow him if he was absent above a quarter hour, and not make himself available to speak with the lovely Annie whenever she managed to break free from her hostess duties. Frustrated at the trail of his thoughts, he shook his head. Spying made him question a friend, and that didn't set well.

"Madelynn isn't sixteen?"

"What?" Mr. Swanson now spoke with a widow. John had been introduced to her but couldn't recall her name.

"You shook your head when I asked if Madelynn was sixteen." A tiny frown formed.

"I didn't hear you correctly." At all. "That's her age. Mam believes her suitor, Todd Caudill, will soon propose. He works at one of our shops where they met. If they marry, I'll train him on every task. My parents trust him. He's responsible. Steady. He could eventually manage the whole business, if necessary."

"If they marry?" She tilted her head. "Do you doubt his intentions?"

"It's this war." He tugged his ear. "I talked him out of mustering into our regiment but ..."

"He may enlist if the war lasts very long."

"Yes." He met her concerned brown gaze.

"Then you may relax." Leaning forward, she patted his arm. "My father believes the war will be over with one big battle."

~

The muscles in John's arm tensed under Annie's fingertips. "Don't you agree?"

He glanced across the room toward her father. "Don't wish to disagree with a smart man like Mr. Swanson. Let's hope he has the right of it."

Her fingers slipped from his arm. "But you doubt it."

"Never underestimate the enemy."

Annie's heart skipped a beat. Her brother was...*No. Never the enemy.*

"I will go where my country sends me." John straightened his shoulders. "And fight whatever battles it faces."

Pride bubbled over at his bravery in preparing to fight for their country.

Against her brother.

Her hand jerked. No, one battle would settle it. Her father was right. He must be right.

John glanced at guests leaving in groups of two or three. "The party's over." He sighed and turned back to her. "Before I go, please give me news of your brother. He hasn't replied to my letters of late."

Annie's heart plummeted. Will's secret weighted her down. She never wanted to lie to John, yet her father had sworn her to secrecy. "He...he and Frances are very busy planning for the babe's arrival."

"That must be it." His jaw tensed. "What of war news? Has he written of troops forming in North Carolina?"

She drew back. Was he asking her to reveal Confederate secrets? Troop information was a topic her father had told her to repeat to no one but himself. "I know naught of such things." Her voice came out as a whisper. "You, as a soldier, know the truth of this."

His gaze dropped. "Aye."

There had never been an awkward moment between them before that one. Annie stared at his bowed head. Did he imagine Will heading north to join the Federal cause?

Movement at the door caught her glance. Widow Greenhow gave her a gracious nod. Annie rose, and John followed suit. "Pardon me one moment. I must speak to someone."

～

*J*ohn, his heart heavy as a stone, watched Annie greet the widow at Hiram's side.

Annie had avoided his question. Because she didn't want other guests to hear her reply?

Possibly. He understood why she preferred to keep information about Will to herself. He'd wait until they were alone and ask again. There was something else he wanted to ask her tonight.

He stood apart as Beatrice joined the small group by the

parlor entrance to bid farewell to the widow, who was a family friend, if their animated faces were any indication.

He looked around the parlor, decorated in shades of dark pink that complimented the floral wallpaper. The furniture was expensive cherry wood—an excellent choice.

The widow left with Hiram. Two gentlemen in ordinary frock coats followed.

John ambled over, and Annie met him a few steps away from Beatrice.

"Thank you for a pleasant evening." He clasped her gloved hand, reveling in her touch. She gave his fingers a gentle squeeze, lending him courage to make his request. "Tomorrow is Independence Day. Our regiment has planned a public drill, and our band will perform. May I escort you and your sister?"

"That will be lovely." A blush infused her face.

His heartbeat quickened. It was as if their relationship picked up where it left off after the magical week of Will's wedding. "Our troops are learning well. It will be quite a display."

"You wouldn't deceive me, so I'll hold you to that promise." She laughed and released his hand.

Deceit. He flinched. Spying on Hiram couldn't end too soon.

Annie beckoned her sister. "Bea, John has invited us to his regimental drill and band concert to celebrate Independence Day."

"A concert?" Beatrice clasped her hands together. "I'd love that above all things. Thanks for including me in your invitation." Her glance slid from him to her sister.

"Wonderful." Annie's sparkling eyes heightened his anticipation of the promised entertainment. "I have no duties with the drill, so I will watch them with you. I'll come for you at eleven o'clock."

Hiram reentered the room alone.

As John was the last guest, etiquette demanded his swift departure.

"That will be lovely." Her smile widened. "Father, John offered to escort Bea and me to his regimental drill and band concert tomorrow."

"How fortuitous since I will be busy tomorrow. It sounds like a delightful entertainment." Hiram tapped John's shoulder. "I regret we didn't get the opportunity to talk. Come again next Wednesday."

Annie tilted her head with an upraised brow.

"I will, thank you." John looked around the empty room. "It seems Lieutenant MacDonnell left without me."

"Perhaps he didn't wish to disturb your conversation." Hiram shook his hand as they strolled from the room. "Don't worry. There will be plenty of opportunities to talk while you're in the city."

Annie followed them to the long table near the front door. The butler offered him the only hat remaining on the table with a flourish.

"Much obliged."

The white-haired butler inclined his head and opened the ten-foot tall, ornately-carved oak door.

John turned at the entrance. "I will see you tomorrow." He tipped his felt hat as he donned it.

She inclined her head. "Eleven o'clock."

John hurried toward the dark avenue. A difficult conversation awaited him this evening. Best get it done.

CHAPTER 4

*U*nderbrush rustled in the woods to the right of the dark avenue.

John reached to his side for the firearm he'd left at his tent. A Rebel soldier? He tensed for a fight, drawing comfort that men standing picket were within shouting distance.

A man emerged from the woods. "Good evening, Sergeant-Major Finn."

"Lieutenant Farmer?" The officer wore the plain clothes of a working man. Should he still salute?

"The same." Quick strides brought him within a yard of John. "No need to salute. We'll dispense with formality while working together. Call me Christopher unless we meet in uniform in other soldiers' company. Then, of course, you'll address me as an officer."

"You're in civilian clothes." John gave his head a little shake. "To what purpose?"

"Our conversations are less likely to be noticed." He glanced around. "Discover anything this evening?"

John's gut clenched. "The Swanson's cook makes delicious lemon snaps."

"Noted." Christopher lowered his voice. "See anything suspicious?"

"Precious little." Better to tell what he saw and get back to camp. "It was a pleasant evening attended by local families, officers, and a couple of undersecretaries."

"Who do they work for?"

He named the senators, watching as Christopher made a note on a piece of paper with a pencil stub. It was too dark to see one another clearly. How did he expect to write anything legible?

"Anything unusual happen?"

"Mr. Swanson was absent from the main party for nearly an hour. Presumably in the refreshment parlor with other guests. Sorry, I should have followed him."

Christopher looked up. "Recognize who returned with him?"

"A civilian—perhaps a neighbor or local businessman."

"Anyone else at the soiree who stood out to you?"

"A widow. Lively woman on friendly standing with the whole family." John frowned as Christopher's pencil scratched across the page again. "Nothing of note there."

"Perhaps not." He pocketed the paper and pencil. "When will you see the family again?"

"I'm escorting Miss Annie and Miss Beatrice to our military drill tomorrow." John folded his arms.

"Very good." Christopher gave a crisp nod. "I'll meet you here tomorrow night before *Taps*."

"No need. Mr. Swanson is busy tomorrow and cannot accompany us."

"I see." Christopher rubbed his chin. "Keep your wits about you anyway. The sisters may reveal something in innocent conversation that will help us." His fingers touched the brim of his straw hat. "Tomorrow."

So this was how it would be...outranked without a uniform no matter his opinion. "You'll be wasting your time." But he said it to Christopher's back as the man disappeared into the darkness.

~

*D*istant musketry, bugles, and drums from other regiments lent a patriotic Independence Day backdrop as Annie stood in blazing sunshine beside her handsome soldier, her fingertips resting lightly on his arm. Gleaming rifles in the hands of several hundred uniformed soldiers impressed her as they went through the various drills. Shouted orders meant nothing to her or Beatrice at her side, she was certain, yet something stirred in her soul to watch the young men sworn to protect her country handle their rifles nearly in unison. These must be the Union's finest soldiers.

John seemed to believe it as well, for pride blazed from his eyes beside her.

An earlier flag-raising ceremony had stirred a depth of emotion that surprised Annie. In the midst of this nation's terrible troubles, displays of devotion and loyalty touched her core. She wondered if Southern states celebrated the day as they did here in the city with dress parades, band concerts, and speeches.

Did Will feel the same patriotic stirrings toward the Confederacy as she did to the Union? Did those sentiments divide them as a family?

The mere thought chilled her despite the pleasant warmth of the sun high in the sky.

Audience applause jolted her back to the present.

"Our troops performed well." John leaned over, his voice a whisper.

"Indeed." Annie flushed that her attention had wavered.

"Thrilling." Beatrice gazed at the soldiers marching away.

"They started as raw recruits and worked hard to become

good soldiers." John searched Annie's expression. "Officers trained them on Long Island in the Boston Harbor."

"An inspiration to behold." Pride bubbled up inside Annie. "You and your officers trained them well."

"Not me." He shook his head. "I'll have responsibilities guiding men in battle, but maintaining records for the regiment is a big task of mine."

"I'm certain you excel at it." Annie's heart swelled as she stared up at her handsome escort in his blue coat. She dared to dream he'd become her beau.

"I hear music." Beatrice looked across the field toward a band of some twenty members.

Drums, bugles, guitars, fifes, violins, and banjos played an unfamiliar song. "What are they playing?"

"That's *The First Gun is Fired.*"

"Ah. George Root's song about the Battle of Fort Sumter." Beatrice chuckled. "Don't look so surprised at my familiarity with it, Annie. You know my love of music."

"I do, indeed." Annie opened her blue fan—a long ago gift from her mother—and fanned her face.

"We can hear the band from the copse of trees." John indicated the shaded area with a nod. "Afterwards, we'll share in a meal, one that women in the vicinity have graciously embellished with their own offerings."

"Rebecca promised a batch of chicken croquettes and potato cakes." Annie rested her hand on John's right arm as he offered his left to Beatrice. "I recommend them."

"Don't forget her lemon snaps." As they strolled, Beatrice looked over her shoulder. "I don't recognize this song."

"Our music lover doesn't know a song?" Annie teased.

"It's *May God Save the Union.*" John chuckled. "The war seems to have inspired our writers and composers."

They had reached the welcome coolness of the shade, where local families lounged on colorful quilts or chairs. Annie greeted them and introduced John. She turned to him as the strains of *Home, Sweet Home* swelled in the air. Did he feel at home when with her?

~

The Declaration of Independence had been read after lunch, ending John's regiment's entertainment for the day.

"Shall we sit?" He indicated an unpopulated area under a mighty oak tree. At her nod, he spread the quilt she'd brought. He took her hand and helped her sit, thankful that her blue skirt didn't fan out with the current wide hoop style. He liked her sedate, lady-like manner of dress. In fact, she was nearly perfect in every way.

Except her honesty about her brother, or lack thereof. He intended to introduce the topic before Beatrice returned with Patrick. Hopefully requesting specific songs from the band would take several minutes.

"What a lovely day." Annie fanned her face.

"'Tis a grand aul day. All the better for the beautiful guests who graced our humble celebration." He tipped his hat at her.

"Why, thank you, kind sir." Her dimples showed.

That sweet smile of hers was going to be his undoing. Best change the subject. "My compliments to your cook." He patted his stomach. "Those chicken croquettes were delicious."

"I told you." She twirled an escaping tendril of brown hair with her finger.

"You had the right of it." Suddenly he was back in North Carolina beneath another tree, where he'd kissed her for the first time. He'd sure like to do it again, but not here in this crowded field.

"I'm looking for Bea and Patrick." Annie scanned the crowd. "Ah, they're standing with the banjo player. I can't distinguish the tune over the crowd. Not to mention the neighboring bands adding to the din."

"Plenty of other drills and bands to keep everyone in the city busy all day."

"Thanks for making this a day to remember."

"'Tis my pleasure."

"You are as impressed as everyone else about our cook." Annie leaned back against the trunk. "Did Will tell you Rebecca's story?"

"No. She's not your slave, is she?"

"Certainly not." Eyes snapping, she pushed against the tree as if ready to stand.

"'Tis glad I am to hear it." He laid a gentle hand on her shoulder. Unfortunately, slavery was legal in the city. "Yet I'm not surprised. My apologies for asking."

She averted her eyes. "I despise such assumptions. Rebecca and her husband are paid, the same as the rest of our staff."

"Nay. Not my assumption. Merely a thoughtless blunder I deeply regret." What a dimwitted fool he was. Rebecca obviously was an important person in Annie's life. "Please tell me about her."

"Rebecca and her husband, Tom, have been with us since 1850." The fire receded from her brown eyes. "He's a farrier, gifted with horses. I have great admiration for all he's accomplished."

He raised his eyebrows. Men who shoed horses were plentiful and necessary in a city this size. "Both have earned your respect."

"They were enslaved by the same master. A decent one, as it turned out." Annie glanced at the refreshment tables, plates and bowls nearly empty after a hearty meal. "Tom trained as a farrier from boyhood. He took to it with astonishing skill. His master allowed him to work in their village and share in the profits. Tom negotiated with him to apply it toward the purchase of his freedom."

John blinked. "That's amazing."

"Tom fell in love with a kitchen maid. Rebecca was sixteen at the time. Tom proposed and then negotiated to buy her freedom as well." Her eyes hardened. "They waited to get married until given their papers because they didn't want to have to purchase their children's freedom as well."

John's mouth tightened. It was a terrible system—one he fought to squelch.

"They traveled to Washington City in 1850. My mother met Rebecca at the market one day and learned of her experience. She hired the couple immediately."

"The more I learn of your mother, the more my respect for her grows."

"She was the most remarkable woman I've ever known. Rebecca's second." Annie gave him a tremulous smile. "Tom manages my father's horses, our two carriages, the landau, and other vehicles with the help of a stable hand, yet there isn't enough work to busy them all day. He also works as a farrier at a local stable. Everyone recognizes his gift."

"He must be quite a man."

"He is."

He removed his bowler hat and twisted it in his hands. "How did you come to be so close to Rebecca?"

"Well, of course, knowing her background stirs respect in any heart." Annie gazed at groups mingling in the field. "But it's more than that. I was eight when she came. She spoiled us children with sweets. She rewarded our almost daily visits to the kitchen with something to 'tide us over' until our next meal. We held her babies while she cooked, and she listened to our childhood troubles. Mother, who hired a maid to take care of the children, was often there as well. There were many afternoons we all took tea together in our parlor while Father worked."

"She's a treasured employee." John understood. He appreciated the people managing his family's furniture stores.

"Far more than that." Tears glistened in her eyes. "My father lost his way after Mother died. I finally see signs of him taking an interest in his business, his community again—thanks to the war." She extracted an embroidered handkerchief from the sleeve of her pale green dress and dabbed at her eyes. "Rebecca was the one we turned to, the one who kept us strong. I cried on her shoulder once only to look up and see tears staining her own face." She met his gaze squarely. "She understands loss, grief. Perhaps it's because we have no other family in the city, but she's become almost a second mother to me."

They were as close as that? John's jaw slackened. He sandwiched her gloved hand between his own. "I'm glad you have her in your life. Your home."

"Me, too." She placed her free hand on top of his and then looked away. After a moment, she removed her hands, folding them in her lap.

Aware that she struggled to recover her composure, he sank back against the rough bark of the oak tree. Her cook's story was inspiring. What then must Annie think of her brother's decision to serve in the Confederate army? "I wish Will were here. I've a hankerin' to see me old friend."

"I miss him too." She paled.

"Annie? Are you all right?" He clasped her hand, drawing it close to his heart. "May I get you a glass of lemonade?"

"That would be most welcome." She stared at their clasped hands.

Releasing her, he sprang to his feet. "I'll return shortly."

∼

*S*haking, Annie braced herself against the sturdy trunk to raise herself to her feet. The pain of Will's choice to serve on the opposing side struck her afresh. This was supposed to be his country too. He'd chosen differently.

Heat coursed through her body. Her brother had betrayed their family…a wrong that couldn't be remedied.

Teasing laughter, a ready smile, inherent honesty, and family loyalty made him the best of brothers. Her pride in him had deepened when he went to West Point.

Will had been a favorite with the staff. He'd pretended to steal more than his share of sweets from Rebecca's kitchen while she pretended not to notice. He had spent many hours with Tom in the stable, learning to care for horses. How had he forgotten his roots so quickly? It seemed he'd put their mother's abolitionist teachings behind him. What had so changed him?

He fought for the enemy. Had he lunged at her with a knife, she could scarcely be more wounded.

She didn't trust herself not to unburden herself to John. The horrible secret was too fresh not to betray herself by some word, some unbidden facial expression, to alert John that all was not as it should be. Certainly not as she wanted it to be.

Angry as she was, she didn't want to drive a wedge between the two friends. Fighting on opposing sides in this war between the states might be one of the few things strong enough to divide them.

CHAPTER 5

Fireworks lit the night sky. Smoke temporarily masked the moon and stars. John left for his meeting with Christopher amid the noise of his camp's artillery salutes, cheers, and laughter. A waste of time, just as he'd warned the officer last evening.

But it was another worry that consumed him now.

When he had returned to Annie with a cool glass of lemonade that afternoon, she'd insisted on finding her sister. Beatrice and Patrick had found a shady spot to enjoy the band that John couldn't hear until within two hundred yards of them, so loud were boisterous conversations, neighboring celebrations, drills, and musketry.

Annie had taken her sister aside. After an animated discussion John didn't hear, the ladies asked to be escorted home. Beatrice's mutinous expression as she glanced at the band suggested that leaving was solely Annie's idea.

John enjoyed the glimpse Annie had given into her childhood, especially with Rebecca and her family. Her happy expression told him she enjoyed his company. What went wrong?

45

Annie had rejected his offer to return for the evening's festivities, which included a bonfire. There had been a bonfire at Will's new home that she'd enjoyed so it wasn't the entertainment. A headache brought on by heat?

Perhaps…though she hadn't claimed a headache.

Curious.

John peered ahead on the darkened avenue. Lots of folks out tonight. Soldiers stood together. Families and couples strolled past him with a nod. Horseback riders and an occasional landau or carriage passed while he waited on the side of the road where Christopher had appeared the night before.

Thoughts of Annie pressed in. Patrick's and Beatrice's presence on their stroll home prevented him from probing the reason for Annie's agitation. It didn't seem the right moment to suggest another outing, nor did she ask him to call on her. All his dreams of courting her had been resurrected today. He tried to find comfort that he'd see her at next week's soiree.

"Evenin'." Christopher strolled up in uniform.

"Good evening." Remembering the informality Christopher had requested just in time, John didn't salute.

"Long day. Promises to get longer." Christopher glanced around at the groups chatting nearby. "Care to walk with me?"

"'Twould be a pleasure." John fell into step beside him, noting they walked in the opposite direction from Annie's home. Probably smart. He didn't want her to know about these meetings.

"Did you escort Miss Annie Swanson to your camp's celebration today?" His voice lowered as a wagon passed.

"Aye. Beatrice also attended." It stuck in his craw to report on his dear friends. Yet—better him than someone who didn't care for them. Hot heads often prevailed these days… and misconstruing someone's words was too easily a consequence. Nay, it was best that someone who cared for them monitored their actions.

"Learn anything?" Christopher gave him a piercing stare that seemed to penetrate the darkness under the canopy of trees.

John shifted his shoulders. The poor man's grief over losing his wife was a safe topic. "Not much. Annie said that Hiram has been mired in grief since losing his wife."

"That was two years ago."

"Aye." The man had studied Hiram's background. John's eyebrows lowered. "The war has given him something new to think about. She didn't say so, but perhaps that's the reason they entertain often—to fill Hiram's evenings with activity so he doesn't think about his wife."

"Possible." Christopher pinched his lower lip. "Anything else?"

"She told me about her cook's background. It's unlikely to be of concern to General Scott."

"Maybe not, but I've got some time." He crossed his arms. "Tell me."

John summarized Rebecca's background for him.

"Interesting." Christopher studied him. "Did either sister mention Will?"

"No. I asked Annie for news of him, but she felt poorly. Our day was cut short. I think she got a headache from the heat."

"Felt mild to me."

"We're soldiers, accustomed to being outside." The canopy of trees above them thinned as they approached his camp. "Anyway, Annie sought out her sister, and soon Patrick and I were escorting them home."

"Lieutenant Patrick MacDonnell?"

John quirked an eyebrow. How did Christopher know Patrick? "The same."

"You said that Annie had to find her sister. Where was Beatrice?"

"We had separated when Beatrice asked Patrick to take her closer to the band."

"Ah. They were alone for a time."

John folded his arms. "A mere half hour with plenty of chaperones around. There was no impropriety, if that's what you're suggesting."

"Did Patrick tell you of their discussion?"

John clenched his jaw. "Music. That's as much as I know." They were within a hundred yards of the first row of tents in his camp.

"When will you see Annie again?"

"As I said, she didn't feel well. We made no plans. Mr. Swanson invited me to their soiree next Wednesday. I hope to see her before then." He wanted to escort her to church. Failing that, he'd attend the church where her mother's funeral services had been held and search for her there.

"Find a reason to see her again."

"'Tis busy I'll be until the Sabbath." John stopped outside his camp. The bonfire still burned brightly, though the crowd had dwindled a bit. "I have duties to the army." And his new duty of spying on her father. Mustn't forget that.

"Then plan to see her for Sunday services." Christopher studied him. "Do you know where Willard's is?"

The hotel? "Yes. I stayed there when I was in the city for Mrs. Swanson's funeral."

"Excellent. Meet me there for breakfast on Monday morning." He stood at attention. "You'd best salute me this time, old boy. A few soldiers are looking this way."

John complied, a little irked that he hadn't been given the choice about their next meeting. Then, remembering savory meals he'd consumed there, he strolled to his tent and convinced himself it was a small enough sacrifice for the cause.

~

*L*uncheon had been served two hours before with at least another hour of sewing ahead. Annie stuck the needle into the white fabric of the soldier's shirt in front of her and then rubbed her aching hands, a common pain that accompanied long days of sewing for the Union army. The whir of two sewing machines rarely halted. Each of the dozen or so women who sewed here almost daily since the firing on of Fort Sumter were determined to clothe their soldiers without delay. Forty-one shirts had been completed this week alone. Five girls under the age of twelve sewed handkerchiefs in a smaller parlor in the back of the house.

"Hands hurt?" Beatrice, who sat beside her at one of the four long worktables in Mrs. Jackson's expansive parlor, pulled white thread through the top button on a man's shirt.

"A little." Annie massaged her wrist. "You've almost completed that one."

"Two more buttons." She held up the shirt and stared at it with a critical eye. "I like making these over-the-head blouses where the opening reaches only to the chest."

"Me too." At twenty, Esther Jackson lived with her parents in this spacious New York Avenue home. "They're faster to make."

"Especially with Ruth and Reba stitching side seams on the machine." Beatrice bent over the cotton fabric.

Annie glanced at the Abbott sisters behind the sewing machines at separate tables, who only paused when reaching for the next blouse that Mrs. Clara Johnson and Mrs. Charlene Abbott cut from various sized patterns. The sisters sewed as if competing for the highest number of completed shirts.

"I live in such dread of this war." Sitting at another table, Mrs. Amelia Jackson spoke with her back to them.

"Agreed." Charlene Abbott paused, scissors in hand, at the cutting table. "If this unpleasantness is unavoidable, let's finish it."

49

"If women ran things, there'd be no battles or division." Amelia sighed. "A pity."

No divisions—in their country or within their family. That sounded like heaven to Annie. How she longed to return to simpler times when folks with opposing viewpoints still respected one another.

"Ladies, let's not sink into doldrums." Standing as tall as her five-foot stature allowed, Mrs. Clara Johnson put her hands on her hips. "Maintain a positive outlook. Now, how about another topic entirely."

Silence. This wasn't the first day Clara had stepped in to keep their gathering from growing maudlin, yet all Annie could think of was her brother's choice—and how it divided her family. It also would affect his friendship with the man who so captivated her. She tried to calm her breathing by staring into the sunshine on the bustling city street. What was John doing now? Did he want to court her? If so, why hadn't he suggested a concert, a country drive, or even offer his escort to church? Was it a reticence, as Beatrice had suggested, to discuss plans with others present?

"Any news from Will and Frances?"

Esther's voice broke the silence. Annie's throat constricted at the hint of suspicion in her eyes.

"Oh, didn't we tell you?" Beatrice's voice held an artificially bright tone. "They expect a blessed event by Christmas."

A chorus of gasps pulled Annie from her melancholy reflections.

"What joyful news." Clara clasped her hands together. "That little one will be a blessed addition for your family."

"Indeed. We'll be excited to meet our little nephew or niece." Annie's animation ebbed as she wondered if Will's Confederate service altered their ability to see the newest member of the family...at least until the battles ended.

"I've begun knitting already." Beatrice's blue eyes shone with her joy.

"The baby will be born before you know it." Charlene cast a proud glance at her unmarried daughters busy at the sewing machines. "The years afterward fly as well."

"Did Will muster into the Union army yet?" Esther studied his sisters.

Annie squirmed like a butterfly pinned to a branch. "I don't believe so. He will do everything right and good." At least, the Will she used to know would have done the right thing.

"A finer, braver man never drew breath." Beatrice's tone held conviction and something else Annie rarely heard from her—a warning to let it be.

She must do something to ease the rising tension. She cinched the fabric and held it up. "This sleeve is puckered. Should I rip it out and start over or leave it as is?"

Beatrice and Esther examined it.

"I'd leave it be." Beatrice eyed Esther. "There's enough here to keep us busy for weeks."

"Agreed." Esther flushed. "I'm ready to begin another shirt."

Annie exchanged a relieved look with her sister as Esther flounced away. The daughter of her mother's old friend might suspect all was not as it should be, but the topic, for today at least, was closed.

CHAPTER 6

*J*ohn, seated inside the tent he shared with Patrick, was scanning the latest notations in his books midmorning the next day when two shots rang out.

The back of his chair struck the grass. That musketry sounded as if they came from the other side of the farm—not the woods behind the Swanson's mansion, thank the Lord. Had the pickets found Rebels?

He burst from his tent and saw men huddled across the field.

Racing toward the commotion where Corporal Ben Boyle drilled with his company, John's stomach turned to find two men writhing on the ground, one bleeding from the shoulder, the other from the leg. Kneeling soldiers applied strips of cloth to stanch the wounds.

"What happened?" John was barely at the corporal's side before he'd barked the question. A drilling accident?

"Two shots fired in rapid succession from the woods." Ben stared into a section of the woods. "Both bullets found their mark. McManus and Wiley have been hit."

John's blood ran cold. He wasn't ready for fighting to start in Washington City, especially this close to Annie's house. Before he could reply, Patrick and several other officers arrived. He quickly explained what he'd learned while Ben crossed the field to question his men.

Two men were sent to search the woods. While they were gone, John felt his senses alert for every cricket, every snapping branch as he peered at the underbrush.

Their soldiers returned without finding Rebels. The camp of the Twenty-seventh New York Volunteers, a German unit, was at target practice and it was believed to be an accident.

A tragic one. John didn't like his soldiers getting shot by other regiments this side of the Mason-Dixon line. It turned out that their regimental commander didn't either. In fact, Colonel Cass feared his wounded soldiers had been shot by Rebel scouts.

Their pickets guarded that area because the officers, especially Colonel Cass, believed there might be Confederate soldiers hiding inside the cover provided by the trees. John had been comforted that the woods so close to Annie's home were daily scoured for the enemy...and possibly a hidden depository of their weapons.

John figured Confederate scouts would have been found by now if they were in the vicinity. Was this extra patrolling an overabundance of caution?

He worried about his men and civilians. One family in particular.

A target practice accident put them all at risk.

It was after supper before he settled down to his work again. After the day's scare, he wanted to see Annie more than ever.

Tomorrow was Sunday. He'd attend her church and talk to her afterward. He resolved to wait for her to talk about her brother. If she knew, she'd tell him.

Services couldn't arrive soon enough.

~

*A*nnie's smile refused to dim once she spotted John awaiting her on the church steps.

To think he sat beside her, his leg brushing against her blue dress. She didn't know the scripture text. She heard nothing of the sermon. In her daydreams, John still strolled with her at the picnic with his regimental band playing.

Her mother had warned her to settle for nothing less than a church-going man. A God-fearing man. And here he was, sitting beside her on her family's pew.

Things had felt unsettled between them when he escorted her home the other day. Uneasy. As if Will becoming a Confederate officer was something he already knew, something that stood between them.

Not today. His twinkling green eyes proved all was well between them. Father was right—John need never know about Will until the battles ended. If her prayers were answered, all this would be over by the end of summer. Birds sang outside the open doors as if giving her a sign that peace was on its way.

Annie stood beside John afterward and introduced him to friends and neighbors. More than one unmarried lady glanced at the uniformed officer a second time. His gaze returned to hers after every introduction, as if no one he met mattered more.

"Please come to our house for luncheon," she said as they exited the church behind her family.

"'Tis happy I am to accept," he said, teasingly, "once I receive your invitation."

"Consider this an invitation." She laughed. "You don't have to be back at camp, do you?"

His grin broadened. "Not until later this afternoon."

"Father?" She waited until he turned back. "John has the afternoon free. It's such a beautiful day. Let's take the landau and go for a ride in the country."

"That sounds lovely." Beatrice smiled up at her father. "A ride in the open countryside is precisely what we need."

He shook his head. "I'm meeting a client after lunch, but you young folks go. Ask Tom to drive you. Jacob is home with his family today."

"Jacob's my father's driver." Annie explained at John's questioning look. "Father, if you're certain you can't join us—"

"Go. Enjoy yourselves." He studied the cloudless sky. "Take your parasols."

"It's all settled then."

John's glance lingered on Annie, causing a delicious tingle that warmed her heart and calmed her doubts.

She was growing more certain that he was the right husband for her.

It was time he figured it out.

~

*A*nnie couldn't remember when she'd laughed so much. At John's suggestion, Rebecca and her daughters rode with them while Tom handled the reins for the landau's team. John had kept them all entertained with soldier training stories on Long Island. Who knew raw recruits made such hilarious mistakes?

Or perhaps John had a bit of a storyteller's flourish in him.

She decided with a smug smile that it was both.

All the ladies held pretty parasols. Annie's blue one matched her frock, as did Beatrice's peach one. Annie had given Nancy a pink one and Hannah a yellow one from her childhood. Rebecca's was the color of a spring sky.

Rebecca had balked at the invitation when Annie went to the kitchen after lunch. "That's your young man. Spend time with him and your sister before this war gets its ugly grip on us."

"The war already has an ugly grip on us." Annie's thoughts

had flown to Will. "Come with us. Tom will drive. The girls will love a ride in the landau."

"They've never ridden in one, so it'd be a treat." Rebecca studied her. "This invitation came from your young man?"

Annie nodded. "I told him how special you are to me. That you've been like a second mother to us since…"

"Land sakes, child. We all miss her, don't we?" Rebecca had wrapped her in a warm hug, tears glistening in her eyes. "If we can be back before I have to get supper on…"

Annie had assured they'd return in plenty of time, so when an hour had passed, she reluctantly asked Tom to head back.

Other than ending too soon, the afternoon was just about perfect.

❧

*T*hey were well outside the city when Annie asked Tom to turn around.

John had been focused on entertaining his audience and failed to notice their surroundings. Studying the countryside, he wondered where they were in Maryland. This green wilderness was part of the Union, but it was an uneasy relationship. Railroad bridges had been burned. Severed telegraph wires had cut communications for a time. Secessionists in Baltimore had thrown stones at Union soldiers. One officer was even killed.

It reminded him of yesterday's target practice accident. Everyone now seemed satisfied that was what it was. Yet the incident had heightened John's determination not to let his guard down.

Which he'd done for the last hour.

Unless he missed his guess, the big battle that everyone anticipated would happen in the coming weeks. Annie had been wise to turn back to Washington City.

56

Too bad he'd left his rifle and sword back at camp because he hadn't wanted to take them to church.

Best not tell any more stories, though amusing his companions had been the most enjoyable part of a good day. No, he'd keep his wits about him until they returned to the city without raising undue alarm in the children.

His head jerked toward movement to their right. An animal?

"John?" Annie stared at him as he studied the trees lining the dirt road. "Do you feel queasy?"

Gripping the side of the landau, he peered at bushes. No one crouched there. His nerves were getting the better of him after yesterday's incident.

Tom glanced back at him. The horses picked up the pace.

Rebecca, tilting her head, considered John's expression.

"Not after that delicious meal." Time to lighten the mood. "You're a fine cook, Mrs. Parker."

"Thank you kindly, Sergeant-Major Finn." Her glance darted to the branches above them. "I have help in the kitchen, and the upstairs maids pitch in when we have parties."

"'Tis grateful I was for you stretching the meal to serve one more." The children might be lulled into complacency. Rebecca Parker was another story.

"Always room for one or two more." Rebecca raised her hand, palm up, toward Annie and Beatrice. "Your mother taught me that. She often invited unexpected guests to dine with her for luncheon. Your father has picked up the hospitable habit your mother ingrained in us."

Annie said, "Father is from the South. He always extended hospitality when we were growing up. Mother fit right in with her welcoming spirit." Annie folded her hands. "She was very gracious."

"Always." Beatrice squeezed her sister's hand.

John peered at a farm up ahead. His tense shoulders relaxed at this sign of civilization.

"That she was. Blessed lots of folks." Rebecca covered their hands with her own. "My family included."

"Yes, Annie told me a bit of your story." As they passed another farm, John sank against the leathered cushion. They were close to Washington City with plenty of Federal camps ahead. "Mr. Parker, your experience is an inspiring one."

Tom sat straighter. "Much obliged, Sergeant-Major Finn."

"You all may call me John. That sergeant-major name is a mouthful."

He looked back. "Name's Tom. Thank you for inviting my family along. These girls will talk about this drive for a long time."

"'Tisn't right to ask a man to give up a Sunday afternoon. Hope having them along makes up for it."

"That it does." Tom focused his attention on the road as they passed a row of homes.

Annie gave John a radiant smile that befuddled his thoughts. What a sweet, beautiful woman. Perhaps it wasn't so far-fetched to pursue this courtship. His father must loosen the reins on him now that he was in the army.

He must be free to pursue his own life, and dreams, outside of the family business.

CHAPTER 7

*A*nnie and Beatrice accompanied John and Patrick to a concert in the White House garden the following Saturday after one of Rebecca's delicious lunches. Laughter and pleasant conversation with brave, handsome soldiers set Annie's spirits soaring. Or perhaps that was due to John's attentive courtesies and the way he anticipated her every glance. Listening to the United States Marine Band playing *Columbia, the Gem of the Ocean* with John at her side stirred dreams of standing beside him always.

Despite spending four days sewing for the soldiers—trousers this week—in the Jacksons' parlor, she'd been happy to stroll with John two evenings. Regrettably, she talked with him for a scant quarter hour at her father's weekly Wednesday soiree. That didn't matter as much now that they were courting. He'd already accepted an invitation to luncheon after services tomorrow.

"Do President and Mrs. Lincoln sit in the garden sometimes to listen to concerts?" Patrick, standing at Beatrice's left side, leaned over during a pause between songs.

"I don't see them"—Annie scanned the crowd—"though I'm certain the Lincolns sometimes attend. Have you seen our president about the city yet?"

"Not I." Patrick's tone held regret. His glance lingered on Beatrice.

"You will." Beatrice lifted her parasol higher and shifted so that she was under its shade. "I've seen him once in his landau and twice on horseback."

Looking at her, Patrick shook his head in wonder. "What a sight it must be to see the leader of our land out and about on business."

"He's always accompanied by soldiers guarding him." Annie hated to think of President Lincoln in danger. Their nation needed strong leadership to guide them through this tragedy.

"I'll keep me eye open for the great man." John peered at the open windows on the second floor of the White House.

The band struck the beginning chords of *Yankee Doodle*, and they sang along with other bystanders. Some whistled the tune. A festive atmosphere belied the apprehension that had settled on the city. When the crowd sang along with *The Girl I Left Behind Me*, Annie gave a side glance at John...until she noticed Patrick singing the song to her sister.

Beatrice laughed and turned her attention back to the band, but Patrick continued to stare at her as he sang in his baritone voice. Was he flirting?

Annie turned back to the band. The couple were chaperoning her and John and definitely not courting, but Patrick's actions suggested otherwise.

They all sang every verse of *Amazing Grace* before the band took a break.

John hadn't suggested any plans beyond the concert. She hoped he didn't mean to escort them home so early in the day.

"Ladies, I propose we stroll down Pennsylvania Avenue to

Willard Hotel for supper." Patrick, his gaze holding Beatrice's, took off his hat and bowed with a flourish.

Beatrice took a slight step back.

"My dear, might I have the honor of escorting you down the avenue?" Grinning, he donned his hat with eyes only for Beatrice.

Annie wasn't amused. Patrick was betrothed to a woman back in Boston. Was his manner a shade too friendly toward her sister?

~

*J*ohn raised his eyebrows at his friend's flirtatious manner. If Patrick wasn't careful, Bea might misconstrue his conduct to indicate a level of interest unbecoming in a man with a fiancée. Did he treat all women with such charm? John was courting Annie, and he wasn't about to allow anyone to trifle with her sister's affections, though Beatrice treated Patrick more as a friend than a beau. She knew he had a girl back home. John would have a few questions for him this evening.

Annie's frown disappeared. "I'd love that above all things." She looked up at him, her brown eyes wide and glowing.

His insides turned to jelly. "That's grand then."

"Father took us last October." Her eyes lost some of their luster. "Before the election…and before secession began."

Difficult days, to be sure. Her mouth drooped, and John wondered whether her thoughts had turned to her brother's family in North Carolina, now part of the Confederacy. He longed to comfort her, to have the right to face life's challenges with her. Annie's attentiveness and actions showed she cared for him. Might it develop into something strong enough and deep enough to convince her to venture the railroad to the West as his wife? It was the stuff of dreams. "Does your father expect you for the meal?"

"Let's ask Jacob to drive us to the bank to inquire about his plans. I doubt he'll object. He's been quite distracted lately, hasn't he, Bea?" Annie rested a pink parasol against her shoulder.

"Oh?" Her comment alerted John's senses.

Beatrice stared at something in the distance. "The war seemed to bring him back to us and out of his terrible grief."

"Yes, that's it." Annie glanced at her. "Now his clients desperately need him."

"How so?" John leaned closer to hear past the festive crowd going their separate ways after the patriotic concert.

"Some customers require assurance their money is safe in these troubled times." Annie waved her fan so quickly that tendrils escaping her brown combs danced in the breeze.

"A few have removed their savings and moved South." Beatrice lowered her voice. "This must worry Father, of course, yet he never complains."

"That's why he's asked us to curtail our spending." Annie's eyes widened. "I hadn't puzzled that together."

"I fear that's the cause." Beatrice caught Patrick's eye and flushed. "Forgive us, gentlemen. It fell into place for me this moment."

"And I was but a moment behind you, dear sister." Annie touched her shoulder.

John hadn't considered that the Swanson family suffered the shortages of war, especially with the number of guests attending their weekly soirees. "Another reason we're praying for this conflict's short duration."

"Amen to that." Patrick lifted his forearm as an invitation for Beatrice. "Shall we find our driver and ask him to take us to your father?"

"Let's." She placed her fingertips on his arm.

John clasped Annie's delicate hand and laid it on his arm. Her radiant smile lit a spark in his heart. What a blessed man he was to have found her favor.

As they followed Patrick and Beatrice, John scanned faces in the crowd. The warmth of the sunny day scarcely blocked the chill he tried to squelch when meeting the gaze of Christopher Farmer.

Had the man who asked him to spy on Hiram Swanson followed him to make certain he performed the task?

~

"I hope you didn't wait long." Hiram Swanson ushered all four of them into his office that didn't seem quite as spacious as normal.

"Not at all." Annie gave him a brief hug and stepped aside for Beatrice to do the same. The smell of leather drew her attention to the new chair behind a table. Ledgers filled a floor-to-ceiling bookshelf dominating the wall behind the desk. She studied the large painting of a beautiful young bride—one of her favorites of her mother. "I haven't been here since you replaced your chair."

"Your grandfather's old one had worn out its usefulness. The new one is quite comfortable." Father indicated for his daughters to sit in the two empty seats and then sat behind the ornately carved oval table that had previously belonged to his father-in-law. "How was the concert?"

"Heavenly." Beatrice's face glowed. "We knew most of the songs. The crowd sang along."

"An unexpected benefit to hosting regiments is band concerts." Father's expression lightened at her obvious delight. "What brings you here?"

"John and Patrick have asked us to supper at Willard Hotel." Annie glanced at John, who stood by the door with his friend.

"We said nothing about that to you this morning and didn't want to worry you."

"I have a meeting after supper." Hiram studied the two men. "I hadn't planned to go home to eat."

"Please join us then," John said.

Patrick shot John a raised-eyebrow look.

"Yes, do come, Father." Bea's face lost its animation as she glanced at Patrick.

Annie, noticing her frown, was glad that her sister wasn't falling for the handsome lieutenant. "Can you spare an hour to dine with us?"

"I'd like that." He rubbed his hands together. "Jacob can drive us to Willard Hotel, go home to eat and explain to Rebecca that we're dining out tonight. Then he can return for us to bring me back to the bank and take my daughters home."

"It's all settled then." Though Patrick sounded uncertain.

Annie fought to keep a pleasant demeanor. His unwavering attentions to her sister grated on her nerves. Should there be cause for concern, her protective Father would notice.

"Please give me a quarter hour." He stood.

"We'll wait on the sidewalk." Annie kissed his cheek. "It's quite pleasant for mid-July."

Or was it a beautiful day because of the company of a certain Irish soldier whose brogue grew more pronounced when his emotions were engaged?

And she was becoming more certain every day, even though he hadn't said as much, that his emotions were very much engaged.

~

They only got as far as the luxurious lobby at the Willard when John spotted Christopher sitting on a cushioned chair outside one of the parlors. The lieutenant spoke with one of the many officers milling about the spacious, elegant room. Had he followed them? What was the man about? No one in the Swanson family must know of their connection. John couldn't wait to put this unsavory job behind him. This family had done nothing to deserve such scrutiny.

Christopher had never sought him out in such a public place so his presence here probably had nothing to do with John. Little doubt that others reported to Lieutenant Farmer. More likely he met with another spy.

His stomach churned. *Spy.* An ugly word for an ugly deed. Yet it described him, whether he liked it or not.

One of the Willard brothers crossed the high-ceilinged lobby to Hiram and engaged him in conversation. John glanced at Christopher, who indicated the parlor at his right with a slight nod.

Was the man daft? He wanted John to leave supper with his companions—the very family the army lieutenant insisted he spy on—to give him a report? This after cancelling their breakfast in this very place six days before.

Hiram introduced John to Henry Willard. John shook hands with one of the brothers who'd built the hotel to prominence. President Lincoln had stayed there before his inauguration.

Annie and Beatrice seemed familiar with the hotel owner. With Hiram's bank a short walk from the restaurant, John imagined the banker often dined here.

John glanced at Patrick as he shook Mr. Willard's hand. Thankfully, John had maintained his silence about the matter surrounding Lieutenant Farmer to Patrick, for he didn't seem the type to keep a secret under scrutiny.

John felt the weight of Christopher's stare. Did the man expect him to leave his party immediately?

As Hiram's conversation with Mr. Willard continued, John didn't look again. He'd wait until they'd ordered supper before excusing himself.

He hoped to prove this spying business was a waste of everyone's time…especially with their country in crisis.

John certainly didn't want to add to the turmoil, though it awaited him if Annie ever discovered his betrayal.

May it never be.

CHAPTER 8

*A*nnie and Beatrice were back from the dressing room. John excused himself and left the elegant dining room, where Union soldiers filled half the tables.

Long strides took him to the sparsely populated parlor. Christopher smoked a cigar in a corner by a piano, blessedly alone, though others talked in groups nearby. He stood and returned John's salute. "Please seat yourself."

John sat on the edge of a side chair. "I dare not tarry."

"Yes." Christopher leaned forward in his chair. "Sorry to miss our meeting. What news is there?"

"Perhaps nothing. Mr. Swanson is preoccupied with the war that we can all claim. Methinks you'd best set your sights on someone else." He waved wisps of cigar smoke away.

"I disagree." He shook his head. "Mr. Swanson keeps late hours."

"True. Both daughters have commented that bank clients are concerned about losing their wealth. Some clients have withdrawn their money and moved South. The girls have been cautioned against unnecessary expenditures. Perhaps the conflict merits such worry."

Christopher eyed him. "Notice anything unusual at the Swanson's soiree?"

"Nay. Fewer refreshments. Annie suspects the expense of entertaining is becoming exorbitant." Heat rose in his neck to be answering such personal questions about Annie's father while the man awaited his supper in an adjacent dining room.

"Who attended Wednesday's party?"

"Many of the same neighbors. A few new officers from New York regiments in the area." After giving their names, he consulted his pocket watch. "I must get back." It had been above ten minutes since he'd left. Hiram must wonder at his long absence. Nothing escaped his notice, especially where his family was concerned. John rose to his feet.

Christopher stood. "My duties bind me close to the city. Pay close attention to conversations at the party—like with whom local citizens linger. Listen for soldiers who give details on weaponry, troop movements, fortifications, specific orders, and the like. Watch for an opportunity to sneak into Mr. Swanson's study. Bring me anything written in cypher. Look for notes about our military. Memorize them, leave them as you found them, and report to me on Thursday at my home." He gave an address to a boarding house on Sixteenth Street. "Come whenever you can get away. If I am from home, write me a letter, seal it, and leave it with my landlord. You can trust his discretion."

John tapped his foot. "I must go." He saluted, barely waiting for it to be returned before turning on his heel.

Before he'd stepped out of the parlor, Patrick strode toward him. "The girls are concerned. The food has arrived and Mr. Swanson is waiting on you before asking the blessing. What kept you?" He looked over John's shoulder.

John wheeled around. Christopher was gone.

~

*T*he sun dipped toward the horizon in a beautiful array of pink and lilac. Annie sat beside John on the ride home. Raising her parasol against the rays beating down even at this advanced hour, she glanced at him. He stared at the city streets without speaking. So unlike him, for he was wont to feel her every gaze with flattering attention.

He'd brooded over something since he returned to their table at supper. His apologies for delaying their meal were explained by a chance meeting with an acquaintance.

If Father regarded this regrettable lapse as inconsiderate, he had smoothed over the incident with his innate Southern charm. However, his manner had cooled toward Patrick during the meal, who had showed an excessive fascination in every remark Beatrice made.

Beatrice and Patrick, facing them toward the back of the vehicle, were also quiet. Her sister hadn't addressed any direct remarks to the lieutenant at supper. Annie decided to draw John's attention to the matter when they had a moment alone.

Silence stretched uncomfortably long.

"I love riding on these beautiful summer evenings." Annie employed her fan to coax a breeze toward her face.

"Reminds me of Mother." Beatrice gave her a grateful look. "Remember how she bundled us up with wraps and mufflers on sunny winter days for long rides?"

Nostalgia for those simpler days overcame Annie. "She claimed the fresh air was healthy."

"We'd take leisurely drives across the Potomac into the Virginia countryside." Beatrice contemplated the southern skyline. "Such a beautiful state."

"That it is." After a brief glance at Beatrice, Patrick averted his gaze to a church on their right. "Majestic mountains. Green valleys with clear rivers and streams. My uncle has land outside

Richmond. I spent several happy summers there as a child. Fond memories."

"My father's family lives in and around Richmond." Beatrice gripped her parasol. "I miss my aunts and cousins."

"As do I." Annie paled to think of the border that now separated them.

"This hardship will soon pass from our nation." Compassion lit John's green eyes.

"I pray that's so." Annie searched his concerned expression.

"The Confederate army is no match for ours." Patrick's hearty tone seemed a little forced. "Nothing for you ladies to worry your pretty heads about."

"Our city is overrun with Union soldiers." Beatrice's eyes narrowed. "Cannon blasts and musketry are daily occurrences. One hears the beat of drums and the blare of bugles issuing commands to soldiers in their drills. I think there is plenty to concern us, Patrick."

Annie raised her eyebrows. Not at the comments but at the harsh tone. "You surprise me, Beatrice. You've always seemed so unconcerned."

"I strive to trust that all will be well." The fire left her eyes. "I don't like the bickering. And I don't appreciate the sentiment that our neighbors to the South have become our enemies. Living in a particular location is the only fault that can be laid on some."

"'Tis my opinion that most folks don't want to fight their brothers, neighbors, and ..." John gulped, "friends." His hands clenched. "Speaking for myself, I promise you that is my deepest fear."

"What is?" Annie feared John's answer.

"Looking across a battlefield"—tormented eyes met hers —"and seeing a friend in enemy lines."

Will. Annie pressed a hand against her lips to keep from crying out the truth.

John didn't know his dear friend had elected to fight for the Confederacy.

But Annie knew it. And it sent chills to the core of her heart.

~

*U*nless John missed his guess, something was afoot. He, along with other officers, had been drilling companies for three days straight, reminding them and then repeating what to do when bugle tunes and drum beats sounded orders for advances, charges, and retreats. Infantry had to learn forty-nine different bugle tunes in addition to thirty-nine different drum commands. John spent most of his time drilling troops on battle commands. Shouted orders were often lost in the noise of battle that a bugler's blast penetrated.

Recognizing a musical command was vital. It saved lives...or cost them if soldiers misinterpreted it.

"Sergeant-Major Finn." Corporal Ben Boyle approached. "My men have benefited from an afternoon with you."

John inclined his head at the compliment. He'd seen vast improvements himself. "They've worked hard. So have our bugler and drummer. I believe these soldiers more ready for battle than yesterday."

"Hope they don't need to use what they've learned in battle for some time yet. *Never* suits me just as well." Ben rested his hands on his hips. "If you're finished, they are due for target practice."

John frowned. "Corporal, these men have been hard at it for two hours in the blazing sun."

"Yes, sir. They'll have a quarter hour break and then another two hours before calling it quits at supper." His glance darted to the tree line, where a group of soldiers relaxed in the shade. "Company D will be here shortly to drill with you."

Rumors abounded throughout the city of a looming battle,

making these drills a crucial preparation. Colonel Cass hadn't given orders about marching out, but he and Patrick both suspected it was coming soon.

The men dismissed for a short break. John removed his hat to swipe sweat from his forehead. Two more hours. Then he'd wash and dress for the soiree at Annie's home. He feared he wasn't going to be a good guest, as worn out from the heat as he already felt.

He'd be going without Patrick, who hadn't been invited. He frowned to remember the confrontation between them on Saturday night.

They'd barely left the girls' home when John rounded on the lieutenant. "What are you thinking, man? Flirting with Beatrice when you've a fiancée at home. Never say you have forgotten Deborah so quickly?"

"How can you ask?" Patrick stammered. "My heart belongs to Deborah."

"Then act like it." John felt little mercy. His friend's behavior was inexcusable. "I'll not allow you to trifle with Bea's affections."

"She knows I am engaged to be married."

"That's one thing you've done right," John fired back as darkness thickened under the canopy of trees along the avenue. "You've been invited on our outings as an escort for Bea. Not a suitor. Did ye forget?"

"Nay." Patrick's face flushed darker than his red hair. "Deborah hasn't written me. Not a single letter since I arrived in Washington City. My attention had wavered with the miles between us."

John's tone softened. "Mail delivery is uncertain. Letters and packages can get delayed." Movement among the trees reminded him their pickets were on duty. He lowered his voice. "If a matter of weeks makes ye forget yer girl..." John hadn't forgotten Annie in the year that separated them. Nor had any woman tempted him to forget her.

"You have the right of it." Patrick had looked away. "I've some thinking to do."

Fortunately, on Monday, the mail wagon brought five letters from Deborah and a box filled with marble cake, apple pie, molasses cookies, and jars of strawberry jam and blackberry jelly. Patrick devoured a quarter of the pie while reading and re-reading every letter. He wiped a bit of apple from his mouth. "My Deborah. Always thinking of me. Praying for me." He held up the open box of baked goods. "She's a peach of a girl."

John had been working in their tent by lantern light. He studied the lieutenant's blissful expression. "That she is."

"I'm the luckiest man in the world."

John stared at him.

"Don't worry. I'll not forget again."

"See that you don't." He relaxed. "Are you going to offer me a cookie?"

Patrick extended the box. "She's the best cook at our church."

"Delicious. I'll wager you're right." Another bite, and only crumbs remained on his fingers. "You are a lucky man."

"Me feet are on solid ground again. If the Swansons invite me to their home, I'll not forget meself."

"I'll talk to Annie." His conversation with her after church on Sunday had been uncomfortable. After all, he'd been the one to introduce Patrick. Annie said that her father noticed things in his behavior toward his daughter that, in light of his engagement, he couldn't abide. John didn't think Patrick would receive another invitation to join the family any time soon. Perhaps never.

CHAPTER 9

*A*nnie spent most of the evening talking with other guests despite her desire to sit with John. He had left the room for a half hour anyway, presumably to take refreshments with other guests in the upstairs parlor. That didn't bother her. What had agitated her were the murmurings from officers within her hearing. They were preparing for battle. According to the military men, it must come soon.

Men would die. Her heart nearly stopped to think of John and Will on opposing sides. Her brother had written Father that he was camped in North Carolina, without divulging his location, but for how long? She shifted on the sofa beside a Massachusetts officer. What was he saying? Something about drills. She'd been sitting with him for five minutes and hadn't distinguished above ten words.

Her mother would be appalled.

But Mother had never entertained soldiers in her parlor on the brink of war.

Excusing herself, Annie sought *her* soldier. He didn't seem to feel her gaze as he listened attentively to an army captain. To think that parties this summer had taught her to recognize straps and stripes on officers' sleeves. How Will would tease her if he were here.

She grasped the back of a chair at a sudden wave of dizziness. No, her brother couldn't safely step inside the parlor of his boyhood home with Union officers present. A sobering thought.

Annie stole another glance at John. To all appearances, he was still attentive to the captain, yet his gaze darted toward a nearby group of soldiers. Had he overheard troubling news? She'd ask when there was a free moment.

Beatrice sat on a sofa with another officer, a man old enough to be her father. All seemed well.

Annie searched the room for neglected guests and spotted a man by himself near the piano. Sighing inwardly, she moved toward him with a smile.

She reminded herself that John wouldn't leave without talking to her as she settled into a chair to make the lonely stranger, an army sergeant, at ease in her parlor.

∿

*A*s John listened to a New York army captain speak of his family, his ears perked up. A group four feet distant mentioned General Irvin McDowell. A quick glance. One of the speakers was an undersecretary in the government. Another was a sergeant-major, like himself, and the third a corporal.

"General McDowell marched out yesterday." The undersecretary spoke in low tones.

The foreboding mixed with excitement in his voice gave a clue that troops leaving had a special purpose. The first big battle was on the horizon, as he and Patrick suspected. John's body strained to hear the reply. He could scarcely believe the captain he was talking with didn't hear the ominous news.

"Where'd they go?" The corporal raised his chin.

"Virginia." The undersecretary peered around him.

Droplets of tea from the cup in John's hand splashed his coat. So it had started.

"You all right?" The captain across from John removed a handkerchief from his coat pocket and offered it to him. "Hope the tea had cooled some."

"It did. Much obliged." John swiped at his arm, silently cursing his clumsiness when the undersecretary supplying the information glanced over. They moved out of earshot. John strained to hear. Christopher needed to know the undersecretary divulged secrets, even if it was to Union officers. Perhaps he'd even tell civilians to spout his own importance at knowing military details. If there truly were Confederate spies here, this was valuable information. Perhaps Hiram?

John returned the handkerchief with his thanks. Needing to gather his thoughts, he excused himself and moved toward the maid next to the beverages.

"More tea, sir?" The pretty brunette lifted a dainty porcelain tea kettle.

Mind in turmoil, John set his cup on her tray. "May I have lemonade, please?"

She gave him a tumbler full.

Mumbling his thanks, he moved toward the group discussing General McDowell's troops. Was it true? A twinge of disappointment rose that his regiment was still in the city. He'd dreamed of marching into battle during his days at West Point. If one major battle decided this conflict, he wanted to be there. It was a story to tell his children and grandchildren.

His slow advance on the group was halted by a gloved hand on his sleeve.

Annie.

He forced a smile, wishing she had waited ten minutes. The opportunity to discover further details was lost.

~

"*I*t's my duty as hostess to make certain all guests are entertained." Annie's brown eyes glowed up at him. "I noticed your conversation with the captain concluded. Do you have a destination in mind, or will you sit with me?"

"'Tis no greater pleasure afforded to me than to speak with my lovely Annie."

Heat surged into her face. "I thank you, kind sir." In anyone else, such compliments seemed overdone. Was it his Irish brogue that made the difference? Or her own heart's response to him?

He looked behind her and frowned.

"John?" She turned but saw none of his acquaintances. "Is there someone you need to speak with before we sit?"

His troubled green eyes cleared. "Not when I've longed to talk with you all evening. Please. Let's sit."

Annie complied, sitting as close to him on her favorite mauve sofa as her dress allowed. "Is there any news in your regiment?"

"Why do you ask?" His brow puckered.

"You're aware that Beatrice and I sew for our soldiers with a ladies' group."

He nodded. "Many are our thanks."

"It's rumored that the big fight approaches quickly." She clasped her hands. "I know not when it will happen, but I don't want you there."

John drew back his shoulders. "Annie, I mustered into our army to fight for our country. Unless the Confederacy decides to surrender peaceably, I will eventually see fighting."

"I understand." She picked up her fan from a side table and waved it across her face. "The older women are fearful. After hours of listening to their dire predictions of death and dying..."

"Soldiers get wounded in battle. It's true." His head ducked toward hers. "It's important you remember one thing. If it's my time to die, I'm at peace with my Maker."

Her heartbeat thrashed in her ears. While it comforted her to know his soul was right with God, even the possibility of his death dimmed the lamplight shadowing his face. She couldn't find him again only to lose him.

"But not to worry. I will return to you." His hand on hers stilled the wild motion of the fan.

"What's this?" Her father stopped beside them. "Are those tears in your eyes, daughter?"

John released her hand, though he continued to regard her with compassion. "Annie fears a coming battle, sir."

"Do you know more than the rumors then?" Father studied John's face. "Have you received orders to march away from our dear city?"

"No, sir." John glanced beyond Annie's shoulder.

"Then there is no cause for alarm." Father knelt beside her. "Guests have already begun to leave. I will send the rest away. Rest is what you most need, dear child. All this sewing, hour after hour. It has exhausted you, I fear."

"No, Father." What she needed was time with John. Giving into her own emotions had caused this. "I'm fine now. It was a momentary lapse."

"If you're sure..." At her nod, he stood again. "I'll see to our guests." He joined a group gathered near the door.

"Your father is right to be concerned." John stood. "A good rest will restore you."

"Will you call tomorrow?" She rose. "I hate that my emotions got the better of me. Father is very protective of his daughters. And his son."

"'Tis glad I am to hear it. Though 'tis no surprise." He reached for her hand. "I will be busy tomorrow until after supper. May I come for you at half past seven for a stroll?"

"You may." Her small hand was engulfed in a large, strong grasp. If they strolled near her home and then sat in the garden at twilight, her father might allow her to walk without Bea as a chaperone.

CHAPTER 10

With another long day of drills behind him, John strode toward Sixteenth Street underneath an overcast sky. His stomach growled loudly enough that a man in a passing carriage could have heard it.

If you ate a hurried lunch and skipped supper for an evening stroll with your girl, your stomach might gurgle too.

There were still no marching orders from Colonel Cass. However, he noticed new regimental camps while walking to Christopher's boarding house.

Curious. It lent credence to what he'd overhead last night. He shook his head, wishing he'd learned General McDowell's destination out of his own curiosity. As someone working for the army's commanding general, Christopher likely already knew.

Though John's search of Hiram's study had been thwarted by an attentive butler, this time he had information for Christopher. Hiram had been gone from the parlor while the young man spouted his knowledge. Yet Annie's father was highly inquisitive about any military-related topic.

John found the three-story brick building with no trouble. A

middle-aged man answered his knock. "Good evening. I'm looking for Lieutenant Christopher Farmer. He expects me."

"Are you certain?" The bearded man raised his eyebrows. "For Lieutenant Farmer is having supper out this evening."

John extracted his pocket watch. Half-past six. "He asked me to leave a note should he be called away."

The landlord extended his hand. "I will see that he receives it."

John flushed. "I didn't write one because I expected to speak with him directly. Have you a sheet of paper I may use for the task?"

The man seemed unsurprised by the question. Perhaps John wasn't the first to make such a request. "Follow me." He led John to a sitting room with a dozen chairs, side tables, and a writing desk. "Wait here."

Christopher's absence might work to his advantage. John calculated a half hour walk to Annie's home. He'd best hurry and write that note.

~

"I'm happy you tore yourself from your duties to stroll with me." Annie held John's arm. "Especially after expressing my fears to you. I assure you that I'm proud that you're courageous and brave. And of your rank."

"'Tis no great rank. But happy I am to hear of your pride in me." He tilted his head toward her. "'Twill keep me strong."

"You won't need me for that." Her hand tightened on his arm as they strolled under the shade of majestic elms.

He halted and turned to face her. "You're a strong woman, Annie Swanson. Having you by me side makes me a better man."

Staring up at him, she dared to dream of a future together. "That's the nicest thing anyone has ever said to me."

"It's the truth." He brushed her hair back off her cheek.

Her heart thudded. *Kiss me.* Her gaze dropped to his lips. *Kiss me like you did last summer.*

Almost as if he read her mind, he bent closer. Slowly. Did he expect her to refuse? Then his mouth covered hers for one delicious moment—

"Whoa." Horses clomped on a stone in front of a carriage.

They broke apart. Her cheeks flamed. One moment later, and she'd have missed their kiss altogether.

They stood awkwardly, him shielding her from curious stares until the carriage passed.

"My apologies," he said.

"No." Looking into his eyes, she clasped his hand. "Don't apologize."

His stomach rumbled.

"Did you miss supper?" She laughed.

"I wanted to see you."

What a sweet man. Her heart melted. "I can't allow a man to miss supper." She turned toward her home, pulling him along behind her. "Come with me. Rebecca always keeps bread and meat or cheese for sandwiches."

∾

*J*ohn had been working on his notes all Saturday morning when marching steps on the road snagged his attention. He walked to the end of his row of tents to where Patrick stood with Corporal Ben Boyle. "What is it?"

"Regiments are marching out." Ben faced the street with arms folded.

"We've watched staff officers and orderlies riding toward the different camps in the area." Patrick's expression was more serious than was his wont.

John's heart hammered as soldiers filed past with bedrolls,

haversacks, and rifles on their shoulders. Marching toward battle. "How about us?"

"Don't believe so." Ben stared at passing soldiers. "No orders from Colonel Cass."

John's chest tightened. Why not them? Their men were trained and ready.

"This isn't the first regiment that's marched south." Patrick widened his stance. "A great battle will soon be fought. Possibly, it's already happening."

"Question is, will we be needed?" John studied the man who, unlike him, had completed his military education.

Patrick shrugged. "Hard to know. But I'd prepare myself if I were you."

~

*R*egiments continued to march past John's camp all afternoon. Too agitated to settle back into his book-work, he stood near the road with his comrades and cheered them along. Bands playing *Yankee Doodle* and *Columbia, the Gem of the Ocean* stirred his patriotic fervor. He longed to join those marching to battle.

Those pounding feet caused a slight tremble in the ground where John stood yards away. Annie must realize something was afoot. He had no news, but he must ease her mind, if he could.

He found Patrick in their tent. "Hundreds of soldiers have passed Annie's home this afternoon. She is bound to worry."

"True." Patrick folded a shirt. "But there may be little time to prepare for what's ahead."

"I must go to her."

"Then go now, before orders are received." Patrick stuffed the shirt in his knapsack. "Make haste, man. We may have a matter of an hour or two should orders come."

"I shall return within the hour." John strode down the row of tents, grateful Patrick hadn't pulled rank and insisted he stay close.

As companies continued to fill the avenue, John strode in the opposite direction inside the first line of trees. Intent on seeing Annie, he ignored the underbrush that slapped his legs. The woods blocked the heat of the sun until the mansion was within sight.

Standing a few feet from the avenue were Annie and Beatrice with Rebecca, her daughters, and two maids. Soldiers paused, cups in hand, in front of one of two large black kettles to receive a dipper of beverage and then quickly stepped back in line. Each lady employed a dipper. They worked quickly, offering a kind word along with what was likely lemonade.

The sight warmed John's heart. He lengthened his stride.

Annie looked up with a gasp. "John!" She ran to him with outstretched hands. "I feared you already left. I wanted to come to your camp but Rebecca and Bea prevented me."

"Wise women, both." He clasped her hands. "Army camps are no place for a lady."

"What's happening?" Fearful brown eyes searched his face.

Best say it quickly. "No doubt these men march toward Virginia. My regiment has not received orders to join them."

She closed her eyes. "God be praised."

"We may yet receive them."

Her eyes opened wide.

"The Ninth Massachusetts stands ready to defend our country." His hands tightened on hers. "We're well-trained."

Her face paled underneath the shade of a wide-brimmed hat. "Fight bravely, my dear soldier."

"I will." He cupped her face. With his thumbs, he gave a gentle caress on her soft cheeks. "If ordered, I will fight for you, my family, and my country."

"I had so looked forward to sitting with you in church

tomorrow." Her gaze dropped. "I will spend the whole service praying for you instead."

"I can ask for no greater thing." He kissed the hand that squeezed his almost convulsively. Uncaring of the crowd, he bent and kissed her cheek. "I must go. I'll return as soon as I can."

"Yes, you must go." She blinked rapidly. "Godspeed. My prayers go with you."

CHAPTER 11

"More troops are likely to pass our home." Annie peered at the dwindling lemonade in the twenty-gallon pots normally used to boil laundry. They'd earlier been scrubbed to serve lemonade and water to the soldiers. "We'll need more."

"I'll make enough to fill one of these pots. There's enough blackberry shrub to fill another." Rebecca rubbed her back. "Want me to use that?"

Her father's favorite. Annie frowned. "Hold one jar back for Father. He works hard and never complains."

"Agreed." Beatrice glanced down the road to where the last regiment had dropped out of sight minutes before. "We can't neglect Father in our desire to serve our soldiers."

"Leftover desserts from the last soiree disappeared with the first group." Half-turning, Rebecca lifted her skirt. "Can you serve the crowd while I take the girls inside to bake a big batch of cookies?"

"Yes, please bake whatever is easiest for you." Gratitude filled Annie for Rebecca's hospitable spirit—the same one in her own gracious mother. "Donna and Barbara will return soon to help us serve."

"Please ask Jacob and the gardeners to carry out the shrub and lemonade." Beatrice called after them. "It's too heavy for you and the girls."

"Jacob's here?" Annie's brow furrowed. Her father was working this Saturday, as was his custom.

"Yes, Father took the chaise again today and is using the stable near the bank. That frees Jacob to drive us, if need be."

"Besides seeing John, my only task is offering our soldiers a cool drink."

Beatrice peered up the avenue. "I hope Rebecca quickly prepares the beverages."

"I don't hear marching feet from that direction." Annie looked toward John's camp. "Perhaps they have enough. John's not certain that his regiment will be ordered to fight. It's difficult...the not knowing part. I fear for him."

"Yes." Beatrice spoke in muted tones. "I'm praying for him and Will."

Fear gripped her. "Will is in North Carolina. Never say you think..." She recalled that John's greatest fear was seeing a friend on enemy lines. "No. It can't be."

"Probably not. It's a long distance. Yet there are trains to take him into Virginia." Beatrice averted her eyes. "Many things have happened that no one could foresee. Who knew heated disagreements between states and government officials would lead to hateful words that cut deeply enough to sever our nation?"

Annie had seen it too, yet she'd never heard it vocalized so eloquently. "The impossible is happening to our country. We must pray for the safety and protection of those we love." She met Beatrice's anxious gaze. "Bea, we will not falter. We will stand."

"Yes, we'll do all we can from our own little avenue." Beatrice squeezed her fingers.

"More soldiers are on their way." Faint sounds of drums, bugles, and banjos grew louder. Annie peered down the road toward flying dustclouds. "Get ready. I see them now."

~

The anticipated orders had come hours before—minutes after John returned to camp.

Prepare to march. Men were to carry three days of rations in their haversacks and thirty cartridges in their cartridge boxes.

They cheered as regiments from other states passed the camp. They'd soon join them.

John's pride in them had never run so deeply. The men had gone about their preparations with willing spirits. It took courage to face an army on a battlefield. These brave men possessed that in abundance.

All was done now, and they had yet to receive orders to march. The Second New Hampshire filed past them as the sun dipped below the tree line.

The Irish Ninth soldiers gripped their rifles as they lined the tent street rows of their camp, each arranged by company.

Waiting.

John's thoughts strayed to Annie. The tears in her eyes had never reached her cheeks. Strong, brave woman that she was, she'd fought them back. He could do no less than equal her courageous example.

Darkness fell as they waited. Then the order came.

Cheers erupted. John joined in. They filed away from camp, marching swiftly toward the battle. The men quieted. John thought of Annie, trusting her prayers accompanied him.

Late in the night they halted when a staff officer rode up and spoke to Colonel Cass.

What happened? Was the battle just ahead? John shifted his rifle to his other shoulder, ready for anything.

"About face."

Return to camp? John had steeled himself for every order… except that one.

"About face," John shouted to the soldiers in his vicinity as the unbelievable order was repeated down the line.

He shared the frustration on the faces of his comrades as they glanced at one another. They'd mentally prepared themselves to fight. But it wasn't to be.

No regiments followed them. The moon was the only witness to their march back to the city.

Despite the predawn hour, once back at their familiar camp, the men were formed into a square. John was glad that Colonel Cass intended to address his disappointed men.

"Soldiers, tonight you've done me proud." The colonel walked back and forth in front of them. "I fully expected you all to march toward battle as enthusiastically as you have done. 'Tis proud I am to lead such fine, courageous men."

John thrust his chest out. He feared the buttons on his jacket might burst off in the pride that their leader's words aroused in his soul.

Tomorrow was another day. There'd be other battles. Unless this one ended the war—his deepest desire.

Colonel Cass dismissed them with his thanks. The men went to their quarters. John yawned and trudged to his tent for whatever sleep the night still afforded.

As his head touched the pillow, he knew he'd miss church with Annie. He'd see her as soon as he could to tell her that her wish had been granted.

The Irish Ninth wasn't participating in this battle.

~

*a*nnie attended church with her family with a heart full of dread. She heard nothing of the service. True to her word, she prayed for John the whole time.

As she had done through the wee hours of the night when the escape of sleep eluded her.

Beatrice reached over occasionally to squeeze her hand. Though grateful for her sister's sympathy, Annie kept her head bowed.

She drew a ragged breath as the congregation sang the final hymn.

Father ushered them into the landau with little more than a nod to their neighbors. "Are you all right, Annie?"

"I worry for John." She flapped her hands toward her face as the driver guided the team through the crowded road. "I will be fine once we hear news. Did you learn anything, Father?"

"I did. Not very pretty, I'm afraid." His lips tightened.

Annie gasped. "Did we lose the battle?"

"Rumors are that the battle is planned for today. Some senators and congressmen have packed picnic lunches for their families and are traveling to watch the fighting." He grimaced. "I'd not have believed such a thing had several church members not confirmed it. A few spoke with regret that it was too late to take their phaetons and buggies to Manassas Junction to view the battle through telescopes and opera glasses."

Annie's chest tightened. Men died in battle. *Not John or Will. Please, God, not the men I love. Protect them.*

"Outrageous." Beatrice opened her fan with a snap. "Reminds me of the Roman gladiators. I suppose government officials have advance knowledge of military orders."

"It seems so in this case." Hiram glanced at Annie. "I'm certain all will go well for John." He looked away. "And Will."

"Yes, Father." Annie mustn't forget her father's worry. It

strengthened her. "They're both safe." And suddenly she was convinced it was true. How, she did not know—nor how long they would remain that way.

$\sim$

"*P*erhaps there is news of the Ninth Massachusetts at their camp." Hiram walked with his daughters toward the front drawing room after a subdued lunch. "I will ride over if you like."

"Why did I not consider that?" Annie touched his sleeve. "May we ride with you?"

"An army camp is no place for a lady." He patted her hand. "I'll return with all speed. You'll not be left to wonder long, my daughter."

A knock on the door drew all eyes.

Mr. Irving Grant, their butler, crossed the hall and opened it. "Sergeant-Major Finn. How pleased the family will be to—"

"John." Joy flooded over Annie at the sight of her soldier. Her beau. She ran to him, hands outstretched.

"Good afternoon, Annie." He clasped her hands to his chest. "'Tis me hope that ye were not overly concerned about me safety."

"I feared you'd been ordered to battle."

"I was." He nodded. "I came as soon as I could. I didn't want to worry you."

"You look exhausted."

"I own to that. 'Twas a long night." He looked beyond her. "Good afternoon, Mr. Swanson. Beatrice. I regret missing church services."

"Come. Sit with us in the parlor. Irving, please request refreshments for our guest." Father waved his arm toward the large room, where the family hosted guests for the soirees.

"Rumors abound in the city." He quickly told him what he'd discovered. "I'd be pleased to know true events."

John sat beside Annie on the sofa. "I do not know what happened outside my view. 'Tis pleased I'd be to tell you my story."

CHAPTER 12

*E*veryone John talked with the next morning seemed as on edge as he felt. Dark, ominous clouds brought pouring rain, confining them to their tents. Patrick stretched out and soon slept restlessly. John tried to catch up on notes but finally gave up. His mind was too engrossed with wondering what happened at Manassas Junction, for it seemed the rumors Mr. Swanson heard were correct—at least about the location.

Rain pelted the tent canvas as he started an overdue letter to his family. He'd finish upon learning the latest news.

"It's still raining?" Patrick sat up and stretched.

"Dark and gloomy as dusk." Rain splashed into mud puddles forming outside the tent.

"Any news?"

John shook his head. "Let's see what we can discover."

"We'll be drenched within seconds."

He shrugged. "Perhaps you'll not need a bath then."

Patrick gave a half-hearted chuckle.

They stepped outside. John shoved his hat over his ears. Its short brim barely prevented rain from striking his eyes.

"Captain's as crazy as we are to be out in this downpour."

Patrick pointed at Captain Michael MacNamara talking with Lieutenant Lantry at the end of their tent road.

"Maybe he heard something."

"Can't get wetter," Patrick grumbled as long strides took them to the officers. "Any news?"

"Nope." The captain stood with arms crossed. "Thinking about walking to the Second New Hampshire's camp. They left before we did and didn't come back when we did. It'll kill a few minutes."

They all agreed and were soon outside the camp. Only it wasn't empty. A soldier inside the first tent was bent over a letter.

"Did you see fighting, son?"

"It was bad." Staring miserably at the wet grass, the young man flushed scarlet.

They waited but he said nothing more.

Hair lifted on the back of John's neck as they stepped a few paces from the tent. What had happened?

"The captain's an acquaintance of mine." Captain MacNamara exchanged an uneasy glance with John and Patrick. He turned and strode down the tent road. "Let's pay him a visit."

The captain was in his quarters. He put down his pen to greet them.

Captain MacNamara made hasty introductions and then studied his friend. "What happened, Fred? There was a battle at Manassas Junction?"

"There was." Fred rubbed his bearded face. "Gentlemen, we were defeated. Our army ran in full retreat." He shook his head. "If I live to a ripe old age, I'll never forget the road to Centreville and on to Washington. Supplies of all kinds strewn on the path, flung about by terrified men. Destroyed wagons on the wayside. Dead horses. Wounded men lying about with no one to dress their wounds. Soldiers even dropped perfectly good weapons on their headlong flight back to the city."

John's heart thundered out of his chest. What was this? Retreat?

No one expected this terrible news.

Then another possibility struck. Had the Confederate army followed them back to their nation's capital city? Was President Lincoln in danger?

Was Annie in danger?

His head reeled.

Their first big battle was supposed to end the whole conflict. This was a disaster.

~

*A*nnie preferred to walk with Beatrice to Mrs. Jackson's home for a day of sewing. The weather didn't cooperate, so they set out in the closed carriage with poor Jacob huddled in the rain to drive them there. They were stopped, even in the rain, to show their passes.

The group gathered in the Jackson's parlor was half the normal size.

Mrs. Jackson hurried over with her daughter, Esther, on her heels. "My dears." She clasped her hands together. "Have you heard the terrible news?"

A feeling of foreboding swept over Annie. Was there news of Will? "Tell us quickly."

"Our soldiers were defeated near a place called Manassas Junction. Our very own Union army...in full retreat from the Rebels." She extracted a handkerchief from the shoulder of her dress and dabbed at her eyes. "Didn't you notice our soldiers on the sidewalk down the street?"

Annie exchanged a dumbfounded look with Beatrice.

"We had our shades down against the pouring rain." Beatrice's voice shook. "What are you saying?"

"Our soldiers ran headlong into our city after a grueling

battle. A tragedy, to be sure. For all of us. I'm certain they fought as bravely as they should." Another dab. "Our streets are crowded with dazed, defeated soldiers. Spectators aplenty abound even with this rain, you may be sure. Some folks try to give those poor men something to eat."

"The Union army lost? Are you certain?" Annie couldn't comprehend their army losing even one battle. Everyone had assured her it would be over before it began.

"Poor dear. I didn't want to believe it either." Mrs. Jackson patted her arm.

"Ambulances bring wounded. Shops and stores are closed." Esther wrung her hands. "Several poor soldiers sleep under an awning down the street, their heads resting on the curbstones as if they were pillows."

"Many sleep in the pouring rain, dear."

"Others return to their camps with bandages around their arms or legs or heads." Esther shook her head as if in a daze. "It's a sad day for our country."

"That's not the worst of it." Charlene Abbott joined them, her face ashen. "It's said that our leaders are just as shocked as we are."

"President Lincoln?" Annie frowned. He seemed a strong, capable man—exactly the type of president the country needed to guide them through these unprecedented days.

"I haven't heard specifically about our president, but it's said our city is in grave danger of attack."

"We are surrounded by thousands of our own soldiers to protect us." Annie sought to reassure the older women. "I can't believe the danger is as great as you fear."

"Don't you see?" Esther stared at her. "Our soldiers didn't return as they left. They're scared."

What if John's regiment hadn't been ordered to return to Washington City en route? Would that have altered the outcome?

"Mother and I went out this morning." Esther looked out the window. "We saw the poor men with our own eyes. Weak. Dispirited."

"Beaten down, they are." Mrs. Jackson gave a tiny shake of her head. "Broke my heart to see it."

"Is there anything we can do?" Beatrice looked at fabric on the tables. "Are we sewing shirts today?"

"No." Mrs. Jackson put her handkerchief back in the shoulder of her dress. "Our army needs bandages."

"Let's get started." Annie took Mrs. Jackson's arm and walked with her toward the cluttered tables. Though her heart ached for their beaten-down army, she needed to do something positive for them.

At least it sounded as if Will was safe, if he had even been at Manassas Junction. She sighed as she tore a long strip of cloth. The way things stood, it might be days or weeks before they heard news of her brother.

～

*J*ohn, sick at heart over the crushing defeat, trudged back to his camp. He shared what he'd learned with fellow soldiers hungry for news. Moments later, he stood with them as soldiers stumbled up the avenue toward their regimental camps. Though it wasn't bullets and cannons pelting them today, the rain multiplied the misery engraved in their faces. Weariness marked their painful progress. The same soldiers who had answered the Irish Ninth's cheers with confident shouts didn't raise their eyes from contemplation of the muddy road. They walked bent over, as if the terrible burden of what they'd endured was beyond their comprehension.

His shoulders slumped from the weight of his heart, John looked up at the sky as the rain slackened. Dark clouds lightened. The rain stopped, and a ray of sun touched his drenched skin.

Broken men, in groups of two or three, trudged past.

"Send us to the fight." A soldier behind him spoke in fervent tones.

"We'll turn this thing around." Another man's voice carried from the back of the crowd gathered at the end of their tent road.

"We'll whip 'em."

John turned and drew in a quick breath at the renewed hope on several faces that had been gloomy moments ago.

Yet it was what was beyond them that captivated him.

Two men stood in the back holding flags. One held their nation's flag with the stars and stripes floating gently on a breeze. The other was their regimental green flag, its sunburst and eagle emblems reviving John's pride in his Irish Ninth *and* his country.

Not the country of his parents' birth, but his nation nonetheless. Beloved.

Worth fighting for.

CHAPTER 13

nnie had asked Rebecca to prepare chicken croquettes for supper because John had praised them at the Independence Day picnic that seemed months past instead of a mere two and half weeks before. Father didn't return home for the meal, but John ate a second helping, bringing a contented smile to Rebecca's face. Not wanting to bring up unsavory topics while they ate, Annie pushed aside her questions about the retreat until dessert was consumed.

Beatrice accompanied them to the parlor after supper. "Can we ask about the battle, John?"

"Tragic." He sat beside Annie on a sofa and across from her sister. "My heart is heavy for those who fought."

A door clicked behind them. "Father, you're home." Annie rushed to his side. "Rebecca has your supper in the warming oven."

Exhaustion lined his face. "I'd rather eat at the table in here and talk with my family. John, I'm glad you're here."

"I'll ask Mr. Grant to get your plate." Bea left the room quickly.

"You can eat there." Annie pointed to a long table two feet

wide near the pianoforte. "We'll arrange our chairs around the table with you."

"That will be fine." He looked at John. "I trust you will not mind the informality of us treating you as family?"

"'Tis an honor to be treated as such, sir." He bowed his head slightly. He followed Annie's instructions and the table was soon arranged for them.

In spite of the turmoil in her city, a delicious sense of well-being washed over Annie. John being there at such a time was a deep comfort. He'd warn them if there was danger, for he'd always be honest with them. As Will's friend and her beau, she trusted him with her life.

~

*J*ohn answered Mr. Swanson's probing question with growing unease. The man ate with a nearly insatiable appetite, but John had a feeling his hunger for knowledge was even greater.

"We made bandages for our wounded soldiers today." Annie sat at John's side opposite her father.

"Excellent." John gave an approving nod. "They are much needed now the fighting has begun."

"It's said that our army didn't return with the same confidence as they displayed marching out." Beatrice glanced at John.

How could they, after such a retreat? He must choose his words carefully with the whole family, as he didn't want to scare the ladies or give what little information he'd learned that wasn't already common knowledge. "Brave men will rally."

"What of the rumors that Southern troops plan to attack this fair city?" Eying him, Mr. Swanson shoved a bite of chicken croquette into his mouth. "I've even heard mention of plans to attack Fort McHenry."

"You are remarkably well-informed." He'd heard the same

rumors. Baltimore's Fort McHenry was a weak garrison, but the Union didn't want to lose it. Did his host know that? Troubled by Hiram's many questions, Christopher's suspicions rose to the forefront of his mind. Were Hiram's concerns those of a citizen who feared for his family? Or did his probing questions stem from a need to supply information to the enemy? He'd best guard his tongue.

"The only topic on my customers' lips these days is our conflict with our neighbors to the South. Naturally, I hear many things in the course of my day." He studied John. "Discerning truth from rumors is the difficulty."

"As in any war." John hoped his guarded tone didn't offend. Citizens of this capital city had learned a great deal. Without knowing specifics about general knowledge, he'd best put a lock on his tongue.

"So many troops occupy our city that I feel safe." Annie gazed up at him with trust reflected in her brown eyes. "Especially with your camp less than a mile away."

Her confidence in his ability to protect her thrilled him to his core. "Our Irish Ninth stands ready to defend." He returned her smile with a niggling of trepidation. How long would his regiment stay there? Whether he liked it or not, recent occurrences might lead to changes. The captain had hinted as much.

"Something happened in the streets near the bank that disturbed me." Hiram drummed his fingers on the table.

"What is it, Father?" Beatrice asked.

"Even though the North lost the battle, Federal soldiers managed to capture groups of Southern soldiers. Our fair citizens jeered at them. Lined the roadsides to do so." His lips tightened. "Some threw mud and rocks at men who could not defend themselves."

The atmosphere suddenly felt charged as with electricity.

Annie's face stiffened.

"Did you see...familiar faces?" Beatrice spoke in a whisper.

John's thoughts flew to Will.

"I stood in the streets with them. I studied the prisoners' faces. Some scared. Some angry. But no." Hiram turned a serious gaze on his daughters. "I saw no one I knew."

The sudden silence was broken by the tolling of the clock.

John panicked, for he must be back before *Taps*. It was eight o'clock already, and he had much to say, most of it for Annie's ears alone.

～

"I'm thrilled you suggested a stroll." Annie's arm rested lightly on his forearm. No bands played to accompany their walk this evening. An owl hooted as a lone chaise buggy passed them. "With all the bad news assailing us, nothing brings me as much comfort and strength as moments with you."

John halted. "Do you mean that?"

Annie's heart skipped a beat at the intense look in his green eyes. "I do."

"I could not be happier than to know I'm your hero." He covered her gloved fingers with his strong hand.

"You must believe you are." Her skin tingled at the wonder on his face. He cared for her. Did he love her?

"Recent events will likely precipitate orders to leave this vicinity."

"No." More bad news? Her heart plummeted. "I don't want you to go."

"Nor do I want to leave." His smile wavered. "Yet the army may command it."

She looked away. He had a job to do, and she wanted him to do it.

"Since I can't predict what those orders will be, there is something I wish to discuss with you." He turned and resumed the walk. "Did you wonder why I rarely wrote to you after Will's wedding?"

"Yes." Finally, he meant to tell her why he hadn't pursued a courtship with her. "We were often in one another's company that week. You sought my company at every outing. You even —" No. She wouldn't mention their kiss under the stars. "Then you wrote only two letters. I'd like to understand why."

"Ye deserve that and more." Scarlet stained his cheeks. "As you know, my family owns a furniture factory and three stores in Boston. What you don't know is that my da and mam came to this country with nothing but a pair of strong hands and a knowledge of carpentry. I was but a babe when we settled in Boston. It took years of hard work for him to build the company to its current state. His success ensured a comfortable living for my family. I'm proud of him."

"I understand." Annie's father had left a thriving Richmond law practice to marry her mother. "My father worked hard to learn the banking profession after marrying Mother. She had one younger sister and her father needed to train someone to take over the bank after his death. Father didn't inherit his father's plantation. Wealth wasn't given to him. He worked for it."

"I've no doubt of it." John glanced at the sky. "Let's turn back. We'll stroll in the opposite direction until the sun sets, and then I'll walk you home."

"Father wants me to stay near our home because of the late hour." The sun approached the horizon. "We have a few minutes. Please, tell me quickly."

"For several years, I worked at our factory when not in school. Long enough to know it wasn't to be my life's work."

"What do you want to do?" These details from his boyhood captivated her.

"The railroad has always fascinated me. I'd hear the whistle blow on passing trains and get a hankering to climb aboard. I wanted to go with them, see what those passengers saw...even as a boy." His eyes had a faraway look. "A teacher told us that folks were talking about building a railroad across the country to the Pacific Ocean. I feared they'd build it before I grew up."

"No fear of that." Annie laughed. "As far as I know, it's all still a dream."

"A grand, *doable* dream." Enthusiasm enhanced his Irish brogue. "That's why I went to West Point. I'd heard that graduates don't always follow military careers. That education lends itself to other careers. Like one in the railroad."

"That's thrilling." With a light in his eyes that she'd seldom seen, he never looked more handsome or appealing. She was relieved he didn't want a military career because the army kept men away from home months at a time.

"Yes." The animation in his face died. "And then my father's illness left no one to lead the company. I put aside my dreams."

Family obligations had cost him years away from his chosen career. Admirable yet tragic. "It doesn't have to remain that way. Your father took over the company's leadership when you mustered into the army. Isn't that true?"

"Aye. Part leadership anyway. He wants me back as soon as the conflict ends. He believed I'd be home before Christmas. He said he can handle the reins for six months."

"You said your brother must mature before he's ready to help significantly."

"Aye." He sighed.

"Is there no one else? Perhaps a trusted employee?"

"We think alike, Miss Annie Swanson." His expression lightened. "I've trained two men in all aspects of our furniture business. My sister Madelynn is courting, and her young man will eventually manage a store."

"Excellent. You mentioned that before." Her fingers tightened around his arm. "That all sounds promising."

"What gave me courage to finally speak to you is me mother's last letter. It came this morning. Me father seems to be doing well. Her opinion is that running the business has not taxed his strength beyond what is normal."

"Then you are free to pursue your dreams." Her heart swelled with thankfulness. The sun had dipped below the trees. "You may yet be part of building that railroad reaching the Pacific Ocean." *Ask me to marry you. Take me with you.*

"I pray so." They'd reached the canopy of trees that offered welcome shade in the daylight hours. Now it was dusk. He stopped walking and turned to her. "It may be a rugged life. Far different from the one enjoyed by the daughter of a wealthy banker."

"Perhaps that daughter is ready for the adventure as the wife of a railroad businessman." Joy bubbled up. "Perhaps that daughter would follow a certain sergeant-major in the Irish Ninth were he to propose."

"Are you certain?" He caressed her cheek.

"You'll never know until you ask." She held her breath.

"I love you." He bent and kissed her.

She gave herself up to the joy of his kiss. *He loved her.* She finally heard the magical words that altered her destiny. "I love you, John."

"You are an amazing woman. I will ask when the time is right." He gave her a lingering kiss that left her breathless. "I promise."

Why not now? What held him back? His commitment to the army? Perhaps he wasn't ready to commit to her.

She stepped back from him. "We'll wait on the kisses until you make up your mind."

CHAPTER 14

"We've received our marching orders." Patrick strode into their tent early the next morning. "We're breaking camp and moving."

Annie. Last evening's stroll hadn't ended well, and now this? Blood receded from John's face. "Where are we going?"

"That's not clear. Colonel Cass may know specific details." Patrick folded a shirt. "We're to build up fortifications for Washington City. We're moving out of the capital."

"How far?" John rubbed his hands through his hair. This wasn't a good time to leave Annie, who had misconstrued his question about their courtship to mean a marriage proposal. What kind of scoundrel proposed to a woman while spying on her father? He was not so lost to his moral roots as that.

"Miles from here, certainly." Patrick packed his shaving mug and brush in his knapsack. "Other than that, I cannot say."

Wait a minute. Miles away? Then Christopher couldn't expect him to spy on Hiram Swanson any longer. His spirit lightened. "When will we leave?"

"Later this afternoon."

"Look, I need to go into town."

"You want to tell Annie?"

"Yes." And Christopher. Patrick didn't need to know that.

He rubbed his chin. "Pack up and help me get the tent down before you go. All the men are packing, so I doubt it matters that you won't be here to oversee their activities for an hour or two."

"I owe you." John rolled up his blankets tightly.

"Be back by lunch so you can help with last minute tasks." Patrick stuffed a change of clothing into his knapsack. "And give my regards to Bea—and the family."

John stuffed letters from his family into his knapsack. "I will." It scarcely mattered if Patrick harbored feelings for Beatrice now.

He was hard-pressed to figure out how he'd see Annie in the future. It had been easier to finagle an hour or two away from camp when his destination was a ten-minute walk. Now, what must he do to see her?

Chances were very slim that they'd return to this camp.

～

"You're joking." John stared at Christopher's impassive face. The man made a good spy because he gave little away. "How can I be expected to monitor Hiram Swanson's conversations from miles away?"

"You aren't traveling as far as you imagine." Christopher leaned back in his chair. His boarding room was large enough to allow ample space for a writing table and two spindle-back chairs. "Do you own a horse?"

"In Boston." John crossed his arms. "'Twill be waiting for me there when me army days are done."

"You'll need one here." He extracted some bills from his pocket and tossed them on the table. "It's not unheard of for someone of your rank to bring a horse to camp."

"Are you serious, man?" John stared at the cash. "I always figured to march with my men."

"Purchase it after you arrive at your destination. No harm in letting a higher-ranking officer without a steed ride it during marches." He pressed his fingertips together. "What have you learned?"

"Mr. Swanson has admitted to a great deal of knowledge of our current difficulties." John glanced out the window to where the top of the President's house could be seen from the fourth-story room. "He daily hears news from clients."

Christopher drummed his fingers against the desk. "Anything specific?"

John hesitated. "He asked many questions about what I'd learned of the battle. Of our troops' morale. Numbers of wounded and killed."

"What did you tell him?"

"I only answered what was general knowledge. Annie and Beatrice had learned quite a bit at a ladies' sewing group that was fairly factual."

He raised an eyebrow. "Tell me about the sewing group."

John tugged at his collar. He hadn't intended to place Annie and her sister under scrutiny, but he told him what he'd learned. "They sew for our troops. Their latest task is making bandages. I'm certain there are no nefarious activities originating there."

Christopher grunted. "You'd be surprised." He straightened his shoulders. "I realize you won't be able to see the Swansons as often, but buy that horse. Arrange a weekly visit—the Wednesday soirees, if you can manage it. Anything else?"

"There was mention of clients who removed their money from the bank before moving South."

"Ah. We suspected as much, of course." His pencil scratched across the paper in front of him. "What else have you learned?"

"Nothing. Other than he keeps long hours at the bank."

"If you attend the soiree, I'll meet you in the usual place. If not, stop here before riding back to camp...no matter the time. If I'm away, leave a sealed note only with my landlord." He stood.

"Understood." Pocketing the bills, John rose. "Will there be problems obtaining the appropriate passes to travel to the city?"

"I will have what you need sent to you today by messenger. It will be sealed. Open it when you're alone so as not to arouse curiosity."

John picked up his bowler hat. "'Tis curious it's this important to spy on the Swansons."

"There are things afoot that we must get to the bottom of." Christopher eyed him. "And I suspect you've had moments of doubt in your conversations with Hiram Swanson."

"Aye." John couldn't stem the guilty heat that charged up his face.

"Exactly." Christopher extended his hand. "I'll be in touch if necessary."

"Of course." John shook it.

"It's unfortunate that your camp has to move. This secret duty is as important as the official duties that brought you to Washington City."

"Yes." If both duties were of equal standing, he'd better find a way to search for written evidence in Hiram's study. John's stomach churned while running down the stairs.

Now to see Annie. Pity he didn't have a horse yet. After this long meeting with Christopher, he'd not have above a quarter hour to spend with her.

❧

"*M*r. Grant, please ask Jacob to bring the landau around whenever it's ready." Annie rubbed her temples. Her headache had delayed their departure to sewing group long enough.

The white-haired gentleman inclined his head. "I'll see to it, Miss Annie."

After he left the parlor, Annie rested her aching head against the cushioned armchair.

"Are you certain you feel like sewing today?" Beatrice studied her. "Perhaps you should rest. I'll go alone."

"No. Our soldiers need bandages." She closed her eyes. "I didn't sleep well. I'll retire early tonight, and all will be well tomorrow." But would it? After her conversation with John the previous night, she didn't know. It was the first time he'd told her of his dreams to participate in the railroad's expansion. His excitement had been contagious. As his wife, she'd support his decisions and follow him into the vastness of the West.

But he hadn't proposed. He'd discussed future plans and said he planned to propose. Then why didn't he? She was willing to wait until the end of the hostilities.

"You've been out of sorts since your stroll with John last evening." Beatrice perched on an opposite chair. "Anything happen?"

"No." Her tone came out harsher than she intended. "Sorry, Bea. I'm scared about what's coming." It was true. Thoughts of war scared her, but that wasn't at the forefront of her thoughts.

"Pardon me." Mr. Grant entered the room. "Sergeant-Major John Finn is here to see you, Miss Annie."

"John's here?" The clock on the mantle showed it was half-past nine. "Something's amiss."

"Please invite him into the parlor, Mr. Grant." Beatrice glanced at her. "Nod to me if you'd like privacy."

"I will." Annie moved forward as her handsome soldier hurried into the room. "John, I didn't expect you."

"Forgive me." He clasped the hand she lifted toward him. "Good morning, Annie. Bea."

They murmured their greetings.

"I apologize for arriving so early." He looked at her fingers curled around his. "I have only a few moments to let you know that we've received new orders."

"Another battle?" Her breath caught in her throat. The last one had gone so badly.

"No." He spoke quickly. "At least...not yet. We're packing up the whole camp and marching out."

"Where are you going?" Her body went cold.

"I don't know." He looked away. "Maybe not far."

"What do you know?" He must know something. Sometimes when he answered father's questions, John had the same evasive look in his eyes.

"Nothing specific. And I'm unsure of facts. I'll let you know more later."

"How? Will you write to me?"

"Of course."

Annie nodded to her sister.

"John, we look forward to seeing you as soon as may be." Beatrice inclined her head.

He released Annie and stood when Beatrice did. "If I am within riding distance, I will visit weekly."

"But you have no horse." Annie gestured to a sofa as her sister slipped from the room.

"I'll buy one."

Joy bubbled up into laughter at his fervent tones. He cared for her enough to do that? "Then I'll pray your regiment remains nearby."

Laughter eased the tension from his face and just as quickly evaporated. "Last evening didn't go well. I meant to explain my long silence after Will's wedding. Even though I'd met the prettiest girl in the world and she'd stolen my heart, I wasn't free from family obligations. Wouldn't be for years. You bring me hope that it's all possible."

"It is possible." Her headache eased at the hope in his eyes.

"That's what I needed to hear." He gave a shaky laugh. "If I can manage to be at your soiree next Wednesday, will there be a place for me?"

"There will." *Always.*

"If I am able to do so, I will let you know where I am camped."

Her brow furrowed. "*If* you are able?"

"Many activities, if known by the enemy, gives them an advantage." His expression turned serious. "Some things I will not be able to tell you."

Annie drew back. "I'm not the enemy, John."

"Of course not. But that doesn't change my ability to speak of military secrets." He glanced at the mantle clock and stood. "I apologize, but I must go."

Her heart plummeted. "If you must."

"If I find myself free on a Sunday…"

"I'll ask Rebecca to set another place at the table."

He held out his arms.

She stepped into them and rested her head on his muscular chest. "I wish you didn't have to leave." She looked up at him.

He touched her lips with a gentle finger. Then his lips followed with a kiss that held all the love she'd longed for from her Irish soldier.

"I'll return as soon as I can," he whispered against her lips and then kissed her again, longer this time. "Good bye, my sweet Annie."

"Good bye."

He strode from the parlor. At the door, he gave her one backward glance. Then he was gone.

CHAPTER 15

*W*ithin hours, the baggage wagons bulged with their regiment's supplies. They'd marched through Washington City in the afternoon sun on Tuesday, July twenty-third, to the lilting tunes of their regimental band and smiling waves from bystanders. When they crossed the Potomac River into Virginia, John paused to look behind him. Unsure of their final destination, he prayed this road didn't take him far from Annie—a desire that had nothing to do with Lieutenant Christopher Farmer's orders and everything to do with his heart.

As he marched, John pondered Christopher's assertion that his spying and military service were on equal footing. If so, he'd best give the matter the serious consideration it deserved rather than the half-hearted attempt that best described his work. He'd resented that *anyone* spied on Hiram Swanson.

No more. A messenger had delivered all the passes required for John to travel to the Swanson's weekly parties, and also to see Annie. A blessing, though some might say he used their courtship for his own purposes. The thought rankled like a burr hidden in a boot. He never wanted her to doubt his love that burned strong and true.

The band played *The Girl I Left Behind Me*. It struck a chord in his soul. *I'll never leave you, Annie. This spying business will soon be behind us. Then the only barriers between us will be the miles that separate us.*

Night fell, and still they marched along roads showing imprints of hundreds of boots and leather shoes.

Loud cheers burst from woods ahead. John lengthened his stride to catch up with Patrick. "What's this?"

Their band quieted.

"Union regiments are camped in those trees." Patrick nodded toward them.

"They're cheering for the Ninth Massachusetts?"

Men of the Irish Ninth returned the cheer.

"A beautiful noise." Tension eased from John's back. "Look at those bonfires."

"Huge." Patrick looked to his right as they continued past. "Quite a welcome."

The bonfires continued along their route. Was it possible reports of their courage and resolve had preceded them? It seemed so, for periodic cheers broke out.

John's exhaustion seeped away at such a grand welcome.

It was late when they halted in the woods behind a mansion where they were to eat and then sleep. The home's size reminded John of Annie. He hoped she'd been sleeping for hours.

Patrick strode over. "Know where we are?"

"Nope."

"That's Arlington House." He surveyed the large home in the moonlight. "The home of Robert E. Lee. Confederate Colonel Robert E. Lee."

*a*nnie walked alone on Wednesday afternoon to the site of John's camp listening to the sound of distant drums. He really was gone.

No one had asked to see her military pass that morning when she and Beatrice had walked to the Jackson's home. What she had once resented she now longed for because showing those passes meant John was close.

She ambled along well-worn paths in the field that had housed a city of tents the morning before. John didn't think his camp was moving far away—though too distant to walk. A delicious sense of comfort welled up that he planned to purchase a horse to visit her.

He'd try to attend her father's soirees, where her responsibilities as hostess demanded her attention to other guests. Sunday services and then lunch with her family afforded more time for conversation. Perhaps a drive if the weather was fine.

If he must choose, she hoped to see him on Sundays.

Annie avoided deep ruts from tent spikes as she wandered the vacant field so recently filled with activity.

She loved a military man. Her Irish soldier was brave and strong. She blushed to recall his muscular chest as he'd embraced her. She lifted her parasol higher so that anyone seeing her scarlet face would attribute it to the sun's warmth.

No word yet from him. Her mother had striven to teach her patience... Annie had waited a year for John to renew his courtship. How patient must a woman be?

Sounds of bugles and drums drew nearer as she approached an army camp. Knowing her father would disapprove of her venturing closer, Annie turned toward home.

Their father arrived as she and Bea finished eating an early supper.

Rebecca and Mrs. Grant, their housekeeper, brought his meal while he greeted his daughters.

"Thank you." Gratitude swelled Annie's heart that her staff needed no prompting. "Mrs. Grant, how is your arthritis this evening?" The dear woman suffered so that she avoided stairs. Maids cleaned the upper floors, and her husband communicated with staff on the housekeeper's behalf so everything ran smoothly.

"Tolerable, Miss Annie." White curls peeked out beneath her white cap. She positioned a steaming plate of roasted beef, mashed potatoes, and corn pudding in front of Hiram. "Thank you for asking."

Father murmured his thanks. Rebecca slipped out while he bowed his head for a brief, silent blessing. Mrs. Grant made her way slowly from the smaller family dining room.

"How was your day, Father?" Beatrice, a glass of lemonade cradled in her hands, settled back in her cushioned chair.

"Tolerable." He answered between bites of roasted beef. "I've heard rumors."

Sensing the warning in his ominous tone, Annie tensed. "What's being said now?"

"There may be an attack on our city."

Annie gasped. "But...John's regiment marched off yesterday."

"Yes. There is movement of troops that we may learn about from our evening guests. Listen carefully so that you can tell me verbatim what is stated."

Annie met Beatrice's wide-eyed gaze.

"Are we in danger, Father?"

"Not at all." His face relaxed. "We'll take precautions. General Beauregard led the Confederate army to a resounding win on Sunday—just three days ago. Who knows but that he plans to follow that victory with an attack on our capital city? But not to worry. I doubt it will come to that."

Annie wrung her hands. "How unfortunate that John is not here to protect us."

"There are other troops still in our city."

He didn't seem upset. In fact, his countenance had lightened, as if sharing the rumors lent them less credibility. "Nevertheless, I want you to stay home the next few days." He gave them each a long look. "No strolls. No walks to the market. No meetings in the Jackson's parlor. If you must sew, do it here."

"Should we cancel our soiree?" Beatrice's glass chinked against the table.

"No need." He smiled. "If military guests do not come, we'll know to be on our guard. If they leave in haste…" He raised his hands expressively. "Remember to come to me with any information. Those bits of knowledge help us protect ourselves."

It wasn't clear to Annie how knowledge protected a person from a soldier wielding a musket.

Not clear at all.

~

*A*nnie looked up every time Mr. Grant ushered in another guest. In vain. John wasn't coming. Even knowing it was impossible to march out one day and return to virtually the same location the next, her heart had held out hope for the first hour. Now, it was time to help her father acquire the knowledge he desired to feel secure about their safety.

She'd visited with an undersecretary of some representative for five minutes and now sat on a sofa with an army officer. Usually, she allowed the men to speak on any topic they chose. Tonight, she hoped to steer the conversation. "Captain"—having forgotten his name, she widened her smile in the hope he didn't notice—"I've heard the most frightful rumors."

"About the war?" The young man's mustache twitched.

"Yes." Annie searched his face. "Will General Beauregard attack this city?"

"Don't worry about Beauregard."

"He beat us once."

"Once." The captain's face darkened.

"I worry for my family...and President Lincoln."

"No need." He spoke with growing confidence. "Forts guard our city."

"Forts?" Perhaps this was what her father wanted to know.

"New ones have been built—Fort Corcoran, Fort Haggerty, and Fort Bennett to name a few."

"How comforting." Annie memorized the names.

"Those forts guard the Aqueduct." His chin lifted. "Fort Runyon and Fort Albany guard the Long Bridge."

She raised her brows. "These forts will protect our city from threats coming from the South?"

"Precisely. It's impossible to cross into Virginia without a pass."

"That must be inconvenient for local merchants."

"War's inconvenient to everyone, Miss Swanson, one way or another." He leaned forward. "Perhaps you've heard that Colonel Robert E. Lee has moved his loyalties to fight for the South."

"I'm uncertain if I did." Such details had mattered little to her in the spring.

"Regrettable." He pursed his lips. "He abandoned his home—Arlington House—and we started building fortifications on it."

She blinked. Beatrice was right—soldiers loved to boast.

"I know another thing that will make you feel more secure."

"Oh?" She waved cigar smoke out of her face with her fan.

"More forts will be built shortly."

"That's...quite amazing." Annie's breath caught in her throat. Had John's regiment left to build a fort to guard the city? He'd hinted that he didn't believe they'd go far. "May I ask you something, Captain?"

"Anything." He leaned forward.

"Is such information...secret?"

"Once they've been standing a while, a fort's location is likely known to the enemy. A fort's weaponry and number of troops guarding it is another matter. Most of what I said is generally known," he sputtered, looking away. "I told you no specifics."

"Of course not." He'd given her the answer she craved—either John hadn't known these details or he was bound to secrecy—and better at keeping secrets than this officer. She understood. After all, wasn't she keeping a secret from him? "It's hard to discern truth from rumor right now. That's all I meant."

"I understand." His face reddened. "It's been a lovely evening, but I must take my leave."

Ten o'clock already? "Thank you for coming." She stood and curtsied, refraining from inviting him to return. That was up to her father.

Within a quarter hour, all guests were gone. Father asked the maid to pour hot tea for the three of them and then dismissed her.

He sank back into his cushioned chair. "So, my daughters, what did you discover?"

CHAPTER 16

*A*fter supper on Sunday, John waited on the densely-wooded hillside by their camp for Patrick and a few others. After writing a quick letter to inform Annie he was nearby in Virginia, there had been plenty to keep him busy.

There was an air of excitement because his regiment had been charged with erecting a new fortification called Fort Ramsay, joining other forts recently built, like the nearby Fort Corcoran. They'd already cleared enough of the woody hillside to pitch camp and create an abatis to protect their front.

John crossed his arms and surveyed the sharpened tree branches that had been laid in a row with the pointed ends outwards. Good work for men new to the task.

Footsteps behind him caused dirt to spill down the hillside.

"Looking at the results of our hard work?" Patrick stopped beside him.

"Thinking what a privilege it is to build it." John studied the partially-cleared hill. This was something tangible about his contribution in this war to tell his children. He knew the woman he wanted to be their mother. Annie.

"Reckon so. You ready to buy a horse?" Pat clapped him on the back. "Everyone's here."

John picked up his rifle, and they set out to find a local family willing to sell him a horse. Several others learned of their errand and joined them, including Corporal Ben Boyle. All carried rifles.

"Nice evenin' for a stroll." Patrick surveyed the lush green countryside.

"Aye." John grunted. His mind was on buying a steed to see Annie.

"Can't venture too far afield." Ben lengthened his stride to match theirs as they passed Fort Corcoran. "The enemy's close."

"Agreed." John sighed. Picket duty had become more serious, because a large number of Confederates were camped near Fall's Church, some two to three miles from the Union location. "Ten of us are no match for a regiment."

"A company, maybe." Patrick quirked an eyebrow.

John grinned. "Ten men from the Irish Ninth against a hundred?"

"Sounds about right." Ben chuckled.

"Maybe we'll have luck here." Patrick pointed ahead to a two-story white clapboard farmhouse with a barn and outbuildings.

"Looks promising." John fingered the bills in his pocket hidden beside the passes for Washington City. "Hope they need money."

When they reached the property, John asked Patrick and Ben to accompany him while the rest lounged under one of the lane's shade trees.

A woman in her twenties answered the door. Three children, the oldest one a boy of perhaps six, held onto her charcoal-colored skirt. Her glance swept their uniforms. "Yes, gentlemen?"

John took a step back at her frosty tone. Perhaps her husband had mustered into the Confederate army. Their camp was in Virginia, after all. "Good evening, ma'am. Pardon our intrusion. We don't mean to trouble you, but do you have a horse for sale?"

"No." She reached for the door as a baby cried from the upstairs.

He held up his hand. "Do you know of another family nearby with a horse they don't need?"

"No." The door closed firmly.

"Thank you kindly." John placed his hat on his head and shifted his rifle against his shoulder.

"Let's go." Patrick led the way to a dirt path back to the road. "Either that woman was busy or she doesn't like Union soldiers."

"Both." John glanced over his shoulder at the house, where a little boy watched them from behind a lacy curtain. "Doesn't bode well."

At the next home, a black man met them on the porch steps. He told them all their extra horses were now owned by the Confederate army.

John's spirits sank with the sun. How was he to see Annie?

Some of the men who'd come along turned back to camp, claiming it a lost cause.

"Let's try once more." Ben stared at a house on a hill. "Buying a horse isn't working. Perhaps this time you can offer to pay for the use of a horse for, say, a month at a time."

"There's an idea. Never heard of renting a horse." Patrick sighed. "But no one seems to have one for sale. You want to see Annie, don't you?"

"Of course, man." John rubbed his chin. "Sounds fair. They retain ownership and earn money for a month or two."

"Hopefully longer." Ben studied the wooded hills. "We dare not go farther tonight. This is it."

John scoured the woods for movement. Nothing…but no need to push their luck.

A boy of perhaps ten emerged from the barn, a large brown and white dog at his side.

They met him halfway between the dirt road and the house. "Good evening."

"'Evenin'." The boy eyed them warily. A mop of blond hair fell across his forehead.

"We're hoping your pa has a horse he'll sell us." John crossed his arms, thankful the dog stayed at the boy's side. It seemed watchful rather than unfriendly. "Can you fetch him for us?"

"Nope." The boy tilted his head. "He ain't here, but it ain't gonna matter. Ma can't spare either of our horses."

"Is your Ma in the house?" A dog barked in the distance.

The boy widened his stance. "What fer? I done told you we ain't got no horses for sale."

"I don't need a horse more than twice a week. Can I pay your family for the use of a horse? Say, ten dollars a month?"

"You'd pay that much to stable our own horse for a month?" Behind the boy, a horse neighed. His gaze darted to the barn. "Fifteen."

John liked the young lad's attitude. "Fifteen it is." They shook hands. "I'll come for the horse Wednesday afternoon and return it Thursday morning." He wasn't certain how long he'd be gone, especially since he had to meet with Christopher after Hiram's soiree. Those conversations could lengthen already long days.

"Agreed."

"My name is Sergeant-Major John Finn."

"Zachary Beets. But you can call me Zach, being's we're in business together."

"Good to meet you, Zach." John shook hands with the budding businessman. "I may need it on Sundays."

"That'll cost a dollar extra."

John quirked an eyebrow.

"Ma likes to go for drives after Sunday dinner." He brushed back his hair. "She might not mind giving it up so much if she's getting a little extra money."

"Let's keep your ma happy." John counted out the bills. "I'm paying you for one week in July—even though it ends on Wednesday—and the whole month of August."

Zach counted it. "Want to rent a saddle to go with it?"

John, tapping a finger against his chin, regarded him. "I think the saddle can be included in what I've already paid."

"Agreed." Zach gave a cheeky grin. "Just thought I'd ask."

John couldn't hold back his laughter as Patrick and Ben chuckled. There was something likable about the incorrigible boy.

He now had transportation. His captain reluctantly gave his permission to an evening's leave on Wednesdays when his daily duties were done.

～

*J*ohn's second letter had assured Annie he'd attend their soiree. She'd hoped that he'd dine with her family before the party—a vain hope since the first guest had arrived a half hour before.

Annie greeted an army lieutenant and sat to talk with him. Or pretend to listen was more accurate. With her fan stirring a breeze on her flushed cheeks, she looked up each time Mr. Grant ushered in a new guest.

"May I escort you around the forts of Washington City?"

Annie lowered the fan. "Pardon me, Lieutenant Waters?"

"I'm not surprised you didn't hear me with the number of conversations going on around us." He leaned closer. "I asked if I could escort you around the forts of your city. There are a number of them now."

On the verge of a refusal, she paused. Her father wanted

information on the military. Some forts were in plain view of citizens. Apparently, officers weren't supposed to share this information unless it was widely known. "Are new ones being built then?"

"I'd not take you to any that the general public doesn't know about. I don't want to worry you"—he patted her hand—"but it's common knowledge that the enemy is amassing in Virginia."

For an attack on Washington City? She gasped. Her father had been wise to curtail their activities, even if she did tire of remaining close to home.

"Virginia is a large state. I didn't say there's a large army nearby. No need to panic." The officer maintained a confident air. "There are pickets and barricades on our bridges over the Potomac River."

"To keep the Confederate soldiers from reaching our president."

"That, and we must retain control of the railroads. Transportation is critical for moving our soldiers."

The parlor door opened. Mr. Grant gestured a white-gloved hand toward Annie.

John stood in the doorway, even more handsome than when he'd left a week ago. His expression was just as warm and welcoming.

Annie stood, and Lieutenant Waters stood when she did, halting his words mid-sentence. Annie knew she was being rude to her poor guest. She hadn't realized how afraid she'd been that something prevented John from coming. "Forgive me, Lieutenant Waters. There is someone I must greet."

CHAPTER 17

*A*nnie's beauty, enhanced by a pink dress with a lacy overlay that he'd seen before, captivated John. He could not look away. He was glad that Rebecca's husband, Tom, had been in charge of stabling horses. When John had arrived a half hour before, sweaty from the sweltering heat and smelling of the stable, Tom showed him where he could wash and change into the fresh uniform he'd packed in his knapsack. He was doubly happy for a clean uniform as he gazed at Annie, who was as lovely as a slender pink rose in any garden.

"John." She glided forward and clasped his hands. "I worried something prevented your attendance tonight."

"Something tried." He grimaced. "Our regiment is engaged in new tasks taken on since we marched away eight days ago. Regrettably I couldn't obtain permission to leave camp until we broke to prepare our suppers." Forgoing his meal, he'd left immediately. His stomach protested missing the supper that his heart did not regret. "My apologies."

"Tell me everything."

He gave a start. There was little within his power to share at this early stage. Guilt gnawed at him for spying on her father. Still, if there was something of importance to report, he had to find it. In the meantime, he trusted that Annie was unaware of any wrong-doing by her father. Her loyalty was firmly on the side of the Union.

When Christopher released him from spying and this was behind them, he would propose with a bouquet of flowers in hand. Roses or daisies? Roses were more romantic, but his favorites were daisies. How often had her beauty struck him with the same wonder he felt when gazing on God's handiwork in nature...like a field of daisies.

"*B*ut first, allow me to introduce you to Lieutenant Waters." A slight frown stole her smile as she looked at the tall blond-haired man who had followed her.

The reproach in her eyes as she made the introductions was a rare lapse in her impeccable manners, though her fan likely masked her displeasure from the stranger. She must have wanted a private word with John. Worry for John must have consumed her. "A pleasure, Lieutenant Waters." He shook the officer's hand.

"Thomas. Always a pleasure to meet a fellow officer."

"John." The man had an open, honest face that he liked.

"Did I hear you say something about new tasks?"

John darted a glance at Annie's watchful eyes and then gave a slight nod. "In these early days, many tasks are new." John silently shot the man a warning look. Thomas ought to know better than to pursue the matter in front of a civilian in a crowded parlor.

"Ah, the secrets of war." His eyes gleamed. "I've asked Miss Swanson to accompany me on a ride around the city to see our forts. Such a drive is certain to relieve her fears."

"I am unable to accompany you, Lieutenant Waters," Annie

said, "as my father has asked us to remain near home for the time being. He feels we are safer here."

John pulled at his ear. His desire to ease her fears placed him in a quandary, since he was unable to tell her about the forts he'd seen across the Potomac and those now under construction. "I could scarcely bring meself to leave you if I believed you and your family in imminent danger." It was the best he could do to reassure her.

"I believe you." Her face relaxed. "I trust you."

Shame seared his face. His despicable spying on her father wasn't the act of a gentleman with serious intentions on that man's daughter.

"If you saw those forts, Miss Swanson, you'd sleep easier." Thomas bounced on his heels. "You're as safe as a baby in her crib."

Annie smiled at both men. "How can I live in fear with such brave men as yourselves guarding our city?"

❧

A frown from her father recalled Annie to her hostess duties. Excusing herself, she roamed from group to group.

John left the room with several others, presumably to enjoy refreshments in the upstairs parlor. Her father followed within moments.

The evening brightened when Mrs. Greenhow beckoned her a few minutes later. Neither John nor her father had returned, and Annie was glad for the opportunity to speak to an acquaintance she'd known since girlhood.

"Mrs. Greenhow, how lovely you could join us this evening." Annie chose an empty arm chair beside her. "There are so many strangers at these soirees that it is a true treasure to converse with my mother's friend."

"Thank you, my dear. We do miss her, don't we?" The widow, mourning the loss of a daughter, wore a ruffled black dress.

"Yes." Annie's breath hitched. She paused to regain her composure. "I need her wisdom more than ever."

"It's true, my dear. We are much beset, aren't we?" Mrs. Greenhow nodded to one of the soldiers glancing her way, possibly a new acquaintance. "Southern prisoners from the recent battle have been confined to the Old Capitol Prison on First Street. I've given them food, blankets, and clothes." Mrs. Greenhow's bitter tone surprised her.

"How kind of you. I had heard we took prisoners."

"Do you remember that I lived in that big brick house that's now the Old Capitol Prison in my girlhood? It's fallen into disrepair." She closed her fan with a snap of her wrist. "To think it is now a prison. Disgraceful."

"I wasn't aware Southern soldiers were being held in your old home."

"Thank you for not referring to them as the enemy, my dear." Mrs. Greenhow leaned forward. "I have difficulty thinking of our Southern neighbors as enemies, Annie, when they were so recently our friends."

"As I do." With a flounce of her skirt, Beatrice perched on a sofa to the widow's left. "I hate this fighting. Why can't we all just get along?"

Annie raised her eyebrows at her sister's vehemence.

"I wish that could be so." Mrs. Greenhow jerked her head in a nod so hard that her high-crowned bonnet shifted. "Alas, that is not our reality. Pardon me, ladies. The crowd has dwindled. I must speak with someone before I take my leave."

Her crinoline skirts rustled as she moved away.

"There's no help for it. We must mingle a few more minutes." Annie rose.

Beatrice sighed. "Yes. But John returned to the parlor. Go. Talk with him while he's alone."

"I will." Annie squeezed her hand. "Thank you for understanding."

A shadow crossed her face. "Someday I will feel the same way about a beau. Then, I really will understand."

~

*J*ohn had filled his stomach with ham sandwiches cut into small triangles, lemon cake, and a slice of apple pie while talking with fellow officers. No civilians were in the room, so they spoke freely.

"My regiment is ready to march out." Lieutenant Tom Waters speared a bite of lemon cake as he glanced at uniformed men encircled near the well-stocked table. "Our troops are ready."

"We're raring to head south ourselves." Captain Jerome Wustrack crossed his arms. "We figure we'll be sent to Tennessee but no orders yet."

"Same here." Helping himself to a cookie, First Sergeant Conner Sheets bounced on his toes.

"I expect your cavalry men will see lots of our countryside." John tugged on his ear. The others were still camped in the city, but he didn't divulge his location.

"Fine by me." Conner rubbed his hands together. "I've never been more ready."

"We may be sent to Virginia." Tom shrugged. "But no orders have been given. Who knows but that we'll be tasked with guarding the city?"

"It's an honor to guard the city, should that be your task." John placed his empty plate with the others and then stiffened. They weren't alone. Hiram Swanson lingered at the refreshment table within easy hearing distance. The enemy was always interested in troop movements, and John's host had heard their conjectures. A coincidence? It was getting harder to believe his host was completely innocent. John wasted no time steering the conversation by asking about folks back home.

Hiram carried a plate of apple pie to a nondescript fellow whom John didn't know. A civilian. An undersecretary for some official? The men sat in a corner and spoke in tones too low to carry more than a few feet. Were they sharing secrets?

Blast. Christopher had him questioning everything. Innocent parlor conversations had grown sinister.

Yet he could not discount the possibility, especially since his army's commander was suspicious of Hiram. Aye, and John's own suspicions were aroused. Time to discover if there were notes to prove or disprove Hiram's involvement in spying for the Confederates.

The last time he went searching for Hiram's study, the Swanson's attentive butler had stopped him with his hand on the open doorknob. Thinking quickly, John had asked for directions to the water closet. If caught again, that wouldn't work a second time.

He'd think of something else.

A furtive glance showed Hiram was comfortably seated in the corner with the undersecretary. Excusing himself to the officers now reminiscing of home, John strode from the parlor.

The back hall was empty. Good. Maybe John would get those few minutes alone in the study after all.

Wait. He needed light to read documents. He lifted the lantern hanging by the study door from its metal hook and peered in both directions.

No one.

Hardly daring to breathe, he turned the knob and pushed the door open.

In a flash, he was inside the dark room. Lifting the lantern, he hurried to the large table on the left. Under the soft glow, he scanned the few stacked pages. A list of names with dollar amounts. Customers? The banker was known to work from home. He returned the stack as he found it.

What else? John spotted a roll top desk with drawers to his right next to the curtained windows. As noiselessly as possible, he raised the rolling folds. Excellent. Those cubby holes contained letters and documents.

Starting from the top left corner, he scanned the first letter. It was from a bank customer withdrawing funds in preparation for a move to South Carolina. Was this important?

That letter was back in its place before he read a similar note. Hmm. Were the Swansons suffering financial difficulties due to folks leaving the bank?

Sweat broke out on John's forehead. This was personal information no one needed to know, right? It shamed him to be reading it while enjoying the privileges of a guest.

Keep reading, he could almost hear Christopher say. His own gut told him there was more to discover.

Footsteps in the hallway.

John extinguished the light. Then his eyes flew to the open roll top. It had been closed when he came in.

Footsteps ambled past the door toward the front of the home.

That was too close. He lowered the roll top as soundlessly as possible.

The clock chimed the half hour. John gave a start. Nine-thirty already?

Opening the door, he peered both ways. Movement by the kitchen. He closed the door and waited precious seconds while footsteps passed, then mounted the stairs.

Another look. No one. He'd best get out now. He replaced the now unlit lantern and made for the dwindling crowd in the parlor, where the sisters were in conversation.

Heat surged up his face as Annie's face lit up at the sight of him. If she knew where he'd just been... Long strides brought him to her side as Beatrice turned to the maid serving lemonade, coffee, and hot tea.

"John, I've longed to see you. Guests are leaving. Let's sit together." Annie nodded to three military men walking out of the parlor with her father. "I figured you were eating your fill of refreshments."

The happiness on her beautiful face robbed him of the power of speech for a moment. Or was it guilty shame that locked his tongue? He offered his arm. All too soon, the soft gloved fingers slid from his sleeve as they sat on a sofa near the front window.

"I hoped you'd arrive early enough to dine with my family."

"I regret my tardiness more than ever." The slight pout of her lips increased his longing to kiss her. Best turn his thoughts to something else. Like his spying duties. He'd discovered personal secrets, not the military ones Christopher expected. Granted, he hadn't completed his task. He sighed, for he'd have to search another day. "My time belongs to the army."

"For how long?" She inclined her head at neighbors exiting the parlor.

"I mustered in for three years."

She gasped. "Three...years?"

He raked a hand over his clean-shaven jaw. It seemed an eternity to him too. "No one expects this trouble to last that long."

"Your letter told us that your camp is in Virginia."

"Yes, John." Hiram strode over with Beatrice in the otherwise empty parlor. Even the maids were gone. "Where is your camp?"

"Just across the Potomac." He swallowed as Hiram scooted an armchair close and sat on it.

"Are you closer to Falls Church or Alexandria?" Hiram regarded him with clasped hands.

"That I cannot say, Mr. Swanson." His regiment's exact position was of interest to the Confederate army and might not be widely known yet. His earlier suspicions mounted. "I am not as familiar with Virginia as you are."

"You say you're right across the river?" He leaned forward.

John frowned. "We crossed it. It was a good long march." Was that too much information? Perhaps not. They could have gone in any direction after crossing. Vague replies mustn't give offense…a fine line.

"We missed you at supper." Hiram sat back, fingertips touching.

"Father, he was not dismissed until breaking for supper at the end of their day." Annie turned to John. "We'll plan on you next week and hope for the best." She forced a smile. "We didn't realize how fortunate we were when you were a mere mile away."

"'Tis grateful I am for the invitation." There wasn't anywhere else John preferred to be. "Yet I cannot say with certainty that I'll be here for Wednesday meals. We're quite occupied at camp."

"Oh?" Hiram tapped his fingertips together. "Is your regiment tasked with erecting a fortification then?"

Curiosity? Or something deeper? John felt a rush of adrenaline. "I cannot say, Mr. Swanson. The army has its secrets."

Beatrice sat in a chair beside her father. "Seems to be a lot of those around here."

John raised his eyebrows at her bitter tone. Did she allude to her brother's service to the Confederate army? "It appears so." He longed for Annie to tell him about Will…even as he prayed this family never discovered his own secret. War had the power to divide family and friends—and might erect an insurmountable wall between him and Annie if he let down his guard.

"Will you attend church with us Sunday?" Annie peered at him anxiously. "Of course, you're welcome to dine with us. Spend as much of your day here as possible."

"I plan to see you all at church." It was a long ride. Meeting at church gave him a little breathing room if he got a late start. "Perhaps we can go for an afternoon drive before I must leave."

"Of course." She lifted her chin. "We must bow to your military duties. Lieutenant Waters mentioned that our bridges into Virginia are heavily guarded. Is that your task?"

He pinched his lower lip. Did that worry her? Perhaps it was acceptable to ease that apprehension. "Nay. That task is not mine." He glanced at the mantle clock. Nearly ten-thirty. All other guests were gone. How had he so forgotten himself? "Thank you for your gracious hospitality this fine evening."

Beatrice and Hiram said their good-byes. Annie took John's arm and walked with him to the front door, where Mr. Grant awaited with his bowler hat.

"Hurry back," she whispered, "and Godspeed."

He raised her gloved hand to his lips. "Take care, my precious Annie. I will return."

CHAPTER 18

a man stepped out from the woods near Annie's home as John approached. "Christopher?"

"Late night."

John sighed. "Not over yet." He dismounted. "Can we walk as we talk?"

"Certainly." Christopher fell into a brisk walk beside him. "Which way will you go?"

"I'll cross on the Long Bridge." John peered into the woods that lined the avenue. "Our pickets are long gone from these woods."

"What did you discover?"

"I was late arriving and missed supper." He had news tonight. "I greeted Annie, who was talking to a lieutenant, who offered to drive her around the city to see the forts so she might rest easier."

"Name?"

"Lieutenant Thomas Waters. I think he meant merely to comfort her."

"Understandable. But unwise. Citizens who are out and about the city certainly see trees toppling and the forts going up. It's impossible to hide them. If Lieutenant Waters neglects to share military details, little harm will be done. We're concerned about information reaching the enemy through Confederate sympathizers." A heavy frown marked Christopher's brow in the dim light. "Or spies."

"Information can be used against us. I'd appreciate knowing similar facts about what's going on near Richmond and other Southern cities."

"Exactly."

"There's news about Hiram Swanson. Want to hear it?" They left the awning of trees behind them. The moon and stars lit their path. He regretted his duty to share his suspicions.

"If you'd be so kind." Christopher grinned.

John chuckled. Sometimes it seemed he and Christopher were friends. Nay. Friends didn't ask friends to betray loved ones. "Hunger led me upstairs for refreshments with a few other officers. There were no civilians in the room at first, so they all conjectured where they might next be sent. I noticed Hiram lingering at the table. He was certainly listening."

Christopher eyed him. "Go on."

"I changed the topic and he moved away. He sat in the corner talking with an undersecretary. Low tones. I couldn't hear the conversation." John stared at the dirt road as he walked. He gave the man's name with a deep sigh.

"Are your suspicions finally aroused?"

"Aye." The agreement was torn from him. "While he was with the undersecretary, I went to his study."

Christopher's back straightened. "What did you find?"

"A list of names with dollar amounts on a table. I figured those were bank customers."

"Possible. Since they weren't hidden. But there may be other meanings. What else?"

"There's a roll top desk. I was only able to read two letters before footsteps in the hall convinced me I pushed my luck to remain."

"Don't leave me in suspense."

"Sorry." Heat surged up John's face. It shamed him to pass on what might be construed as gossip. "Those two letters were bank business. Two different customers wrote that they were withdrawing their money to move—one to South Carolina, the other to Virginia."

"Nothing else?"

"There was no time." A weight as heavy as a gold bar settled on John's chest. "I'll have to go back."

"Yes." Christopher pounded his fist in an open palm. "You may have been one letter away from finding incriminating evidence."

"Aye."

"Anything else?"

"Hiram wanted to know where I'm camped." A long day of hot work followed by an evening of conversation, no matter how pleasant, had tired him. He was ready for his tent. "He asked if my regiment is building a fort. Annie and Beatrice were there."

"What did you tell him?"

"That the army had its secrets. When he asked where our camp was, I pleaded ignorance of Virginia geography."

"Very good." Their footsteps and the horse's clopping steps were the only noises besides a hoot owl. "Which neighbors attended?"

"There were several. Mr. Walter Johnson and Mrs. Clara Johnson. A widow…I believe her name is Mrs. Rose Greenhow. The Abbotts, a couple with two unmarried daughters. There may have been others."

"Whom did they speak with?"

"Officers. Undersecretaries. Government officials." John

quirked an eyebrow. "As normal. The family friends help the Swansons entertain."

"Pay more attention to citizens next time. And get back inside Hiram's study. Read everything, even if it seems unimportant to you. Cyphers aren't the only codes being used by spies." He clapped John on the back. "Good work. Your courtship of Annie gives us an inside view we lacked."

Shame made it difficult to breathe. How it went against his heart to provide the information requested by his country. He hated it.

He mounted his horse.

"If you see Annie on Sunday, stop by my boarding house after you leave."

He nodded and trotted away, hating himself.

He feared Annie would hate him too—if she discovered his deceit.

~

*A*nnie was glad that John had rallied himself to take her and Beatrice for a drive, though he was moving slower than normal on Sunday. Her father had left them directly after lunch in the chaise buggy, leaving Jacob free to take the reins of the landau. Annie and Beatrice took turns telling John the history of city buildings while the August sun took its toll on all of them.

When John rode away late that afternoon, Annie noticed the tired slump of his shoulders.

What was he doing back at camp to so exhaust him? Was he building one of the fortifications that her father had hinted at during lunch? It didn't surprise her that John didn't confirm their suspicions. Her hero was well-suited to keep military secrets.

Her father's distraction over the next ten days concerned

her. Often, he arrived home at dusk to continue working in the library. Unannounced guests were escorted back to him, and Annie and Beatrice sometimes retired before these strangers left.

Mrs. Greenhow arrived at their soiree on the second Wednesday in August before John. Annie took advantage of a smaller crowd to sit with her. "Mrs. Greenhow, I worry about Father."

"Oh?" The widow scanned the room. "In what way?"

"He leaves before I come down for breakfast in the morning, often eats his supper out, and then continues working late into the night."

"It's the war, my dear." Mrs. Greenhow sighed. "Difficult days for everyone, that's for certain. I can't blame citizens for desiring to vacate the city's turmoil."

"Never say that you are leaving us too?" The widow was a link to her mother Annie didn't want to lose.

"Washington City is my home." She patted Annie's hand. "I'll stay no matter how difficult it becomes."

"What do you mean?" Annie's brow puckered. "Are you having difficulties?"

Small lines marred her forehead as she stared at her folded hands. "Let me simply say that all is not as it seems."

Annie stared at her. "I don't understand."

"I know, my dear. I pray you never do." She rose. "I believe your young man has arrived."

Annie's gaze flew to the parlor door, where John waited. She stood.

"My courting days weren't so long ago that I don't understand your longing to see him. I believe your mother would approve." Mrs. Greenhow patted her arm. "There are others with whom I need to speak, but I cannot tarry this evening. I'll bid you good-night."

"Thank you for a lovely conversation, Mrs. Greenhow." She

glanced at John, who waited patiently a few feet away. "And thank you for coming."

"My pleasure, my dear." She embraced Annie and then strolled across the room and sat on a sofa beside a government official.

"John, how lovely that you're here. How long have you been waiting for me?"

"An eternity." Grinning, he clasped her outstretched hand. "Nay, not long. Five minutes perhaps. I didn't want to involve myself in another conversation before greeting you. Was that Mrs. Greenhow?"

"Yes." She tilted her head as she recognized the woman's laughter in the background. "She was a friend of my mother's and seems to know everyone. My father often invites neighbors and bank customers to our parties. She comes whenever free to do so. I wonder if she has an account with my father's bank. I don't think so. There has been so much upheaval this year that I scarcely know his customers any more—unless they come to our house to meet with him."

His expression grew serious. "Do his customers often do that? Meet him privately here, I mean?"

"Some have of late." She took his arm. "I'm certain you need refreshments after your long ride. Lemonade?"

~

*J*ohn dismounted when he reached the familiar tree in the darkness.

Christopher emerged, smoking a cigar. "You're early. Not quite ten o'clock."

"You'll not hear me complain. The guests were not so numerous as other evenings."

"Learn anything?"

"This will be quick. I didn't speak to Hiram until just before leaving. Then he merely invited me to church on Sunday."

Christopher blew a ring of smoke toward John. "What else?"

"Annie was in conversation with Mrs. Greenhow when I arrived so I waited for her. Annie feels close to her mother's old friend."

"Learn anything about the widow?"

"Aye, though I'm not certain it means anything. Mrs. Greenhow may have had money deposited at Hiram's bank in the past, but, even if that's true, it's doubtful she's a customer there now. Annie says this year has been such an upheaval that she doesn't know his customers. He works long days, and customers sometimes meet him at home."

"Did he talk with Mrs. Greenhow?"

"For a bit. He walked out with her, presumably to say goodnight. A lengthy parting for it took ten minutes."

Christopher rubbed his chin. "Did you search Hiram's study?"

"Nay." He shook his head regretfully. "The butler lingered in the hall when I arrived and was there each time I left the parlor."

"Hmm. Did you leave something out of place last time?"

"I don't think so." John had wondered the same thing and dismissed it. "I believe the butler is simply remarkably loyal to the family. I wasn't able to search it last week either. Methinks Sunday afternoons may afford more opportunities. Mr. Swanson often has errands after lunch."

"Agreed. Try that. Your country appreciates your service." Christopher ground his cigar under his heel. "I will see you Sunday afternoon."

"I'd prefer to only come on Sundays." He caught Christopher's sleeve as he turned away. "Wednesdays are very long days." Annie was often too busy with other guests to spend more than a quarter hour with him. He had arrived late tonight and didn't observe any suspicious behavior on Hiram's part.

"Our whole regiment is working hard and I don't learn enough to make it worth the effort."

"Allow the general to make that decision." Christopher eyed him. "For now, maintain the same schedule."

He strode away.

John's shoulders slumped with exhaustion. He mounted his horse and rubbed his neck. "Sorry about the long ride, old girl. I know we'd both rather be sleeping by now. At least the guards at the checkpoints know me and it doesn't take long to show my pass anymore. But it's worth the trouble to see Annie."

They set off. The horse's clopping hooves echoed in the silent avenue.

hough John had cantered on the dirt roads in Virginia under a cloudy sky, it was still half past seven when he rode up the beautiful drive to Annie's home a week later. Curious. There weren't any carriages dropping off guests at the front steps. He urged his horse forward, where Tom Parker awaited him at the stable door.

"Good evening, Tom." John dismounted and gave him the reins. "Did I mistake the day? It appears I'm the first to arrive at the soiree."

"Evenin', Sergeant-Major."

No matter how many times John had invited Rebecca's husband to address him by his given name, Tom always referred to him by his rank. "May I wash and change before going inside as usual?"

"Room's empty and waiting for you." Tom led the sweat-soaked horse into the stable, and John stayed at his side. "No one else is coming. Mr. Swanson cancelled the party."

"Cancelled? Can't say I'm sorry. Too tired to talk with strangers all evening." John paused in easing his knapsack from the saddle. "Am I welcome, then?"

Tom rubbed the mare's mane. "From what I understand, Miss Annie does everything possible to make a certain officer from Boston encounter a welcome."

"She's everything that is kind and sweet."

"With her mother's strength. That be a powerful combination." Tom tossed the saddle on top of a stall wall.

John shifted his knapsack containing his clothing…and his latest worrisome letter from his mother…over his shoulder. "I'd best hurry and get inside."

~

*A*nnie knew the moment John rode up the drive toward the stable. He was too late for the supper she'd shared with Beatrice, but he was certain to be hungry. Rebecca had asked to be told the minute he arrived.

Annie hurried down the long hallway to the right of the stairs to the kitchen. "Rebecca, John is back with Tom at the stables."

"Well, then," Rebecca wiped wet hands on her green apron, "I reckon we have a few minutes to prepare a plate for him."

"It's a two-minute walk from the stable." Her brow puckered.

"I'll tell you a secret"—Rebecca peered out the window—"but don't let on to John."

"I won't." Annie stepped closer.

"Your young man has such a long ride to get here that he brings a change of clothes with him." She sliced a generous portion of roasted beef. "He doesn't want to come courting while smelling of the stable."

Annie flushed. She had wondered how he managed that feat. Rebecca was right. They had a few minutes.

"I believe that young man cares for you"—she gave her a measured look—"the way you want your husband to feel for you."

"Oh, Rebecca. I dearly pray you are right." Joy coursed through her heart. How wonderful it was to confide in the wise woman. "He said some things this summer that give me cause to dream. Yet he stops short of proposing."

"Humph." A large serving of stuffed cabbage nestled beside slices of beef. "Must have something weighing on his mind. You said he has responsibilities with his family?"

"True." Her spirits, already low from a burden she intended to share with John this evening, plummeted further. "His ambitions do not lie with running his family's business. Nor does he desire an army career after the war's end."

"Oh?" She prepared a dish of pickled beets. "What does he want instead?"

"You'll never believe it, Rebecca." Annie clasped her hands together and told her of his dreams of working for the railroad. "Just think of it. What a thrilling adventure such a life will be."

A throat cleared.

Annie looked at the open doorway at her butler.

"Pardon the intrusion, Miss Annie." Mr. Grant lowered his gaze. "I knocked but should have waited until you answered."

Had he heard her gush about John's dreams? She gave a slight shake of her head. It scarcely mattered. The whole household would learn of his plans when John proposed. "It's no intrusion, Mr. Grant. What is it?"

"Sergeant-Major John Finn has arrived, miss. He awaits you in the parlor with Miss Beatrice."

"Thank you." This evening there were no other guests to steal her attention from him.

"You can take him to the family dining room whenever you've a mind to." Rebecca patted her shoulder. "Donna and Barbara have readied it for you."

Annie thanked her and turned away. The joy of seeing him was marred by the turmoil faced by a friend.

~

*J*ohn hadn't expected to dine in the company of both sisters, making the delicious meal all the more welcome. "Thank you both for that wonderful supper. And please thank Rebecca. 'Tis a pleasure to eat her meals." He folded his napkin while wondering at tense undercurrents. "'Tis a shame your father dines from home this evening."

A maid came in quietly and took his empty plate.

"Yes." Annie sighed. "Yesterday, Father cancelled our soiree. Then he sent word this afternoon not to expect him all evening."

"Is everything all right?" Something to do with Will? John hadn't heard any news concerning Will's regiment but that didn't mean he hadn't been wounded in battle.

"No." She glanced at Beatrice.

"Can you be trusted, John?"

He stiffened at Beatrice's question. Did she know about his betrayal of their family to Christopher? Nay, he didn't believe so. There was no accusation in the eyes of either sister. Yet he was in a predicament. What if they told him something that he'd be duty-bound to tell Christopher?

"Look there, Beatrice." Annie gave her sister a look of reproach. "You've hurt his feelings. You know we can trust John. He'd never betray us."

His stomach lurched.

"Let's talk in the garden. I feel the need for fresh air." Annie tilted her head.

"Of course." He forced the words out. "I have a wee bit of news of my own."

"You'll not require a chaperone while sitting in plain view of the avenue." Beatrice stood. "I will excuse myself to reply to our cousin's letter."

"Yes, thank you, Beatrice." Annie rose and walked with John to the door. "Please give my love to Meg," she said over her shoulder. "I'll write soon."

"I'll tell her." Beatrice ascended the stairs as they strolled into the warm evening toward the side of the house.

John steeled himself for bad news about Will, forcing himself to wait until Annie settled on a white cast iron garden bench decorated with an intricate floral and vine design and then sat beside her. "Please tell me what's troubling you."

She took a deep breath. "You remember Mrs. Greenhow?"

"Is she not well?" He suppressed a sigh of relief that the bad news didn't concern Will.

"As well as can be expected." Annie leaned closer. "She fears she's being watched."

"Watched." The widow was suspected of spying? His heart thundered. "By whom?"

"I don't know. I haven't seen her since last week's soiree." Annie frowned in the waning light. "Father talked with her then, but she advised him to keep his distance."

"Why?" John was beginning to feel Christopher's influence... asking questions so as not to take important information for granted.

"If someone accuses her of something unseemly—like spying on the Federal government or the army and passing along secrets to the Confederates—then she doesn't want Father to be implicated." Her voice dropped to a whisper. "Or us."

"You and Beatrice?" His eyebrows shot up.

"Yes." She raised miserable eyes. "We're friends of the family, after all."

A setback, indeed. This was worse than he imagined. If the widow had been spying—and he couldn't discount the possibility—her associates would be scrutinized. Had John fueled the flames that might consume Mrs. Greenhow by mentioning her conversations with Hiram?

"Father says not to worry. Go about our days as normal. In fact, we rejoined our sewing group this week."

"He no longer worries about an imminent attack on Washington City?"

"No." Her face took on a pinched look. "Not imminent anyway. The rumors lost their fever pitch."

"That I didn't know. I'm only in your fair city to see you." He strove to speak gallantly but feared it fell flat. Then he flushed. That wasn't quite true, with his spying on Hiram. Yet he could hardly say that aloud.

"It means so much that you're here." She laid a soft hand on his. "Forgive me for monopolizing our evening with my concerns. Please, tell me your news."

"'Tis glad I am you shared your worry with me. As for me... I've had a letter from my mam." Unable to keep still, he stood and paced.

"I trust everyone is well."

"She worries for my da."

"He's ill?" Annie's hand clutched her throat.

"Not to my knowledge." His pace increased. "But she wrote that he is overly tired and pale. Weak. Things she noticed before his last attack."

"Has the doctor seen him?"

"Nay. He refuses to send for him." Sitting beside her, John shook his head. "My da is a stubborn man."

"What can be done?"

"She asks that I quit the army and return home. Accept the reins for the family business." John rubbed his jaw. "She doesn't understand my military duties. 'Tis not so easy as she imagines."

"What about your brother. He didn't muster into service, did he?"

"Carl is still in New York City searching for a new store location." He ground his teeth. Mam wouldn't be in such a frenzy if Carl would act like the man he'd been raised to become. "For six months now. Nay, nearly seven. Methinks he is having a good time on my da's money."

Someone rounded the corner of the home with a lantern, illuminating the darkness that had fallen on them unaware. Annie withdrew her hand from his.

"Rebecca suggested I join you." Beatrice placed the lantern on a round white table and sat on a cast iron chair that matched it. "The sun has set. We feared you were so deep in conversation that you didn't notice."

"'Tis growing late." John regretted their time together ended. It was too precious in these anxious days. Yet protecting Annie's reputation was important. "Rebecca was right to send you."

"John was just telling me that his mother has concerns for her husband's health."

"I regret to hear this sad news, John." Beatrice folded her hands.

An owl hooted from a nearby oak tree.

John must leave. Annie's pinched face kept him rooted to the bench.

"I will pray for him." Beatrice spoke quietly.

"As will I." Annie squeezed his hand and released it quickly.

"And I will pray for your dear friend."

Beatrice darted a glance at Annie.

"John knows her." Annie shifted to face her sister. "He understands our family's close connection."

"Aye. I do, indeed." John was duty-bound to speak of the matter to Christopher. *Please, Annie, don't tell me anything else in confidence that's connected with the war or spying.*

"Remember to tell no one else." Beatrice's face hardened. She gave him scarcely a glance as she stood.

"It's late, John." Annie gave him her hand. "I will look for you at church on Sunday."

CHAPTER 20

*A*nnie was still upset over Beatrice's harsh tone with John when they returned from the Jacksons' home on Friday afternoon. They had switched from making bandages back to shirts. Annie's fingers were sore from sewing, and she was thankful to reach the solace of home.

"Good afternoon, Miss Annie. Miss Beatrice." Mr. Grant shut the door behind them and pointed to the long table, where a sealed envelope rested on a silver plate. "Jacob delivered a message from your father."

A rare occurrence, indeed. Father often sent verbal messages through his driver, but never had he sent a written note.

"Thank you, Mr. Grant." Annie met Beatrice's wary glance and then picked up the letter. "We will read it in the parlor."

"Very good." Inclining his head, he opened the door for them.

"I have a bad feeling about this." Beatrice sat beside Annie on one of the sofas as the butler closed the door.

"Will?"

"That was my first thought." Beatrice stared at the parchment as if it were a serpent ready to strike.

Annie broke the seal with shaky fingers. Beatrice leaned closer and read silently with her.

My Dear Daughters,

I write in haste. The despicable thing we feared for Mrs. Rose Greenhow has happened. She has been arrested on suspicion of spying. She and her daughter are held at their home on West Sixteenth Street. Her house is being searched—for what, I do not know. What can the authorities expect to find in a respectable widow's home? It's a disgrace to our government and to our city. Those involved should be called to account for their actions.

Do not speak of her arrest to anyone until it is common knowledge. I know I may trust your discretion. We must not drag a good woman's name through the mud by participating in gossip. Often one bad thing follows another in matters such as these. Other arrests may be forthcoming and will almost assuredly be mistakes that cost good people their reputations. Since Mrs. Greenhow has visited our home in recent days, suspicion may fall on us. It's best that you keep close to home until we talk. Do not wait supper.

Burn this note once you both read it.

Your loving Father

Beatrice crumpled the note. "This is intolerable."

"Little Rose is only eight." Just the thought of dragging an innocent child into the unwarranted arrest ignited her anger. To say nothing of Mrs. Greenhow's innocence. "Mrs. Greenhow... arrested. For *spying*. Outrageous."

"Agreed." Beatrice smoothed the page and then scanned the letter again. "A new secret to keep."

"What about Rebecca? I tell her nearly everything." Annie wrung her hands. "Jacob knows about the note. And Mr. Grant. What can we say to satisfy their curiosity?"

"Nothing." Beatrice shook her head. "At least not until Father comes home this evening."

"I wish John were here." Annie looked at the parlor door, willing him to enter.

"I'm glad he isn't." Beatrice stiffened. "You've already said too much."

"How was I to know Mrs. Greenhow would actually be arrested?"

"You couldn't." She sighed.

"I hate all this secrecy." Annie's heart broke for the mother and daughter.

"There's no help for it."

"Father instructed us to burn this letter." Why was it so important it be destroyed? She looked at the cold stove in the corner. "Let's build a small fire."

"I'll light the kindling." Beatrice crossed the room.

Annie scanned the note once more as she trailed her. Her nails sunk into her palms. Even if Mrs. Greenhow were guilty—a possibility she refused to consider—her poor daughter was innocent. The nerve of some people.

After Bea had lit the kindling, Annie dropped the letter into the flames.

~

*L*ate Saturday afternoon, John took a long draw from his canteen then upended it over his head. Building a fort was difficult, even with many diligent men. They'd cleared trees from the hillside to prepare space for a magazine. Then the digging of the breastworks began. The fort that was planned for five guns was speedily taking shape, and they'd only been working about a month.

One more week of a sweltering August. He swiped his brow. Milder autumn temperatures would bring welcome relief—especially since he no longer slept in a leaky tent.

They'd begun to build quarters. He and Patrick shared the

small wooden building with two other officers. John worked by candlelight until *Taps* played every night, trying to catch up on notes pushed aside for building the fort. Still, he wouldn't trade this opportunity to participate in something so significant. He figured that folks a hundred years from now would remember the fortifications around Washington City.

Just like the railroad that would someday reach from the Atlantic to the Pacific. He yearned to be part of that history, life-changing as it promised to be for so many citizens longing to head west. What was now a trip of months by wagon train and weeks by stagecoach would be manageable in a matter of days. His blood pumped to consider it.

The bugle blew. Thank heavens. Men put down their axes and shovels to break for supper.

"Fort's taking shape." Patrick sauntered over.

"That it is."

Soldiers rubbed their lower backs and their necks. They flexed their fingers.

"We're all growing stronger, but still get sore after digging all day."

Patrick grunted.

Even he was, and he hadn't done any heavy digging. John folded his arms across his chest and waited while the equipment was stored.

"You going to Annie's tomorrow?"

"Aye." His stomach rumbled again. How he'd savored the meal at her home three days before—baked fish—but seeing Annie was the most precious gift of all.

"Everything going all right for them?"

John turned a piercing look on him, wondering if he heard gossip concerning Mrs. Greenhow. Patrick had likely met the widow at the Swanson mansion. "Why do you ask?" After a few days' reflection, it seemed plausible that the widow was a Confederate spy. John had witnessed private whispered conversations with officers, undersecretaries, and Hiram—who was mighty curious. Christopher hadn't been waiting the other night. A bit of Irish luck, that, for it gave him time to ponder what he'd learned. But John would tell him at their next meeting.

"Just missing their soirees, I suppose."

"Talking with people I don't know at a party isn't my idea of a fun evening—not when I must start a similar conversation with another stranger a quarter hour later. Then you do it all again the next week." John yawned. "Annie's the reason I go." And his spying on Hiram.

"She's a peach of a gal. You're a lucky man." Patrick surveyed the green valley below the hill where they camped. "Virginia is a pretty place. Got an itching to explore it. Too bad it's dangerous to venture far from camp."

"When it's quiet—no bands, drills, sawing, or digging—I imagine this conflict is all a bad dream." John studied the line of trees beyond the small valley. Pickets remained vigilant, reminding him that enemy soldiers were near. "Then the bugler blasts another order, and I know I'm wide awake after all."

They were silent as the men headed to their quarters.

"You haven't been yourself since you got a letter from home." Patrick's expression softened as he stared at the valley. "Everything all right?"

"You know about Mam's letter. A letter from my sister, Patricia, voiced the same worries." According to his sister, their parents had written Carl at the beginning of August with a request to return home immediately. No response. Patricia's concern was that he had fallen in with a disreputable crowd who tempted him to greater misdeeds. "Not only are they worried for his health, me brother is causing a bit of a dust."

"Let's talk over supper. I'm starving." Patrick turned toward their camp.

"Be there in a minute."

Patrick's footsteps, muffled by the grass, faded.

Glad for the solitude, John rotated his shoulders as if to shed the bonds placed there by his family. His dream of marrying Annie and heading West to work on the railroad seemed farther out of reach than ever.

Nay. He'd fight for their future—his and Annie's together. There must be another answer besides the one pressed on him by his parents.

For now, there was a fortification to be built. For now, Annie's family might be under stricter scrutiny because of Mrs. Greenhow's troubles, and he must do everything within his power to protect them. For now, his family needed him...and he could not go to them.

~

"More bad news for our dear friend." Hiram Swanson strode into the parlor after supper on Saturday night, where Annie and Beatrice worked on gifts for Will's baby. Exhaustion lined his face.

"What is it, Father?" Bracing herself, Annie laid aside a tiny nightgown.

"Rose was wise to warn us away." He sank onto a nearby seat and rested his head against the cushioned high-backed armchair. "All visitors since her arrest have suffered her fate."

"No." Beatrice's knitting needles halted mid-stitch. "Every visitor has been arrested?"

"Unbelievable. But it seems to be true." He sighed. "Lillie Mackall and her sister are among those held at Rose's home."

"Preposterous." Beatrice's face set. "How long will this last?"

"No one knows."

Annie exchanged a look with Beatrice. "Do you believe they will find anything incriminating?"

"I know not what those detectives will deem to be evidence.

In these troubled days, an innocent correspondence from a friend may be suspect." He yawned. "Pardon my manners, daughters. I have not slept well of late."

"Are you hungry, Father?" Annie glanced at the mantle clock. Nearly ten. "I'm certain that Rebecca—"

"I ate at Willard Hotel."

"Is it safe to talk to neighbors and friends about this?" Mind racing, Annie perched on the edge of her seat.

"Many already know. There are rumors, as always." He studied her. "Folks will certainly expect you to know about it, especially since we are acquainted with the family."

Acquaintances? Annie's brow puckered. They were more than that. "Then we are free to speak of the incident."

"Certainly." He hesitated. "One word of caution—it's more prudent to listen than speak in such a case."

"You are saying not to fuel the flames of gossip surrounding her." Annie met Beatrice's watchful eyes.

"Precisely."

Wise council. Annie was almost as concerned about her father's exhaustion. "It grows late, and we have church tomorrow."

"You girls go on to bed." He gave a dismissive wave. "It's been a long week."

CHAPTER 21

"*J*ohn, you've spent much time here this summer. I'm curious about your tasks." Mr. Swanson forked a bite of cherry pie Sunday at lunch. "One hears so much about forts going up around the city. Is that happening near your camp?"

This again? John couldn't say that his would be a lunette, a temporary fort in the shape of a half-moon, with two sides and a stockade gorge when completed. Or that his regiment sheltered behind the lunette. He drew a deep breath. "I'm certain you can appreciate my reticence to speak on the subject." They'd already spoken of the war, the women's sewing group, and troops leaving city camps.

"I'm not asking you to divulge military secrets, my boy." He sipped his coffee. "Yet you are courting my daughter. Can you tell me anything to satisfy my curiosity?"

"Far more interesting is how I came by my horse." He grinned.

"Pray tell us, John." At his side, Annie sipped her lemonade.

"As you know, I am camped too great a distance from your home to walk here. That necessitated buying a horse. That plan did not prosper." He settled into his story about the feisty young fella. "When I told him I'd need a horse on Sunday, Zach demanded an extra dollar a month because his mother likes to take drives after dinner."

Annie giggled. "Did you give it to him?"

"I agreed to his demands until he implied he'd charge me extra for a saddle."

"I like the sound of that boy." Mr. Swanson chuckled. "Tell him to see me for a job when he's older. What did you say his name was?"

"Zachary Beets."

"I'll remember that."

Then John realized his mistake. If Mr. Swanson wanted to discover their location, he could inquire about the whereabouts of the Beets family. John's face burned. Such an innocent mistake. On second thought, Mr. Swanson merely joked about hiring a ten-year-old.

"I'll be out all afternoon." The older man laid his folded napkin to the side of his plate. "I will bid you farewell."

"Thank you for your hospitality, sir." John rose from the family's dining table, uncertain if he was dismissed. None of the Swansons had mentioned Mrs. Greenhow's arrest all day. Yet murmurings in hushed tones from the pew behind theirs had alerted him. He'd anticipated the topic during their meal.

"Are you working today, Father?" Beatrice stood when Annie did.

"No, friends have asked me to call." He kissed his daughters' cheeks. "If I am not back by six, do not wait supper." He shook John's hand and then strode from the room.

"Do you wish me to stay?" John looked at Annie.

"Please do. Father didn't mean for you to go."

"In that case, how about a ride?"

"Sounds lovely." Annie raised an eyebrow at Bea.

"Of course. But I want to change into a cooler gown."

"Great idea. I'll do that too. Please give us a few minutes."

"Aye, and take as long as you like." This was his opportunity to search Hiram's study. He tapped his foot by the front window until a chaise carried the banker toward the city.

He stepped in the hall. Mr. Grant wasn't around. First obstacle eliminated. As soundlessly as his boots allowed, he hurried into the study and closed the door. Enough sunlight streamed behind the closed curtains to light the room.

The table was clear today. He opened the roll top desk and began reading. The top row of cubby holes seemed to be bank-related business. Same with the second. And the third.

No cyphers. No cryptic notes.

Maybe the drawers. There was a bundle of old letters tied with a red ribbon in the top one from Charlotte Clements. The maiden name of Hiram's wife. Touching that he kept the stack close.

Time was passing. John replaced the letters to rifle through the next drawer, which was filled with correspondence. One more minute and he'd have to leave. Nothing war-related here. Was there a cyphered message...anything to help Christopher—

He dropped the pile. Help convict Hiram. That's what he was trying to do.

Right before he escorted his daughters for the afternoon.

What kind of scoundrel did such a thing?

He straightened the letters and closed the drawer. Running feet down the hall had him scrambling to shut the desk. The cook's children? They ran past the study.

Swiping his wet brow, he opened the door. He was almost to the parlor when Mr. Grant descended the stairs.

"The young ladies sent me with their apologies. They'll be right down." The butler studied him. "Miss Annie asked me to inquire if you'd like a glass of lemonade while you wait."

"Aye. Thanks." Boy, that was close.

He couldn't relax, even as he downed the lemony beverage

when it came in one long draw. Nothing seemed out of place in the study. It bothered him a little, for his own bookkeeping efforts got messy at times. Wasn't everyone like that?

One squeaky step alerted him that the ladies were ready. He schooled his expression, hoping he didn't appear as guilty as his heart told him he was.

John soon sat in the open vehicle beside Annie, looking as beautiful as a daisy in a yellow dress and matching parasol. Beatrice sat opposite them wearing blue. "'Tis a lucky man I am to escort two beautiful ladies. Where shall we go?"

"I want to see the forts." Beatrice fanned her face beneath the shade provided by her white parasol. "Can you, as an officer, explain what we're looking at in each?"

"Your family has a fascination with forts." He grinned to remove any sting from the words. "Some are in plain view of citizens, that's certain. Fort Runyon and Fort Albany guard the Long Bridge. There are forts that guard the Aqueduct, as you probably know. Unfortunately, I know little about the locations of our fortifications." That was true on this side of the Potomac River, anyway.

"Let's drive toward Georgetown." At a nod from her companions, Annie leaned forward. "Jacob, take us along Rockville Pike."

"Yes, Miss Annie."

"Oh, lest I forget," she added, "you're welcome to dine with us Wednesday, but Father has cancelled the soiree again. He's too busy these days."

His exhausted body thanked her. It took better than two hours to ride here if he included the walk to pick up his mount. "As appealing as that is, we're so busy at camp that I can't leave again on a weeknight." John didn't want to explain how he dashed away when the bugler dismissed the troops to supper or the ribbing he gladly took at his courtship of a beautiful woman that kept him from camp twice weekly.

Her lips turned down.

"Sundays are best, unless we have to march out." Like the soldiers had who formerly occupied the ravaged field they were passing. A cow lowed near the farmhouse on the opposite side of the road.

"Is that possible?" Her brown eyes widened.

"In war, anything is possible." As much as he hated worrying her, he had to be honest. Then he flushed. His honesty had conditions.

She gave him an apprehensive look.

"I don't believe it will be soon." Best change the topic. "You were worried about Mrs. Greenhow last Wednesday." Glad of the breeze stirred by the team's slow trot, John settled against the cushion. Buildings and a church spire up ahead told him they approached Georgetown. "I heard something at church this morning…"

"I'm certain you did." Annie's face darkened. "She's been arrested."

"Her home was searched." Beatrice's lips tightened.

"And her poor daughter is under house arrest with her," Annie added.

"Father heard that her visitors have also been arrested." Beatrice's shoulders stiffened. "Disgraceful. Why, if we had taken her a meal or visited to inquire how she fared, we would have been arrested also."

Chilling possibility. "Ladies, this is unfortunate. I never really thought…" He caught himself before mentioning his own surveillance at their soirees. That was close.

"How could you?" Annie snapped her fan open. "How could *any* intelligent person suspect Mrs. Greenhow of spying on our government, our military? She's been nothing but kindness itself to us since our mother died."

"No one spoke to me directly of her trouble at church this morning. I did hear mutterings behind us. I wanted to turn around and defend her good name." Beatrice gave a nod to ladies in a passing chaise. "I don't know if I can contain my tongue if anyone speaks disrespectfully of her to me."

"Agreed." Annie's cheeks turned crimson. "It drives a deeper wedge to divide us as a country, don't you agree, John?"

"Aye." His burning face could not be blamed on the sun. Nay, shame was the culprit.

Especially since he had to report to Christopher upon leaving them today.

$\sim$

*J*ohn arrived at Christopher's boarding house and pulled out his pocket watch. Half-past five. He sighed. It'd be late before he ate supper. If he found an opportunity to eat.

As he stepped inside, Christopher pounded down the steps. "Missed you Wednesday."

"Aye. There was no soiree. I ate a late supper when I arrived and talked with the family."

"Speaking of supper, I'm heading out now. Care to join me?"

"If it's quick."

"Not the Willard Hotel then." They stepped into the sunshine. "That your horse?" He pointed to the mare tied to the hitching post.

"For the next couple of months."

"Leave her there. There's a family restaurant two blocks from here. We'll walk."

He easily matched Christopher's long stride. "You asked—"

"Not here."

Groups were engaged in conversations on the sidewalks. Couples strolled by. Families out on Sunday drives crowded the streets. John flushed. Not the best place to give a private report.

Every window was open in the cozy restaurant, providing a

pleasant cross-breeze. Only a third of the dozen tables were occupied. Christopher chose a table near the back, away from flapping curtains at an open window, where he sat facing the door.

They both ordered fried chicken, the day's special. "Ordering the special ensures we'll be quickly served," Christopher said. "This is one of my favorite restaurants in Washington City. Good food fast."

"Perfect." John's stomach rumbled at delicious smells wafting from the kitchen. "I'd resigned myself to missing supper. I stayed too long at Annie's house. Or it's more correct to say that our drive lasted longer than I intended." But he'd not complain about an extra hour with Annie. Every minute with her grew more precious. Was the regiment slated to leave the vicinity when the fort was done? No one knew.

Or no one was saying.

A matronly woman brought them each a cup of coffee.

"Thank you, Mrs. Knowles."

She inclined her head and left.

"There was no soiree this week. Interesting. Any idea why?" Christopher settled back in his wooden chair.

"You remember Mrs. Greenhow? The widow?"

Christopher cocked his head.

"She's been arrested. You probably already know that." John's temples began to throb.

Christopher's eyes remained watchful.

"The family is close to her, as I've said. They've cancelled this week's party as well. Hiram works long days. He cannot entertain while he is so busy."

"Was Hiram with you today?"

"He attended church and ate lunch with the family." Mrs. Knowles placed two loaded plates in front of them. "Thank you, ma'am. That fried chicken looks as delicious as my mam's." One of the few meals she still prepared because it was his father's favorite. It had been months since John had eaten this meal. His mouth watered.

"Quite a compliment from a homesick soldier. Save room for peach pie." Smiling, she returned to the kitchen.

Was John homesick? Perhaps. Especially with the recent news from his family. He uttered a quick Irish blessing on their meal and then demolished a chicken leg in three bites. Tasty, though not as good as his mother's.

"What's the verdict?" Christopher ate just as hungrily.

"Delicious." John shoveled in several bites of mashed potatoes before attacking the next piece of chicken. He scanned the room. Two tables had emptied since their arrival.

"Hiram left after lunch?" Christopher prompted.

"Yes. It gave me an opportunity to search his study."

"And?"

"It was mostly bank correspondence similar to what I found last time. There was a stack of letters from his wife. Some were written during their courtship because they were from Charlotte Clements."

"By all accounts, they had a happy marriage."

"Aye." John grieved for Annie's loss too. "One thing I didn't find was a cypher."

Christopher looked over his shoulder. "Good thing you're speaking in low tones."

"No unusual message that made no sense. Nothing." He sighed. "I didn't have an opportunity to look at all the documents. Everything is so tidy."

"Too tidy?"

"Maybe."

"You said he left. Where did he go?"

"Didn't get specific." John took a long swallow of coffee. A sight more palatable than what he'd been drinking in camp. "Said he was seeing friends and expected to be late."

"Anything else about events that happened last week?"

John quirked an eyebrow. "You mean about Mrs. Rose Greenhow's arrest?"

"How do the Swansons feel about it?"

Christopher bit into a golden-brown biscuit.

"Upset. Angry, for they believe she's falsely accused." To think that the widow might have obtained information in Annie's parlor sickened him. "They've known her for years. She was friends with their mother."

"We suspected as much." His eyes gleamed. "Good work."

His appetite fled. "That does not mean the Swansons are guilty of anything, assuming Mrs. Greenhow hasn't been wrongly accused."

Christopher lowered his voice. "Detectives uncovered incriminating evidence at her residence. The woman *is* guilty of spying."

John's fork clattered against the plate. Difficult news for Annie. And it added credence to the suspicions of Hiram's activities. Not good.

"Do Hiram or his daughters inquire about your duties? Or want to know about fortifications? Ask you about troop movements?"

"Aye. Hiram has twice asked if I'm involved in building a fort. He's tried to discover my location. His excessive curiosity may be explained by his protective instincts. Perhaps he's merely a father who wants to know more about his daughter's beau."

"Do you really believe that in light of the widow's guilt?" Christopher eyed him.

"I'll warrant I have suspicions about Mr. Swanson." John shoved his half-filled plate to the side, too upset to focus on anything but the spying done by a widow right under his nose. Though she wasn't the one he was sent to monitor, he should have noticed the little clues now so clear to him. "Annie has a natural curiosity. She worries I'll be sent to battle. She asks because she wants me to stay in Washington City."

"Of course." Christopher's tone showed a tinge of doubt.

"Here now." The motherly woman was back. "I've brought you both a nice plate of peach pie. Eat up."

A generous portion, indeed. John had no heart for it. His stomach agreed.

CHAPTER 22

*A*nnie and Beatrice trudged home on Friday afternoon under overcast skies.

"Why doesn't it just storm already?" Annie glanced at the gray clouds. There was a feeling of foreboding in the air that had made her restless since last evening.

"The wind is whipping up." Beatrice held onto her hat while grasping her parasol. "You are in a mood today."

"I know. My apologies." The wind swept her small hoop skirt to one side like a bell. "I'm miffed at John for not coming to supper."

"Still?"

"Rebecca kept food warming for him until eight o'clock." Annie rolled her eyes heavenward. Didn't he want to see her as much as she longed to see him? The coming storm fit her mood exactly.

"Annie, he has a long ride both ways." Beatrice frowned at the sky. "He mentioned that his whole regiment is working hard. They're probably building a fort. Can't you understand?"

"I suspected it, but he didn't say so when Father pressed him." She wavered between betrayal that he hadn't told her and pride that he might be involved in such vital work. "Even if it's a secret, he should have told me. We must build trust between us."

"Obviously, I do not *know* it." A gust of wind blew blond ringlets across her cheek. "If he simply wrote army reports as he did while camped here, don't you think he'd tell you?"

Annie shook her head. "When did you get so wise?"

"You're the wise sister. I abhor secrecy. That's why I noticed."

"I also hate the secrecy...especially about Will. I want to tell John that Will fights for the South. If he has a proper amount of time to consider Will's views, I'm certain he'll put their differences aside for friendship's sake."

"No." Beatrice halted. Their mansion loomed a hundred yards ahead. "You can't. You promised Father."

Annie's cheeks burned. "Try concealing a confidence from the man you love about one of his dearest friends. A secret that will hurt him. Especially when that friend happens to be your brother. You can't hate that more than I do."

"No." Color drained from Bea's cheeks.

A raindrop splashed on Annie's face. "Hurry inside."

The rain picked up to a sprinkle. Laughing, they stepped inside and wiped moisture from their faces.

"I was about to send the carriage for you, Miss Annie. Miss Beatrice." Mr. Grant shut the door behind them. "Alas, I tarried too long. Forgive me."

"Not to worry." Annie laughed, exhilarated from their run. "See, we're barely wet."

"Very good." He inclined his head toward the hall table. "Your father sent another letter. For your eyes only."

Annie's restlessness descended full-force as she stared at the sealed envelope, so similar to the previous yet more sinister. This was what her restlessness, her premonition had been about. Not John or Mrs. Greenhow.

Her brother.

"Thank you," she whispered, darting a glance at Beatrice,

who stared at the letter with huge eyes. Annie reached for it with trembling fingers. "We'll read it in the parlor."

He nodded, concern in his gaze. Perhaps the butler who had long served the family felt the weight of the single page as she did.

The parlor door closed behind them before Annie grasped her sister's hand. "Bea, this one is about Will, I'm sure of it." She feared to read of his death.

"Yes."

"Let's discover the worst." Releasing her grip on Beatrice's icy fingers, Annie broke the wax seal and unfolded the page.

My Dear Daughters,

I wish I could give you this news while with you but, given the city's unfortunate fondness for gossip, the terrible news may reach you before I can.

Brace yourselves. Will's regiment has been guarding Hatteras Inlet along the North Carolina coast. They built two forts there, Fort Clark and Fort Hatteras, that were but lightly armed. Will was at Fort Clark when it was attacked by Union ships. I'm certain my brave son did all he could to protect himself and his comrades. They ran out of ammunition and abandoned the fort for the shelter of nearby Fort Hatteras. The next day, Union ships fired upon Fort Hatteras, which soon waved the white flag of surrender. I regret that virtually the entire regiment has been captured. Very few escaped. Your brother must be a prisoner of war for I cannot believe he's gone to Glory.

I know you are as devastated as I am. Please pray for him and for Frances. This news is doubly hard on her. You may tell our staff and seek their prayers on your brother's behalf. Normally, I would wait until the news spreads but names of local soldiers captured in the battle will no doubt be published in newspapers soon. It may not be long before neighbors come to offer comfort. I leave it to your discretion whether to receive them.

Ask Rebecca to prepare my supper, but I cannot say when I will see

*you. I am seeking further news of your brother's safety. It's my hope
and prayer that both forts surrendered without loss of life. I will try to
discover as many details as possible before coming home.*

My heart is with him and with you, my daughters.

Yours always,

Hiram Swanson

Will, a prisoner of war? Tears streamed down Annie's cheeks as she blindly reached for Bea's hand.

"How can it be?" Beatrice whispered, her eyes awash with her own tears. Her fingers clutched Annie's as if she swam in deep waters and groped for a rope to pull her to safety.

"Of all the things I feared to read." The words blurred. "This isn't... It can't be true."

"Father would not write of it if there was any doubt." Beatrice's voice broke.

"No." Annie released her sister's hand and covered her face in the horror of it. Will. Captured. In her wildest nightmares, she'd never imagined such a thing.

At least he was alive. In her spirit, Annie somehow knew it. Her senses reeled as she tried to cope with her brother's plight.

They were both silent.

"I'm certain his captors will treat him respectfully. He *is* a gentleman, after all." Annie swallowed past the lump lodged in her throat. She could scarcely bear the thought of anything less.

"I dare to hope so." Beatrice wrung her hands. "I have not heard reports to the contrary."

"Mrs. Greenhow told me Confederate soldiers captured after the Battle of Bull Run were treated shamefully." She met Beatrice's shocked stare and gathered her close for a long moment. "Perhaps she exaggerated the facts?"

"To what purpose? Why should she lie?"

Excellent observation. What was to be gained by lying? "I

don't feel like entertaining guests—not even those who long to comfort us."

"Unless Will's name has been announced as a prisoner, they will not know of his capture." Beatrice spoke bitterly. "This is one of the few occasions I'm thankful for our secrecy."

Small comfort, though, when his Southern loyalties would soon be known publicly. Her father was right. Newspapers were likely to list names of Southern prisoners with connections to Washington City. She crossed her arms in a vain attempt to shield herself and her family from pain. "John will know what to do. I must get a message to him."

"No." Beatrice's tone hardened. "Not yet. He won't know those forts' surrender affects Will. There's no rush."

"I need his strength and comfort. And Will is his dear friend." Annie swiped at her wet cheeks with a dainty pink handkerchief.

Beatrice blew her nose with a handkerchief from her pocket. "Neither of us will have the comfort of a beau in this trouble."

Surprised, Annie looked up. "I guess not." Did her sister miss one of her old beaus who now served the Union army? "Bea, is there someone special…"

"No."

Her tone was almost harsh. Annie decided to shift the conversation. "At least we can tell Rebecca and the staff. I think it best to simply read Father's letter to them."

"Which means they'll learn that Will fights for the Confederacy."

"It can't be hidden. It will be a relief to discuss it with others who love Will."

"Agreed." Beatrice waved her hand with a sigh. "We need the support of their prayers."

"The letter will explain the worst. I don't feel strong enough for questions." Annie forced herself to stand on shaky legs. She longed for John's reassuring presence, even if he didn't understand the battle she faced. "I'll ask Mr. Grant to assemble everyone in here." She opened the door, and there stood Rebecca.

The compassionate woman took one look at Annie's face and wrapped her arms around her. "Something inside told me it was bad."

"It's Will." Clinging to her, Annie sobbed on her shoulder. "He has been captured."

Mrs. Grant gasped from behind them and reached for her husband's hand. Donna and Barbara exchanged a look of horror where they waited in the hall with Rebecca's daughters.

"Then we'll pray for his release." Keeping an arm around Annie, Rebecca stretched her hand toward Beatrice.

They clung to one another, crying together.

CHAPTER 23

"Did you hear?" Patrick took a long drink from his canteen as they sat for an afternoon break from overseeing the building of sleeping quarters.

"Hear what?" John hadn't slept well for two days and was in no mood for riddles. He'd see Annie tomorrow, who made everything seem better—even worrisome letters from home. Another one from his mam had arrived two days before. His da had missed several days of work. Again, Mam asked John to come home.

"Good things are happening for us in North Carolina."

A sense of foreboding chilled the pit of John's stomach. Will lived and served in North Carolina. He reminded himself that Will's company could be anywhere.

"We captured two forts and nearly a whole regiment." A triumphant gleam lit Patrick's eyes. "Our ships bombarded Fort Clark and Fort Hatteras at Hatteras Inlet. Can you imagine it? Cannons bursting from the ship... I can almost smell the gunpowder. What I wouldn't give to have witnessed the battle."

John's inability to focus on Patrick's face must be from the blinding sun. Or the fear gripping his soul. "Tell me, man. Which regiment was captured?"

"North Carolina troops. I believe it was the Seventeenth Regiment."

No. Will's regiment.

Patrick frowned. "Why so glum? This is good news."

John fought a desire to punch the smirk from his face. "Were men killed?" Had Will been killed? Did Annie know?

"Maybe a few." Patrick eyed him. "I thought you'd be as thrilled as I am. This is war, remember?"

As if he could forget. He turned his head to mask his agony.

"After the beating we suffered at Bull Run, our army needs a victory."

"Aye." John forced his fingers to uncurl. Patrick didn't know Will fought for the Confederacy, much less the Seventeenth North Carolina. A sudden urge to comfort Annie made it difficult to breathe. "Do you think the captain will give me leave for a few hours? I need to go into Washington City."

"Doubtful." Patrick's face tightened. "Especially since you plan on going tomorrow. You have no idea how much of yer slack I take up when you're gone, and do I ever get yer thanks?"

John stared at him, dumbfounded. "'Tis sorry I am, Patrick," he stammered. "I never knew."

"That's right. Ye don't know. Do you believe you're the only man out here with burdens too weighty to bear?" Patrick crossed his arms. "I regret your worries for your family. I know they're valid. But consider the crosses someone else carries every now and then." He spun on his heels.

He watched Patrick stalk into the woods. What was that about?

John rubbed his stubbly chin. He'd talk to him later. For now, his highest consideration was Annie's difficulties. And Will's. He bowed his head to pray for his friend.

Had he been wounded? Killed? The possibility tore at his

heart. If he felt that way, how much worse for his sister? John must go to Annie.

According to Patrick, requesting another evening's leave from camp wouldn't go over well with the captain.

He had to try.

~

*A*nnie sent regrets that she and Beatrice were unable to attend a luncheon at the Jackson's and stayed at home all day Saturday, willing the day to pass. John was coming tomorrow. Though she wanted to sit on the garden bench in front of the avenue where they'd often talked, it was too public. Since she'd given instructions not to receive any visitors except John, she didn't risk her presence in the garden as an invitation for uninvited guests.

The staff understood her reasons, for she'd read her father's letter to them. Everyone now knew that Will fought for the Confederacy and had vowed to keep the secret—though how long they'd have to maintain secrecy was anyone's guess.

As the hours dragged toward evening, she wondered why she went to so much bother. No one had called to comfort them about Will's capture.

It seemed that Beatrice was right. No one knew trouble had befallen her family.

She clasped her hands together as she stared out the window. Annie was happy her mother had perished before suffering this all-consuming pain for her son.

"Supper will be ready soon." Beatrice wandered into the parlor and joined Annie at the window. "Any sign of Father?"

"No." Nor of John, her heart whispered. "Since yesterday's search for information bore little fruit, he's out again today. I've hardly ceased praying all day that he'll discover Will's location. I'm certain he plans to go to him, no matter where that may be."

"He's speaking to friends in government today." Beatrice, her pale face cast down, perched on the edge of a sofa.

"Not President Lincoln, who could surely unearth the information we crave." Annie sighed. "Though he met him this spring, Father doesn't want to cause undue questions about his own loyalties."

"Father is always careful."

"And protective of his children." Annie pushed the window open wider to coax a breeze inside on the hot summer day. "The last day of August. What a terrible month. First, Mrs. Greenhow is arrested and now... Will's capture is far worse."

"Yes." Beatrice's fingers trailed the back of a chair as she wandered about the room.

"Bea, I need John." Annie gripped the windowsill. "If only he were here."

"What can he do that Father isn't already doing?"

"Nothing." Annie's sigh came from deep within. "Except comfort me."

"Be grateful he doesn't know." Beatrice joined her at the window.

"I cannot hide my distress."

"No. But you can steer the conversation to Mrs. Greenhow's continuing difficulties."

"Her troubles are mounting. Mrs. Jackson said yesterday that detectives found incriminating evidence, if gossip can be believed."

"We cannot distinguish truth from gossip." Beatrice shrugged. "Your despair can be easily explained by mentioning those rumors."

"I don't like this lack of candor between John and me." Annie closed her eyes. "If we are to be married, there can be no secrets."

Beatrice gasped. "You are betrothed?"

"No." Her stomach fluttered in hope, as if the wings of a

butterfly took flight. "We have merely discussed the future. There has been no proposal."

"I think we can rest assured there will be." Beatrice touched her arm. "John loves you. That much is certain. In these troubling times, it must be comforting to have a good Christian man to rely upon."

"It is." Annie's heart was full. John loved her. Bea was right.

He'd do everything within his power to help them. He was honest. Upright. God-fearing. Traits her mother had advised them to look for in a future husband.

CHAPTER 24

John strode to the Beets farm on Sunday as the sun peeked over hills on the eastern horizon. Having made a friend of their dog, he no longer knocked on their front door before saddling the mare. He'd talk to Zach when he returned.

Patrick had been wise to warn against asking the captain for leave to go into Washington City yesterday. He was befuddled by the captain's stern refusal. In fact, he learned he was lucky to be gone every Sunday. Other soldiers and officers also visited the city on Sundays, yet only a few courted a woman there.

The dog wasn't sleeping on the porch when John entered the yard. Good. He didn't have a spare moment for the boy's pet. Hungry for news of his friend, he hoped to talk to Annie before services started.

"Morning, Moonbeam. Ready for a long ride?" He stroked the mare's neck and then reached for the saddle. It wasn't resting over a side stall as normal. "Hmm. Someone seems to have misplaced your saddle, old girl. Let's look for it. I'd rather not bother the family this early."

"Mornin', Sergeant-Major Finn." Zachary stood in silhouette

at the barn's entrance. "Ma asked me to get this month's payment before you ride out."

"Top of the morning to you, Zachary." John's heart sank. He hadn't remembered the date. "I don't have the whole amount with me. Will you accept half now?"

"Nope. I'm the man of the house with Pa off fighting." The ten-year-old crossed his arms. "Confederate bills ain't good across the Potomac River. Ma says she needs it today."

He extracted a few bills from his pocket. "Here's ten dollars. It's all I have with me. I'll bring the rest this evening when I drop off the horse."

Zachary eyed him. "I reckon that'll be agreeable with Ma." He counted the bills.

"Thank you. I'm good for it." John shook his hand.

"Reckon you are, since I know where you're camped." He stuffed the money into his slouch hat and shoved it down over his ears.

John crossed his arms, annoyed at the first disrespectful comment Zach ever made to him. He had been nothing but kind to the boy. They'd worked out a generous plan to make his family money while keeping their mare. And this be his thanks? "Trust me. I'll bring six dollars when I return."

"I'd be obliged. Ma says times are getting tough." Zachary pushed his hat up. The corner of a one-dollar bill peeked out. "I'll get that saddle now."

So the boy had hidden the saddle to ensure they talked. John chuckled, his irritation evaporating. He was one shrewd little businessman. No telling what he'd pursue as an adult. Little doubt he'd figure out a way to succeed, no matter the obstacles.

The sun warmed John's back as he rode away five minutes later. He sighed. A talk with Annie before church wasn't going to happen.

*A*nnie scanned the church grounds for John as soon as her family arrived in the closed carriage. Jacob extended his hand to help her out of the vehicle. She cringed to meet the glance of Mrs. Charlene Abbot standing with her two daughters. Usually happy for a chance to talk with the Abbots, especially daughters Ruth and Reba, who were her age, Annie hadn't recovered from the shocking news about Will. Her thoughts swirled chaotically. She doubted her ability to refrain from blurting the truth. Attending church was a challenge when all she wanted was to hide until John came.

She gave them a smiling nod and then averted her eyes, praying her friends did not take offense.

They ambled over, Annie's slight snub apparently missed by the normally alert women.

After exchanging polite greetings, her father excused himself. Learning little of value yesterday caused his preoccupation at breakfast. It had been a silent ride to church while Annie's heart cried out for reassurance of her brother's safety, something her father couldn't provide.

"There's interesting news connected with Mrs. Greenhow. Have you heard?" Reba's eyes flashed with excitement.

Curious despite her qualms about participating in gossip, Annie gave her a wary glance. "I've heard of the arrests." Old news that invited her friends to share new information. She berated herself for her weakness even as she stepped closer.

"I can scarcely believe it. Mrs. Greenhow is a spy." Reba glanced from Annie to Beatrice. "Detectives found a stack of partially-burnt papers in a laundry stove."

"The notes looked like scribbles," Ruth leaned closer, "like a message in cypher."

Annie's stomach turned queasy. Was it true? Her mother's friend…a spy for the Confederacy?

"Do you know what that is?"

"Yes, everyone knows cyphers are used in coded messages to protect secrets." Annie clamped back her rising irritation. It wasn't Ruth's fault her nerves were in tatters. She softened her tone. "Not that I've seen one."

"Of course not. Who among our acquaintances has…except Mrs. Greenhow?" Reba lowered her voice. "Can you believe it? We have a spy in our midst."

"I'm convinced Mrs. Greenhow is loyal." Annie said. Yet her defense didn't ring true. The widow said Confederate prisoners' treatment at the Old Capitol was shameful. Had it been as reprehensible as she had claimed?

"Oh, I'm certain you're right."

Tension eased from Annie's shoulders.

"Question is, which side is she loyal to?" Ruth raised her hands, palms up. "I don't know what to think."

Annie yanked her white gloves over her wrist. What was the truth? Every event seemed washed in tints of gray. Nothing was clear.

Church bells pealed. The clear tones ended the painful conversation. She strolled beside Beatrice toward the church with a renewed resolve to keep Will's capture a secret as long as possible. Especially from friends who loved to gossip for even worse might be said about her brother in coming days.

On the other hand, the Abbots were the perfect people to tell if she wanted news spread quickly. A good thing to remember.

At the bottom of the steps, she gave the crowd a final sweeping glance. Where was John? Desperation to see him reached a fever pitch. She waved a fan in front of her face to mask her agitation.

Even if she was barred from explaining her heartache to him, she needed him. His mere presence soothed her spirit. *Come to me, John. Don't fail me today.*

~

*L*ate to church again, John had slipped into the back pew. As soon as the last amen was uttered, he craned his neck for a glimpse of his sweet Annie's face.

A stranger beside him cleared his throat.

John started. "Pardon me. Did you say something?"

The bearded man with hair graying at his temples inclined his head. "My name is Tobias Wilson, and you are Miss Annie Swanson's beau."

"You have the better of me, sir. I don't recall our meeting." He glanced at Annie, who had turned to talk with folks sitting behind her family's pew. "I've met a great many men since coming to your city. My apologies for my rudeness. I can only say in my defense that current events have befuddled me."

"Think nothing of it, Sergeant-Major Finn. I believe we all can claim the same bewilderment in these troubling times. We were introduced in passing." Mr. Wilson smiled graciously. "I was very happy to hear the good news yesterday."

"Good news, sir?" How could he politely extricate himself from a casual conversation he had little patience for when Annie needed him?

"The capture of the Rebel forts. Hadn't you heard?" He twisted his beaver hat in his hands. "After the beating we took at Bull Run, this news is a breath of fresh air."

Not to John in this instance, for it meant the capture of his school buddy. He clenched his fist. "I may have heard something about that."

"John."

He turned from the uncomfortable conversation at the sound of Annie's voice.

"I was worried." Her voice faltered as she focused on the man beside him. "Mr. Wilson. How lovely to see you this Lord's Day."

"And you, Miss Swanson." He inclined his head. "I was mentioning to your young man—"

"War news. Nothing of significance." John covered the icy hand clutching his sleeve with his own. Talk about bewilderment. Her expressive eyes told the tale. She knew. "Annie doesn't like to hear such particulars." *Steer the conversation to more savory topics, Annie, as you do so well.* He prayed she read his thoughts.

She glanced at him. Something she saw there made her face lose its color. "True." She whispered. "I cannot bear...I pray you will forgive me."

"Of course, my dear." Mr. Wilson patted her hand, the one not clutching John's arm. "Why, you are ice cold. Quite amazing. I find the atmosphere inside the church to be quite stifling. Perhaps—"

"I'll take her outside. The sun will warm her." John pounced on the opportunity to get away from the gentleman. "Please excuse us."

"Good day, Mr. Wilson." Annie's lips trembled into the semblance of a smile.

John led her outside into the thinning crowd. "Annie, are you well?"

"Not unwell." She tightened her grasp on his arm. "That's not the problem. You are coming for dinner."

"Yes." He didn't want her to tell him—yet he did. He wanted her to trust him with the dreadful news about her brother. How it must terrify her. "Let's talk after lunch. There's your family by your carriage."

While strolling to her family, Annie gave him one beseeching look before shifting her glance to her pink-and-white fan. Her pale cheeks matched the pink of her dress. He longed to take her in his arms and comfort her.

On other occasions, John had tied his mare to their landau and rode with the family to their home. Today he rode behind their closed carriage because they had taken off at a good clip while he strode to a shaded hitching post for Moonbeam.

Hiram left the house while the girls freshened up before lunch. John, standing at the front window, watched him drive off alone in the chaise. What was so important that he didn't eat Sunday dinner with his daughters?

Curious, to be sure. He'd mention it to Christopher.

Guilt gnawed at his soul.

John slumped in a chair in the parlor as he waited for the girls. How he abhorred the position he'd allowed himself to be placed in. Yet had he refused to spy, another man would have done it, one who could not care more for this family than John did.

Did that compensate for his betrayal?

At lunch, John expected the girls to tell him about Will. His heart shrank when they instead talked about Rose Greenhow. When would Annie trust him with her burden for her brother?

"I don't want to believe she's a spy." Annie pushed her untouched apple cobbler aside. In truth, none of them had done justice to Rebecca's delicious meal. "But why was there a partially-burned cypher in her stove?"

"I'm at a loss to explain it." The evidence was rather telling, to John at least, yet he hesitated to cast their friend in a bad light. "All will be made clear soon."

She held up open palms toward him. "You always know what to say."

He flushed. The truth in the widow's case wasn't going to bring Annie comfort. "'Tis me Irish brogue." Seeing her dimples, he chuckled.

"And I love that brogue, kind sir." She giggled.

"'Tis happy I am to hear it since it comes and goes when it pleases."

"It comes when your emotions are engaged." Annie blushed.

"That it does." He hoped his teasing coaxed her worry away. Since she still hadn't mentioned Will, he imagined Beatrice's presence silenced her. Perhaps they needed solitude. "Do you want to stroll?"

"What a lovely idea." She looked at Beatrice.

"I'm feeling rather pensive this afternoon. Besides, I have some knitting for Will's baby. You two go on." Crimson stained her cheeks. She rose. "Annie, please accompany me to my room. John, pray excuse us for a moment. I will see you upon your return."

"'Twill be a pleasure." John inclined his head. He didn't miss the irritation that flashed across Annie's face. What was going on? "Annie, I will await you on the lawn. Take as long as you like."

CHAPTER 25

*A*nnie's irritation mounted with each stair step. She didn't need a reminder from her sister to keep her silence about Will.

They were quiet until inside Beatrice's spacious bedroom with its canopied brass bed and pink coverlets that matched the wallpaper. Annie spun to face her sister. "No need to warn me about maintaining my silence."

Beatrice took a step back. "I merely wanted—"

"Yes, I'm aware that you don't want him to learn Will's a prisoner." She crossed her arms.

"Of John's army."

No. Annie's breathing stopped. She sank onto a chaise lounge near a broad window. "You're wrong. John has no part in this."

"Not in this specific incident. That's true." Beatrice sat beside her. "You must face reality, Annie. John and Will have become enemies."

"Impossible." She leaped to her feet. "They're friends. They will *never* be enemies to one another."

"I pray you're right." Beatrice walked to the window. "For that would divide our family."

Annie froze. "What do you mean?"

Distant drumbeats were the only sound.

"Bea?"

"John is your beau. You love him, don't you?"

"You must know the truth." Annie had never expressed her feelings in words for John. "I love John more with each passing day. If he proposes—*when* he proposes—I am ready with my answer."

"The way you look at him ..."

"Do my eyes betray my love for him?"

"You trust him implicitly. As you formerly trusted your brother." She turned tormented blue eyes toward Annie. "You cannot believe, should Will and John become sworn enemies, that I'd support the cause of your beau at the expense of my beloved brother."

Annie stiffened. Unmoving, as if icy fingers gripped her core and held her captive. Her own sister...catapulting her into an impossible choice.

Betrayed by her brother and now her sister. Who was next?

⁓

ootsteps rustled dry grass behind him. At last. John turned to greet the woman he loved. His smile froze. Annie's face was nearly the color of the white lace trim on her pale pink bodice.

"Me dearest Annie." He clasped her gloved hand. "What is it? What's stolen the luster from your beautiful brown eyes?"

"My apologies to keep you waiting." She gave him a dazed look. "I'm aware your time is not your own."

"Me time is yours, sweet Annie. As much as I'm able to give." Alarmed, he gathered her trembling frame close to his side and led her to a garden seat. "Please, tell me what has upset you." He fought back fears that something worse had happened to Will. Beatrice's restless agitation was now reflected in Annie's eyes.

Obedient as a child, she sat. "I can't."

John, retaining his clasp of her limp hand, sank beside her. "Something happened that you can't explain to me."

"Yes." Her voice fell to a whisper.

"Does it have something to do with your family?"

Her gaze dropped to their clasped hands.

Sworn to secrecy? Perhaps. He understood such a vow. Didn't his promise to Christopher of silence also plague him? "Is there anything I can do? Anything within my power will be done."

A tear rolled down her cheek. "I had a disagreement with Beatrice."

Relief flooded over him as he wiped away the tear with his thumb. A sisterly spat. "I'm sorry you quarreled. Want to talk about it?"

"Yes." She sniffed. "But it's impossible."

"Then I will pray for peace to reign again between you and your sister. You are too close to allow anything to separate you."

Her eyes captured his, then fell to their clasped hands. "I never dreamed anyone...that is, anything had the power to divide us."

Had they fought about him? Was it Will? His mind raced back to their lunch conversation. Nothing of importance there except— "Does this have anything to do with Mrs. Greenhow's arrest?"

"I feel betrayed by my—her. Yes, that's it."

John searched her woeful expression. "Did you just realize this?"

"Yes...no, that's not quite it." Her fingers tightened around his. "Had she been arrested and falsely accused, I'd have been angry with the authorities who have harassed an innocent widow trying to raise her daughter alone."

"However..." John risked anger directed at him this time unless he tread lightly. She was already upset.

"However, I cannot understand why detectives discovered a partially burned cypher code in her stove. I can think of no reason that explains it away." She raised bleak eyes. "Unless she is truly guilty of spying."

"Sanding the wood reveals the true grain underneath the rough lumber. In the same way, the truth has a way of rising to the top...or so me da was fond of saying." His da imparted lots of wisdom about life while training him to run the family business.

He feared his da's words would apply to himself. The truth of his own spying must not surface.

"That is so. Jesus said that the truth will set us free." She sighed. "Perhaps it will not save my mother's old friend."

"Perhaps that's not the truth Jesus spoke of." He brushed a loose tendril behind her ear.

"Why didn't Mrs. Greenhow warn me of her activities?"

"And put you in danger?"

"So many secrets." She stood suddenly and turned her back to him. "I hate this war."

Was she thinking of the wedge driven between her and her brother by his choices? John's brow furrowed at her unexpected vehemence. "What...secrets do you speak of?" His own guilt rose up to shame him. Did she suspect him?

"Nothing of significance." She clasped his hand. "At least you and I support the Union."

So, she was talking about Will. Wait. Did she imply the rest of her family were Southern sympathizers? His uneasiness multiplied. Christopher feared this family's allegiance was for the South. *Please, sweet Annie, don't give me any information to prove him right.* He patted his uniform signifying his willingness to fight for their country.

"You're my hero. You know that, don't you? In this mad world where nothing is as it seems, I depend upon you." Her eyes softened with trust. "Now. How about that stroll?"

A knife twisted in his gut. He wanted to be a hero in her eyes. The hero she thought he was.

A hero did not spy on the family of the woman he loved.

CHAPTER 26

"*M*oonbeam, you're moving slowly, old girl. You seem as tired as I feel." John dismounted a mile from camp and rubbed the mare's nose. "Do you sense my agitation? Nothing is going as it should. Though I cannot be sorry that Christopher was not at his boarding house. I had scant desire to speak to the man." Sighing, he looped the reins around his wrist. "Nothing wrong with you that a nice bit of hay won't cure. Wish I could say that eating supper will restore me spirits. We both know that's false. Your ears perk up at a lie too, don't they, girl?"

He trudged on beside the horse, too emotionally spent to scan the woods for Federal pickets that guarded the area. If the enemy surrounded him at this moment, he'd not even put up a fight.

Fortunate he was for Union pickets.

A lone figure sat on a log at the bottom of the hill near their camp. "Patrick."

"Been waiting for you." The red-haired man pushed himself to his feet. "Thought I'd accompany you to the Beets farm."

"Appreciate the company." The air between them had been

strained since their disagreement yesterday. "I have to return to our cabin first. Will you wait with Moonbeam?"

"Sure thing, but why climb that hill twice if you don't have to?" Patrick patted the horse's mane.

John glanced at the newly-dug road and hundreds of stumps dotting the recently forested hillside. His exhausted body rebelled at climbing it even once. "Mrs. Beets demands the fee for the month of September today."

"How much you need?"

His spirits rose a fraction. "Six dollars. You have that much on you?"

Patrick nodded. "Pay me back tonight."

"As soon as we return. Much obliged." He summoned a grin.

A turtle could have outrun the pair as they continued to the farmhouse. The crickets' song didn't drown out distant drumbeats.

"'Tis right you were about the captain. 'Twas foolish to ask for another evening away when I had permission to go today. I should have held my tongue."

"Tried to warn you."

"That you did." John darted a look at Patrick's stony face. "Has my absence from camp created such a stir?"

"Not while we camped in Washington City. A couple of hours away from camp was no great hardship, but it takes you nearly that long to travel one way to her now." Patrick scanned the tree line. "We're too busy for you to leave twice a week."

"You agree with the captain." The farmhouse loomed on the horizon. John slowed his steps, determined to clear the air between them.

"Aye."

"Why?" John stopped to turn to him.

"Just as I said…we're too busy for you to shirk your duties."

"There's no shirking of duties." His anger boiled. If Patrick knew of his spying activities, he'd change his attitude. "I burn the midnight oil to maintain the books."

"I've been meaning to thank you for keeping the rest of us awake." Patrick put his hands on his hips.

"My apologies. I'll take me work outside the cabin after *Taps* from now on."

"Good." Patrick continued toward the Beets farm.

"Something else is wrong." John matched his stride. "Is it Deborah? Your family?"

"Finally. An inquiry about my family." His pace quickened.

"Patrick, wait." Exhaustion prevented him from maintaining his friend's pace.

He halted with his face toward the homestead, a mere hundred yards away.

"'Tis sorry I am that I've been so preoccupied with myself." That was all Patrick knew he was worried about, anyway. "Is Deborah well?"

"One of the fellows in our company wrote to his girl about those of us who were courting ladies in Washington City. She learned I accompanied Beatrice on various occasions. That I attended soirees at her home." He turned slowly to face John with tormented eyes.

"She's angry?"

"'Tis a mild word for her feelings."

John's heart sank. "Did you explain that you merely escorted Beatrice to chaperone Annie and me? That you accompanied her in service of a friend?"

"It began that way."

John took a step back. "What do you mean?" Had Patrick's feelings run deeper?

"Beatrice and I were drawn together by our love of music. She's so beautiful"—crimson traveled up his neck—"that after a while Deborah's face faded in my memory."

John sucked in his breath. "If you've mistreated an innocent—"

"No, nothing like that. I respect both ladies."

"Then what?" He lengthened his stance.

"'Twas all in me own mind. Me own heart." He stared at the ground. "Never a stated thing."

"So Mr. Swanson was right to banish you."

"Me flirtations got the better of me."

John stared at his downcast face. He scarcely blamed his friend for falling for a Swanson sister—hadn't he done that himself? "Do you still wish to marry Deborah?"

"Aye."

"Do you love her?"

"Lots of nights have I lain awake pondering that very thing. Talking with you has shown me the answer." Resolution marked his expression. "I love Deborah. I'll marry her on my next furlough...if she'll have me."

"She's a good woman." John clapped him on the shoulder. "But a mite jealous. Perhaps with good reason. Curtail your flirtatious behavior, for she may not forgive you a second time."

"No worries. There will not be another woman for me."

As they continued onward in silence, John's thoughts turned to Annie, the only woman for him. He'd propose once this spying business was behind him—and the turmoil of Will's captivity passed.

❧

lease, don't leave. Everything inside had screamed for John to stay in the city. Annie uttered not a word to betray her turmoil when he gave her a chaste kiss good-bye.

Annie, her heart as cold as the Potomac in winter, sat in the garden long after John turned and waved one last farewell from the avenue leading to the heart of the city. Her spirit had calmed while he was here. The moment he mounted his horse, her agitation returned. *Please, return quickly.*

Fear for her brother battled anger toward her sister. Their argument was the worst they'd ever had. She couldn't face Beatrice yet. Certainly, she did not plan to dine alone with her. The harsh words hadn't meant Beatrice sympathized with the South…had they?

Someone cleared a throat.

She gave a start. Then her eyes focused in the gloom beneath the trees. "Mr. Grant. You startled me."

"Forgive me, Miss Annie." He bowed slightly. "I thought you would hear my footsteps on the dry grass. Mrs. Rebecca sent me to say that supper is served."

That late already? "Has my father returned?"

"No, miss. We've had no word of him."

"He seeks news of my brother." Useless to keep secrets regarding Will from the staff. Besides, they were nearly as apprehensive as her family. In truth, the staff were family, too.

"Your father won't rest easy until he finds his son." The butler inclined his graying head. "And he will find Will sooner rather than later, mark my words."

"Thank you, Mr. Grant." He and his wife had been with the family since Will was an infant.

"May I inform your sister that you will be in directly?"

She gave an emphatic shake of her head. "I'm not hungry. I'll sit here a bit longer and then go up to my room."

His face puckered. "As you wish. I'll inform Miss Beatrice."

She stiffened at her sister's name.

War had started at Fort Sumter in April. How had the country's division invaded her home by September?

CHAPTER 27

"You know much about the parole and exchange of prisoners of war?" John fell into step beside Patrick. Lunch break was over and a busy afternoon fashioning simple tables for officers outside in the blazing September sun awaited John.

"It started back in February. Major General Twiggs is one of ours. His troops were in Texas when that state seceded. He surrendered all our troops within the state." Patrick's stride slowed. "Confederates gave them paroles and released them with the understanding they'd not fight as soldiers until a formal exchange happened."

"Far better than holding men in prisons until the war ends." An uneasy atmosphere had lingered between them the past two days that John was anxious to mend.

"'Tis certain my choice would be an exchange if fate demands my capture." Patrick halted beside tables in various stages of creation. "Why the sudden interest?"

"Been thinking about that Confederate regiment captured last week. Overcrowding our forts and prisons with extra

mouths to feed. An exchange of prisoners seems best to me."
Good news for Will.

"Agreed. We'll get some of our own officers and soldiers
back in the exchange." Patrick raised his hand as if to clap John
on the back. Then he dropped it. "Keep up the good work on
those tables."

No friendly smile. No frown either. John watched him walk
away, longing for restoration of their old camaraderie.

John hated seeing the worry in Annie's eyes. Men died in
prison. Spending weeks, months, or even years in prison camp
was a fate he didn't wish on anyone. Certainly not his best
friend.

John directed the erection of soldiers' quarters in between
building tables. Good-natured bantering, the whirr of saws, and
the pounding of hammers among the men convinced John he
was free to concentrate on his own carpentry work. He applied
the small sharp wire of his bradawl to make a nail hole in the
wood. Unseasoned wood, at that. His da would never allow
them to use unseasoned wood in their shop, but the army must
make do with supplies on hand. Besides, no one imagined these
tables would be used after this divisive war ended.

Better for the country by far to release the animosity felt by
both sides.

Easy to say. Soldiers dying on battlefields and in hospitals
made forgiveness mighty hard to achieve.

He selected wood for his third table of the afternoon and
pondered Will's fate. There was a way to shorten his friend's
time in prison. Once John learned Will's location, he'd pen a
letter pleading with Will to swear allegiance to the Union, an
oath that went a long way toward his release. He'd earn his
freedom from prison camp upon vowing never to take up arms
against the United States again.

Preferably to fight for the North. Maybe even in John's
regiment.

Otherwise, Will must await a prisoner exchange for his release. Difficult circumstances for a man raised in luxury. John muttered at the wood beneath his aching fingers.

He took a long drink from his canteen and splashed his face. As glad as he was that his carpentry skills bore fruit outside his father's factory, it was still grueling work.

"Looks good." Patrick strode over later that afternoon. "Who gets this one?"

"This whole lot"—John waved a hand at six tables, each three feet square—"go to Company C officers."

"The practical jokers in the Cow Bell headquarters?"

"Aye." Tension oozed from John's shoulders to remember some of their antics. "Company C's Street is always lively."

"Want to get their goat?" Mischief lit his eyes. "Or should I say their cow bell?"

John raised his eyebrows.

"How difficult is it to etch something under a tabletop?" Patrick folded his arms over his chest. Waited.

That's what had been missing. It had been too long since John had joined in the practical jokes galloping throughout camp. He'd been too guilt-ridden by his spying to participate in the merriment. They excelled in it. Even in the midst of difficult days, his buddies soon rallied themselves to make a joke or two. Patrick had instigated a few practical jokes with John's full support...in the early days.

Grinning, John swiped sawdust from a table. "Time's a wast-ing' if we want it ready this evening."

<hr />

"There's more news about the forts we captured down at Hatteras Inlet." Esther Jackson entered the parlor of her family's home.

Annie tensed. The battle had been discussed briefly when

the women gathered on Tuesday. Too upset to listen, she'd steered the conversation. Now, two days later, she fought the desire to learn the information while hiding her distress at the details.

"Isn't that old news?" Beatrice didn't raise her eyes from the trousers she stitched.

"Not to the *New York Times*." Esther tapped the newspaper in her hands. "And not to me either. I'm interested."

"Of course, we all are, dear." Mrs. Jackson peered over her daughter's shoulder. "A mere week has passed. No great mystery it's still being reported."

"On the front page." Esther smirked at Annie and Bea.

Esther's smug look annoyed Annie. Still, her curiosity was aroused. She'd read every newspaper account that her father brought home since learning of Will's capture. A tear-stained letter from Frances, received yesterday, had confirmed their fears. An escaped soldier had brought her the terrible news that Will was a prisoner of war. He hadn't been harmed during battle, news that left Annie nearly limp with gratitude.

"What does it say, Esther?" Ruth Abbott glanced up from the blue fabric resting on the table in front of her.

Beatrice, at Annie's side, sucked in her breath.

"Fascinating. It's the news as our neighbors to the South see it. There's a section quoted from the Petersburgh *Express*, which in turn quotes last Friday's edition of the Newbern *Progress*." Esther scanned the page. "It says that the entire Confederate force was eight hundred fifty-three. Some fifty escaped."

Oh, that Will had been one of the fortunate fifty. Annie changed her mind about learning the hurtful specifics. Her forehead nearly brushed the fabric in her fingers as she bent over it, so great was her need to hide her expression from her friends.

"A Lieutenant Citizen says he believes forty were killed. About twenty wounded."

Annie shifted. Far worse for those soldiers and their families than what her family suffered at this hour. Mother had always tried to look for positive aspects in every situation. That was the only one that Annie had discovered.

"I hate to hear of so many dead." Ruth's face lost color. "Captivity is a better fate."

"Agreed." Annie's voice was more fervent than she'd intended.

Ruth glanced at her. "Much better to send imprisoned men home to their families."

Was that possible? John knew the army's rules and regulations. Might the authorities release Will and send him home?

Beatrice darted a glance at Annie and then stared at Ruth. "Have you heard of this circumstance happening before? I am sympathetic to those poor soldiers and their families awaiting them back home. I confess that my sympathy has born a keen curiosity."

Annie raised her eyebrows at her sister. *Don't show too much interest, Bea. We don't wish to draw attention.*

"I know little of such matters. That's what *I'd* like to happen. Men who used to be our own countrymen...prisoners of war. So sad." Ruth sighed.

"It's a victory for us, Ruth." Esther looked up from reading. "You're looking at this the wrong way. We are that much closer to ending this war."

"I suppose that is the best way to view it." Ruth threaded a needle. "Where is Hatteras Inlet anyway?"

"North Carolina." Esther glanced at Annie. "Your brother lives there. Are those forts near him?"

Annie blinked at the conversation's turn. "I have no notion where the forts are located."

"Look at this map in *The New York Times*." Esther sat beside her and pointed to the sketch. "You attended Will's wedding. Did you go there?"

Two dots marked Fort Hatteras and Fort Clark on a curved

land arc in the water. "Will doesn't live on an island." Her thoughts swirled. She must sway the conversation in a new direction.

"He lives inland, near the Chowan River." Beatrice spoke quickly.

And not many miles from the Albemarle Sound that the river emptied into. The very spot where the wedding party had enjoyed a picnic luncheon after a pleasant morning's journey to get there. Will and Frances had ridden in a landau with Annie and John on that not-to-be-forgotten day—the last time she spent an entire day in her brother's company. Christmas last year had been a festive occasion with many people always on hand. Had she known that time was so short... She shook herself from her reverie, hoping these women didn't know much about the country's geography. "He's developed quite a love for fishing since his marriage," Annie said.

"Men do love to hunt and fish." Esther studied her. "What news do you hear of Will?"

A chill spread up Annie's face. This was dangerous ground, especially in light of the newspaper articles. "Their days are filled with preparations for the upcoming birth of their first child."

"Yes, that is what you said." Ruth nodded. "Is Frances well?"

No. Definitely not. She fears for her husband. "The doctor is pleased with her health."

"What of war news?" Esther tapped the map. "Has Will mustered into the Union army?"

"I don't believe so." Sweat beaded on Annie's brow. "He has immersed himself into learning how to run a plantation. Why, he knew nothing about growing cotton when he married Frances."

"His father-in-law has vowed acreage as his wedding gift, though nothing is settled yet." Beatrice's bright look that didn't reach her eyes. "Is that not generous of him?"

"Amazingly so." Esther dropped the paper on a table beside the parlor door and then returned to her seat beside Annie. "May we all be as fortunate."

Annie glanced out the window at gathering clouds. She didn't want a thousand-acre plantation. Her dreams included riding the rails west with John as her husband.

"It's good to know what is keeping Will from mustering into the army." Ruth pulled a needle through the fabric. "And here I wondered if he hadn't become a Confederate soldier."

CHAPTER 28

*R*uth's seemingly innocent observation hung in the air that seemed to dissipate from the room. Annie choked on her own breath.

Her gasps were echoed as a dozen pairs of eyes speared her and Beatrice. *Don't allow this thought to take hold in the minds of our friends. Don't let it become an accusation.*

"I must confess to entertaining that same possibility." Esther's blue eyes pierced Annie's facade.

A stiff upper lip now, Annie. Her mother's oft-repeated advice reverberated in her brain just in time. "I don't know why you'd question the loyalty of a boy you attended school with, Esther." Annie's mild tone surprised even her.

"I...I didn't question—"

"Why, you most certainly did." Annie tried to maintain a pleasant demeanor when all she wanted to do was scream. "Within hearing of everyone in this room."

"But I didn't mean—"

"Then you should better guard your tongue." Annie's back stiffened. "Such words can plant doubts in the hearts of those listening. You must beware of this tendency in yourself."

Beatrice shot her a look and then bent over her fabric.

"You sounded like your mother just then, Annie." Mrs. Abbott covered her mouth with her hands.

"Thank you." Gratefulness washed over Annie. "There is no higher compliment."

"I'm sorry." Esther gave her a stricken look. "I didn't mean anything by it."

Her anger receded into a puddle of remorse. After all, Esther had only questioned Will's loyalty...a correct assumption, considering the facts. "I'm certain you didn't." Annie patted Esther's tense arm. "Let's speak no more about it."

"I will not. Thank you." Esther whispered.

No one spoke. Feeling the weight of a stare, Annie looked up and met Ruth's curious gaze.

She was the one who'd originally voiced the concern. Annie's heart sank that her friend remained unconvinced.

She barely stifled a sigh. The truth of Will's capture would soon be known, no doubt causing the friendship of many to grow cold.

Whom could she trust to remain true?

$\sim$

*H*iram strode into the family dining room the next morning, where the sisters lingered over a late breakfast.

Beatrice glanced at the mantel clock. "Half-past nine? Father, I didn't know you were still here."

"I have been to the bank and back already this morning." He gripped the back of an intricately-engraved dining chair. "I may have found your brother."

"Where is he?" Clutching her napkin, Annie rose from her chair.

"The same ships that fired upon his fort have spirited his regiment to New York."

"New York?" Beatrice's blue eyes widened. "Why could they not have brought him here where we could visit him daily?"

"I know not why the army chooses to do as it does." Father waved her question aside. "In any case, we have a place to begin."

"They may not keep him in New York?"

"Perhaps not." He grimaced at Annie's question. "Hundreds of men became prisoners at the same time. A single prison camp may not hold them all."

Annie's mind reeled with possibilities. "Then he might be moved here to Washington City."

"Prisoners from the fiasco at Bull Run were held here." He rubbed his clean-shaven jaw. "I did not expect that we'd have the gift of Will's captivity in our city. It doesn't appear that we will receive such a boon."

"You've spent a long time considering this." Compassion filled Beatrice's eyes.

A feeling Annie shared. She felt closer to her sister, indeed to her whole family, than she had since their argument.

"I've thought of little else." Hiram extended his arms to them. They clung to him. "I am going to New York. I have information that he is to be held on Governors Island in New York Harbor."

"I'll go with you." Annie wanted to help. Her father needed support. Shadows under his eyes and deeper lines on his forehead showed the strain he endured.

"I will as well." Beatrice's voice was muffled against his coat.

"No." He shifted them to an arm's length away and retained a hand on their shoulders. "Prison camps are no place for ladies."

"Even when that lady's brother is among the captives?" Annie raised her eyebrows.

"Even then." He gave a deep sigh. "Why, your mother would

206

turn over in her grave if I took you to such a place. Do not ask it of me."

"She'd turn over in her grave to see a lot of atrocities the newspapers speak of."

Annie agreed with her sister's softly spoken words.

"True. Let's sit a moment."

They settled back into their chairs. Annie pushed aside her plate, her appetite gone.

"It's such a gloomy day. Exactly fits my mood." Beatrice, from her place beside her father, stared out the large window overlooking the garden.

"Yes, rain is likely later today." Annie hardly knew what to say yet strove to lighten the heaviness that engulfed her and must surely affect her family too.

"If you two are ready to talk about something besides the weather..." Father turned serious eyes on each. "I'll leave tonight. There are a few things at the bank that require my attention before I leave."

Beatrice turned back to him. "Anything we can do to help?"

"I assume you're going to your sewing group today?"

Annie nodded. "My heart's not in it today." She hadn't told him about yesterday's conversation about Will.

"Understood," Father said. "My heart has not been in my work this week, and I've still been there. I want you to behave as naturally as possible. To my knowledge, Will's name hasn't been reported in any newspaper in connection with the battle. I've checked as many as I could lay my hands on."

"If recent conversations in our sewing group are any indication, our friends may turn their backs on us." Beatrice stared at her folded hands.

"Some may." Annie couldn't argue. "When the truth is revealed..." Her thoughts turned to John and his reaction. His friendship with Will was strong, and so was his love for her. He'd never betray her.

"We must be strong, my daughters. Stand in the strength of your mother and your faith in God."

Annie straightened her shoulders. She was her mother's daughter.

"In any case, I rely on you both to watch over things here." Hiram swept his hand around the room. "At the house and at the bank."

"What do you mean?" Annie's brow furrowed. She'd visited him there many times but never worked an hour.

"You must remember Philip Tomlinson, my assistant manager, who has been with me the last decade."

They nodded.

"Annie, in my absence, Mr. Tomlinson may require your signature on bank documents from time to time. You may trust him. Make a note of everything but sign whatever he brings you."

Annie caught her breath at the unprecedented request.

"I had you both sign some documents after Will moved to North Carolina. Do you recall?"

She had a vague recollection of signing official papers.

"That allows you to transact business on my behalf. Should circumstances require it, Mr. Tomlinson will send for you to come to the bank or bring the documents to you. I'll be in correspondence with him. This responsibility will not tax you overmuch." He patted her arm. "It's only for a week or two."

"Then may I go with you, Father?"

Annie stiffened at her sister's request. She'd rather go to New York than bear responsibility for the bank.

Father turned to Beatrice. "It's no place—"

"I'll help other ways." Beatrice's raised clasped hands. "Like with correspondences. My penmanship is fine. You've said as much."

"It's true my time will be divided between visiting Will and bank business. I could use your help." He tapped his fingers

together. "Very well, as long as you can be packed by eight o'clock."

"I'll be ready. Thanks, Father." Beatrice hugged him and then hurried from the room.

Annie lowered her eyes. The last time they'd all been to New York City was the year Will graduated from West Point. Mother had been alive, and they'd combined a trip to celebrate Will's achievement with a shopping expedition. Annie had never been there without her sister. And now Beatrice was going without her.

"Here is a list of items we'll want to take to Will." Hiram extracted a page from his pocket and scanned it. "Perhaps it's best if you send your regrets to the sewing group for today and help gather these few comforts for your brother."

"I'll be happy to pack them." She took the note. "Rebecca may want to bake some cookies or a cake to satisfy Will's love for sweets. Is that allowed?"

"I don't see reason for an objection from his captors. One can never know for certain." He rose with a sigh. "But we'll eat the confections should Will not be on Governors Island. I'll speak to Mr. Grant about packing my trunk and then head back to the bank. Ask Rebecca to prepare supper early, say half past five."

Annie agreed and stared out at the garden shrouded in gloom. She hadn't mended the relationship with her sister and now had little desire to do so.

After all, Beatrice was leaving Annie to bear the responsibilities of home and business. Leaving her to face the ill will from acquaintances once it became public knowledge that Will was a captured Confederate lieutenant.

Leaving her alone to face the coming storm.

CHAPTER 29

"*A* telegram for you, sir."

In the waning light, John stared at the folded page in the soldier's hand. He'd just returned from the Friday evening prayer meeting to his small wooden quarters that smelled of freshly cut lumber. After a long day working in the rain, his only desire was to drop onto his cot and sleep until the bugler played *Reveille* in the morning.

The message must be from his family, probably his mam. His da couldn't be... No. He wouldn't borrow trouble. He rubbed the back of his neck before snatching the paper from unresistant fingers.

"Sorry, soldier. I'm on edge this evening."

"Probably the weather, sir. Sure has been a wet one." The private saluted and splashed away in the muddy aisle between the basic wooden shelters.

The telegram was getting wet in the drizzle. John ducked inside his quarters, which were blessed empty.

Every sense on high alert, he unfolded the page and read his mother's words.

My dear Son,

Your da suffered apoplexy yesterday. The doctor does not say how well he will recover. His left arm is paralyzed, and his leg will not yet carry him. He speaks little though seems aware of everything happening.

John, tell your commanding officer that you are needed. Resign from the army. Hurry home.

With love, Mam.

Eyes closed, John rested his head against the rough plank wall. It had required nearly six months for his father to recover his strength last time, another year before he returned to work. This attack seemed more severe.

Now what?

The chains that bound John to the family's business tightened so that he could hardly breathe.

He paced. His mam expected him to drop everything and hurry home. *Resign from the army.*

John gave a low whistle. Unless sickness or battle wounds prevented his service, he'd volunteered to defend his country, his home. Everything inside told him he'd done the right thing.

Mam demanded too much.

There were others at home to see to his da's care, his mam's needs.

Like his little brother. Hardly little any longer. Twenty-one, and Carl acted as if he were a boy on a lark. It was high time he acted his age. His brother had no desire to fight for his country, more's the pity. The army'd make a man of him quicker than the crowd he'd likely taken up with in New York City. His brother had sunk deeper into depravity during his stay there.

Carl needed to go home. He knew little about the family business other than the fact that it provided for his comforts. He could learn the same way John had—by laboring dawn to dusk at their furniture factory.

John tossed his wet hat on his cot as he passed it by. It wasn't wise to turn over management of the factory and stores to Carl until his brother took his responsibilities seriously.

In time, his brother would return to the Christian values he was raised to follow. It might take an unfortunate occurrence, an unforeseen circumstance, to shake him up. Like the war going badly or losing a friend in battle.

Or losing their da.

He gulped. That fear struck too close.

What about Patricia's husband? Scott was an intelligent man. His brother-in-law would learn to manage their business with advice and training from trusted employees. Unfortunately, his gifts lent themselves toward bookkeeping, not management. John foresaw him running one of their stores before he'd run the entire business. Besides, he already had a job, where he was thriving.

It wasn't fair to ask Scott to give up a promising insurance career.

Madelynn's beau, Todd Caudill, wasn't ready for such responsibility. John had written his da over the summer, encouraging him to train the lad on each job in the factory, keeping him in each position until he mastered it and then moving him to another area. Given time—if he married Madelynn—Todd had the makings of a manager.

If Carl wasn't interested, John figured that was the company's future.

John wished that Patrick had accompanied him to this evening's prayer meeting. He had opted instead for the festivities taking place on Company C's Street. The carousers hadn't yet discovered the cow bell that John had etched under their table. Patrick had been a different man since confessing his own hardships, and John wished he was there now to mull over his mam's summons with him.

Booted steps thudded on the dirt ground as a knock came. "Enter."

Corporal Ben Boyle opened the door and shut it behind him. "Evening, Sergeant-Major Finn."

"Hi, Ben." John sighed. "As I've said before, just call me John whenever enlisted men aren't around. What can I do for you?"

"Heard you received a telegram. Wondered if it was bad news."

"It was from my mam. My da has suffered another apoplexy."

Ben sucked in his breath. "Is it as bad as the first?"

"Worse." It was a relief to speak of his worries. "He hasn't been able to walk yet. Nor can he move his left arm."

Ben clapped him on the shoulder. "What now?"

"Mam asks that I resign from the army. That I'm needed at home to run the family business."

"A furniture factory, right?"

John nodded and turned away.

"Not as easy as she imagines to quit the army."

John gave a bitter laugh. "No."

"The fort's taking shape. I believe we'll be here long enough to finish building sleeping quarters."

John rounded on him. "You've heard something?"

"No." Ben shook his head. "A hunch. We've got a strong regiment. We'll be sent to fight, not left to guard our nation's capital should the enemy be foolish enough to attack."

"An important task, guarding President Lincoln and the citizens of this city." And Annie. He'd rather be the one guarding her than leave the job to another regiment.

"'Tis. Just don't think it'll be ours." Ben's eyes darkened. "Your leadership, your training, will be needed in upcoming battles."

"I'll be here for them." John stared at the telegram lying on his cot. "Mam has no idea how to go about without my da...and I don't know when he'll recover." Or if he'd recover his vigor.

"Don't you have a brother?"

A brief nod.

"He didn't muster in. Might he step in to fill your father shoes?"

"No man alive can fill me father's shoes." His face stiffened at the mere suggestion. "Not me. Certainly not me, brother. Carl prefers the insides of a tavern to a factory."

"Perhaps you can convince him otherwise."

"He hasn't listened to me for a year or better." John raked a hand across his jaw. As far as he knew, Carl had not replied to his parents' summons, sent some six weeks prior. "Nor our father."

"You were once close, right?"

John grunted. "It's been a while."

"Look, I know you'll want to go home for a furlough at least. Why not talk also to Carl?"

The idea had merit.

"You're fighting for your country," Ben added. "Isn't your brother worth fighting for as well?"

John drew his shoulders back. "I am a simple soldier, Ben. I can wage but one battle at a time."

"Then leave the war's battles behind when you go to Boston." Ben adjusted his hat closer to his forehead. "Take them up again when you return."

Long after Ben left, John pondered his suggestion. Then he put on his soggy hat and left in search of captain.

~

*A*nnie rode with Beatrice and their father to the train station. "I put two wool blankets, sheets, and towels in Will's bag."

"Thanks, Annie." Beatrice sank against the cushioned seat of their closed carriage used for ill weather and night travel.

"Tom offered to go to the grocery and purchase a generous supply of beef jerky and coffee." Annie met her father's troubled gaze. "He brought back enough to last Will a month or two. Along with a tin cup. He said it's also useful for cooking food like soup over an open flame in army camps."

"I imagine guards bring prepared meals to prisoners. They likely treat officers better than enlisted men."

"No doubt Will had to leave possessions behind. Tom also purchased a knapsack for his clothes, a haversack for his food, and a canteen."

"Very good." Father nodded. "I do not know how well they feed him. That beef jerky will restore his strength. Please thank Tom for me."

"I will." Annie was glad they had pleased him.

Her sister said, "It was difficult to think clearly this afternoon. Such a whirlwind of activity it has been. Why, I hardly know if I pinned on my hat properly." Beatrice gave the brim of her blue felt hat a gentle tug. "No, it's snug. It was difficult to decide what to pack."

"This isn't a social visit, Bea." He rubbed his forehead. "Our primary purpose is to comfort your brother."

"Sorry I couldn't help you decide on the clothing to take." Annie felt sorry for her sister. Lantern light outside the windows showed Beatrice's crestfallen look at Father's mild reprimand. "I gathered lye soap, a shaving mug and brush, and clothes from Will's old wardrobe before working in the kitchen with Rebecca. She baked him a batch of lemon cookies and an apple pie. I made his favorite almond cake. There's enough for both of you."

Beatrice reached for her hand. "Thank you. And I'm sorry."

It was the first time she'd referred to their argument all week. Was she sorry for saying that she supported the Southern cause because of Will's involvement, or did she apologize for her comments about Annie's future husband? Either way, this wasn't the moment to question her. She only wanted to heal the rift between them. Annie's fingers tightened around her sister's. "I know." She didn't want the harsh words to stand between them along with the miles.

"What's this? Is there some problem I need to be aware of?" Father frowned. "You don't resent your sister going without you, do you, Annie?"

Her resentment had stemmed from Bea's comments about John. "I merely wish to come along."

"You're needed at home." He raised the shade. Dim light from a street lamp illuminated the strain on his face. "Besides, your young man will likely escort you to church in our absence."

"Yes." Annie's face grew warm. "I don't want to miss his visit."

"Please give him our regrets without informing him of our mission."

Annie's heartbeat quickened. Her father denied her the comfort of telling John.

He peered out into the darkness. "It doesn't appear the rain is heavy enough to affect our travel."

Annie suddenly dreaded their leaving. "You will let me know of your safe arrival in New York City?"

"Of course." He patted her arm. "I'll send telegrams of news that cannot wait. Otherwise, expect letters from your sister at regular intervals."

"Thank you. Please give Will my love."

"And mine." Beatrice reached for Annie's hand again.

"I will." Father gave them a tired smile. "Your brother knows you both worry for him."

"I'll pray that you may visit him immediately." Annie worried about her father's exhaustion.

"As we all will." He stifled a yawn. "Forgive my ill manners, my daughters. It's been an exhausting day. Bea, there were no sleeping quarters available in this train. I didn't like to delay our trip until tomorrow in order to wait for another one. If you don't mind, I will sleep in my seat."

"Not at all." She exchanged a worried glance with Annie. "You've earned the rest."

"Yes, Father, please rest as much as possible. Both of you." Annie sensed the weight of all her father faced in the drooping of his shoulders. "I will pray for you both, and, as always, Will."

It was too late to say more. They had arrived at the depot.

CHAPTER 30

"Sorry to bother you so late, Captain." John had waited for his superior to return to his quarters for half an hour.

"It must be important, Sergeant-Major Finn, to wait for me past *Taps*." The officer shook droplets from his felt hat and tossed it on a cot just like John's. In fact, this rough cabin was the same size as the one he shared with three other officers. There was only one cot here. A stack of papers cluttered a field desk. Otherwise, the table with a bowl and pitcher and lantern were the same. "What is it?"

"I've received a telegram from my mam." He gave it to his captain. "My da has suffered apoplexy."

"Sorry to hear it, John." He scanned the page. "She wants you to resign. That why you're here?"

"No, sir." John gently pocketed the limp telegram. "That is her request, not mine."

"Good." His shoulders relaxed. "I didn't want to remind you of your commitment. The regiment needs your experience."

"Thank you, sir. It's an honor to serve with you and the Irish Ninth."

"So, you're here to request a furlough?"

"For one month, sir." He nodded. "It will take that long to understand my father's condition and arrange for his care. I also want to see that our family business is in good heart. I must find someone to step in until Father recovers or my brother accepts the reins."

"I see." The captain rubbed his bearded chin. "When do you want to leave?"

"I hope to leave at dawn."

"Let me speak to the colonel. We will inform you of our decision."

John had expected an immediate answer but thanked him and saluted. Walking back to his quarters in the drizzle, his mind raced with preparations to be made upon receiving his furlough papers.

Not the least was seeing Annie. He'd stop by her home on the way to purchase his train ticket and deliver his latest report —potentially his last report because he'd be in Boston for weeks —to Christopher.

Restlessness overtook him. He walked to the edge of the tree line and looked out over the dark valley. His country's enemies were within a couple of miles of their picket line.

If Annie's father was spying on the Union, then he must be counted an enemy as well.

The toe of his leather shoe dragged in the mud. Hiram's views were bound to be affected by his son's service to the Confederacy.

Certainly, John had seen evidence to support his Southern sympathies. After all, the banker spent the first twenty years of his life in Richmond. The man acted as a Southern gentleman at all times, with a pleasant hint of a drawl. Annie had said that his family still lived in Virginia. It made sense that he didn't want to go to war with loved ones on the opposing side, especially his own son.

Did it go deeper? Did Hiram spy on Union officers and government officials who attended soirees in his home?

He owed it to Christopher, to his country, to reason this out.

Too agitated to keep still, John walked along the tree line away from camp in the drizzle though mindful to stay inside the area under guard by their pickets. Conversations at West Point with Will hadn't usually turned serious, but they had spoken of slavery on occasion. Will's mother had been an abolitionist, and her views had affected her husband and children.

Yet Hiram seemed to sympathize with the South's plight.

Recollections of Hiram pressing John for details of his own regiment's activities gave him pause. Officers who believed themselves in the home of a staunch Union supporter were not always mindful of their words. Annie had said as much.

John had witnessed Hiram's sharp interest in military comments. John wanted to believe it was mere curiosity.

Yet there was evidence to the contrary.

Such as his connection to Rose Greenhow. If newspaper articles and rumors were true, evidence against her mounted. A widow who lived four blocks from the President's House was guilty of spying for the Confederacy. Hiram's wife had been her friend. His daughters held her in esteem. Hiram may have been her banker in the past.

Not enough to convict him of wrongdoing.

If he was still her banker, he'd be aware of money going in and out of the widow's account. John had no way of knowing if the activity was enough to raise an alert...*if* the widow still had money on deposit at Hiram's bank.

Widow Greenhow had been at several soirees where Hiram had private conversations with her. That didn't mean anything illegal had happened.

Other neighbors who knew them suspected nothing because their behavior didn't change when Hiram talked with the widow. Not even a raised eyebrow on the part of a neighbor.

John's searches of his study uncovered nothing that hinted at spying.

Besides, any smear of blame on Hiram Swanson would attach itself to his daughters under the whiplash of a gossiper's tongue. His chest tightened to think how his sweet Annie might suffer. How devastated she'd be if her adored father was arrested as a spy. Even if she discovered John's part in the treachery and never wanted to speak to him, a severed relationship between her and her father was not what he wanted.

Yet he must tell Christopher all he knew. He gripped a low-hanging branch and rested his forehead against the damp bark. The duty belonged to him.

He'd spied on Hiram to clear his name and discovered enough to warrant concern, but no tangible evidence. Perhaps the wisest course would be to write of his observations and allow the authorities to determine Hiram Swanson's innocence.

Yet this man was to be his future father-in-law.

Sweat mingled with rain on his face as he folded his hands in prayer that he still might marry Annie.

The government was interested in discerning the banker's loyalty. When John spoke to Christopher, he would include that the savvy businessman had a compassionate heart. He was a grieving widower who loved his children.

John turned back toward camp to pack for his furlough and then write his report for Christopher.

He drew comfort knowing Annie would never know what he'd done.

~

*A*nnie arose the next morning to a gray dawn. No sunrise, but it had stopped raining. She sighed. One must accept small blessings at times like these.

She washed and dressed herself before Donna arrived to

help her with the buttons on her dress. Then she went down to the kitchen and sniffed. Biscuits and bacon.

"Do you mind if I eat my breakfast in here this morning?"

"Sure don't." Rebecca hugged her. "Child, you look like you was run over by that train your family took last night."

"I feel like it." Annie didn't mind Rebecca's plain speaking. Her honesty was a refreshing gift. "I hope Father and Beatrice were able to sleep."

Rebecca looked out the window. "Might be they're still sleeping."

"Thank you for packing meals for them." Warmth rose in her cheeks. "You were more thoughtful than I was yesterday."

"You had plenty enough on your mind." Bacon sizzled in a skillet. "Everything is easier to take on a full stomach."

"Sandwiches. Cheese and crackers. Cookies. You gave them food that's easy to eat while traveling." Annie sank into a spindle-backed chair. "I was so involved in baking for Will that I didn't spare a thought for the needs of Bea and Father."

"Don't fret none." Rebecca took a pan of biscuits from the oven.

The scent of them whetted her appetite.

"You all have a lot to contend with," Rebecca added. "No need to make things worse by jumping on each other for stuff that don't matter."

Annie had wondered if she noticed the rift between her and her sister. What Beatrice said still had the power to slice away at Annie's confidence in John. It was a good thing she was certain of their feelings for one another.

"Hope you don't mind a simple breakfast." Rebecca set a loaded plate in front of her.

"It's perfect. Thanks." Annie reached for a slice of bacon. "I almost wish that sewing group was meeting on Saturdays to give me something else to think about."

"If you ask me, what you need is a day of rest." Rebecca

patted her shoulder and then moved to the sink basin. "Yesterday was a whirlwind."

A couple of hours to herself held a certain appeal. "Perhaps I will go back to my room for a while." She ate the rest of her meal in silence and pushed back from the table. "Come for me if someone calls. Father said that Mr. Tomlinson may require my assistance while he's gone."

"I'll tell Mr. Grant. Get some sleep now."

Annie trudged upstairs. She had fallen asleep praying for her family's safety and John last night. Father had asked her not to reveal to him the nature of their New York trip. Their conversation might not go exactly that way.

It went against the grain to disregard her father's wishes. However, Annie's very soul screamed to release Will's secret.

It was time John learned what happened to his friend.

CHAPTER 31

*J*ohn bid Patrick good-bye and then strode toward the Beets farm. Two weeks of furlough had been granted when he'd requested a month. Sighing, he acknowledged it might have been denied completely. Best accept what he was given.

It was an hour past sunrise. No doubt Zach was already milking the cows and feeding the chickens and such. John, having never lived on a farm, knew little of the work it demanded.

Asking a favor of the family was going to cost him. He had all his money with him, and it needed to get him as far as home.

He strode up the dirt path leading to the Beets homestead. A dog barked. They didn't expect him and especially not this early on a Saturday. "Good morning," he called out. "Zach, are you here? It's Sergeant-Major John."

The boy, wiping the back of his hand across his mouth, stepped out of the house with his mother behind him. "Didn't expect you 'til tomorrow. You need Moonbeam today too?"

"Morning, Mrs. Beets. Zach." He halted at the bottom of the porch steps.

"Good morning, Sergeant-Major Finn." She folded her arms across her bib apron.

"Forgive me for calling so early." John figured it was best to get right to the point. "My father is ill."

"Sorry to hear that." She inclined her head to the side, eyes crinkling in concern.

"I've been granted a furlough of two weeks. I need a ride into town."

She exchanged a look with Zach.

"I've been renting your mare. Still got about three weeks left that I already paid for." John looked at Zach's furrowed brow. The lad was likely figuring how he could make the most money possible from this unexpected occurrence. "There's a couple of ways we can do this."

"I'm listening." The boy leaned against a porch post badly in need of a coat of paint.

"You can drive me to town in your wagon, and I'll pay you five dollars for the ride."

Zach's eyes widened. "What's the other way?"

"I ride Moonbeam into Washington City, stable the horse near the depot for two weeks, bring the mare back here, and pay you eight dollars." That was his preference, but it wasn't his horse.

Zach exchanged a look with his mom. "The eight dollars is extra, on top of what you already paid us for September?"

"Aye."

"We'll take the eight dollars." Mrs. Beets extended her hand, palm up. "We'll expect the horse back in two weeks. If you're a day late, it's an extra dollar."

"Agreed." John extracted the bills from his pocket. "Much obliged. I'll saddle up Moonbeam."

"Thank you." A tear shone in the mother's eyes as she stared at the bills. "Oh, and, Sergeant-Major Finn."

John, nearly to the barn, turned back.

"I will say a prayer for your father."

His heart softened toward the family determined to make every possible penny off him. War wasn't easy on anyone. "That'll be grand."

They were back inside when John led Moonbeam from the barn a few minutes later, presumably to finish breakfast. He'd buy breakfast in Washington City if Annie wasn't home, but he didn't want to lose a moment with her. If she was out, he'd buy his train ticket and then return in the hopes that she had returned while he was gone.

Maybe today she'd trust him enough to tell him about Will.

❧

*A*nnie awoke with a guilty start for sleeping comfortably while Will slept in a prison.

She whispered another prayer for her family and then made a face at her brown dress, as wrinkled as if she were the one sleeping on a train.

Pushing her gloomy reflections aside, she changed into a peach sateen dress, wondering how to fill her day. If only she had a distraction.

Her eyes fell on white fabric folded and tucked into a basket on the floor. There'd been little time to complete little night-gowns for her nephew or niece. She'd do that in the upstairs family sitting room. The main floor drawing room that Beatrice preferred was too vast and empty without her.

A knock on her bedroom door. "Come in."

Donna stepped inside. "It's good to see you awake, Miss Annie. A certain Sergeant-Major Finn is here to see you."

"On a Saturday morning?" Annie covered her suddenly warm face with her hands. "Oh, but my hair—"

"I'll help you, Miss Annie, after asking Mr. Grant to have him wait in the drawing room."

226

"No, Donna." The maid turned back. "The family sitting room, please. Not the drawing room. I'm missing my sister this morning."

"Of course. I'll return shortly."

Annie threw back the lacy curtains. The gloom outside no longer penetrated inside her bedroom.

Joy bubbled up, warming her heart. John was there.

~

ohn looked at the mantle for the third time in two minutes. Ten o'clock. He'd arrived half an hour earlier and changed his uniform in the stable. He imagined that he had awakened Annie. There'd been no sign of the rest of the family. After penning what he hoped was his final report, it would be difficult to greet the home's owner with a pretense of normalcy.

Even the butler was absent. A pity, for now he didn't need to sneak into the study. He patted the coat pocket holding his report for Christopher. Feeling only fabric, he patted it again. Ah, it was in his knapsack he'd left with his horse. Good. It seemed almost blasphemous to have the pages inside this house.

Nothing was as it should be these days. Except Annie.

Crossing his hands behind his back, he stood before a clean hearth as he might if a fire burned there. Perhaps he should have purchased his ticket and dropped his report off at Christopher's boarding house first. Time was short, and so was his furlough.

"Good morning, John."

He spun, Annie's soft voice and sweet smile bringing him back to earth and taking him to Heaven on angel's wings. "Annie, 'tis good of you to rearrange your morning. 'Tis hopeful I am that it was not a great sacrifice."

"Silly. You and your Irish brogue. How it does things to my

heart." She laughed. "There's no question of rearranging my schedule for you. You must have left camp early. Did you eat breakfast?"

He hadn't, but it no longer seemed important. "'Tis lovely you look in that orange dress."

She giggled. "It's more the color of a peach than an orange, but I thank you for the compliment, kind sir."

He gave her an exaggerated bow. His heart lightened with her teasing. Seeing her was like a breath of spring air after his anxious night.

"Sit with me." She sat on a sofa and patted the cushion beside her. "Did army business bring you here?"

His heart plummeted again. How he wished this were a simple social call on the woman of his dreams. "I have news."

"Tell me." Her face paled.

He quickly gave her the details he knew, including his mother's request. He clasped her cold hand. "I'm going there to make different arrangements."

She looked away.

"Ye know my heart is not in building furniture."

"I know. You dream of following the rails westward."

She understood him. No wonder she commanded such a hold on his heart. "What a lovely way with words you have. That's my heart's desire exactly. Save one thing you neglected to mention."

Pink infused her cheeks.

The time wasn't exactly right, not with the worry of reporting about her father on his back. But he couldn't wait another moment. "In my dreams you are beside me. As my wife."

∾

"*I*s that a proposal, Sergeant-Major John Finn?" Her heart told her it was, but she'd been wrong before.

"No. This is." Clasping her hand, he dropped to one knee. The teasing light in his green eyes was replaced by a new intensity. "Miss Annie Swanson. Will ye do me the sweet honor of becoming me wife?"

"Oh, John." Her heart swelled with love. "I will."

"Ye will?"

She nodded, marveling at the wonder on his face.

"Ye have made me the happiest of men." He stood and enfolded her in his arms. He bent slowly, his eyes on hers. Then his gaze dropped to her mouth. He kissed her. Once. Twice. A third, leisurely kiss that stole her breath. "I love you, Annie Swanson."

Those were the words she'd longed to hear. This was the sweet proposal her heart had craved. "I love you, Sergeant Major Finn."

"'Tis music to me ears." His eyes lightened. "Ye love me." He clasped her close to his fast-beating heart. "Usually, Bea or Rebecca shows up about now with a cup of tea and a plate of cookies to act the chaperone."

Will.

Annie shifted in his arms. "Bea isn't here. Neither is Father."

"I expected your father to be at the bank, but where is your sister?" He removed his arms and scooted a few inches away.

Staring into each other's eyes, they sat on the comfortable sofa.

Annie shifted and smoothed her dress. This man was to be her husband. All the more reason to eliminate the secret between them. She tucked her hand inside the warmth of his. "They will soon arrive in New York City."

He raised his eyebrows.

"It's a long story." She took a deep breath. "It's time you

learned the truth. About Will."

~

*W*hen Annie rose and crossed to the window overlooking the garden, John followed. "Tell me."

"He…he didn't muster into the Union army as you did. He chose to serve the Confederate army." Her fingers trembled. "He's in the Seventeenth North Carolina regiment."

John closed his eyes, grateful she had finally trusted him. He must choose his words carefully and not reveal his prior knowledge. "Were you as shocked as I to discover it?" A horse's kick to the stomach better described his original astonishment.

"I feel he betrayed our family, our country. I had no notion how to answer inquiries by friends." She peeked at him and then half turned away. "I felt that you, as Will's friend, had a right to know. Father made us promise to tell no one."

"I understand his position."

"John, you are too good to me." She turned back to him. "But there is worse news. Brace yourself."

He clasped her hand to his heart, dreading the need to maintain the pretense.

"Will's regiment was stationed at Hatteras Inlet. Remember the recent battle where two Confederate forts were captured? Fort Clark and Fort Hatteras?"

A brief nod. Oh, yes. He remembered.

"Will was there. He's been captured." Her whole body shook.

"My dearest Annie." He drew her close, and she rested her head against his chest. "How I wish I could rescue him and all of you from this trouble."

"Father searched for him and finally learned that the very ships that fired upon his fort carried nearly an entire Confederate regiment to Governors Island."

"In New York Harbor. Which is why Hiram and Beatrice are

in New York City."

"Yes." Her voice was muffled against his coat. "To find him. Father wants to negotiate his release."

"Unlikely for a civilian to be able to negotiate that." He led her to the sofa and sat beside her. "However, the army has a system for an exchange of prisoners. A Union captain for a Confederate captain. A lieutenant for a lieutenant. A private for a private."

"To return home?"

"Yes."

"That's wonderful." Her face brightened. "My brother will be exchanged for a Union officer of equal rank."

"There's also a possibility of parole. If paroled, they'll force Will to promise not to take up arms against the Union until he is formally exchanged for an officer of equal rank."

"I feel as if a weight has fallen from my shoulders." Her hands trembled. "I should have told you immediately so you could explain it to Father."

"It may not happen quickly." Looking into her beautiful eyes, John clasped her hand to his chest.

Her brow furrowed.

"Some seven hundred men became prisoners that day. It may take months for them all to be paroled or exchanged. Your brother will be in prison for some time." He hated to see the glow fade from her eyes.

There was another possible avenue for Will. Swearing an oath of allegiance to the Union provided a way for him to return to his wife and their plantation, perhaps to be there for the birth of his first child. If only someone could convince him. Perhaps the words of Will's father would sway him.

Best not to mention that possibility to Annie. He didn't cherish the idea of dashing her hopes again.

Footsteps stopped outside the door. He released her hand and stood as it opened.

CHAPTER 32

*R*ebecca brought in a tray of tea and a plate of lemon cookies. "Why, Miss Annie, what's troubling you?"

"I told John about Will."

The cook drew in her breath. "Mr. Swanson won't be pleased."

"I know." Annie's gaze dropped to her hands. "May I speak with you in private, please?"

"Of course." Rebecca poured two cups of tea. "Sergeant-Major Finn, please help yourself to tea and cookies. You must be parched."

More than he could say. "Thank you, Rebecca."

"I need only a moment," Annie said. "Please excuse my rudeness."

"Not rude at all. These are trying times for everyone."

The women hurried away. John wondered which news took precedent—their engagement or her brother's possible exchange and parole. Trying times, indeed.

He hated himself for not being as honest with her as she was with him. He'd agonized over each word in his report. In the darkness of night, he'd scrutinized each sentence to make certain it was reported accurately.

He raked his fingers through his thick mane.

Aye, the weight of what he'd written grew heavier as he contemplated the possible outcome. What if Christopher and General Winfield Scott didn't agree with John's assessment that there was not enough evidence Hiram Swanson was a Confederate spy?

Rather than showing there was no hard evidence of wrong-doing, John's report instead might be the proof used against Hiram. A man fighting to free his son from prison camp didn't need to wage another battle for his own freedom.

He clenched his fists. In his mind's eye, he read his words again as if they were a serpent poised to strike at his future father-in-law.

Words could be misconstrued. Taken out of context. His letter might be used to place him behind bars.

Not worth the risk.

He wouldn't show the report to Christopher. Instead he'd make certain to measure his words when talking with Christopher, while still being honest.

The report must be destroyed before it destroyed the life of a good man. Should he burn it here? He strode to the wood stove in the corner. His pocket was empty. That's right. He'd moved it to his knapsack while changing in the stable. He'd take it with him to Boston and burn it at home.

He gave a guilty start as the parlor door swung open.

~

"*A*re you cold, John?"

Annie had been bursting to tell someone her good news and made certain to be gone only a minute or two. Bea was always her first choice and she regretted the inability to tell her sister immediately. Under normal circumstances, she'd have waited with her mother while John spoke privately with her father. A stem of grief for mother melted with a new realization.

Strange that John hadn't mentioned obtaining Father's permission. No matter. It was a mere formality since she knew her father held John in high regard.

No man courted Hiram Swanson's daughters unless he did.

The men could speak when Father returned from New York and John returned from Boston. Two weeks...a long time to keep this secret to herself. A happy secret for once. She'd seek out Rebecca, who was already sworn to secrecy, and explain they'd wait to share the news.

"A mite chilled." John's face reddened. "I considered building a fire."

"I'll help." She started toward him.

"Nay, I'm fine without it."

"If you're certain." She sat and arranged her skirt. John barely looked at her when he sat by her side. Strange. There was no denying his love, his passion for her. His cup of tea sat nearly untouched. "You didn't drink your tea."

"I'm parched so I'll drink it now." He upended the cup until it was empty. "We worked all day yesterday in the rain, and it was still drizzling last night. I was soaked to the skin."

"I hope you don't catch a cold, working outside in such weather." Something was wrong. He still wasn't looking at her.

"Winter will be worse. Snow. Icy winds." He ate a lemon cookie in one bite.

"It chills me to think of it." She poured him another cup of steaming tea and then served herself.

"Being out in all kinds of weather trains us to endure it." He munched on another cookie before sipping his tea.

Did she imagine that he avoided her eyes? Then she blushed. Their kisses ended shortly before Rebecca's arrival. He granted her a moment to compose herself.

"What are your plans for today?" He sank back onto the sofa beside her.

"To spend it with my betrothed."

"'Tis good to hear that word from your lips." He gulped down the tea. "I must purchase a train ticket. I'll return and remain with you until departure time nears."

Anticipation of a day with him filled her with joy. "I'll get my shawl and accompany you."

"No."

His abrupt tone halted her mid-step to the door.

"I have a short meeting with an army officer before I leave. It won't take long." He reached for another cookie without looking up.

She frowned. "You said your regiment's camp is outside the city. Who will you meet inside Washington City?"

"Army business that I'm anxious to end. Then I will return to you." Another cookie.

"Did you eat breakfast?"

He flushed. "As a matter of fact, I didn't have that opportunity."

"Rebecca probably has biscuits—"

"No, please don't bother her. I'll just go and return for luncheon, if I may?"

"Of course." Their time together was so short. She wouldn't see him for two weeks. "I can wait outside the office while you meet with the army official."

"No." He held up his hand. "It's quicker to go by myself."

"All right." She didn't understand the importance of going alone. Admittedly, she had a lot to learn about the army. Then she blushed. She'd soon know as much as he wanted to tell her. "I'll wait for you."

"Those words are beautiful music to my ears, my sweet Annie." He took her in his arms and kissed her. "You are more precious to me than my humble words can express. 'Tis blessed

I am that you'll be my wife."

His words touched a chord deep inside. "How wonderful to love and be loved by you, John. Our life together will be an adventure."

"Aye. A grand adventure. I'll speak to your father when next we meet. Good fortune may smile upon us and send us both to Washington City at the same time." He kissed her once more and then stepped away with seeming reluctance. "I must go. Don't worry. I'll not tarry."

"You'd better not," she teased. "I miss you already."

He chuckled. "Good bye, sweet Annie. I'll hurry back to you."

CHAPTER 33

*J*ohn trotted to the depot and purchased his ticket, pleased that his train departure at seven that evening gave him several hours with Annie.

No matter what happened, he must not bind his future to the drudgery that awaited him in Boston. He'd find a different solution for his family's problems.

Pocketing his ticket, he rode toward Christopher's boarding house. Shame burned him at the report nestled in his knapsack. He'd talk to Christopher in person instead of leaving him the written evaluation he'd penned in the pre-dawn hours.

Guilt sat heavily on his chest for even writing the treacherous words. Thankfully, Annie suspected nothing.

A dunderhead like him didn't deserve such a fine woman. Nay, he'd spend the rest of his life trying to be worthy of her.

John dismounted outside Christopher's boarding house at half-past eleven. He whistled. Dinner at Annie's was in an hour. Best make this quick.

Once inside, the owner directed him to the room Christopher rented.

He knew the way. Four flights of stairs. First door on the right.

"Sergeant-Major Finn. Just as I expected." Christopher widened the door. "Come in."

John raised an eyebrow. This wasn't a planned meeting. Christopher's words were meant for someone else's ears. Whose? "Lieutenant Farmer." He took his cue from the officer. "Thank you for seeing me." The door closed behind him to reveal a small bachelor's quarters sparsely furnished with a bed, desk, table, chest, wardrobe, and two chairs.

"I didn't expect you, of course, but my landlord does tend to keep an ear to what his tenants are doing." Speaking in low tones, he gestured to a spindle-backed chair. "We haven't talked for a while. I wondered if you avoided me."

"Avoidance has no part of this delay. The captain has curtailed me to one day weekly away from camp."

"I see."

John bristled at his disbelieving tone. "And you are not the easiest person to locate on a Sunday evening."

"My apologies. What have you to report?"

"I learned today that Hiram Swanson and Miss Beatrice Swanson are in New York City seeking an audience with his son." John, though he'd rather stay standing and take his leave quickly, finally sat. "Annie finally confessed that Will's a Confederate officer and a prisoner of war."

"General Scott learned that Lieutenant Swanson was among those prisoners taken to Governors Island." He nodded as he sat in the chair beside his desk. "How are the Swansons taking this news?"

"They're devastated. Worried."

"Understandable." Christopher folded his hands. "Did you uncover any evidence that Hiram Swanson is a Confederate spy?"

"No hard evidence." John straightened his back. "Searches of

Hiram's study didn't bear fruit. As I reported earlier, there were no cyphered messages."

"Any maps hidden in a drawer?"

"None."

"Did you find sketches of Union forts?"

"Nay. An excessive curiosity and attentiveness to all military conversations is the most I can charge him with."

"Did Mr. Swanson ask you about your location, or officers in your regiment, or specific numbers of troops?"

"Aye." Wait. That was more than one question. "Mr. Swanson tried to discover my location. He asked me to invite Colonel Cass, my commanding officer, to the first soiree I attended. The colonel couldn't attend and it wasn't mentioned again."

"Your location?" Christopher's brow furrowed.

"He tried to discover the location of our camp. I believe I mentioned that to you."

"I recall that." He nodded. "Any concerns that he aided Mrs. Greenhow's spying efforts? Supplied her with information?"

"I can't prove either. They spoke privately on occasion and seemed to hold one another in esteem." Heat surged up John's cheeks. "'Tis sorry I am that I didn't notice the widow's treachery. After her arrest, I pondered what I'd observed of her actions. Her friendly manner to officers and private conversations with undersecretaries should have alerted me."

"Yes, we suspected some information was coming from those parties. Widow Greenhow has been vocal in her support of the Confederacy."

"Not to me." John frowned in thought. "I was introduced to her but had no private conversations with her. I concentrated on Mr. Swanson's activities."

"The widow's associates are being investigated. Nothing has led to Hiram Swanson." Christopher tapped his fingers on his desk. "Perhaps the widow was the main culprit at those soirees after all."

"It may be worth investigating those undersecretaries who spoke with her in quiet corners." John was cheered to hear Christopher hadn't found anything to incriminate Annie's father. Maybe this nightmare was ending.

"We are. You provided those names."

"Aye." John looked at the blank page on Christopher's desk, happy to see that he hadn't written any notes from today's meeting. It made him feel better about his decision not to give a written report.

"You understand why we scrutinized his activities."

"Aye. I had my own suspicions." John was duty-bound to admit it.

"Not anymore? Did Hiram—or his daughters—give you reason to suspect them of supporting her spying activities?"

"Nay." Christopher wasn't dragging Annie into his suspicions. "I'll not deny that some guests spoke too freely to other guests. Perhaps to Mrs. Greenhow herself, though I have no direct knowledge of it." John straightened his back. "I've spent much time with Miss Annie Swanson and will vouch that her loyalties are bound to the Union."

"A spirited defense indeed." Christopher sank back in his seat. "Is Hiram Swanson a Southern sympathizer?"

Would that hurt his future father-in-law to admit? "The man's son fights for the Confederacy. He was born in Richmond and raised in the South. He cannot enjoy this conflict with folks so recently our countrymen." He prayed his answers didn't damage a good man's name and reputation. "Are we finished with this task?"

"Yes, you've done your country a great service." Christopher studied him. "We know you're courting Annie. Your feelings seem to be genuine."

"Aye." Sweat beaded on his forehead.

"Spying on her father can't have been easy."

"Nay." It had been the most difficult service he could render his country. John rose to his feet, his emotions spent.

"Thank you, John. I believe you gave an honest evaluation." Christopher stood. "By the way, what brings you to Washington City on a Saturday?"

He told Christopher of his da's illness. John believed, under other circumstances, the two of them could have been friends. As matters stood, he preferred never to lay eyes on the man again.

"No need to report to me again." Christopher extended his hand. "But I trust that, should you learn something that needs to be reported, you will contact me."

"Should we meet again, I pray it's under other conditions. With all this unpleasantness behind us."

"We're in agreement on that point." Christopher nodded as he ushered him out.

A weight lifted from John's back. One unwanted responsibility was gone. Tomorrow, he'd be in Boston with his family. He prayed they didn't replace the unwelcome responsibility he'd just shed with a new one.

CHAPTER 34

*A*nnie awaited John's return at the drawing room window, both her mother's and Bea's favorite parlor. He was ten minutes late for their meal. Purchasing a train ticket was accomplished in a matter of minutes, so the reason for his tardiness had to be his meeting.

With an army official. What was that about? He hadn't explained, and she'd been too euphoric from his marriage proposal—and his kisses—to ponder it.

Hurry, John. We have such a short time together before you leave for Boston.

Restlessness drove her from the room. Her butler hurried over from the hall where he'd no doubt been waiting to admit John. "Mr. Grant, I prefer to wait in my sitting room upstairs. Will you call for me when Sergeant-Major Finn arrives?" Her betrothed, she thought with a blush. "Since our meal is ready, I'll come down immediately."

"Very good, Miss Annie." He handed her a sealed letter. "Tom found this after Sergeant-Major Finn left and believes it belonged to the officer."

"I'll give it to him. Thank you."

Back upstairs, she stared out the window that provided a glimpse of the avenue. No sign of him yet. She stared at the sealed pages in her hand. No address or writing on the outside. Another look out the window. Not here yet.

She hoped to drive along the beautiful Potomac River after they dined, no doubt a romantic ride with one's betrothed even in daylight.

Annie stared back down at the letter. What was in it? It might not belong to John. She'd best check it. Besides, the only secrets her fiancé kept from her were military ones. She'd close it immediately if that was inside. She broke the wax seal. What...?

John's handwriting.

In my surveillance of Hiram Swanson—

Annie drew back. Surveillance. Did he mean to say spying? On her *father?*

Chunks of ice gathered in her core. No, it couldn't be. There was another explanation.

In my surveillance of Hiram Swanson at the request of General Winfield Scott and Lieutenant Christopher Farmer—

Her heart skipped a beat and then thundered in her chest. General Winfield Scott, the Commander of the Federal army, had asked John to spy on her law-abiding father? It made no sense.

I have found no hard evidence to support your suspicions that Mr. Swanson is a spy for the Confederacy. His family has a connection to Mrs. Rose Greenhow, the Washington City citizen who is being investigated for spying on our government and military officials in order to supply secret information to the Confederacy. Mr. Swanson is undoubtedly sympathetic to her plight due to his deceased wife's friendship with her, yet I've witnessed nothing beyond a few private conversations between him and the widow, all of short duration. She is a family friend—"

The pages fluttered to the floor. If she hadn't recognized John's handwriting, she'd believe someone played a terrible trick on them.

Her vision blurred at John's treachery. Her heart felt encased in ice as she stared in horror at the pages that fell print side down.

What else had he written about her father and Mrs. Greenhow? Did John mean to persecute the poor woman who had suffered enough, even if proven guilty?

No matter. What she'd read was enough.

John wasn't the man she'd thought him to be.

She'd considered him honorable. Trustworthy. Her future husband. The man of her dreams.

A derisive sound gurgled in her throat. More a nightmare than a dream. Father had been right to caution her against telling John about Will.

Now, not only did he know that his West Point roommate was a Confederate officer, but also that he'd been captured. Then the man had had the gall to propose after spying on her father.

Where she'd been ice cold moments earlier, her face burned as hot as a blaze.

Ah, the meeting John attended at this very moment with this Lieutenant Farmer...perhaps with General Winfield Scott himself.

John had betrayed her, her father. Indeed, her entire family would suffer from the blow he dealt.

Everything had been a lie. John had courted her in order to discover whether her father was a Confederate spy. For how long? Had he betrayed her from the outset? Their chance meeting on the avenue that first afternoon might have been part of the plan to deceive them and not a coincidence at all.

She dashed away the tears on her cheeks. He wasn't worthy of them.

At a knock on the door, she snapped, "Enter." Her tone sounded harsh to her own ears.

~

"Sergeant-Major Finn, Miss Annie. He asked to escort you to the dining room." Mr. Grant opened the door wider.

John thanked him and stepped inside. Mr. Grant closed the door behind him, perhaps surmising rightly that he desired a moment alone with her.

Annie, her back as straight as a bayonet, stood with her back to him with pages littering the floor. "Annie?"

She turned around, her face red and splotchy. Tears glistened in her brown eyes. She snatched the pages from the floor and flung them at him. "Why, John? Tell me why you spied on my father? A man as honest as you are treacherous."

He picked them up, his heart shrinking at the look of betrayal in her eyes. His report. But how... *No. Not now that I've finally dispensed with the task and the guilt of spying on friends.* "Annie. Me sweet Annie, please underst—"

"Courting me was only a means to an end."

"Nay! It was never that. Me feelings for you are deep and true—"

"They can't be." She shook her head. "Or you'd never have agreed to General Scott's scheme."

A lightning bolt could not have struck with more force. She knew General Scott was behind his spying. "How much did you read?"

"Only that you spied on my father and Mrs. Greenhow's conversations." She spat the words. "I don't care what other lies you've written."

"I did it to protect ye. Twas intolerable to see the name of a good, honorable man besmirched—"

"Honor? What do you know of honor?" She pointed to his report. "Even if you courted me to gain access to my father, it sinks to a new level of treachery that you proposed to me while performing your evil deed."

Her tone sliced through him like winter sleet. Every instinct had warned him to wait until this mess was behind him to propose. "Aye. I'm guilty of an evil deed."

She gasped.

"Guilt has eaten away at me since I..." The words caught in his throat at her forlorn look. He took a step forward.

Hands shaking, she backed into the wall.

Dare he tell her all? That he did it to free her father of suspicion. That Christopher would have assigned the task to someone else, someone who might have misconstrued innocent actions and comments, placing on them a sinister cast. No, it wasn't his secret to tell...not during war. He'd been at West Point long enough to appreciate his duty.

"Some truths are not mine to reveal. Please trust that I'd tell you if I could."

"Why should I trust you now when you've proven yourself unworthy of even friendship with my family?"

John hung his head. He was not sorry that, if the deed had to be done, someone who loved the family had done it. His heart broke that his actions had destroyed Annie's faith in him.

"It's time for you to leave."

"Aye. 'Tis that." He'd broken the heart of the woman he'd have died to protect. There was no going back now. "Ye must believe..."

She raised her chin.

"Nay. Of course. Ye cannot believe me now." He turned away. Halted at the door. "'Tis sorry I am to have broken your heart. Me will regret it to my dying day." He didn't profess his love one last time. She would not believe anything he said.

And he bore the shame of it as he walked away.

She said nothing to stop him.

He left, leaving his heart behind him.

CHAPTER 35

*A*nnie listened to John's halting footsteps take him down the winding stairs. As if he tarried to give her an opportunity to stop his exit.

Stopping him was the last thing she wanted to do. In fact, if she saw him again a decade from now, it would be too soon.

The heavy front door latched closed. He was gone.

She ran to the window, waiting for one final glimpse of the man who had been her betrothed for one morning only. Too short a betrothal to ever mention its reality to anyone. She regretted having told Rebecca. The disappointment of his betrayal must be hers alone.

A lone rider appeared on the road. There he was, his proud shoulders bent under a weight of guilt and shame. "You should feel ashamed. You did this, John. The fault is yours alone."

The horse and rider ambled out of sight.

The curtain's edge fell from nerveless fingers as the street blurred. She crumpled to the floor.

"Annie?" Rebecca sank to the floor beside her and gathered her close. "What is it, child? Why did your beau leave before eating his meal? Has his regiment been called to battle?"

"I wish." Annie fished a handkerchief from the shoulder of her dress and swiped at her face. "No, he has gone away. For good."

Rebecca gasped. "But he just asked your hand—"

"Please, say nothing more." Annie pulled away. "Ever. There is no betrothal. I was wrong about him."

"He seems like a fine, upstanding gentleman. What has you so riled?"

"I cannot tell you. Just trust"—tears gushed at the dreaded word—"that what happened would be sufficient to satisfy you, were you to learn the truth."

Rebecca raised her chin, a fierce look in her eyes. "Never say he tried to take advantage. There are people who love you here in this house who will speak to him in your father's absence."

"Nothing like that." Her father was the one who'd been dishonored. "Please. Let us speak no more of it."

"Very well." Rebecca stood and helped Annie to her feet. "Lunch is ready."

Her stomach revolted against food. "None for me. I'll lie down."

"You go right ahead." Compassion shown from her brown eyes. "Let me know if you need anything."

Annie turned away. Rebecca lacked the power to turn this all into a bad dream. That was what she needed most.

∽

*J*ohn somehow filled the empty hours before his train departure and scarcely remembered to send a telegram with his arrival time to his family. He reached the station in Boston, and Patricia's smiling face was the first he saw as he stepped off the train.

"John, we've missed you so." His older sister hugged him with one arm while cradling her baby. "It's good to have you back in Boston. Philip has grown in the months you've been gone."

"Hello there, young fella." John rubbed a finger across his nephew's soft chin. "What is he now, eight months?"

"And growing like that proverbial weed." Standing behind his wife, Scott couldn't keep a proud smile from bursting across his bearded face.

"You're a lucky man."

"Don't I know it. Your turn will come when the war ends."

John shook his brother-in-law's hand with more than a twinge of envy. Their happiness wasn't to be John's, after all. "How is Da?"

"Not good." Patricia's brow wrinkled. "This one was worse."

"Perhaps not worse." Scott sent his wife a cautious look. "But it hit him harder, possibly because it's the second. He never recovered completely from the first, in my opinion."

"Makes sense." John shifted his knapsack on his back. "Does he speak?"

"Slowly." Philip tugged on his mother's curls, and she winced. "He's moved his arm a bit."

"No movement on that left leg yet." Scott took the baby from his wife and wrapped him in a blanket against a chilly breeze.

John frowned. "How is Mam?"

"Strong when she's at his side." She exchanged a concerned glance with Scott.

"Yes, she falls apart when she's away from him. It's as if she doesn't want him to see how upset she is."

John rubbed his jaw. "Should we encourage her to spend more time with him?"

"That's not the problem." Patricia shook her head. "All her thoughts are of him. She steps away only when he falls asleep. That's when she realizes her exhaustion."

"Let's talk in the carriage." Scott pointed to a familiar vehicle with a familiar driver. "Do you have a trunk?"

"Nay. Soldiers learn to travel light." As he approached, John extended his hand to their long-time employee. "Mr. Jones. It's good to see you again."

"And you." The family's driver of nearly a score of years opened the door for them. "And may I express my regret for the circumstances."

John tipped his hat in acknowledgement. "Thank you."

"Supper's in an hour," Patricia said once they were on their way. "That will give you a few minutes with Da."

"Good. Any news from Carl?"

She gave a resigned shake of her head. "Mam sent him a telegram. I wrote him a letter the day it happened, pleading with him to come home. He should have received both."

John bit back a frustrated groan. Then a new worry struck. "Think he's in trouble?"

"Scott and I wondered about that." She took the baby back from Scott and settled him against her shoulder. "It's possible. No one has heard from him in nearly two months. Our parents asked him to come home six weeks ago. Has he written to you?"

"No." His neck grew warm. "That's my fault. My last letter to him was mailed mid-July. I told him to forget about a store in New York and go home. He never replied."

"Da may not be the only one in our family to worry about."

John feared she had the right of it. First things first.

His mam cried when he arrived at his childhood home. He'd never once seen her cry, and the sight only escalated his fear for his father. "Is Da worse?"

She sobbed into his coat.

John looked over her head at his younger sister, Madelynn. Tears coursed down her cheeks as well. He extended his free arm to her, and she rushed to his side and buried her head in his shoulder.

Truly alarmed, he looked at Patricia. "Please, look in on Da.

I'll be there as soon as I can." She left the room with her husband. "Let's sit for a moment, Mam."

His petite mother, gray streaks more plentiful in her black hair, allowed him to guide her into the parlor to a sofa. Madelynn's black hair and blue-eyed beauty was marred somewhat by her tears as she sat beside her.

He knelt before his distraught mother and patted her hand, trying to forget that he'd knelt before Annie just yesterday. "Mam, please tell me what's happened."

"Your father isn't getting better."

His heart sank. "Is he worse?"

She shook her head. "I don't believe so."

Thank you, Lord. John released a breath.

Lines had deepened on Mam's forehead and around her eyes. "You're exhausted. When was the last time you slept?"

"I can't disturb your father's rest, John. Be reasonable."

He hid a smile at this spark of his mother's normal feisty attitude. "Sleep in Patricia's old room and let Da sleep."

She touched his shoulder. "You certainly are a sight for sore eyes. I've missed you, me boy."

"I've missed you, Mam. Which do you want first, supper or a nap?"

"Oh." Her brow furrowed, and she turned to Madelynn, who'd perched on her chair. "Is the meal ready?"

"Not yet."

"Since you're here, I think I'll go up now, John, if you'll be all right for a few minutes."

"I'm fine. Take a good long nap." He quirked an eyebrow at his sister, who stood to escort their mother upstairs before she changed her mind.

Whispering a prayer that she'd feel better after sleeping, he slipped through the open door of his father's bedroom. Creeping to his father's bedside, he took in the ashen face and the slight droop in the left corner of his mouth. His heart plummeted to see his beloved da suffering the same malady as he had nearly four years before.

Da opened his eyes. "Johnny. My boy."

"I'm here, Da." He reached for the frail hand, once so strong.

"You came...back."

"Of course." He saw compassion and concern on Patricia's face where she sat on the opposite side of the bed.

"That's good. The company...will be...in good hands...now." He closed his eyes.

Nay. John's head bowed. Not this time. Even if he wanted to stay, the army wouldn't allow it.

CHAPTER 36

*A*nnie was grateful for her father's telegram the evening before. He had seen Will, who was doing infinitely better than they'd feared, for they hadn't known the conditions of the prison. He hadn't been wounded in battle. Father had sent Frances a similar message, so there was no need for Annie to dash off a note to her sister-in-law. The telegram also told her to expect a long letter of explanation from Bea.

Though Annie sympathized that telegrams by nature were meant to be brief, it frustrated her to wait to learn what the rest of her family already knew.

She hadn't attended church the day before. Her heart wasn't strong enough to answer well-meaning inquiries about the absences of her father and sister. Yet it had been a long day, spent alone.

Better to keep busy than grieve for what might have been had she fallen in love with a man worthy of her regard. Life trudged on.

Even as she dreaded questions about Beatrice's absence leading to others about Will, Annie dressed in her plainest gown for the sewing group meeting.

Thankfully, few people guessed her courtship with John was more than a casual acquaintance. No one would mention him. If they did, tears she'd cried last night might easily start again.

On second thought, it seemed best that Beatrice's absence provided an explanation for the sorrow in her eyes. Everyone knew how close they had always been.

That was, until Beatrice had stopped supporting her relationship with John.

Annie sighed. If only she had listened.

A knock on the family dining room where Annie breakfasted alone proved to be Mr. Grant.

"Pardon me for interrupting your meal, Miss Annie." He entered hesitantly.

"Not at all." Her stomach could handle no more than toast and tea this morning. Again. "What is it?"

"Mr. Tomlinson from your father's bank sent word. He asks if it's convenient for you to stop by the bank today. Something about documents requiring your signature."

"Father mentioned that likelihood." She sipped her tea while considering her schedule. "I'll go before attending my sewing group. Is Jacob available to drive me?"

"He is. Shall I request the landau or the chaise?"

She looked out at the sun-drenched lavender garden. Not at all suited to her mood.

"The landau then, Miss Annie?"

"Yes, thank you. I'll be ready in half an hour."

"Very good. And may I say how pleased me and the Mrs. were to receive the wonderful news that Mister Will has been found in good spirits."

"Thank you. I know you remember him fondly."

As he closed the door behind him, her smile faded. If only Will's friendship meant half as much to John, he'd never have struck them such a blow.

She closed her eyes and folded her hands. Even with as much

as he'd hurt her, she still prayed for the recovery of his father's health.

~

"Two families are withdrawing all their funds from our bank?" It struck Annie as odd that two long-time clients were closing their accounts. "Is this a frequent occurrence?"

"Regrettably so, Miss Swanson." The balding businessman frowned. "It happens occasionally as a normal part of business. It increased with the start of the hostilities."

It explained why they'd begun to curtail expenses over the summer.

"Your father isn't one who desires to burden his children with his financial worries."

"Financial worries?" Annie stared at him, horrified. There must be some truth to this revelation.

"Yes, now if you'll sign here"—he pointed to a line, then another—"and here."

Annie complied, her thoughts swirling. There'd been no frivolous purchases for weeks. Father had stopped serving supper at their soirees and then halted the evening parties altogether. He'd blamed his schedule for the changes, but were finances equally to blame?

"Thank you." He set aside the documents for the ink to dry. "If there's a need for your signature again, I'll let you know."

"Yes, thank you." Her voice seemed to come from far away. "Mr. Tomlinson, may I ask you something?"

He nodded and inclined his head.

"Is the bank in trouble?"

He *tsked* and fumbled with papers on his desk. "I'd hardly say *trouble*. No, definitely not trouble, though that's not to say there's no reason to... Of course, it's nothing for you to worry over."

She drew back her shoulders. Something was definitely wrong. "But I am already worried." Father expected her to take note of what she signed at the bank. She was following orders. "You may explain."

~

"*W*hat do you think, Dr. Spencer?" John had been pacing outside his parents' bedroom for a quarter hour. His legs wanted to keep pacing. Good manners prevented it.

"Not much improvement." The doctor took off his spectacles and rubbed his nose. "Not what you wanted to hear."

Not by a long shot, and he'd never been good with long-range rifles anyway. The man with graying sideburns appeared tired. "Are you hungry? We can talk over a bowl of beef and noodle soup." His family's cook, Miss Stella, rivaled Rebecca's cooking—and that was saying something.

"As I missed dinner," the doctor said, "I will gratefully accept."

"Good." John led the way to the dining room. "Wait here while I see about getting us something to eat."

A few minutes later, the soup in the good doctor's bowl was nearly gone, and John knew little more than when he'd taken his first bite. "You believe my father will begin to improve within the next month?"

"You misconstrued what I said, Sergeant Major Finn." He finished his last spoonful. "I hope your father recovers a portion of his former strength. Watch for signs of that in the next month. Twenty years of doctoring taught me the greatest improvement occurs within the first two months."

"Two months?" John raked his hand through his shaggy hair. He needed a haircut while he was in Boston.

"Yes, with improvements continuing for the initial six months. After that?" He shook his head. "Probably negligible."

"I can't wait that long." He tapped his sweaty forehead. "My army furlough ends in twelve days."

"Then I suggest you place a family member in charge of the business." He removed his glasses and wiped them on his napkin. "That's what you're most worried about, right?"

"Nay." He shook his head. "I'm most concerned about my parents. Yet ensuring their business is in good hands is part of that."

"Your country needs good men like you." He put his spectacles back on his nose. "My advice is to find your brother and discover his intentions. Unfortunately, he may not want the responsibility of running the family's furniture business any more than you do."

John's face grew hot at the bald accusation. Yet it was the truth.

He showed the doctor out, pondering the wisdom of his advice. His latest letter to Carl, written during a mood of agitated frustration, had been mailed the day before. What if neither son wanted to run their father's business?

"Johnny? What did the doctor say?"

He closed the door and turned back at the sound of his mother's voice.

She needed to know what might lie ahead for her husband. That was enough sorrow for today.

CHAPTER 37

*A*nnie's thoughts were in chaos after an hour spent with Mr. Tomlinson. The poor man no doubt possessed good intentions, but his communications skills... "I am aware that different banks employ different currencies. We've established that fact several times the past hour." Annie fought to keep her irritation from showing. This was not the way her mother had taught her to comport herself. "What you have not explained to my satisfaction is why this matters so much."

"Of course, you understand there is a war going on."

Annie bit her lip. Hard. Then nodded with a smile. "I had heard as much, yes."

"Right." He drummed his fingers against his wood desk. "That divided our country, you see. Banks included."

She waited for more. In vain. "Explain, please."

"Southern banks now have Confederate currency that isn't accepted as legal tender in the North."

This was progress. New information. "Go on."

"Folks moving South from Washington City formerly kept their money in banks here."

"Yes." Annie closed her eyes briefly. There must be an easier way to discover why her father's bank was in trouble, for she had no doubt that it was.

"They close their accounts in banks in Union states and move South and place their money in banks in places like Richmond or Atlanta."

She forced the corners of her lips upward. "Yes, go on."

"But those banks don't want our bills. They want silver or gold."

Annie's eyes widened. "My father gives them silver or gold from our vault when they close their accounts."

"Silver, Miss Swanson. Our supply has dwindled."

Annie gasped. Their wealth was moving South with old customers.

"Your father is a man of integrity."

"I am aware of that, Mr. Tomlinson." She lifted her chin. "I'm very proud of his character."

"Rightly so." He took a long breath and blew it out. "Not every bank backs their money with gold or silver. Not every bank is in good financial condition. Men like your father place the needs of their customers above their own."

So, her father's integrity had placed him—indeed, the whole family—in a precarious position. At last, she understood her father's insistence on secrecy about Will. Clients who were staunch supporters of the Northern cause might withdraw their funds from his bank should they discover his son served as a Confederate officer.

~

The store that had started his father's journey into the furniture business was a five-minute stroll from their home. John visited it on Tuesday. His furlough was dwindling fast, and he could scarcely believe all that had to be done before he left.

He was surprised yet happy that Todd, Madelynn's beau, had learned much about selling furniture. The current manager was quite pleased with the boy. "My guess is he'll be ready to manage a store in a year or two."

Though John was happy to hear the news, he didn't have two years to wait.

Their second store, two miles from the first, was blocks from the harbor. Because of its location, this had always been John's favorite place to work as a schoolboy. He'd walk along the harbor, taking the long way home to toss sticks into the vastness of the Boston Harbor.

Their bookkeeper fidgeted at a desk across the room as John studied the books in the small backroom serving as an office. Everything seemed in order...yet it didn't.

"Why was the price of spindle-backed chairs raised?" John looked up at Mr. Ferris, a portly man hired this summer after he left.

"In July, sir." The man with thinning blond hair adjusted his spectacles without meeting his eyes.

"That's *when* it happened, Mr. Ferris." John settled back in his chair. "I asked why."

"Well, sir, the manager, that's Mr. Clayton, and I... Sir, we believe the prices were set too low from the outset." He stood. Ran a finger under his collar.

"Did you seek my father's approval first? He is the owner, after all." John grew more suspicious with every nervous twitch the man made. Unlike Mr. Ferris, John had hired Mr. Clayton himself before he left.

"Your father rarely comes here. There has been no opportunity to approach him. It was thought the greater profit was its own reward."

"My father lives less than three miles away. No great distance."

The man, a decade his senior, flushed.

John stared at the columns of numbers. Not his strong suit, yet something didn't tally up. Had the increased profit made it to the cash box?

"Might I see what's..." Mr. Ferris crept over and craned his neck to peer at the ledger.

John closed the book and stood. "No changes are to be made without approval from my family or someone appointed by my family. Is that understood?"

"Yes, sir." He stared at the ledger book with a wary look.

"I'll take this with me." His brother-in-law could tell him if there were discrepancies. "And books from the previous two years from the shelf behind you."

Mr. Ferris handed him the ledgers with hands that shook. "I trust you will find everything in order."

"I trust I will, too." As they shook hands, John hid a grimace. Like shaking hands with a cold fish from the harbor. "I'll reiterate all of this to Mr. Clayton on my way out."

"Yes, sir. Thank you, sir."

John couldn't shake his bad feeling about the whole place as he strode from the room. Mr. Clayton had hired the book-keeper. He hated to think it of them, but he feared they might be participating in shady dealings. He prayed the third store was in better heart.

~

*A*nnie arrived home from her sewing group on Tuesday afternoon, dejected and spent. She spotted an envelope on the hall table.

She nearly ran up the staircase—something she had not done since childhood.

Inside her room, she dropped her shawl on the bed and sat on her chaise lounge chair.

Dearest Sister,

How I miss you! We are not staying in our usual hotel in Manhattan. Instead, we lodge at a modest Brooklyn hotel in a suite with two bedrooms and a sitting room. It's not luxurious but quite comfortable.

The hotel is near Governors Island. Will is being held at Fort Columbus there. Father visited him on Saturday evening and returned almost a new man. It was as if a great weight had fallen from him.

Will is in Fort Columbus because he is an officer. He describes his quarters as "snug" yet comfortable. Even though he is a prisoner (how I hate that word!) he and the other Confederate officers held there are allowed to stroll in the fresh air on a fair portion of the island.

Tell Rebecca that Will gulped down a dozen cookies while Father was with him that first night. That will bring a smile to her face. He will share slices of your almond cake with his closest comrades because he feels they'd do the same for him. He says to thank you for the bedding and warm clothing. He was especially pleased to find the wool blankets and coat among Father's gifts. He will soon need them here in New York.

He sends his love, and Father assured him ours still burns unvanquished in our hearts for our big brother.

There has been no communication from the guards about releases, so Will fears it may be some weeks yet.

Father asks for news of the bank. Has Mr. Tomlinson requested anything of you? Please include that information in your response, for he is most anxious. He trusts Mr. Tomlinson, though there are matters that require his particular attention. So please ease his mind with any information on that front.

For myself, I miss the company of my sister in this fair city. The last time we were here, Mother was with us. I feel her loss keenly, as I am certain Father does. That must account for the sadness I glimpse in his eyes. Do you remember our shopping expedition in the heart of the city? I'm laughing to recall that our coachman had to return our

packages to our hotel while we were at dinner because there was no
room for us to sit!

You know, dearest sister, that I owe you an apology. I regretted my
words about John almost as soon as they were uttered. I can only say
in my defense that my worries for Will overcame my good sense. I
feared you'd ignore Father's warnings and tell John about Will's
capture. I should have trusted your judgement. Please forgive me.

I know in my heart that you and John are meant for one another.
I've witnessed the way he looks at you, as if you are the most precious
of women. And your face lights up whenever he comes to call. Unless I
miss my guess, John will request a private conversation with Father
soon. Then he'll propose, and no one will be happier than your sister to
see the two of you marry in our church. My vision blurs at the thought
of your happiness, so I will close for now.

Your loving sister,

Bea

Annie choked back a sob. Beatrice didn't know, couldn't imagine the treachery that John had dealt their family. How could Annie have been so wrong about him?

No one must discover the truth about what he'd done. Even after all the hurt he dealt her, she wanted to protect his good reputation in her family's eyes.

She curled up on the chaise. In a few minutes she must share the information about Will to ease the staff's worries.

For now, weeping overcame her as she gave into the sorrow of shattered dreams.

CHAPTER 38

"*D*id you...visit...the factory and our stores?"

"Yes, Da." John straddled a cane chair—his father's first attempt at furniture years before and therefore precious to the whole family—and leaned nearer the bed. His father had been sleeping when John returned home the previous evening.

"Well?"

"The factory is doing well." John had promoted long-time employee, Joe Sanders, to manager that spring. "Joe's doing a great job. He demands quality work, just as you did. Our workers respect him."

"Good." Some tension left his face. Though his mouth still drooped, the slur had mostly disappeared. "The stores?"

"Two are doing well. Todd will be ready to manage one by the time he's twenty."

"I've noticed his work. My guess is he'll be my son-in-law someday. Madelynn...too young to marry. Glad...Todd knows it."

John's mother had been seventeen, one year older than

Madelynn, when she married Da. Unwilling to rile his father, he decided not to mention that.

"Which store...causing concern?"

"The one near the harbor." He'd given the store's ledgers to Scott the night before. It might take a couple of days to confirm his hunch.

"That store hasn't been doing well...since Clayton became manager. Don't like him...or that bookkeeper he hired."

Da had a bad feeling about them too. "I've asked Scott to look over the ledgers."

"Good idea—"

"Johnny Finn." His mother bustled in. "You're not to bother your father with work problems."

"Sorry, Mam."

"Now, Mary," Da said, "don't fuss. I feel stronger tonight. And John won't be here long." He closed his eyes.

She gave John a sidelong glance.

"Carl here?" His father opened his eyes.

"No." John exchanged a startled look with his mother. Da hadn't asked for him before that in John's hearing.

"You've sent him a telegram?"

"Two." Mam spoke in a hushed tone.

"Written him letters?"

"From both Patricia and me."

"And me." John added, hoping his father was strong enough to bear his younger son's lack of response.

"Then something is wrong." Da pressed his right hand against the bed. Struggled to raise his head.

"Dr. Spencer recommends you rest a little longer." Mam eased his shoulders back.

"Then someone else must go to Carl. I don't like this at all." He fell back against the pillow.

Anxiety filled John. He'd dismissed his earlier fears for his brother. They descended on him now like an avalanche. It was possible Carl was in trouble.

"John, go in my stead." Da pointed a wobbly finger at him. "Find my boy and bring him home."

~

*A*nnie pushed open the kitchen door and peeked around it. "May I eat supper in here tonight?" She was tired of dining in her bedroom or the small dining room with nothing but her somber thoughts for company.

"I'd enjoy that." Rebecca stirred something in a kettle. "This tomato soup will be ready soon."

"Smells delicious." She sniffed. "Toasted cheese as well?"

"Hope you don't mind an easy supper. The girls needed my help with their schooling this afternoon, and time got away from us."

"The perfect supper, at least for me."

"It's a mite nippy this evening." Rebecca held a bowl as she ladled the soup into it. "Hot soup tastes good on a cold night."

"Yes." Annie wondered about the weather in Boston, by a breezy harbor some four hundred miles distant. But she put away thoughts of John, as she had more than once.

"Nice and hot." Rebecca placed the bowl in front of her with a toasted cheese sandwich on a plate. "Now I want to see you eat every bite. You've eaten scarcely five bites for every meal since ..."

Annie glanced up fearfully. *Please don't say his name.*

"Saturday."

Annie looked away.

"Look, honey." Rebecca pulled out a chair beside Annie and got comfortable. "I know something happened between you and Sergeant-Major Finn. Something bad."

Annie's throat constricted. "I can't talk about it."

"I ain't asking for details. Keep all that locked up inside you just as long as you want. But if you ain't going to talk, you gotta eat."

Annie spooned in a bite of soup. It soothed her parched throat.

"There. That's better. Another bite."

She bit from her sandwich. The melted cheese reminded her how hungry she felt.

"Now, that Sergeant-Major Finn seems like a mighty good fellow to me."

Annie put down her sandwich.

"You ready to talk?" Rebecca stared at Annie's meal and waited.

She ate some soup.

"The way I figure it," Rebecca said, "there's been a misunder-standing."

"I know exactly what he did." Her sharp tone surprised her.

"Well, then." Rebecca crossed her arms. "Maybe you don't understand why he did it."

"True." And how could she? What could possibly have moti-vated John to spy on the family of his dear friend?

She took another bite of soup.

"Did you allow the man an opportunity to explain himself?"

"He doesn't deserve it." Annie reached for her sandwich.

"Hmm. You're still angry with him."

"And hurt."

"I know." Rebecca touched her shoulder. "Thing is, two hours earlier that day, your face was glowing like candles on a Christmas tree at the thought of marrying that fellow."

Annie rested her spoon in the bowl, unable to meet her friend's eyes.

"It got me curious as to what could happen in those two hours to wrought such a change."

"It's bad, Rebecca."

"I believe you." She studied her. "I ain't never met a perfect man. Except Jesus. You ain't looking to marry your Savior now, are you?"

Annie had to laugh a little.

"Didn't think so." Rebecca folded her hands and rested her elbows on the table. "Take my advice and hear him out. He loves you. I don't believe that man would ever do anything to intentionally hurt you."

Annie's laugh turned derisive. "He claims he was trying to protect me."

"Then maybe he was." Rebecca picked up the empty dishes. "If he were my man, I'd give him a chance to explain himself before spending the rest of my days as a spinster."

A heated flush burned her cheeks, reminding her how John's words had scorched her. How could John possibly justify his actions?

CHAPTER 39

John disembarked from the train in New York City on Thursday morning. Carl's boarding house was about a mile's walk from the station. He was exhausted after hours sitting beside a gray-bearded gentleman who not only prevented him from snatching much-needed sleep but also peppered him with questions about Bull Run. He'd explained that he hadn't been there. It made no difference. The man was a veteran of the war with Mexico and missed participating in battles. John wasn't sorry to bid the talkative stranger good-bye as he strode in the brisk wind toward the address where he hoped to find his brother.

John had visited the city almost annually. Despite that, he was unfamiliar with this particular area and took note of street signs, businesses, and brick homes.

He also kept a sharp eye out for his brother. Carl didn't know John was coming. His brother could be anywhere…from sleeping in his room at the boarding house to seeking a store location.

That was what he was supposed to be doing anyway. John

sighed. Thoughts of his father's anxiety increased his pace. With each step, John's concern escalated.

He found the street and scanned the neighborhood for the three-story red brick building his brother had described in a letter. That one on the right fit the description. Now to find Carl.

"John. You're here?"

His gaze dropped from the upper floors to the stoop at the sound of his brother's voice, deeper than he remembered. "Carl? Are you waiting for someone?"

His brother lounged on the boarding house steps. His brown hair was unkempt and too long. His coat sleeve was torn.

"I sit here for the bit of warmth that escapes under the door."

"Why not go inside?"

Carl shrugged and looked away.

Could he be out of money? That was the only explanation that made sense. "Besides living expenses, Papa gave you the advance for six months' rent on a store. It's all gone?"

"Yep."

John fought to control his temper. He waited for his brother to face him. When he didn't, he sat on the steps beside him. "Since when?"

"About six weeks. Mrs. Jordan, my landlady, kicked me out when I skipped paying her for three weeks. Said she has bills to pay and needs boarders who respect that."

"Where do you sleep?"

"There's a deacon's bench in the side yard where I sleep most nights. Mrs. Jordan takes pity on me when it rains. If she has a vacancy, I can stay there one night. I wash my clothes...and myself...when I can."

John sniffed, then recoiled as the smell of body odor wafted over. "You can use a bath now, brother."

"Yep." He sighed. "I've got a dime left. Been saving it for when I get really hungry. There's a restaurant nearby that sells soup for ten cents. Someone gave me a crust of bread yesterday. I figured on buying soup tomorrow."

John's head reeled. "How did this happen?"

He stared at his dirty hands. "I've had lots of time to sober up and ponder that. You won't be happy."

"Let's talk about it over a meal."

"I wouldn't refuse it." Carl pushed himself to his feet.

"Let's see if Mrs. Jordan has a vacancy first."

His face turned scarlet. "She'll want her unpaid rent."

"I got you, brother." John put an arm around the thin shoulders and did what he should have done at first sight. He hugged his brother.

∼

*C*arl had always had a healthy appetite, but the way he shoveled the pile of roasted beef with gravy, mashed potatoes, and biscuits forced John to wipe a tear from the corner of his eye. His anger seeped away. Even if his brother had known about their father's illness, he didn't have money to purchase the train ticket, something none of his family had considered.

"You must believe I wanted to come home." Green eyes pleaded for John's trust.

"I do." What he didn't understand was how Carl managed to squander funds his family could ill afford to lose with their father's illness and one of the stores being mismanaged. "We'll take you back to the boarding house when you've finished. Mrs. Jordan mentioned a bathing room?"

"I never liked getting a bath as a kid." Carl shook his head. "Used to argue with Mam about it. She'd never believe that sometimes I dream at night about dipping into that nice warm water."

"She'd be surprised." John tried to grin, but it got stuck in the

272

mire of his guilt. Not only had he failed Annie, he'd failed his brother. His anger over Carl's bad choices had caused him to give up on his brother. "We both need a haircut. We'll get you that bath and then buy you some clothes."

"I need them." He moved a plate of plum cobbler closer and took a smaller bite. "Turns out that clothes don't last as long when you're out in the weather."

"I've learned a bit about that myself, being a soldier."

"Tell me about it."

"Later. You first." Carl looked better for a healthy meal, but not good. Not yet. "What happened to your money?"

"It's not a pretty story."

John didn't doubt it. He waited to hear it anyway.

"I went to a tavern the first night I was here. Didn't know anyone. Thought I'd have a drink, strike up a conversation."

John's mouth tightened. His brother's love of liquor wasn't a new story.

"Everyone ignored me, so I asked the bartender to give everyone at the bar a drink on me." He flushed. "They talked to me then. Wanted me to return every evening. I did. Bought a round every night. Drank too much to care about finding a new store location for the family."

Friends bought for a pint of ale. Guilt churned like butter in John's gut. He could have prevented his brother's downfall if he hadn't been busy nursing his own grievances about being stuck in a family business he had no heart for.

"I had too much to drink one night. Lots of nights." He stared at the cobbler. "One night in particular stands out, though. I always carried plenty of money with me. I guess I bragged about our family's wealth. Don't remember. Woke up outside the tavern with a knot on the back of my head. My pockets were turned inside out, as if someone wanted me to know they'd robbed me."

"Did they hurt you badly?"

"I was too drunk to notice my aching head." Carl sighed. "At least until the liquor wore off."

"How much did they get?" John braced himself.

"One or two hundred dollars, most likely, though in truth I had gone through part of the store rental money by that time. There was a week's board money left in my room."

John mulled over the loss that soured his stomach. Da didn't need another business loss. Then again, concern for his son was greater. "Did you tell your drinking buddies?"

"They claimed it was a bit of tough luck." Carl clenched his fist. "Never heard from them again. They even stopped going to the corner tavern."

"Carl, they were never your friends." The words spewed from John. The truth must be said. "They're the kind who like you while you're buying a round and couldn't care less about you when you're penniless."

"Reckon you have the right of it." One side of Carl's mouth turned up. "Doesn't sound pretty when you say it though."

"'Tis an ugly tale." John eyed his younger brother. How he wished he'd come soon enough to save him from himself. "Sometimes the truth stings."

"And sometimes it feels just right." Carl met his gaze squarely.

Something in his brother's eyes healed the breach between them.

"I'm here for another reason." John hated to mention their father's health when his brother faced so much turmoil already.

"Da?" The twinkle left his eyes. "How is he? I figure if he'd died, you'd have told me immediately."

"Aye. He's had another attack of apoplexy. Affected his left side."

"I knew that."

John studied him.

"My mail still comes to the boarding house. Getting those

letters from home is another reason I remain close. You all have wanted me to come home. I wanted to go home." He shrugged. "No money."

John shook his head. "Da believed you'd come home if you weren't in trouble."

"He's right." Carl bowed his head and then raised it. "I'm glad Da never gave up on me."

John looked away in shame. He bore his part in his downfall. Now, he'd make certain to help Carl stand on his own two feet. He reached across the table to clap him on the shoulder. "I never will either."

CHAPTER 40

*A*nnie stopped by the bank to sign documents before going to her sewing group on Thursday. One client closed an account, a total of three for the week. She noted the name to include in a letter to Beatrice that evening.

Lively conversations in the parlor made it easy for Annie to enter sewing group almost unnoticed. She found a quiet corner to sew.

"Good morning, Annie." Ruth swooped up all the material in front of her and joined her at a corner table by the window. "It's shirts today. You like making those, don't you?"

"Yes." She was glad for her company. She'd been alone too much the past week. "I can sometimes finish two in one day, as long as they are already cut out."

Ruth bent over a basket of fabric. "This one's ready to sew."

"Thanks." Annie threaded a needle. "How is your family? I notice your mother is absent today."

"Rheumatism. It sometimes troubles her in the morning."

"Sorry to hear that. I'll say a prayer for her."

"Thank you. I'll tell her." Ruth sewed a couple of stiches. "Any news from your sister?"

"Yes, they're having a good time in New York."

"Oh? What are they doing?"

"Beatrice mentioned shopping." She had, but it had been an old memory with their mother. "You usually operate one of the sewing machines."

"I don't get to talk as much from behind a machine. Makes too much noise. When Esther asked for a turn, I was happy to relinquish it." Ruth looked up. "You probably wish you were in New York City, too, shopping with your sister."

"I'm happy where I am." Or as happy as she would be anywhere. The location didn't matter.

"Still makes you wonder why Mr. Swanson just took one daughter with him and not the other."

Annie had answered these inquiries early in the week, when Ruth sat behind the noisy sewing machine. "Little wonder at all. He had business to attend to, and Beatrice asked to go along."

"I know why." Esther stood a few feet away, arms crossed.

Annie searched her stony expression. Yes, Esther did know. She braced herself.

"You do?" Ruth's glance bobbed from Esther to Annie. "I'm not certain why Mr. Swanson is there, but Beatrice is shopping."

"I rather doubt that." Esther's tone was harsh. The room grew silent. Even the other sewing machine stopped humming. "Father told me this morning. She's there with her father to see her brother. Will's been captured, hasn't he?"

Annie's gaze swept the room for sympathetic faces. Some were confused. Others stared as harshly as Esther. Her mouth went dry.

Esther took a step back and turned to address the room. "Will is a lieutenant in the Confederate army."

A collective gasp seemed to draw the air from the room.

"Why I thought—"

"But you said—"

"That's right." Esther's face hardened. "Annie and Beatrice

have been lying to us for weeks. And it might have worked a bit longer if the newspaper hadn't listed Will as among those captured on that island."

Annie forced herself to breathe, then settled her shoulders back. "What would you have me say, Esther?" Annie poked her needle into the fabric and stood. "Would you have been sympathetic to learn my brother fights for the Confederacy while I support the Union?"

"Never." She held her ground. "And the fact that you kept it a secret makes me question your loyalty as well."

The hair stood up on the back of Annie's neck. "No one has ever questioned my loyalty."

"No one expected your brother to fight for the enemy." Esther lifted her chin. "To think that you chastised me for questioning you earlier this week."

Mrs. Jackson came forward. "I find it an appalling lack of candor." She put an arm around her daughter.

"Do you, Mrs. Jackson?" Annie put her hands on her hips. "You're appalled by my lack of candor about my brother's choice to fight for the Confederacy. Were the tables turned and it were your son fighting for the enemy, of course, you'd be forthright and tell everyone you knew. Isn't that right?"

"We've asked you for news of Will and Frances any number of times—"

"And I told you all I could."

"No. You did not." Esther tilted her head. "I don't see how we can trust you."

"Well, then." Annie tried to heed her mother's voice ingrained in her heart, her advice to say nothing malicious. "I will take myself off to save you the need to worry about it one way or another."

"I'll go with you." Ruth snatched a basket and marched to the parlor room door.

"Are you certain you want to be seen with me?" Annie halted at the road. Two soldiers riding horseback tipped their hats as they passed. "I'm glad for your support, but it comes with a price. They may not invite you to return for many months."

"Yes, Esther holds a grudge, all right." Ruth sighed. "In my opinion, she's had a gripe against you and your sister since Harry Lawrence took Beatrice riding in the spring."

"But Harry stopped courting Esther last year." Annie gave a shake of her head. "And Beatrice's interest waned quickly. Why does that matter?"

"It's my opinion she hopes he'll renew his courtship of her. Beatrice is prettier than Esther. You both are. It's jealousy, if you ask me."

Annie glanced back at the house. "They're peering out the window at us. Let's walk."

"Where to?" Ruth fell into step beside her.

"Not home. It's too lonely with Bea gone."

"Will they return soon?"

"I expect them within the week." Annie slowed the pace after they turned a corner. "Now you know where my father is and what's he's doing."

"Visiting your brother."

"Yes." Despite her anger, a weight lifted off her shoulders. The secret was out. It was almost freeing.

"And Will is doing well in that awful place?"

"My brother has freedom—within limits—to stroll the grounds. Officers enjoy some privileges. Still, I can't like him being held."

"No, I don't imagine so." Ruth nodded to two ladies in a passing landau. "Your father doesn't often go to New York, does he?"

"Not as a rule." Until she talked with her family in person, she'd rather keep the private details to herself. She smiled, hoping to turn the conversation. Ruth was more persistent than most when her curiosity was aroused. "But these are unprecedented times, aren't they?"

"I'll say." Ruth shifted her basket to her other arm. "Reckon a bunch of folks are acting strangely, if you think about it."

"I don't know that I want to think about it." Annie considered all they'd endured to keep a secret that all their friends would probably know by day's end. "Folks have their own reasons for acting as they do."

"Some reasons are private."

"They are indeed." Annie kept her eyes on the sidewalk.

"We used to talk more often." Ruth's tone was mournful.

"Before the war, you mean?"

"Yes."

"True." Back when there weren't so many secrets. "You won't see me in the Jackson's parlor anytime soon."

"Don't know as it will matter to me." Ruth pursed her lips. "Because it'll be a month of Sundays before I darken their doorstep."

"You'll probably return before I will," Annie said. "The worst part is that I've lost my ability to serve our soldiers."

"You still want to? Even with Will being a—"

"Confederate officer?" Tension eased with the freedom to speak.

Ruth stopped. "It wasn't a pretense, was it? You sewing for our soldiers?"

"Certainly not." Annie faced her. "My loyalty is to the Union. My mother was an abolitionist. She converted my father to her way of thinking and raised us to believe the same. In truth"— her shoulders sagged—"I can scarcely believe my brother turned his back on those values."

"That's what bothers you most."

"Yes." Multiple hooves clopped on the dirt road, drawing her attention to armed cavalry up ahead.

"Oh, look." Ruth tossed her head toward a crowded street corner. "The cavalry is escorting President and Mrs. Lincoln."

The open carriage gave Annie and Ruth a view of lines etched deeply on President Lincoln's face as he glanced their way. Mrs. Lincoln, dressed modestly with a white lace collar adorning her dark dress, said something to her husband, which Annie wasn't close enough to hear.

"His cares run deeper than mine." Annie stood back to avoid dust stirred by the horses. "Leading a divided country through a war must be a difficult task."

"Without a doubt." Ruth stared after the carriage until it turned right down another street. Then her face brightened. "If you're serious about serving the soldiers, I have a suggestion."

"Let's hear it."

Ruth bounced from one foot to another. "Our pastor's wife collects food to send to our soldiers. Mrs. Shonkwiler doesn't have enough women to help."

"I remember that mentioned at church. I didn't pay enough attention to our pastor's pleas for help since I didn't have time for more volunteer work. I didn't then, anyway."

"Do you have a few minutes to call on Mrs. Shonkwiler now? It's a bit of walk, but I had planned to be out all day anyway."

"Me too. Let's go." Annie was eager to have a purpose again.

They quickened their pace.

Her friend's reaction made Annie long for the old days even more. Nostalgia set in for the innocence of the spring, before she knew of Will's decision to serve the Confederacy.

And before she learned of John's betrayal.

Nothing was the same as before, nor would it ever be again.

"*W*e both got haircuts. We've bought you new clothes—"

"Threw out the old ones." Carl clapped John's back. "And happy I am to see those smelly, stained garments buried in the trash."

"We paid off your boarding debt." They sat in the boarding house parlor. The room that comfortably seated ten was, except for the brothers, vacant that Friday afternoon.

"Thanks for that, John."

"My pleasure." It surprised him to realize it was the truth. After three hearty meals, a bath, and a good night's sleep, his brother looked—and smelled—like his old self. "You're a new man."

"That's the way I feel."

John clapped him on the back. "You've learned what's happened in Boston in your absence—both at home and at the business."

"And I've been thinking about it." Carl pressed his fingertips together.

"Oh?"

"Look, John, everyone knows you hate the furniture business."

"I don't *hate* it," John corrected. "But it's not my dream."

"I don't like to make furniture—except tables."

"Tables?" John's brow furrowed.

"Yes. It may sound silly to you, but I enjoy carving intricate designs on the legs. Leaves and vines and such."

"What?" John straightened in his cushioned armchair. "I never knew that."

"Never told anyone." Carl looked embarrassed. "No one specializes in that at our place."

"Do you realize the value you'd add to each table?" He gave him a sidelong glance. "Are you any good at it?"

Carl laughed. "Better than you. I think...I don't know. Is such carving a talent? Like a gift?"

"You bet it is." John's mind raced with possibilities. "You can learn to run the furniture manufacturing side ..."

Carl looked away.

"You don't want to do that."

"No more than you do."

"Looks like we'll have to hire someone outside the family." John sighed. "You do want to work there, don't you?"

"If I can design tables and chairs."

"Let's talk to Da."

"I'm ready to mount a train tonight." Carl leaped to his feet.

"I have another errand before I leave, but I'll buy you a ticket today if you want to go."

"I do. I need to see Da. And I've been gone too long."

"That you have." John stood. "Pack your bag. You leave tonight. Tell the family I'll be a day behind you."

CHAPTER 41

"You're home already?" Alerted by the noisy entrance of her family, Annie flew down their home's main stairs and hugged Bea tightly. Then she hugged her father. It was a good thing Mrs. Shonkwiler didn't need her and Ruth to help today, or she'd have been away when they returned. "I didn't expect you until Monday."

"We wanted to attend church tomorrow. Got some praying to do." Father gave his beaver hat to Mr. Grant. "There's a lot to be thankful for."

"Yes, there is." Her thoughts flew to John. Her family would never know about his spying activities. She'd simply allow them to believe that his love had grown cold, his interest in her a mere passing fancy. It was better than them being as crushed by his spying as Annie had been. "It's so good to see you both. Now, you must tell me about Will."

"I didn't see him, as you know." Beatrice drew her inside the main floor drawing room and patted a seat beside her on a mauve sofa. "Father has been a happier man for seeing his son, that much I can verify."

"Thank you, daughter." He beamed. "It was as if a sack of silver fell from my back when I saw his smiling face."

Gratitude welled up that worry lines on her father's forehead were less pronounced. "Oh, that we could all see him. Bea's letter spoke of comfortable living conditions?"

"Indeed. His situation could be far worse. We strolled every day. One tries to ignore the guards patrolling the grounds. Will seemed quite adept at looking the other way when they were near."

Annie's imagination conjured up soldiers watching Will with rifles resting against their shoulders. She suppressed a shudder. "Is Fort Columbus an ugly place?"

"It's not as one might think. It seems surprisingly pleasant." Father settled on a cushioned sofa. "Castle Thunder, a circular-shaped fort, holds enlisted men under increasingly cramped conditions. We are fortunate for your brother's West Point training." He sank deeper into his chair. "It's always nice to get home."

"It's lovely to have you back." Annie stooped to kiss his cheek. "Rebecca's been making lighter meals, so luncheon may be delayed."

"Whatever she has planned is fine." He waved away Annie's concern. "I'm ready for a home-cooked meal—and the finest restaurant in New York can't outshine Rebecca's cooking. You may tell her I said so."

~

*J*ohn mounted the steps on an omnibus headed to New York Harbor. Governors Island was then a ferry ride away.

After paying the fare for public transportation, he found every seat was occupied. He grabbed a leather strap and held on. The slow-moving vehicle made frequent stops. At that rate, he figured he could have walked to the harbor quicker. Being jostled by new passengers pushing forward to pay their fare, he tightened his grip on the strap. His nose wrinkled. It smelled none too clean. Someone near him could benefit from a visit to a bath house.

The inconvenience increased his determination to see Will. He'd not come this close to his old school friend without talking with him, as long as the guards allowed visitors. He tapped his blue sleeve, where the chevron gave mute testament that he was a Sergeant-Major, an enlisted rank.

Will already knew, from letters he'd sent in the spring, that John had mustered into the Union army.

Way back at West Point, neither had foreseen fighting on opposing sides. Unforgiving attitudes, hard feelings, bitter accusations, and harsh words between Northern and Southern citizens had fanned the flames of unrest for years.

Worse than that, Will had been captured. If that happened to John, he had little doubt that he'd be angry with his captors. He hoped Will's anger didn't extend to him.

The omnibus stopped at New York Harbor. John released the strap and waited for a stranger pushing past him to exit the vehicle.

The breeze across the water blew away the stench of the omnibus as it pulled away. He took a deep breath.

Just one more leg of his journey to Will.

Please, God. Allow our friendship to survive this war.

~

"Did Will tell you about his days on that island in North Carolina?" Annie ate a spoonful of delicious vegetable soup. Her appetite hadn't returned, though Rebecca had prepared favorite dishes the past few days. At least the family ate in the smaller dining room together, where she felt more at peace.

"The island is long and thin where he stayed. He often watched the sun rise over the Atlantic Ocean and set on the Pamlico Sound." Father sipped his coffee. "The fort, made of sand, brush, and sod, was a small one. His quarters were outside of it."

"Did he like it?" Annie wondered how her brother had spent his days before the battle.

"Yes. Actually, he talked more about the island than the battle." He paused to munch on his sandwich. "There's a village a mile or so from Fort Clark. Wood houses there have a weathered look and little paint, as if the nearly constant breeze had chipped it away. Folks there are fisherman and hunters."

"Makes sense that local folks make their living from fishing." Her father's descriptions painted a picture for Annie.

"Lambs, cows, and calves roam free on the island. Owners know their animals by a mark on their ears."

"Fascinating. I'd love to go there." Annie remembered the battle and flushed. "After the war ends, of course."

"Will liked it, though the weather presented challenges. Islanders are hearty folk. Will was intrigued by the history, stories of pirates." Father finished his sandwich. "He developed a keen respect for the villagers and the way they live."

"Sounds very nearly like paradise." Annie rubbed her finger over the rim of her glass, her bowl half-empty. "Though a lonely one."

"He swam in both the ocean and the sound. Even found time to fish." Father grinned. "He told me about fish that lay flat on the sound's sand. You don't catch them with fishing line."

"Oh?" Beatrice leaned forward. "How then?"

"You spear them with a gig." Father chuckled. "Will said they ate many of them over the summer."

"Sounds like you and Will enjoyed long conversations."

"I promised to return soon." He drained his coffee.

"What of the battle?" Annie pushed her bowl away.

He looked away. "He didn't want to talk about it."

Annie tried to imagine what her brother had endured. Imagination failed her.

CHAPTER 42

*J*ohn followed the guard's pointing finger to a tall thin man wearing the garb of a Confederate officer.

Will's face, as he stood staring out into the harbor, was in profile. John's closest friend stood yards away, and he suddenly feared that everything between them was irrevocably altered.

It would almost be easier to walk away, not knowing, than to face his friend and discover their friendship lay in tatters, shredded to bits by a war neither wanted.

Then Will turned. Saw him. Joy filled his countenance...and then his gaze swept the Union colors, the chevron on his sleeve.

"Will Swanson. 'Tis glad I am to see me old West Point roommate." John ignored the reserve on his friend's face and strode forward with his right hand extended.

"If it isn't John Finn, come to see me." With a strained grin, Will grasped his hand. "I've missed you, old boy."

"It's been too long." John backed up and put his hands on his hips. "I hear you're to be a father soon. Heartiest of congratulations."

"Thank you." His eyes lit up and then dimmed. "Don't know when I'll be released. The guards aren't saying. Did they tell you?"

"No." John shook his head with regret. "Wish I brought the good news you long for." It was too early in their conversation to mention Will taking the oath of allegiance to the Union.

"That's all right." He looked away. "My father was here this week. He drilled the guards for details to no avail. Thought with you being a Union officer ..."

"Low-ranking. An enlisted officer, not commissioned like yourself." Best change the topic. "The guard told me you're able to roam a good bit of the island. Care to take a stroll?"

"Certainly." He set out on a well-worn path. "You know, we made the mistake of allowing our captives to walk around unattended at Hatteras Inlet. We discovered later that, when we released them, they returned home and shared secrets about the formation of our forts, our quarters, and their locations." He raised his hands, palms up. "And who knows what else."

"Want to talk about what happened?"

"The battle?"

John nodded, his eyes on his friend.

"Father said details were reported in many newspapers." Will gazed at the dirt path.

"I'd like to hear about it from your perspective."

He sighed. "Then let's sit. In truth, I've wanted to talk about it, but I didn't want to worry Father."

Hiram Swanson seemed plenty strong enough to John. He raised his eyebrows.

"You should have seen the fear in his eyes when he first arrived. I regaled him with recollections of the island and its villagers to ease his mind."

John nodded. He'd noticed the strain on Hiram's face the last time he saw him.

"I was stationed at Fort Clark. It's located about halfway between the ocean and Pamlico Sound." He chuckled. "That's a misnomer, for the sound is calm, its waters flat with barely a ripple. In contrast, the Atlantic Ocean is never quiet. I've stood on the shore on the darkest nights, watching white capped waves roll toward me. Listening to its constant splash. There's something soothing about those waves crashing onto the shore. I loved living there." His face changed. "Until those last two days."

"What happened?" They settled on a bench facing the harbor.

"A little background first. You see, privateers live on the island. Our army had paid them to capture Union ships and their cargo. They're quite good at it. We held captives now and then. Captains and crew members. Those privateers built towers by planting a pole in the sand and nailing planks into it to form a ladder. Like so." He held one hand straight and leaned the other hand against it with the fingers extending at an angle. "Never seen anything like it. But it worked to show ships off at a distance. Sometimes they captured the ships and returned within the same day."

"Impressive." John wondered what this had to do with the battle.

"They were so successful that we figure it caught the army's attention. The day before the bombardment, we saw a fleet of ships on the horizon drawing closer like black shadows on the water. We saw the ship's mast, soldiers on the deck." He stared out at boats sailing in the harbor as if seeing something else. "Colonel Martin was concerned. So was I. Only some of our heavy guns were in place. He sent for reinforcements."

John tensed, suddenly there on the beach with his friend. Unmounted guns and mounted guns at the fort. A fleet of ships. A formidable adversary, indeed.

"Wind had picked up the next morning, churning heavy surf. Ships were still there. We waited, praying for reinforcements"—he glanced at John—"that didn't come."

"They fire on you that day?"

Will nodded. "Started about ten o'clock. Our return fire fell short. Their ships stayed in motion. They fired their cannons and then moved off."

"Hard to hit a moving target."

"I'll say. In the meantime, they bombarded us at a pace that set all eyes toward the sky and running to avoid the shells. I counted twenty-eight coming at us in one minute's span."

One roughly every two seconds. John gave a low whistle.

"It was likely even higher at times. There were troops outside the fort, cringing against the wall facing the sound. Other soldiers crouched in low brush around the fort. White smoke hid the decks of the ships. The roar of endless firepower nearly deafened us. I wondered if any of us would survive."

This, then, was war. Not pretty or romantic, but fearful and deadly.

"Colonel Martin gave orders to spike our guns and abandon the fort around noon."

"Must have been difficult to destroy your own cannons." Sympathy rose for his friend's plight on that fearful day.

"It was. But it was a sight better than leaving them to fall into enemy hands fully-functioning. Surrendering the fort was hard, though I agreed with the wisdom of his decision. Our cannons weren't effective against their longer-range artillery." Shaking his head, he looked at John with tormented eyes. "Remember when we dreamed of being in battle at school?"

"Aye." John could barely breathe.

"Though it's exciting, what we learned was nothing to the reality of it."

The wind ripped off John's felt hat. He chased it down and then returned to the bench. "Did you run to Fort Hatteras?"

"We tried. The fleet kept bombing us as we ran. Brush and a few low trees provided scant protection—otherwise we crossed in wide open spaces. We lost a few good men that afternoon, for the ships shot at us until darkness fell."

"Terrifying."

"My heart nearly beat out of my chest. All I could think of was surviving the deluge for Frances and our baby." Will tilted his chin. "I hope you never know that fear."

John didn't know what to say. He figured his turn awaited.

"By that time a Union flag flew over Fort Clark. Their soldiers had crossed in small boats to land while the ships fired upon us."

"'Tis small wonder you had such difficulties under those conditions. How could a small force hold out against such an onslaught?"

"Thank you." Some agitation eased from his face.

"I take it you made it to Fort Hatteras."

Will nodded. "Reinforcements began to arrive. Colonel Martin pleaded exhaustion and turned command over to Commodore Baron."

"Glad you got some help."

"Not enough." Will gave him a side glance and then looked at John's sleeve. "It got worse. One of the cannons from Fort Clark fired on us. Then we knew the enemy had captured our fort and repaired at least one of its guns."

Thinking how he'd feel if the enemy took charge of the fort he helped build, John shook his head at the atrocity.

"The fleet resumed their bombardment toward Fort Hatteras. The officers met twice while shells fell at an alarming rate." His face paled with strain. "The second time we all decided to raise the white flag of surrender." He stood and turned away.

"'Tis sorry I am that it went that way for you." John stood.

"Are you?" Will rounded on him. "You wear the garb of the enemy."

John felt as if he'd been slapped. "You and I will never be enemies, Will Swanson."

CHAPTER 43

A long silence.

"I don't want to be enemies with you, Johnny Finn." Sighing, Will sat on the edge of the bench.

"I never thought we'd fight on opposing sides." John sat gingerly, a bit further from his friend than before. "Can't help wondering..."

"Why I fight for the Confederacy?"

John gave a hesitant nod. "You were an abolitionist at West Point."

"Still am."

John's whole body jerked.

"Ah, that surprises you." Will raked his hand through hair that needed cutting. "I married a Southern belle. Frances doesn't like slavery either, though I must say she's been protected from knowing the full extent of all that means. When my father-in-law relinquishes the thousand-acre tract of land he promised us on our wedding day, I'll hire workers to plant and harvest my cotton. My father's wedding gift will go toward the cost of their labor. I figure it'll be enough to see me through one season.

Then, money from the cotton crop will have to pay their wages the following year. I fear Frances' father will want us to fail."

Light dawned. "Until your father-in-law gives that promised land, you must live as if you accept his enslaved workers."

"He's testing my loyalty, or he'd have given us the land already." Will inclined his head. "He's tried to indoctrinate me with his beliefs. I keep hearing Mother's voice."

"Her voice is stronger."

"It is."

John shook his head. "Then why fight for the South?"

"Because the South is where I live. Where my future lies. Where my children will live and play and inherit the land passed down through four generations. Frances's ancestors were on the land before the Revolution. It's their heritage." Will studied him. "Would you not fight to protect your home? Your wife? Your children?"

"I reckon that's what I'm doing." John rubbed his jaw. "Could you not swear an oath of allegiance to the Union?"

"No." His tone was harsh. "Do not ask it of me. Would you swear allegiance to the Confederacy?"

John fought back rising irritation. "Think, man. Taking the oath ensures your early release. You can be home to welcome your baby into the world."

"That was a low blow, John." He raised tormented eyes. "I'd not have thought it of you."

An icy chill formed in the pit of John's stomach. Now he'd done it. The chasm between them deepened. "Forgive me, my friend. I merely thought to give you an escape."

"An escape that destroys those you love most is no escape." The words seemed to be torn from his soul.

A cold wind blew between them. "'Tis the truth you speak."

Will gripped the seat of the bench until his knuckles turned white. "Don't you think I've considered this until I'm nearly sick with worry?"

Shame filled him. Hadn't he learned that there were no easy answers in a war that divided the country? "Forgive me. I spoke out of turn."

They both turned to the harbor. Sailboats. Ferries. A flag flying on the mainland. It all seemed so ordinary.

"I hate this war." Will's words seemed wrung from a tortured soul.

"Aye." John couldn't agree more. Serving his country as a spy had cost him the only woman he'd ever loved. He couldn't take that back any more than Will could swear allegiance to the North.

"I received a letter from you this spring. You're with the Ninth Massachusetts."

"I am. The Irish Ninth."

Will quirked an eyebrow. "An Irish regiment."

"Aye."

"Where is your camp?"

John considered. It seemed harmless enough to give his general direction. "Near Washington City."

"Did you make it into the city?"

"Aye." John didn't want to talk about Annie, though he feared that was who Will wanted to discuss.

"Stop and see Annie when you're in the city. She'd like that."

He said nothing in response, but Will didn't pick up on John's reluctance to speak of it.

"I saw the way she looked at you when you escorted her to my wedding." Will glanced at him and then looked away. "And the way you looked at her."

John took a breath. How he longed to return to those simpler days, when commanding officers didn't ask a man to spy on the father of the woman he loved, of his best friend.

"You should call on her. No one has courted her since the wedding."

Should he try again to mend matters between them? "I have

called on her and your family. She…I…we've had a misunder-
standing."

"Then clear up the matter."

"Aye." Perhaps he could mend the breach between him and
Annie. It comforted him to learn he had Will's blessing.

Both men stood.

Suddenly, it seemed as if they were at a stalemate. Not
knowing when they'd see one another again, John didn't want
to leave. One or both of them might die in upcoming battles.
Will had made it clear he wasn't going to quit, and John wasn't
either.

"It was good of you to come. I appreciate it." Will extended
his hand.

"Godspeed, my friend." John clasped his hand.

"And you."

Will turned away. Took a step. Turned back. "I pray we never
meet in battle."

John's heart leapt to his throat. "May it never be."

Will turned again. This time he didn't look back.

John began to walk away. Was this his last time to see his old
buddy? He turned as Will entered a building.

"Something wrong, son?"

John jerked. "Pardon me?"

"I asked if something was wrong." A bearded guard rested a
rifle on his shoulder. "You look as if you've lost your best
friend."

"God willing, sir"—he looked back at the fort—"I will find
him again."

☙

"*A*re you exhausted from all your travels?" Annie leaned
back against a pillow on her sister's bed.

"Not at all. We didn't do as much as normal." Beatrice extracted a dress from her trunk and shook it.

"Those wrinkles need pressing. What did you do while in New York?"

"I have to confess something." Beatrice looked at her out of the corner of her eye. "I saw Will."

"What?" Annie sat up. Resentment rose up like bile in her throat. "But Father said he wouldn't take you to Governors Island."

"He didn't." She flounced her skirt and sat on the end of the bed. "He drove by the island on Thursday. He had arranged with Will to watch for us to drive by in a rented carriage. I got out when I saw him. We waved to one another for a long time."

Annie looked down at her clenched hands. It was more than she had received. "I want to see him."

"Perhaps Father will take you next time." She got up and took a skirt from the trunk.

"It's good to have you home again."

"It wasn't the same without you, though I'm certain you were glad to be here for John's visit on Sunday. Is he doing well?"

"No, he isn't." She sat up. "He's in Boston. His father suffered another attack of apoplexy."

Beatrice rushed over and gave her a hug. "I should have known something happened. That explains the unhappy look in your eyes."

"Yes, well—"

"I do hope his father recovers quicker this time."

"I'm praying for his recovery." Annie stared down at her hands, so often folded in prayer this week for John's family. For her family. For her shattered dreams.

"I suppose he won't be here for church tomorrow."

"He's on furlough." Annie slid off the bed and dug a pink skirt out of the trunk. "I don't recognize this. Is it new?" She hoped to steer the conversation away from John.

She snatched it away. "Why, you've seen me wear it no less than four times."

"That's right. I remember now." She maintained a pleasant look as if all were well.

But Beatrice was too observant. "Is something else bothering you?"

Annie couldn't share her heartbreak over John but focused her other news, shoving John away from the forefront of her mind. "I'm afraid so. Esther knows Will is a Confederate prisoner."

Beatrice's expression grew stern. "How?"

Annie recounted the events. "I'm most grateful that Ruth left with me."

"Good for her. At least we have one friend."

"There is a bit of good news." Annie turned with a smile. "Do you remember hearing about Mrs. Shonkwiler collecting food and supplies for our soldiers?"

Her brow furrowed. "Vaguely."

"Ruth and I visited her Thursday to offer our help. We helped box donations all day yesterday."

Beatrice straightened. "That must have been satisfying."

"It was. Mrs. Shonkwiler keeps a list for church members of brothers, cousins, uncles, and friends with the regiments they're in. Family members give us their new direction when they move. The list grows daily."

"A monumental task."

"That's only part of it." Annie let the curtain fall. John's name was on the list because she'd put it there yesterday. But not Will's. "She needs help collecting donations and organizing them for items requested by particular regiments."

"And she doesn't mind help from sisters of a Confederate officer?" Beatrice lifted her chin.

"I asked her that. Quite bluntly, since we've already been ousted from one group." Tears rose in Annie's eyes. "She reached for my hand and said, 'I had heard your brother was being held on Governors Island from my husband. We're praying for him. We're all God's children.'"

"She's the kind of person I want to help." Beatrice reached for her handkerchief. "Looks like we can still serve our soldiers."

"Yes." Annie squeezed her sister's hand in comfort. "It surprised me what a relief it was to tell the truth about Will's choice to serve the Confederacy." What still worried her was her father's customers withdrawing their money once it was widely known.

Not much they could do about that now. Except continue to pray.

Too much had happened in the past week. Suddenly she needed solitude.

"I want to write a letter before supper, so I'll see you in a couple of hours." Annie hurried to the door. She'd pen some lines to her cousin Meg to lend it credence.

"To a certain Irish gentleman?" Beatrice giggled.

Her posture went rigid. Her sister didn't know the pain she caused. Annie stepped into the hall and closed the door behind her. She must gather her strength for the coming days. Once her family and friends realized John wasn't coming back, there'd be a deluge of questions.

More secrets. This one she'd keep until her dying day. To protect John.

CHAPTER 44

nnie pleaded exhaustion after supper and retired early for she needed solitude to think about Rebecca's suggestion to give John a chance to explain his actions.

She changed into her nightgown and then sat on her chaise lounge. Distant drumbeats enhanced her melancholy mood.

John had seemed lovingly sincere when he proposed. He loved her. She blushed to remember how right it felt to be within his arms, how she never wanted to leave his embrace. The happiness in his eyes had been real.

He wanted to marry her and spend the rest of his life with her.

Riding the rails westward. What an adventurous life they'd have enjoyed, so different from the society she'd been raised in.

Yet he had spied on her father. His own handwriting convicted him. She tucked her bare feet under her as she pondered his actions.

The few words she'd read said there was no evidence that her father had participated in Mrs. Greenhow's spying.

Did the fact that John supported the Union with his spying make it more acceptable?

It was what her heart wanted to believe.

How tired she was of lies. Secrets. Betrayal.

Conversations with Mr. Tomlinson explained her father's reasons for keeping Will's decision to fight for the Confederacy a secret. Might the reason that John spied on Father be defensible as well?

Certainly not. She drew her knees to her chest and laid her wet cheek on the cotton fabric of her nightgown. *Why did you do it, John? Did you care so little for me? For Will?*

He said he had done it to protect her. She didn't understand.

Will had trusted John. They'd been roommates at West Point. If there was a reason she should not allow him to court her, Will would have been first to warn John away from her.

Her eyes fell on the letter she'd written to her cousin in Chicago. She'd explained to Meg that Will was a Confederate lieutenant in the Seventeenth North Carolina regiment and given her an update on his current position. She ended by reiterating an invitation to visit them whenever she could manage it. A visit from Meg was no doubt what they all needed to cheer them up.

Meg would also keep Beatrice occupied. Perhaps they'd be too busy to inquire about John when he didn't return.

Why did you do it, John?

It was a question that would torment her until she learned the truth. She'd told him to leave when he'd seemed too shamed to speak. Now, she regretted not allowing him to answer.

Rebecca thought him to be a good man. Father respected him. Will, who knew him best, had trusted him.

She crossed to the window and stared out at the garden seat, where they'd spent several happy hours. Would he return to explain? Or stay away as she had demanded?

Suddenly, she did not want to leave it to chance. She picked up her quill pen and began to write.

〜

"*T*is a blessing to have my sons at home again." Mam touched her handkerchief to the corner of her eye. "And you both are a tonic for your father. He actually smiled this afternoon."

"That he did." John rubbed his palms over his pants legs, too restless for long reminisces. They sat in his mother's sitting room for the private conversation she'd requested. His brother spent every spare moment at their father's bedside down the hall. "Carl is going to school to increase his skills before working at the factory."

"I couldn't be happier. My heart had grieved for his choices. He's a changed man." Tears filled her eyes. "And you accomplished it. I can never thank you enough for giving my son back to me."

"You're wrong, Mam. Carl was ready to return home. He merely needed someone to come to him. Da was the one who insisted I find him."

She swiped her wet cheeks with a lacy handkerchief. "Carl will soon be carving ornate etchings on our furniture. What other changes will you make upon resigning from the army?"

He stood and crossed to the window. "It's not as easy as you think to do what you ask."

"Does that include managing our business overall?" She spoke softly.

"It hurts me to disappoint you. I already talked to Da."

"And...?" She joined him, looking down at the crowded street.

"We're selling the store by the harbor. Scott can't prove the bookkeeper is doing anything shady, but my gut tells me something isn't right."

"That's fine then. If you can't trust him, there's nothing else to be said."

"Selling that store will provide money for the family. Carl... he lost everything in New York."

She gasped. "All the money we gave him—"

"Gone. All gone." John and Carl had decided between them to keep the robbery to themselves. It meant his family believed he'd squandered everything, but they didn't want to add worries of the theft on top of health concerns.

Her face paled.

"Da wasn't surprised. It almost seemed he already knew."

She turned away.

"I'll talk to our assistant manager at the factory. He's young, but he may be ready to take on the reins as manager while consulting Papa with his questions. If he doesn't feel up for the task, I will hire someone else. Papa has someone in mind."

Mam sighed. "You'll remain in the army."

"I made a commitment, and I don't take it lightly. Neither does my country."

"You won't move back to Boston after your term ends?" Resignation marked her tone.

"Nay." He touched her shoulder. "My heart is in building the railroad westward."

She stared down at the street.

"It's what I want to do. Can you not understand?"

"'Tis a disappointment that you'll live far away from your old mam." She gave him a tearful smile. "But I understand. Take my advice and marry a good woman who will share your dreams."

Hope flickered for the second time since he'd left Annie. The first had been when Will advised him to mend his relationship with Annie. "'Tis wise counsel, Mam. I hope to follow it."

~

*J*ohn stayed busy the next three days with putting the harbor store up for sale, talking with employees in all locations, and promoting his assistant manager to manager, who burst with pride to be given the task.

On Wednesday, his last evening, his mother cooked a big supper for the whole family. He planned to see Annie before returning to his camp. If she refused to see him, he'd try again the following week. He'd continue until she talked with him...or until his regiment received marching orders.

John had to try to make amends.

"We're dining in the family parlor." Patricia pulled him aside when he arrived home. "The doctor said Da can join us in the parlor if we get him to bed the second he shows fatigue."

John grinned. "His first time he'll be out of bed in two weeks."

She shook her head. "I can't believe all you've accomplished in ten days."

"Carl coming home was the greatest blessing for our family."

"'Twas."

A baby cried from upstairs.

"Philip's hungry." She hurried away. "And you have mail on the hall table. Supper's in half an hour."

John glanced that way, and his heart leaped to see Annie's handwriting. Beautiful, just like the woman herself.

He snatched it up and bolted up the stairs, praying for good news.

Praying she'd forgiven him.

CHAPTER 45

"*I* don't want to be a soldier."

"I know." John met Carl's gaze in the family's closed carriage. Lantern light beside the outside doors gave more shadow than light in the predawn hours. He wouldn't arrive in Washington City until early the following day. He'd sent Annie a telegram, warning her to expect him about eleven. Her letter had been stiff, formal, yet it gave him hope.

"Do you think less of me?"

"Nay." He clapped Carl's shoulder. "You're where you need to be."

"You don't believe me to be a…a coward?"

"Never." His brother had come so far since he'd found him, desperate and homeless, a week before in New York, yet he still required strong affirmation and love to forgive himself. "Not too long ago I thought the army might make the pleasure-seeking boy in you into a man with responsibilities. You've proven yourself. We need good men at home too."

"But I'm not worthy of all I've been given." He folded his arms across a chest still too thin. "I squandered money Da could ill-afford to lose."

"It's true that loss hurt. Da's illness also hurt the family." John waited until his brother looked up at him to continue. "Neither of those are wounds that our parents would never heal from. Do you know what is?"

"Me not coming home?"

John nodded.

"I came home." They stopped outside the train depot. "You come back too, big brother."

"I will, little buddy." John put an arm around him. "I may never live in Boston again, but God willing, I will see you again."

～

*A*nnie told Beatrice that John's telegram announced his arrival at eleven o'clock. She bore her sister's teasing with a stoic smile. Inside, she quaked.

Somehow, she'd convinced Beatrice to pack food boxes without her. Bea and Ruth left at half past nine. Father was at the bank, where he'd worked dawn to dusk every day since his return. Customers had withdrawn funds, as he had feared, but a majority remained. Annie hoped this meant the bank would survive the war.

She paced the floor of the first-floor drawing room. Only a quarter past ten. Too agitated to remain in the place where she had many happy memories of John, she hurried to the kitchen. "Rebecca?"

"Land sakes, child, you almost made me drop this dish." She wiped it dry and put it on a stack of plates. "You never said why you didn't go to the parsonage today. Are you ailing?"

"No." Her stomach felt queasy. "John's coming."

"I see." Rebecca pointed to a spindle-backed chair. "Want to sit a spell?"

"I asked him to come." Annie sat and arranged her dress, the yellow one that John had once compared to a field of daisies.

"Did you now?" She searched her face. "A mighty good idea."

"But, Rebecca, how can I forgive him?" She stared at her friend, her mentor.

"I don't rightly know what he's done. What do you think? Can you forgive him?"

"I don't know. Have you ever forgiven someone of a despicable act?"

"Well, now, I think I know something about that." Rebecca drew back. "But let me ask some questions first. Did he hurt you physically?"

"No."

"Speak to you unkindly? Put his hands on you, raise his fist, threaten you?"

"No, never. Nothing like that."

"Did he play you false with another woman?"

"No. He hardly seems to notice there's another woman in the room when he's with me." Annie's cheeks grew warm.

"The way that man looks at you..." She clucked her tongue.

"How does he look at me?"

"Like you're the most precious person in the world." She tilted her head. "That man loves you."

"He does." Annie nodded. "But he chose a poor way to show it."

"Love like he has don't come around once to most folks. Don't be so quick to toss his feelings back in his face. It's good you're giving him a chance to say what needs said before you shut that door. See if you can find the strength to forgive him, 'cause that's what it'll take. Strength and a whole lot of love." She walked to the window.

"Rebecca? You're thinking of someone, aren't you?"

"Reckon I'm thinking of my father." She stood motionless.

"I've never heard you mention him."

"No."

"Did he hurt you?" Annie joined her at the window.

Rebecca turned to her. "He allowed me to be raised as a slave."

Annie gasped. She'd heard of men taking advantage of female servants. "You mean, your father forced himself on..."

"On my mother, yes." Her face tightened. "This is difficult to speak of, you understand."

Annie touched her arm. "Did my mother know?"

"I kept no secrets from Mrs. Charlotte." She turned away. "He sold me and my mother when I was three. Turned out to be a good thing because Mama and I were safe at the new house. And Tom was there. He bought my freedom and was going to buy my mother's freedom as well, but she passed away before he could do it. We took our papers and came to Washington City." She gripped the shutters. "Mrs. Charlotte was the one who taught me about Jesus, the Bible, and forgiveness." Tears slid down her cheeks. "The man who was my father could have saved my mother and me lots of hardship... Sometimes I hated him. But I forgave him. I forgave him because the load of hurt and anger and resentment was too heavy to keep carrying."

Annie, her heart breaking for all her friend had endured, hugged her close.

"Now, I don't allow my mind to go down that road too often." Rebecca pushed away and blew her nose. "It's in the past. Best it stays that way. He died two years after Mama, and he can't hurt me anymore. Even so, I let it all go a long time ago, and I've no mind to pick it up again."

"Oh, Rebecca," Annie choked back a sob, "I never knew all you endured."

"There was never a need for you to until now." Her face softened. "I still don't know what your young man did, but I think I know what he needs."

Annie stared into the loving eyes of the strong woman she'd known most of her life. She'd never realized how strong. "What's that?"

"Forgiveness."

CHAPTER 46

*J*ohn urged Moonbeam to a trot toward the Swanson mansion late Friday morning. He'd arrived in Washington City in the wee hours of the morning and prayed for guidance the remainder of a nearly sleepless night at the Willard Hotel. The last person he wanted to see at breakfast was Christopher, but the man had entered while he'd been eating and had told John bluntly that he looked like he needed another furlough.

No doubt he did.

Uncertain of Annie's reception, John had left his possessions at the hotel, where he'd stay one more night.

All he could think about was how he had betrayed not only his best friend but also the woman he loved by spying on their father. John believed that Will, trained as a military man, could forgive him more easily than Annie.

But Will didn't know, and John prayed he would never find out. He'd prayed that Annie would somehow retain enough regard for him to keep his secret, which had the power to hurt all of them should it become public knowledge. If word of it got out, it would stain Hiram's reputation, perhaps irrevocably.

He'd ask for Annie's forgiveness. Should she want details, he'd decided to keep them to himself. There was a war going on, and the army had its reasons for their orders, and they rarely shared those reasons with low-ranking enlisted officers like himself. He must not put his country in jeopardy.

Not even to heal his beloved's broken heart.

Finally, the impressive mansion came into view. He studied the well-kept grounds, the spacious three-story home as if committing it to memory.

The garden where he'd kissed Annie.

The nearly floor-to-ceiling window of their drawing room, where he'd come to know and love the family.

The second-floor sitting room, where he'd proposed, been accepted, and then been rejected and sent away. *Annie, me heart, please forgive this soldier his wrongs.*

He passed the home on his way to the stable and dismounted.

"Sergeant-Major John." Tom reached for the reins. "It's good to see you back in the city."

"Good morning, Tom." John rubbed Moonbeam's neck. He wished everyone else in the home felt the same.

He tipped his hat at the stable hand and strode to the house.

Best get this apology behind him. Annie wasn't about to forgive him for spying on the father she adored, but he had to try.

~

*A*nnie let the curtain fall from her fingers in the family sitting room.

She needed all the strength she could muster for her last conversation with John, for what could he say to change what he'd done?

With clenched fists she paced the length of the room. What was keeping the man? Was he too cowardly to face her?

At a tap on the door, she swung around.

"Sergeant-Major Finn is here, Miss Annie," Mr. Grant said.

Her agitation wasn't going to improve until she'd given him an opportunity to plead his case. "Show him in."

John stopped just over the threshold, spinning his hat in his hands.

The door closed behind him.

"My dearest Annie, I can't tell you how happy I was to receive your letter."

I'm not your dearest. "How good of you to come, Sergeant-Major Finn." With a pang, she gestured to the sofa where they'd both sat the last time he was here. "Won't you sit?"

"Thank you." He sat where she indicated.

She chose an adjacent chair. "I hope you found your father in better health than you feared."

"Nay. His speech has improved somewhat. Along with his appetite. The doctor is cautious." He sighed. "It's doubtful that my father will recover enough vigor to run the family business."

"I'm sorry." And she was. John must feel divided between loyalty to family and to his country. Her face grew hot. She knew which loyalty he'd choose, the same one he'd chosen when it came to her.

"I appreciate that." He straightened his shoulders. "I will just say this straight out." He stretched out his hand to her, palm up. "I regret that, while in service to my country, I hurt you."

Aching to feel his strong fingers curl around hers, Annie looked away from his outstretched hand. "I regret it too."

His hand fell to his side. "I can't undo what's been done."

"Why did you do it?"

"Two reasons." His green eyes turned smoky. "We are a country at war. You must believe that only loyalty to my country could convince me to agree."

"Much like your service to the Union army."

"Aye." His gaze didn't stray from hers.

Loyalty to country. Just as Will chose loyalty to the country where he lived rather than the country of his birth. She could not have accepted this as a valid reason at the beginning of the war. Much had changed since then, too much to ever go back to the innocence of the spring. "And your second reason?"

"To protect you and your family."

Protect? She struggled to keep her voice level. "Can you explain how spying on my father protected us?"

His head bowed. "I cannot."

Agitation drove her to her feet. "You say your actions protected me. I say your actions betrayed me. Who is right?"

"Both of us are right." He rose slowly. "How I wish to fully explain. 'Tis not my secret to tell."

Anger shot through her. All she required was an explanation. How could she believe he loved her if he couldn't even offer that? "How convenient."

"Not convenient at all." Torment filled his green eyes. "I'm as sorry as I can be to hurt you. I'll spend the rest of my days making it up to you, if that's what you desire."

Her throat tightened with unshed tears. "How do you expect to do that?"

"I cannot. Not without your forgiveness. Not without your trust." He took a step closer. "Will you find it in yer heart to trust me once more, Miss Annie Swanson? For if you cannot, then there is nothing more to be said."

Trust him? Forgive him a great wrong, just as Rebecca had forgiven her father?

"I've never been false with you, Annie. The army ordered me to keep this one secret from you. They may ask me to keep other secrets during the course of this war."

"Never say"—she backed away—"that you'll spy on us again?"

"Nay. Do not concern yourself." He closed his eyes briefly. "That 'twill never happen again."

"Can I trust you?" The agony contorting his face hurt to watch. Her heart screamed for her to forgive him.

"If the Lord wills it, I will die for you tomorrow with but one regret."

She looked into his tormented green eyes. "What is this regret?"

"That I can die for you but once."

A sob burst from her. "Do you love me, John? Do you really love me?"

"Aye, me sweet Annie." He clasped her hand. "I love you truly. You're the only woman for me. If you send me away, 'tis a bachelor I'll be 'til me dying day."

Tears spilled over. "I love you, John."

He pulled her close, holding her as if she were made of the finest porcelain. "I will love you to my last breath, Annie Swanson."

His declaration of love melted the ice that had encased her heart since she read that awful document. "Then marry me."

"What's this?" He pulled back only far enough to look into her eyes. "Are you proposing to me?"

She shook her head and then nodded, only certain that she wanted to be his wife.

He laughed, the joyful sound filling the room. "Then allow me to first say yes before you change your mind again. And I have a proposal of my own to make." He bent on one knee. "Me sweet Annie, the dearest in all the land, will ye accept me hand in marriage?"

A glow began in her heart and spread to her face. "I will."

He stood and swung her around until she giggled with happiness. Then he kissed her with tender fervor that convinced her of his love. "I must speak to your father."

"He's at the bank." Shyly, she initiated a kiss, the first time she'd done so.

He returned it and then brushed a tendril of hair behind her ear. "Aye, I definitely must speak to your father." He disengaged from her arms as the door opened.

"Annie, I couldn't stay away any longer. Good morning to you, John." Beatrice's eyes brightened as she glanced from one to the other. "Is there news I should know?"

"You'll have to guess." Annie's happiness spread to a fever pitch as Beatrice squealed.

"'Tis not official. I've not spoken to your father—"

"A mere formality." Beatrice wrapped them both in an embrace. "Father told me that he expects you to approach him."

A tap on the door interrupted them.

"Miss Annie, Miss Beatrice," Mr. Grant began, "I have the great pleasure of announcing that—"

"I'm here for my long overdue visit." Meg reached out her arms.

"Meg." Annie rushed across the room and hugged her favorite cousin. "Why didn't you tell us you were coming? We would have picked you up at the train depot."

"I wanted to surprise you." She hugged Beatrice.

"You succeeded. We've longed to see you." Beatrice's eyes sparkled. "You are just in time, but it's Annie's news."

Meg's auburn curls bounced as she spun to face Annie. Her eyes lit up.

Annie looked at John.

His face flushed. "I've not yet talked with your father."

"As Bea said, we already know his answer." Annie placed her hand on his arm, and he covered it with his, warming her. She turned so they both faced her cousin. "Meg, you met John at Will's wedding. He's now Sergeant-Major John Finn of the Ninth Massachusetts...and my future husband."

CHAPTER 47

"I must return to my regiment tomorrow." John clasped Annie's hand as they sat later that day on their favorite bench in the garden, where summer flowers had been pulled and replaced with goldenrod. Autumn showed bountiful red, orange, and yellow in the surrounding woods.

"I'll plan a small church wedding with a reception here." Annie peered at the road.

"It might be months." Now that she'd agreed to marry him, John didn't want to wait a long time. The army had something to say about that.

"I understand." Her hand squeezed his. "I am marrying a soldier."

"I want you to stay in Washington after our marriage." Disappointment filled his gut that he'd not have her with him. "Just until the war ends."

Her head bowed over their clasped hands.

"I trust your father to keep you safe."

"He will." Annie stared toward a yellow patch of flowers. "I began collecting and sending food and supplies directly to soldiers this week. I'll continue with that."

"Good." His chest relaxed into a deep breath.

"I'll pray about it and decide after we marry where I can best serve my country."

"You've served our soldiers continuously for months. We can't win without women like you supporting us."

"Truly?" Brown eyes searched his.

"I promise. Ye have the thanks of our soldiers."

"Come back to me. Always." Her eyes filled with tears.

"If it's up to me"—he wiped away her tears with his thumb—"I will always return. That's a promise."

She rested her cheek against his shoulder. He wrapped his arms around her. Sorrow nearly overcame him to cause her such anxiety. He kissed her wet cheek.

"I love you, John Finn."

"I love you, Annie Swanson." He kissed her lips. "Sometime soon, I'll address you as Annie Finn."

Her cheeks turned rosy, and he kissed her again.

"I don't know where they went."

Beatrice's words broke their embrace. They put a foot of distance between them on the wrought iron bench.

"Perhaps they took a stroll." Meg's voice was closer.

"We're over here," Annie called. "In the garden."

"There you are." They approached, and Bea sat on a chair. "Our curiosity about the wedding got the better of us."

"Yes, what do you plan?" Meg sat, resting a hand on either side of the white bench.

"We didn't get very far with that." Annie tilted her head toward John. "Our dilemma is not knowing when John will receive another furlough."

John nodded. "There are many unknowns. War started in spring. It's now autumn. How many more seasons must pass before it ends?"

An uncomfortable silence descended on the group.

"'Tis sorry I am for casting gloom on a joyous day." He shifted against the metal seat.

"We'll plan ahead and be ready. Meg, you can help us." Annie leaned toward her cousin.

"It sounds fun." She looked pleased to be included. "I don't have a sister. You two are the closest to it."

Annie exchanged a glance with Bea. "We've always considered you as almost a sister. Make it official and make your home with us, at least until the war ends."

"I don't know—" Meg rubbed a finger across her brow.

"Annie, that's a wonderful idea." Bea clasped her hands together. "And I know Father will think so. Please say you'll stay."

"This is generous of you. I confess to feeling a bit lonely lately." Meg placed a hand on her throat. "I'll stay, if Uncle Hiram agrees."

Annie squealed. She jumped up and ran over to hug her. "That's perfect. Plans will go faster with all three of us working."

Bea leaned toward her sister. "The wedding will be here, of course."

"At our church." Annie nodded.

"I'd like my family to come." John's mam and sisters would have his hide if he didn't try to include them. "My father won't recover enough strength for the journey for months."

"Then we'll go there, if necessary." Annie straightened her shoulders. "These are extraordinary days. We must rise above our circumstances, or at least meet them squarely."

"That's a courageous attitude, Annie." Meg's glance shifted to the flowers. "I'm trying to do the same."

"Agreed." Beatrice stood. "Are you ready for that stroll, Meg?"

Meg looked at the couple and then toward the cloudy sky. "I believe we have time for a stroll before supper. Do you two want to come?"

"No." Annie shook her head. "John's had a long journey. We'll wait for you here."

The ladies, arm in arm, walked down the drive.

"You've talked about rising above our circumstances." John waited for them to get out of hearing distance. "You've done that. You're an extraordinary woman, Annie Swanson. Courageous. Strong. Compassionate. Not to mention the most beautiful woman in the world." The afternoon sunlight cast a glow on her brown hair. He clasped her hand. "'Tis a blessed man I am to marry you."

Tears shone in her eyes. "My father will arrive at any moment. He'll want to talk to you."

John's face burned with shame that his efforts to shield this family had the potential to wound them. "Shall I confess my great sin?"

"No." Annie gasped. "Never speak of it again. Especially to my father. I've guarded your secret. Now I want to put it in the past."

"Me precious Annie. No man has ever been more blessed than I am." He closed his eyes in gratitude as a weight fell from his back. "It's behind us."

"Here he is now." She stood and waved.

Hiram Swanson returned the gesture as he drove a chaise up the long drive toward the carriage house.

"Are you ready to talk with him?" She tilted her head.

"Never more so." He grinned. "Let's make this official."

Did you enjoy this book? We hope so!
Would you take a quick minute to leave a review where you purchased the book?
It doesn't have to be long. Just a sentence or two telling what you liked about the story!

Receive a FREE ebook and get updates when new Wild Heart books release: https://wildheartbooks.org/newsletter

Don't miss the next book in Spies of the Civil War series!

Boulevard of Confusion

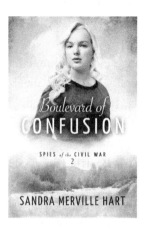

Chapter One

"My Aunt Trudy has invited us to make a prolonged stay with her." Beatrice Swanson held the letter closer to the gaslight lamp in the elegant parlor decorated in shades of mauve and blue. She scanned it again before glancing at her cousin, who sat on a cushioned chair adjacent to hers. "Meg, you remember her, don't you? Gertrude Weston?"

"I'm not likely to forget such a loving, gracious woman." Meg Brooks glanced up from her knitting. "Don't you remember when your mother and my mother took all of us girls to Richmond? We stayed at her home for the better part of the summer."

"That's right. I was nine." Memories of picnics, boat rides on the James River, and lazy days spent at Uncle Isaac's plantation increased Bea's nostalgia for carefree days. Nothing like these days, when one never escaped war news.

"I turned sixteen that summer." Pink tinged Meg's cheeks. "I was courted for the first time there. It's difficult to believe that ten years have passed."

"It wasn't Thomas?"

"Gracious, no." Meg's eyes brightened and then dimmed like the waning moon outside. "I didn't meet Thomas for another year. Mother always fretted that our six-month courtship wasn't long enough, yet time has proved otherwise. We were married almost seven years."

"He was a good man." Beatrice touched her cousin's shoulder, blinking back her own tears at the sadness in Meg's eyes. The widow had finally spoken of her beloved husband, gone nearly two years. Surely that was a good sign that healing had begun.

"The best." Meg straightened her shoulders, and Beatrice's hand fell away. "This isn't her first invitation to you and Annie."

"You are also included."

"That's very kind." Meg's fingers rubbed across the blue yarn soon to be a blanket.

A log crackled, shooting a spark onto the hearth. "Everyone receives a warm welcome at my aunt's home."

"I need a change of scenery, but do you think your father will agree to us traveling to Virginia while the war rages?"

"It's a short trip, only about a hundred miles." Bea gave her a playful grin. "Why would he hesitate?"

"The war."

Bea dropped the letter on to the wood table beside the lamp. The Army of Potomac was in Virginia, with her own brother-in-law camped at Minor's Hill as part of General Morrell's Brigade. "I wish John and Annie had waited until we were all back in Washington City to marry last month."

"The uncertainty of when John will march South...they

324

made the best of a tough situation." Setting her knitting on the chair beside her, Meg knotted her hands. "Especially since we were all in Boston for his father's funeral. Who knows when both sides of the family will be together again?"

"I suppose." Poor Annie hadn't even had her wedding dress. The seamstress had labored over the gown for three weeks, and it still hung upstairs. The pink dress Bea had planned to wear was equally unused, but she could wear it to a party, at least. Those disappointments had paled in comparison to her brother's absence. He was being held at Fort Warren as a prisoner of war. He hadn't been able to see his sister married to his best friend.

Meg weaved her fingers into the sweep of auburn curls gathered with combs. "At least Will has since been exchanged."

"That's another thing that bothers me." Beatrice ambled to the massive first-floor window and pushed aside the curtain to stare into the darkness. Blond ringlets brushing against her shoulders reflected in the glass against the night. "We barely spent three hours with Will at Fort Monroe before the Flag of Truce boat whisked him away."

With a long sigh, Meg joined her at the window. "Two days ago. Just think. He may be holding his daughter for the first time as we speak."

"A comforting thought." Bea's heart lightened at the possibility. "Hannah will be two months old tomorrow. I'm eager to meet my sweet niece. Father decided that North Carolina is too far away to travel until things settle. Our disappointment at this delay is one reason I believe Father will agree to our Richmond trip."

The door opened, and Annie slipped inside. "Are you discussing the invitation?" She joined them at the window.

Beatrice nodded.

"You've been out of sorts for weeks. Maybe a trip will do you good, but I don't know that Father…" Annie looked around the room. "He's not home from the bank yet?"

Bea glanced at the mantle clock. "No, and it's after eight. Perhaps our trip to Fort Monroe this week left him behind on tasks."

"He works too hard." Annie sighed.

"He always has." Bea rested her forehead on the cold pane. "Meg will accompany us if Father gives his consent."

"You will?" Annie's face brightened. "That makes me happier in my decision to remain here. For now."

"Why?" Beatrice stepped back. She had depended on her sister's cooperation to insure their father's agreement.

"Because John may be able to visit a day or two before he marches out. I can't miss the opportunity to see him."

Meg inclined her head. "Any news?"

"Nothing official, though he expects they'll leave as the weather warms." She turned to the darkness of the window. "I miss him already."

"I agree it's best you stay." Meg touched her arm. "Those are difficult circumstances." She turned to Bea. "When do you want to go?"

"There's an Inauguration for Confederate President Jefferson Davis later this month. I'd like to be there. I attended President Lincoln's Inauguration last year."

Annie stared at her. Meg raised her eyebrows.

"Our brother fights for the Confederacy, Annie. No matter our loyalties, it seems like a historic event."

Meg placed another log on the fire. "Is that why you want to go to Virginia?"

"No." Beatrice scarcely understood her reasons. "I simply feel that I must go. Aunt Trudy's spirits are low. She needs the comfort of family."

Annie's shoulders drooped.

Bea gripped her sister's wrist. "She'll understand why you remain at home."

"We must obtain passes." Meg poked at the burning logs. "Traveling won't be as easy as it was before the hostilities began."

"Father will help us." Bea's confidence in her father, a wealthy banker with many connections, was complete. First, she must convince him to allow her and Meg to travel to Richmond for an extended visit.

Meg and Annie had gone to bed when Beatrice heard a noise in the hall. "Father? Is that you?" She left the parlor and peered down the hall dimly lit with lanterns hung sporadically on the walls.

"Bea?" Hiram Swanson's slow stride brought him into view. "I thought you'd be asleep."

"I can't sleep." She reached up to kiss his cheek. "Have you eaten?"

"I had supper with a business acquaintance at the Willard Hotel." He peered behind him. "I came through the back door, wondering if Rebecca had any cookies or pie lying about."

"You and your sweet tooth." Beatrice laughed. "She left you a bowl of cherry cobbler. I'll fetch it. Do you want lemonade with it?"

"I suppose the coffee, if there is any left, is as cold as the night."

"Quite likely." Though Beatrice didn't share his love of the beverage, she wished she knew how to prepare it. "Water, then? Or milk?"

"Water, please."

"Sir, may I take your coat?"

Beatrice swung around. She should have known their gray-haired butler hadn't retired with his wife to their cottage in the woods behind the mansion. Irving Grant took pride in giving excellent service to her family. As long as her father was out, he'd watch for him.

"Yes, thank you, Irving." After shrugging off his coat, Hiram gave it and his hat to his butler. "Up rather late, aren't you?"

"Yes, sir. Is there anything you require tonight?"

Hiram waved him off. "Go on home. I'll see you in the morning."

"Very good, then, sir. Good night, Mr. Swanson, Miss Beatrice."

"I'll bring your cobbler into the parlor, where the fire's still going. I pushed two chairs closer to the fireplace to warm you."

"Ah. Was ever a man more blessed in his children than I?" A twinkle lit his weary eyes.

"Not likely." She laughed, teasing him. "I'll be right back." Despite his sleepy demeanor, she decided as she hurried down the shadowed hallway to make her request tonight. His exhaustion might incline him to agree.

He was lounging against the cushioned back of an armchair when Beatrice set the cobbler, linen napkin, spoon, and a tumbler of cold water on the round table beside him. "This smells delicious...and it tastes as good as it smells. You'd never know it's made using canned cherries."

"Except that it's February." His eyes gleamed at the first bite. "Tell me what's on your mind."

She traced an intricate leaf pattern carved into the chair arm. "Does anything have to be on my mind for me to wait up for you?"

He chuckled. "It's long been your custom to wait up for me when you're troubled about something rather than allow a matter to wait for the morrow."

"Perhaps you're right." She laughed a little at this tendency in herself. "A letter arrived from Aunt Trudy today."

"Did it now?" He shoveled in another bite as if starved.

"Yes, the fighting has upset her. She has invited Annie, Meg, and me to come for an extended visit. She thought President Jefferson's upcoming inauguration would sway us."

"She wants you so soon? That's only a couple of weeks away. What's the rush?"

"To be fair, all her recent letters have hinted at our coming. She wants to meet Annie's new husband, though she understands it's not possible." Beatrice clasped her hands together. "She's lonely since Uncle Parker passed."

"He's been gone twenty years." He set down his empty bowl on a side table. "You'll have to do better than that to convince me."

"She *is* lonely... and perhaps nervous about the fighting. But I guess I want to go as much for myself as for her." Blue flames engulfed the burning logs. "I'm restless. Longing for my Southern family. Will's captivity depressed my spirits to such an extent that only a prolonged visit with him would have eased it."

"Scarcely three hours." Hiram rubbed his hands over his face, rough whiskers making a sandpaper noise, his early morning clean-shaven skin a distant memory. "Not nearly enough for a father starved for his son's company either."

"I know." She spoke softly. Her father was a strong, confident man, yet Will's captivity weighed on him. Stripes of gray hair had thickened in his brown mane the past year. She breathed a silent prayer of gratitude that the heartache of his imprisonment was behind them. "Annie refuses to leave Washington City for fear she'll miss an unplanned visit from John."

He shook his head. "A vain hope, I'm afraid. After the extended leave last fall and the two weeks to bury his father, I'm afraid it'll be some time before the Union sets him loose for any length of time."

"At least they had enough time for a quick wedding."

"Not the grand affair I'd planned for my sweet daughter." His shoulders slumped. "But best under the circumstances."

"True." Neither had it been the day she'd dreamed for her adored sister, yet Annie had been a radiant bride for her groom, who'd had eyes only for her. Would anyone ever feel that way about Bea? Of her many beaus, none touched her heart the way John had her sister's. Bea resolved to wait for such a love.

"As to traveling to Richmond"—Hiram shook his head—"I can't leave the bank for weeks."

"Are we still losing customers, Father?" She searched his wary expression. Annie had explained that some customers had withdrawn their money last year to move South.

"No. For months I feared the loss of great numbers of our customers, but that time seems to have passed." He raised open palms heavenward. "We weathered the storm."

"Good news." Tension eased from her back. Except for wedding preparations, the family had continued to be frugal. Perhaps it made a difference. "Please don't think you need accompany Meg and me to Virginia."

"Troops from both sides are camped in that state." Hiram contemplated the dying flames. "I fear more battles will be fought there."

"As the capital, surely Richmond is the safest place in the Confederacy."

"Agreed." He rubbed the back of his neck until it turned red. "Normally, I would not consider it."

"Meg will be with me." Bea caught her breath, sensing that he was wavering.

"A competent and reliable companion indeed." His fingers thudded against the wooden chair arm.

"Please, Father. I'd experience a special moment in history, especially if the South wins."

His head jerked toward her. "Do you feel that's possible?"

Bea's eyes widened. "I think it's unlikely." Will, her courageous brother, had fought for the Confederacy before his capture and planned to rejoin after seeing his family. Her daily prayers always included a plea for his safety. "Yet certainly, it's possible. I cannot wish defeat upon Will. Nor do I desire the Union to lose."

"That was my dilemma." His fingertips pressed together until they turned white.

"*Was* your dilemma?" Her body tensed. "What do you mean?"

"Will's captivity in a Northern prison altered my thinking. I can't, in good conscience, stand in opposition to my only son."

Her hear skipped a beat. Did he mean...?

"I was born and raised near Richmond. I love Virginia. Still consider it my home. Thanks to your mother's compassionate nature, I cannot abide slavery." Hiram shook his head. "Will agrees. He isn't fighting to preserve it. No, your brother fights to protect his home from an invading army. I can't fault him for that."

Beatrice gasped. "I thought...I—" Her heroic father teetered on the pedestal that she'd placed him on as a child.

"That I was for the Union?"

She managed a nod beyond the chaos in her heart.

"I was, though I did my best to help your mother's old friend, Widow Greenhow, when she asked for it. Nothing much. Information about troops, fortifications, weaponry, and the like, information that seemed public knowledge. Certainly, I considered everything I told her as already known to Confederate generals. I gave it for a time and then stopped, fearing repercussions on the bank and my daughters."

Which mattered most, the bank or his family? Ice formed in her stomach. Her father had provided information to Rose Greenhow before she was arrested as a Confederate spy? Did that make *him* a spy? She covered her mouth with both hands to keep from gasping.

"Never fear. You ascertained my loyalty correctly last summer."

"What about all those late meetings? Times when you left and didn't explain where you were going?"

"Ah, yes." A sheen of sweat dotted his forehead. "I walked a fine line with my customers who support the Confederacy. When they came to me for reassurance, I had to provide it or risk losing their deposits in our bank."

The room spun. "You mean—"

"I allowed them to believe my loyalty is with our Southern neighbors." Hiram lifted his chin. "Just as I allowed my staunch support for the Union to shine when speaking with Northern loyalists."

She stared at a rose pattern on the rug. "That's why you gave the appearance of helping Mrs. Greenhow."

"Just so. She was a former bank customer. And your mother's friend." He ran a finger under his collar. "It was a dangerous undertaking, one that threatened to embroil our family in scandal. In my estimation, the only thing that saved us was that I never wrote any information down for Rose. All was given in a quick, hushed conversation. I left no evidence."

Little things took on new meaning. Father had often seen the widow to the door when she left. Fear gripped Bea. Might her father be arrested if his help became public knowledge, especially since the widow was still in prison?

"As I said," Father continued, "back then I supported the Union. Recent circumstances altered my thinking." His brown leaned forward. "You told me earlier that Will's capture and exchange left you feeling restless, unsettled. Did you expect a protective father to feel differently?"

Shock silenced her. They lived in the North. Had done so all her life. What did this change? "Does Annie know?"

"No." Hiram straightened his shoulders. "Your sister is loyal to the Union. Her husband was recently promoted to second lieutenant in the Union army. As much as she loves him, I doubt she'd have married him if he supported the South."

"Annie's loyalty has never wavered," she whispered.

"I respect her devotion but can no longer share it." He placed a firm hand on Bea's arm. "She must never know."

Beatrice covered her face to block out his agonized expression.

"Keep my secret so that we'll remain close after the fighting ends." Hiram's hand fell away. "War has a way of dividing family. Friends. I'm determined it won't separate my family by anything more than miles."

"Annie felt betrayed that Will fought for the Confederacy." Her hands bunched the folds of her wool dress into tight fists. She forced her fingers to relax in her lap. "I never did."

"Nor did I." Standing, he propped his arm on the fireplace mantle next to the clock.

After eleven already. Her chaotic thoughts caused her head to ache.

"Will you keep my secret? From Annie, John, Meg. Everyone up here?"

Bea wished he had never burdened her with knowledge in the first place. It must weigh on him as well. "I will." To cause further division in the family was out of the question. "Rely on it."

"Excellent." He pressed his palm to his forehead. "About Richmond. You still want to go?"

"Of course." Her father's revelations had so jolted her that she'd almost forgotten her original request.

"I can obtain the necessary passes. No need to worry on that account." Low flames swayed as he paced in front of the fireplace. "I'm giving my consent on two conditions."

"Yes?" Hope swelled like a bubble.

"First, Meg goes with you. When she returns to Washington City, you are to come with her."

"I will." She couldn't restrain her smile. "And the second?"

Father halted in front of the fire. "Your Uncle Isaac has written me. We haven't been close for many years." His back stiffened. "Your mother explained to you children how crushed I felt not to inherit a portion of the plantation as my father told me to expect. I'd always wondered why he..." He shook his head. "As I started to explain, Isaac has written of conditions in Richmond. He's asked for my aid." He turned on his heel to face her. "I've decided to comply with his request. You'll help."

The brothers hadn't been close for years. Mystified, she inclined her head.

"I'm sending money for the Confederate government. You'll hide it among your clothing and smuggle it to Richmond in my place."

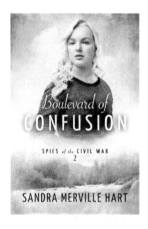

Get BOULEVARD OF CONFUSION at your favorite retailer!

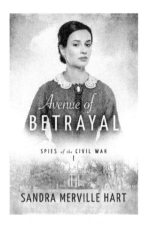

Book 1: *Avenue of Betrayal*

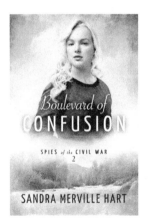

Book 2: *Boulevard of Confusion*

FROM THE AUTHOR

Dear Reader,

When the time came to write a new Civil War novel series, I wanted to focus on an aspect of those turbulent years beyond the battles. I discovered there was a lot of spying. History reports a surprising amount of spying happened in the capital cities of Washington DC (largely known then as Washington City) and Richmond, Virginia, which was the Confederate capital.

Much has been written about Allan Pinkerton and his agents. Pinkerton's agents were loyal to the Union and were active in several southern cities, including Richmond. Pinkerton moved his headquarters from Chicago to Washington DC early in the war. His influence was greater early in the war and those connections will touch this series.

Mrs. Rose Greenhow, a widow living in Washington DC at the start of the war, was a Confederate spy. She built up a network of spies while living within blocks of President Abraham Lincoln at the White House. She had informants within the Federal government and passed on the information to Confederate leaders. One of her spies was a banker, William Smithson, who led a double life as Charles Cables. I kept Hiram Swanson's banking relationship with Rose in the past but attempted to show how easy it might be for vital information to fall into the wrong hands. Rose's real-life story impacts the fictitious Swanson family in our series.

I found a wonderful account of the adventures of the Ninth Massachusetts, the "Irish Ninth", written by Captain Michael MacNamara. The captain's pride in his regiment is reflected in his writing. This historical figure is included in one of the scenes as a small thank you for providing the rich details that add authenticity to the story. For instance, this regiment, while in Washington DC, camped near a wealthy banker's mansion. Two soldiers were shot in a target practice accident. The Ninth Massachusetts marched toward Manassas only to be ordered back to Washington City before reaching their destination. Colonel Cass is also a historical figure that enters the story briefly.

General Winfield Scott commanded the Union Army in the summer of 1861 and did have some spies. Lieutenant Christopher Farmer is a fictitious character.

Miss Elizabeth Van Lew is famous for being a Union spy while living in Richmond. She wasn't alone in her support of the Union. Many "Unionists" lived in Richmond. Readers will learn more about what happened in 1862 in that city in the next two books in the series.

While I have focused on what happened in the capital cities, plenty of spying took place in other important locations. It required greater courage and daring to spy for the opposing side while living in the other side.

I hope you enjoyed this story set in Washington in 1861. I invite you to read the next two books in the series to discover what happens to our characters in Richmond in 1862.

Blessings,

Sandra Merville Hart

ABOUT THE AUTHOR

Sandra Merville Hart, award-winning and Amazon bestselling author of inspirational historical romances, loves to discover little-known yet fascinating facts from American history to include in her stories. Her desire is to transport her readers back in time. She is also a blogger, speaker, and conference teacher. Connect with Sandra on her blog, https://sandramervillehart.wordpress.com/.

ACKNOWLEDGMENTS

I want to thank my agent, Joyce Hart, for her perseverance, guidance, and friendship for the past several years. Thank you, Joyce, for your persistent determination to get this Civil War series in front of a publisher who is excited to bring it to publication.

I'd also like to thank Misty Beller at Wild Heart Books for her faith in me. I'll be forever grateful for her offer to publish not only one but two three-book series. I signed both contracts on the same day for a total of six books! My heart is full. Thank you.

I also want to thank Robin Patchen for helping to make my story better. This is my first experience working with her as an editor and she's quite talented. Thank you, Robin, for all your hard work.

Thanks also to my wonderful Word Weaver critique group. KD Holmberg, Deborah Sprinkle, Starr Ayers, Bonnie Beardsley, and Linda Dindzans have read snippets of this book and given me valuable insights. I love this talented group of writers!

Thanks to family and friends for their continued support,

especially my husband. You give up vacation days to travel with me on research trips. I bounce ideas off you and you give me the male perspective. You keep me grounded. I love you.

WANT MORE?

If you love historical romance, check out the other Wild Heart books!

Marisol ~ Spanish Rose by Elva Cobb Martin

Escaping to the New World is her only option...Rescuing her will wrap the chains of the Inquisition around his neck.

Marisol Valentin flees Spain after murdering the nobleman who molested her. She ends up for sale on the indentured servants' block at Charles Town harbor—dirty, angry, and with child. Her hopes are shattered, but she must find a refuge for herself and the child she carries. Can this new land offer her the grace, love, and security she craves? Or must she escape again to her only living relative in Cartagena?

Captain Ethan Becket, once a Charles Town minister, now sails the seas as a privateer, grieving his deceased wife. But when he takes captive a ship full of indentured servants, he's intrigued by the woman whose manners seem much more refined than the average Spanish serving girl. Perfect to become governess for his young son. But when he sets out on a quest to find his captured sister, said to be in Cartagena, little does he expect his new Spanish governess to stow away on his ship with her six-month-old son. Yet her offer of help to free his sister is too tempting to pass up. And her beauty, both inside and out, is too attractive for his heart to protect itself against—until he learns she is a wanted murderess.

As their paths intertwine on a journey filled with danger, intrigue, and romance, only love and the grace of God can overcome the past and ignite a new beginning for Marisol and Ethan.

~

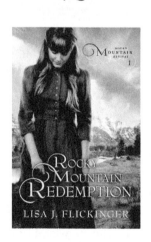

Rocky Mountain Redemption by Lisa J. Flickinger

A Rocky Mountain logging camp may be just the place to find herself.

To escape the devastation caused by the breaking of her wedding engagement, Isabelle Franklin joins her aunt in the Rocky Mountains to feed a camp of lumberjacks cutting on the slopes of Cougar Ridge. If only she could out run the lingering nightmares.

Charles Bailey, camp foreman and Stony Creek's itinerant pastor, develops a reputation to match his new nickname — Preach. However, an inner battle ensues when the details of his rough history threaten to overcome the beliefs of his young faith.

Amid the hazards of camp life, the unlikely friendship growing between the two surprises Isabelle. She's drawn to Preach's brute strength and gentle nature as he leads the ragtag crew toiling for Pollitt's Lumber. But when the ghosts from her past return to haunt her, the choices she will make change the course of her life forever—and that of the man she's come to love.

～

Lone Star Ranger by Renae Brumbaugh Green

Elizabeth Covington will get her man.

And she has just a week to prove her brother isn't the murderer Texas Ranger Rett Smith accuses him of being. She'll show the good-looking lawman he's wrong, even if it means setting out on a risky race across Texas to catch the real killer.

Rett doesn't want to convict an innocent man. But he can't let the Boston beauty sway his senses to set a guilty man free. When Elizabeth follows him on a dangerous trek, the Ranger vows to keep her safe. But who will protect him from the woman whose conviction and courage leave him doubting everything—even his heart?

Made in the USA
Las Vegas, NV
13 March 2023

69009743R00197